D1446114

The Indian Chronicles

José Barreiro

Arte Público Press
Houston
Texas
1993

This book is made possible through support from the National Endowment for the Arts (a federal agency), the Lila Wallace-Reader's Digest Fund and the Andrew W. Mellon Foundation.

Arte Público Press
University of Houston
Houston, Texas 77204-2090

Cover design by Mark Piñón
Original painting, "Diablura," by Alejandro Romero
Cover photo by Georgia McInnis

Barreiro, José
    The Indian chronicles / by José Barreiro
        p.   cm.
    ISBN 1-55885-067-8 : $19.95
    1. Indians of the West Indies—First contact with Europeans—Fiction. 2. America—Discovery and exploration—Spanish—Fiction. 3. Colón, Diego, d. 1526—Fiction. 4. Columbus, Christopher—Fiction. I. Title.
PS3552.A73257I5   1993
813'.54—dc20
                                            93–12810

                                              CIP

The paper used in this publication meets the requirements of the American National Standard for Permanence of Paper for Printed Library Materials Z39.48-1984. ∞

Copyright © 1993 by José Barreiro
Printed in the United States of America

This book is for my tía Lilina and my abuelo Joseíto, who taught me to value the old ways, and for my father and mother, who pointed me to my future.

CONTENTS

Author's Introduction: A Fabulous Find

From 1988 to 1990, while I was completing research on a doctoral thesis, I endeavored to locate descendants of the aboriginal people of the West Indies. I visited the island nations of Santo Domingo/Haiti, Puerto Rico, Cuba, St. Vincent, Trinidad and Dominica. My research led me to interview numerous informants on family oral and documentary history, lifestyle and the genealogical foundations of the islands. This exhilarating work—fueled, in part, by the occasion of the Columbus Quincentenary set in 1992—led to a number of adventures, some personal revelations and the fulfillment, twenty years late, of a doctoral thesis. However, that thesis, which became a curriculum, *The Indigenous Caribbean,* was not the only revelation of those years of research. A far greater discovery resulted: the manuscript that follows this introduction.

In January, 1990, during a research visit to Cuba, a friend from the Oriente region of the island told me of an fabulous find in the remote city of Baracoa, among the elder members of a family of Amerindian descent. My friend, an archaeologist of Indo-Cuban descent himself (from Santiago), insisted that the manuscript was a long-lost set of notes made by Father Bartolomé de las Casas in preparation for his historic book, *Brevísima historia de la destrucción de las Indias,* sometime during the 1530s. He said two investigators from the University of Havana had visited the family in the early 1980s, but had only been allowed to view portions of the manuscript. "The family is very guarded," my friend said.

Such documents have often been found among Indian descendants, so I was not surprised by my friend's assertions. Throughout the Western Hemisphere, the Amerindian peoples have revered and tried to safekeep such material legacies as they have been able to secure. Researchers have often reported otherwise destitute Indian families who could produce old chests full of intricate and high-quality breast plates, quill and bead work, ceremonial bundles and written testimonies and treaties dating back generations, materials sometimes several hundred years old. In fact, there is presently a generalized movement among Indian peoples to recover spiritually important museum pieces. In several places, tribes have reburied human remains taken by archaeologists and have established their own museums or asked traditional societies to hold artifacts, religious icons and other objects retained from the past.

Indeed, I was soon to be pleasantly surprised when the two researchers, both doctoral candidates at the Department of Anthropology of the University of Havana, confirmed that the family had shown them six of the pages, written in the old Spanish script.

They had judged that the paper was probably old, perhaps the log of a merchant sailor, but they had declined immediate work on the subject, having found the material unsuited to their own research on early colonial sugar mills. My friend, whom I had no reason to distrust, assured me that they had viewed but a minor part of it. He surprised me further by informing me that he had translated and read to the Indian family an old article of mine about Indo-Cuban persistence in the Baracoa area. They judged my perspective to be respectful, he said, and asked him to contact me about reviewing their prized possession.[1]

A week later, I was in the village of Guarikén, in the sierras of Baracoa, overlooking the central valley of the Toa River, where I visited the family of Don Francisco Suárez Padrón, a native of the same village. The Suárez Padrón clan is a peasant *mestizo/indio* family which, for several generations at the end of the eighteenth and the beginning of the nineteenth centuries, worked for the estate of a Cuban scholar, Don Ernesto Bosch Samoa near Guarikén, still one of several small Cuban Indian communities.

After sharing a cup of Cuban *cafecito* and reviewing my credentials, Suárez produced a copper box, twelve by eighteen inches in size and almost four inches thick, which he placed on a small wooden table. He said that, except for the few pages shown to the Havana investigators, he had never revealed the inside of the box to anyone outside his family. Suárez recited how he had been entrusted with it by his grandfather, who had received it from his own grandmother. That matriarch from five generations ago, according to Suárez, had said that the box and its contents came to her family via a great-aunt from the Dominican Republic, a migrant to Cuba, who had received it herself as a young woman from a Catholic friar. The friar was a member of the Dominican Order, one of a long line of friars dating back to the turn of the sixteenth century in Santo Domingo. Remembering that Friar Bartolomé de las Casas was a member of the Dominican Order, I took careful note of all the names and their family connections. Suárez then ushered me to the table where he placed the box. He took my hand and put it on the stack of papers.

"Most of it is written by an Indian," Suárez said.

I told him I had been informed it was a Las Casas manuscript.

"Yes," he said, "there are letters from Las Casas, but the bulk is by a Taíno Indian, who claims to have known Columbus." He pronounced it Colón, as in the Spanish. Suárez claimed to understand only about a third of the material, as he found the old Spanish, written in an elaborate twirling script, hard to decipher.

The copper box was indeed full of sheets, pressed tightly. It gave every indication of being quite old. The box had been lined inside with fine wood, of which only a slip remained, dry as last year's tobacco leaf. With great care and under Suárez's watchful eye, I took out one section and then another. There were two types of paper, one slightly thicker than the other and both fifteen inches long. The thinner papers were blank and had been placed between the sheets with writing on them for protection. Many of the sheets appeared blank to the eye, but about halfway into the manuscript a blotting effect had occurred and much of the ink was stenciled onto the thinner sheets, looking backwards to the eye but discernible. I could immediately see that the papers were old. The script was indeed elaborate, in the ornate style of Spanish calligraphy used in the 1500s. Having held in my hands and closely studied verifiable documents from that period at the General Archive of the Indies in Seville, Spain, I could indeed sense that these pages were likely to be a genuine find. Later, in 1990, radio carbon tests at the Bureau of Ethnology in Washington, D.C., dated the paper and wood to the period 1450–1550.

Encouraged by this potentially important find, I rented a room at a "pensión" near the Suárez home and thus began a six-month process of photographing, reading and deciphering the tiny script, and of determining the authorship of the documents.

To report: the contents consisted of letters, some notes and a manuscript of some 440 pages handwritten in very small script. There were indeed letters by Las Casas, two of them, both addressed to a Diego or Dieguillo Colón, at the Dominican convent in Santo Domingo. A long, rambling note by an unnamed friar, dated in 1659; a short note by Don Ernesto Bosch Samoa, dated in 1864, and; the long manuscript of notes and journal entries, comprising the bulk of the papers by a Diego Colón, who I initially assumed would have been either the brother or the son of the discoverer, Christopher Columbus. However, the note by scholar Bosch Samoa seconded Suárez's assessment, guiding me toward a truer analysis. After a short paragraph explaining that he came to read the manuscript on a request from his aunt, Bosch writes, "This is not the writing of the son nor of the brother of the Great Mariner. Neither the argument nor the exposition corresponds with the point of view of the Colón family. This is likely a fraud, though, judging from the paper stock, admittedly an old one."

Immensely intrigued, I read the manuscript pages. Signed by Diego Colón, they were obviously not by a Spaniard, since the journal entries spoke from the point of view of a Taíno or Arawak Indian, one who claimed to have sailed with Christopher Columbus during the Caribbean phase of the contact period. The manuscript of 440 pages, each signed by Diego, was written in a descriptive and natural Spanish. It tells of events lived by the author, mostly around the period 1532–1535, but with episodes that recall the first encounter at the island of Guanahani, site of Columbus' landfall and the author's home island. Thus, the entries tell of memories from the early conquest history of the island that the Spanish named Española, now divided by the countries of Santo Domingo and Haiti. They tell also of the conquest of Cuba and of Puerto Rico.

The full translated text of the Diego Colón journal, plus the two letters from Las Casas, follow this introduction. However, I leave out Bosch Samoa's and the friar's notes, as they are largely unreadable. I am thankful to the eminent Caribbean scholar, Professor José Juan Arrom (Yale Emeritus), who helped me translate the manuscript and authenticated dates used by the author. Professor Arrom, an indefatigable tracker of the Caribbean's Taíno roots, was extremely helpful in deciphering the meanings of Taíno words. However, the final translation is my full responsibility. For the sake of readability, I have sometimes introduced modern usages, such as Puerto Rico, named San Juan Bautista in Diego's time, and the contemporary term, Kwaib, interchangeably with the more historical Carib or Caniba. The two letters of Father Bartolomé de las Casas, one left for Diego and the other sent from Barcelona, are placed at the end of the volume, as they are in fact dated from 1534 and 1543. Diego's final entry, dated in 1546, the work of a shaky handwriting, comes after a full three years of silence following the last of the Las Casas letters. It provides a proper postscript to the narrative and comes after a final encomendation of Diego's worldly goods.

Diego Colón: Points in the Trajectory

I found after a cursory search of the early chronicles the historical personality named Diego Colón, who was indeed a Taíno Indian. Diego Colón was a young man, twelve years old when taken by Columbus as a captive at the first landfall at Guanahaní. A quick study, Diego became Columbus' primary Taíno interpreter within weeks of the first contact. He would not only remain at the center of events throughout the first ten years of the Spanish colonization of La Española, but he lived to full maturity in Santo Domingo. Diego Colón was a native witness to the first half century of that fateful encounter.

Among the early chroniclers, Las Casas himself mentions the Indian interpreter Diego Colón several times in his *History of the Indies*.[2] Dr. Álvarez Chanca, who sailed in the Columbus' voyage, mentions him twice (though not by name) in his famous *Letter to the City of Seville*. Both Gonzalo Fernández de Oviedo,[3] the King's historian, and Columbus' son, Hernando,[4] refer to Diego in his definitive *General and Natural History of the Indies* (1535) and in his biography of his famous father. Diego turns up also in the infamous letter of Michael de Cúneo,[5] raconteur and friend of Columbus, and in Pedro Martyr de Angleria's *Décadas del Nuevo Mundo*[6] (1530).

There are references to a Diego Colón at the General Archive of the Indies, in Seville, Spain, which twice place such a person in Española in 1514; he is also mentioned by an *encomendero* (Spanish grantees who were ceded lands holding whole Indian communities) in Cuba in 1515. Among twentieth century historians, Columbus' preeminent biographer, Samuel Morison, provides several anecdotal references to Diego in his books, *Christopher Columbus, Admiral of the Ocean Sea* and *The European Discovery of America: The Southern Voyages*.[7]

In a twentieth-century novel, Cuban writer Alejo Carpentier twice mentions a "Dieguito, the only one of them to learn some of our words."[8] Writing in Columbus's own voice, Carpentier reflects the final thoughts of the legendary admiral: "Through Dieguito, the last one left to me, I learned that those men neither liked us nor admired us; they had us for treacherous men, liars, violent, choleric, cruel, dirty and foul-smelling ... "

But that was fiction, and in a European (Columbus') voice. Diego's manuscript reopens the historical record and his is an indigenous voice. Sitting in the coastal breeze of the eastern Cuban mountains, under palm and ceiba trees and surrounded by the sounds of the inriri, the Cuban woodpecker, Diego's words resonated in my ears with a vibrancy that is a researcher's dream. Diego's journal narrates a moment in that early history of encounter, when for a brief decade the Taíno people regrouped under the leadership of the young chiefs, Guarocuya (Enriquillo's Taíno name), and actually won a war against the Spanish crown, one that resulted in capitulations that constitute the first treaty between a European power and an American indigenous people.

In any case, Diego's "sheets" provide us with the story of Enriquillo's war and many other historical incidents as well. A narrative written in journal style and making full use of descriptive elements, it can be read for itself, making these explanations already long enough. Except for a glossary that explains Taíno and Spanish words, readers will rejoice that this introduction constitutes the only words extraneous to the noted translator's journal and the letters he saved from Father Bartolomé de las Casas. Without further delay, then, five centuries overdue, we directly proceed to the translation of Diego's text.

José Barreiro
Crows Hill, NY
December, 1992

Notes

[1] See José Barreiro, "View from the Shore: Toward an Indian Voice in 1992," *Northeast Indian Quarterly* (1990).

[2] See Bartolomé de las Casas, *History of the Indies*. Ed. Andree M. Collard. New York: Harper and Row, 1971.

[3] See Gonzalo Fernández de Oviedo, *Historia general y natural de las Indias*. Asunción: Editorial Guaraní, 1956.

[4] See Henando Colón, *The Life of the Admiral Christopher Columbus by his Son Ferdinand*. Trans. Benjamin Keen. New Brunswick: Rutgers University Press, 1959.

[5] See Michelle de Cúneo, "Letter of the Second Voyage," *Universidad de la Habana*, 1972.

[6] See Pedro Martyr de Angleria, *Décadas del Nuevo Mundo*. Trans. Joaquín Torres Asensio. Buenos Aires: Editorial Bajel, 1944.

[7] See Samuel Morison, *The European Discovery of America: The Southern Voyages*. Oxford: Oxford University Press, 1974.

[8] See Alejo Carpentier, *El arpa y la sombra, Obras completas de Alejo Carpentier*. Ed. Maria Luisa Puga. Coyoacán, Mexico: Siglo Veintiuno Editores, 1979.

The Indian Chronicles

Folio I

Our Reality and Theirs

April 12, 1532

One. *The good friar Las Casas requests my witness of the early years.*

The Castillians call this the Year of Our Lord 1532, and today they call the twelfth day of the month of April. This is the day I start.

I write from a small square room in the Convent of the Dominican Order, in Santo Domingo de la Española, where I have resided for six years. These journal pages, where I will inscribe my memories, are a manifest of the kindness of a great man, a priest of the Catholic faith, Don Bartolomé de las Casas, of whom I am a grateful servant and to whom I am greatly in debt for my life and my well-being.

I have had a quill pen, acquired many long years ago, and ink, too, I obtained on my own. But paper has been nearly impossible to come by. The great man of robes, just a few days ago, gifted me with a sheet-book of paper, blank pages for me to fill. Now I have it and today I begin to scratch these Castillian symbols on the page, these drawings that talk. For that, and for his unceasing labor on behalf of my people, I am very grateful to his eminence. I add here, of course, a certainty: that as always in my dealings with the Castillians, the ones my elders called the "covered men," I am aware that the friar has a reason for granting me paper. Don Bartolomé writes now the story of Don Christopherens and the taking of the islands. He requests that I put down on paper the stories of my times with the Admiral.

"Write it now before your mind forgets," the friar told me. "However you want, what you remember, note it down. The actual landfall—how the admiral first set foot on the New World. You were there, Dieguillo." And this is true. I am the only one left who remembers the first landing, from the beach on my home island, my bohío of Guanahani. And I do remember. I remember the ships; their sails like giant gulls; I remember the strange men with coverings like crabs and hairs like frayed rope on their faces; I do, I remember even the clouds, how they formed and what they said to us that day. I remember now, I feel now, a great sadness about that day. It pains me now as I relive it, reminded to remember it by a great man that I love as I come, every day more and more, to hate the twisted ways of his race. I am pleased to do this for Don Bartolomé, though I did warn him he might not like my words.

April 14, 1532

Two. *A reason to remember so much pain.*

Much too busy with convent duties for two suns, today I rush to continue this work, and I am quickly flushed in the greenery of my memories. In this little room that the monks have allowed me, stiff-legged as I am, soft stomach, aching teeth, I still have my mind. For six years, as we have shared an existence in this convent's stone buildings, the friar has asked many questions, bringing up old times and writing down my stories. But now I feel the freedom of my hand, I draw my words on this paper, these words that will carry and be read by others.

I put pen to paper, close my eyes and I am there, almost forty years ago, but now fresh in my sudden memory, during first days when close behind young Rodrigo, my new friend and Captain's servant, I snuck under the poop deck of the Santa María (Marie-Galante, the Admiral always called her), anchored still on the small bay of my home island of Guanahani, right into his master room. The Admiral was bent over a table and quietly Rodrigo and I watched him from behind. He never took notice. That was the first time I saw him scratching the ink marks in his ship's log, engrossed in his mind, resembling one of our behikes in full ceremonial prayer. That act of the Admiral's I pondered even at my early age. Later, as I learned their different ways, this writing on paper that could be taken over long distances and read directly again and again appealed to me. I think on that: that I too now can write, and it warms me.

I confess to the sky and I hope the friar can forgive me when he reads these words. I do intend to tell, to write on paper, what I did see and how I do see it. For the good father and for whomever else might read these pages, I will stall my anger, restrain my hate, retain my cagüayo lizard spirit, my revolving eye, the coolness in my body to see them clearly, and I will write what I have learned of their actions, their speech during the early years and on to the present. But I confess: I am no longer enchanted by anything Castillian, anything Iberian, Portuguese, anything Genoese or whatever else they have across the great open waters. Even as I write, and freely, I still ponder: How will these, my own words scratched on paper, how will they free my spirit? Or will they capture my thoughts, my heart? Will they betray me?

I am nervous to write of those times and those places where once flourished my Taíno relatives. The wounds of these forty years cut deep into my heart and so will most of these pages. So, I sit and I cry and hurriedly before he returns, I sit down to pen these few words of a beginning, on my own. Many things I can say about the Admiral that he will not like. And many things I can tell, too, about the great world of my ancestors, the people of the islands that the Castillians call "Antilles" but which to the eye of my mind I see as our long Cuban lizard (Caymán-Cubanakan), the land of great mountains (Haití-Bohío), the center of dancing (Borikén) and the little Carib turtles, hicoteas, in our language, arching south to the great forest.

And I start with this: What I do for this friar, our great defender, I do because I know what he endures for my people. But it is for my people, too, for that world in which we lived and in which we lost, that I want to write also what I know of who we were, how we felt and believed, and what has happened. I want to be this friar's witness, by Yucahu Bagua Maorocoti, great spirit of my ancestors, I do, and even by the baby Jesus, I do, but in my witness I will write for you, my Taíno-ni-taíno, natural guajiro-ti relatives, for those of you who will survive, for those of you in times to come who will remember that your fathers and your mothers, your grandfathers and grandmothers, were a people.

April 15, 1532

Three. *An introduction of myself.*

My Christian name in the Castillian language, from the time of my adoption by the Admiral, is Diego or Dieguillo Colón. Fifty-two is the count of my rains. Of origin, I am from Guanahani, the first land sighted in my world by the covered men of Castille. I am of the Taíno people and in my native language my name is Guaikán—the remora fish. My mother was Nánichi, from the canoe-building clan of the yukaieke, or village, called Old Guanahani. My father had several names but was most prominently called Coxobanax, after his functions and title in the council of the Cohoba. He was from our island's central village, called Guanahaninakan, but he lived on the coast with my mother's people, who esteemed him as a fisherman of great skill.

I think now of my father's death, only weeks before the Admiral's arrival, how in a moment of joy, climbing tall on a tree of the fruit called mamey, his tight muscular body, like the great maja snake, climbing lazily ever higher on the overlapping branches of a palm tree. With a coral ax, he chopped two, three bundles of ripe mamey. Then, stretching for another fruit, arm extended, body extended along thick broad leaves like a brown ciguayo lizard, a sharp crack and he dropped, long and hard and with no sound, all silent but the snap, the crack when the flat branch broke, as he dropped and dropped and hit rock.

My first sadness comes back to me now, the worst and best, and I must stop. Thinking of my parents, of their generation and their elders, fills me with longing.

This is all in me. I pull away now, lift the pen. I let my father be. Slowly, I will approach it. There is so much. Again today my mind swims with colors and faces, the turns of phrase and the many smells of the sea. The friar's request has filled me with strength, my chest is warm and my mind turns. Even the pain of my right side, past injuries I carry from the time of my betrayal, when even his name that I still carry could not protect me, even the old pain that stiffens my arm and leg, even my tired limbs, have warmed up so that my heart can almost feel glad.

April 21, 1532

Four. *The good friar's argument.*

At lunch today the good friar took his meal, as I usually do, with the Indian servants of our convent. We shared with him our casabe tort, axiaco stew and a fresh red snapper caught out in his canoe in the early morning by young Silverio. Don Bartolomé comes to eat with us quite regularly. Today, before taking a seat, he was already agitated with our cause. As part of his prayer, he said, "Almighty God, help us condemn the encomienda system, brutal destroyer of our good Indian brothers."

The good friar is very forceful. Once he intends to go in a certain direction, he will not be dissuaded. He suffers every day for his ideas about our Indian people. Today, I watched him mop around his soup bowl with a piece of casabe as we heard the first yeller. The shouting came from the stone road that runs down the hill by the convent and you could hear the culprit hurrying by. "Las Casas the great whore son! Buggers the she-dogs and their sons!" he yelled.

Two or three come by every day. They shout their insults at the friar and run away before the younger monks can have a go at them. Most are sons or guards of encomenderos. They hate Don Bartolomé. Once, he was in the vegetable garden, picking our Taíno peppers that he loves so much, when several of the criminals pelted him with stones. They truly hate him and I believe would kill him if given a chance.

As usual, today Don Bartolomé sat quietly through the insults, his hawk face and nose tilted down over his bowl with only the slightest of furrows lining his ample forehead. Two monks came back from a brief chase, empty-handed, and Don Bartolomé ignored them. He put his plate away and re-quested I follow him to my little room.

"How is the writing?" he asked, walking straight to the window as I closed my door.

"I am only starting," I said.

"I need your memory," he said. "I intend to sail to the kingdom, soon. I will pretend I am going to Puerto Rico, the San Juan Island. But from there I will go before the Court in Castille. The King will hear my case."

"Why now, father?" I asked.

"These bastards have no backbone. The whole island is terrified."

He spoke the truth. As we stood and talked today in the convent at Santo Domingo, a young countryman of mine, Enriquillo, the warrior chief of the Bahuruku mountains, remains at large. For thirteen years, Enriquillo and his warriors, among them his war captain, Tamayo, have been free in remote camps in the southwestern mountains of the island.

"Enriquillo's warriors attacked a farm this side of La Maguana just eight days ago," Father Las Casas continued. "The governor is trying to keep it quiet, but four soldiers were killed and their weapons captured."

I asked the good friar if perhaps now the King might not be angrier at the rebel cacique, thus complicating his mission.

"The King will be upset. But with whom? Enriquillo's case is now well-known. Everyone wants the mountains pacified, including the King. My intent is to remind him that Enriquillo is a baptized Indian, a Christian, that he is at war for very good reasons. Others have argued with the King on that account. It is the brutal abuse of the encomienda that brought Enriquillo to war."

The good father was right and as always I was glad to hear him say it, but what he said pricked me. Indeed, Enriquillo was baptized. But, this I do not see as so great an achievement.

I know the story of Enriquillo. I knew his father and his uncles, including his great aunt, the cacica Anacaona, hereditary tribal mother of the Xaragua region, sister of the wise old cacique, Bohekio, and widow of the feared cacique warrior, Caonabó. All are now dead, victims of betrayal, victims of slaughter, almost thirty years ago.

"At the court, they call you idolaters, heathen, barbaric people," he pressed me. "I want to argue that your people's beliefs were actually a form of Christianity, that you worshipped under similar ideas. Do you see? As Christians we are to conquer and wage war upon heathens at will; but a people who hold a measure of Christianity can command more respect . . . "

I nodded, though not with the vigor he wanted.

"Yes or no?" he persisted. "Do you agree with what I maintain, that our best argument to the court is on religious grounds?"

"In truth, father," I told him, "I do not hold as much hope for that argument as you do."

The good friar meant to press on. "I may convince the monarchs by asserting that the religious beliefs you held before our arrival were not so different from the Christian catechism," he said.

Deep in my heart, I refuse to accept this argument from Don Bartolomé. I like what he tries to do, how tirelessly he argues on our behalf, but it angers something within me.

"The closer to Christianity you are, the more the King must care for you. Among all the abhorrent practices of your old behikes, I know some Christian notions were apparent. The idea of a Heaven and Hell, for instance, maybe thoughts about a celestial trinity, things like this, which could lead to a King's recognition. A royal declaration is what your people need."

"We need only to be left alone," I said, with an eruption of words. I must confess that his inquiries and assertions have triggered my memory. I am agitated. I do not mean to be blunt with the good friar, but he speaks sometimes without thinking.

The good father listens to me sometimes, and I feel his acceptance of my truth. But other days he walks as in a waking trance, like a guilty man smitten by the cohoba. Then, he admonishes me: "Only through the Lord Jesus Christ can you find salvation." Or he says: "Bringing Christ on the Cross was our mission to you. Before, it is true, you were lost." When he is like that, when he must own not just my memory but my very own spirit, I shrink from his verbal embrace. Today, at first, it was like that, we couldn't talk. I withdrew into my silence, rather than argue, and my good Castillian friend, this brother of Christ who has suffered so much for my people, he too withdrew, mumbling quietly to himself, his gaze roaming the valley beyond my window.

Five. *The story of Enriquillo.*

A full hour went by before the good friar continued.

"Let's stick to Enriquillo," he said. "As I understand it, twice before going to the mountains, Enriquillo filed complaints. He tried to use lawful means to achieve justice."

I know that story, too. I know exactly who Enriquillo is and how he comes to have hundreds of Indians in the bush mountains of the Bahuruku, how he has changed our lives and what he means to the Indians and African negroes of this island.

"And he is a Christian, is he not?" Las Casas said to pull my tongue.

I reminded the priest that Enriquillo is a survivor of the Massacre of Anacaona's Banquet, which in 1503 destroyed the last major Taíno cacicazgo on Española. I myself saved Enriquillo's father, then brought his young boys to my side, though I did not say so. That was the time when Governor Nicolás de Ovando, a friar, and, in my estimation, an assassin, pretended friendship and accepted Anacaona's hospitality. Then, at his signal, Castilla soldiers attacked the friendly village, shooting and hacking and stabbing. I did remind the good friar of my presence at the massacre.

"But I didn't know Enriquillo was there," he said.

"Yes, he was," I said. "And, you should know, before he was taught the catechism, he was brought up for the cohoba."

"Leave the cohoba out of it. It is drunkenness by any other name."

This is a regular conversation between the good priest and me. He knows I will defend our cohoba ritual to him. I won't attack him, but I will argue with him.

"You have your wine. And you use it in ceremonies, in communion with the Christ."

"This is not fruitful, Dieguillo ... "

"With cohoba, our behikes, our priests, communicated, too, with our Yúcahuguama, our supreme God."

"Enough, you are going too far and twisting my intention. Tell me about Enriquillo's life."

"After the massacre dictated by the friar Don Nicolás Ovando," I said to irk him by reminding him of one his brothers of the cloth, "Enriquillo was educated by the Franciscan fathers, as you know. Then, along with what remained of his village, some eighty or ninety people, he went to an encomendado named Valenzuela when the elder died, his son, Andrés, received Enriquillo and his people for his own encomienda."

"So he was inherited by Andrés Valenzuela from his father?" Las Casas asked.

"Yes," I explained. "The old Valenzuela, named Francisco, died. And, you know, he was a calm man and not given to fits of temper like so many of the Iberians. Under him, Enriquillo's people paid labor tribute, but kept their own cunukus and much of their dignity."

"Nevertheless, by the King's law of 1517, an Indian was freed upon the original encomendado's death. It was an illegal inheritance."

"So it was," I said. "Like so many even today."

I saw Enriquillo occasionally at the convent until 1505 or 1506, when I myself was placed in an encomienda and lost touch with him. He was only seven years old then, but I remember his serious eyes and his alert mind.

It was late in the year of 1518, when the story changes for Enriquillo and his people; that was when they took their fate in their own hands. Young Andrés Valenzuela, an obscene profligate who lives in Santo Domingo even today, took away Enriquillo's mare. The mare was special, a deathbed gift to the young Taíno cacique from Andrés's own father. Enriquillo complained, but Valenzuela claimed it as his own father's inheritance to him. His overseers overtook Enriquillo in a field and beat him up, bruising his ribs and breaking a finger. A month went by. To fulfill his prescribed obligation, Enriquillo took a group of his guaxeris, his working men, to the mines for a four-week period. While he was thus occupied, Valenzuela came to his home and lewdly demanded sex from Doña Mencía, Enriquillo's wife.

"This I had heard," Las Casas said. "It was the rape—how Doña Mencía was raped."

A boy was sent for Enriquillo and he returned immediately. He complained to Valenzuela, and demanded an apology to his wife. "I love my wife," he said to have told Valenzuela, who replied, "Neither Indians nor dogs know how to love?"

"Valenzuela said that?" Las Casas said, taking detailed notes as I spoke. He knows I know the Indian side of this story.

"Of course he did. And this is well-known, how Enriquillo and his wife love each other. Those two were close since early childhood and were brought up together by their families."

"They are lineage?"

"Yes, an arranged marriage."

"But let me finish. Enriquillo, an Indian like me and educated to his legal rights by friars, followed the good course and took his complaint to the Lieutenant Governor, Pedro de Badillo. And again, Badillo laughed him out of court in San Juan de la Maguana. Then he had him arrested for public insubordination and beaten severely."

"It's a miracle he survived!" the friar said.

"It took Enriquillo weeks to recover, but when he did and could get around, he went to the court in Santo Domingo, where he hoped the oidores, or judges, would hear his complaint. But they, too, laughed at him. He stood up, again and again, in court, insisting that they hear his complaint. They placed him in chains for a week, then sent him home, where, at the courthouse of San Juan la Maguana, once again, three Castilla peons attacked him and beat him severely."

" 'I went to them three times,' Enriquillo then told his people. 'All the talk of the priests is for nothing.' This time, when Enriquillo recovered, he rounded up the families under his care and took to the bush mountains of Bahuruku. Valenzuela pursued him with eleven foremen, but Enriquillo easily ambushed them, killing two of the men outright. He caught Valenzuela, stripped him naked, and merely chased him away. 'You are lucky I don't kill you, Valenzuela,' he told his former encomendero. 'Don't let me see you again in these parts or I will.' "

The friar laughed heartily, contentedly. "I have always heard that Enriquillo is not blood-thirsty," he said.

No, Enriquillo is not blood-thirsty, but he is tough. As I write now, thirteen years later, Enriquillo and his many warriors, who number into the hundreds, have this Española island nearly paralyzed. Christians, whether Castillian or Indian, dare not travel the roads without strong guard. The Spanish are not as numerous as they once were on this island, many having gone on to the mainland, although the encomiendas that remain are quite large. Not a few have lost great sums, paying for useless expeditions against Enriquillo, who is one Indian whose cunning is beyond the Castillas' and forceful enough to frustrate them at every turn.

"I think all authorities want to kill Enriquillo," I told Don Bartolomé. "I will do all I can do to save him."

Six. *My own truth I pledge.*

I write this now in a late night of full moon and calm waters. I feel the sea breeze enter my room, lick at my lips. Crickets chirp their long rasp, again and again, and the tree frog bellows back. Beyond earshot but not far, I know the waves caress our shore, once and again an ancient rhythm by which my people breathed. What our world was, how we saw life, how we lived by our heart, by the belly-button of belonging and the memory of ancient teachings—this from my blood and my heart, it seems, the friar does not hear. He has an argument that we were almost like them, nearly Christian, as if this proves us a better people, we who were Taíno—"the good people." No, I respect him, but I have lived too long. I know what we had, the personality of our people that was like a gentle breeze, how they saw only seed in the rotting fruit: what would come forth. But, in forty years, I have yet to hear a Castilla priest express such a thought. Yes, I have seen too much and now, in my time of illness and pain ... my arm and leg on the right side stiffen with their own memory of injury and travail ... [illegible] ... in this providential gift of paper, I pledge my own truth to the mysteries, even if in the foreign language of Castille, which I have commanded since my first weeks with the Admiral.

April 24, 1532

Seven. *What the friar wants.*

I worked the garden all morning, ate lightly at lunch, attended a Mass, then napped. I was washing up after waking, when the knock came and my benefactor, Don Bartolomé, pronounced by King Ferdinand, "Protector of the Indians," entered forthrightly. He announced the continuation of what he called our "historical witness," and requested I take notes.

"I remember a story told by Michelle de Cúneo," the friar began, and he must have seen me grimace, because he said, "I know you did not like Cúneo—but you were there in his story. It happens during Columbus' second trip, when he explored the southern coast of Cuba."

I remember the trip, during the Admiral's second voyage, from April to September of the Christian year of 1494. Don Bartolomé has brought up this episode before. I can tell he wants this episode because of his argument about our Taíno people being almost Christian in their old beliefs.

"Cúneo told my father about the trip. He said that a Cuban cacique spoke of a Heaven and a Hell among his people ... "

It was not quite so. However, I held my tongue. Cúneo was a total bastard, abusive, deceitful, a man who let his balls squeeze his mind, a rapist of women and buggerer of boys. Cúneo was on board only because he was a boyhood friend of Don Christopherens, from his own city of Genoa. He came back from Castille with us, on that second trip, a guest of honor of the Grand Admiral of the Ocean Seas.

"It was the trip to the south of Cuba," the friar continued. "Cúneo told my father that a prominent Cuban cacique, chief of a large yukaieke called Bayamo, feasted the Admiral, then had long words about his own spiritual doctrine. Cúneo said you translated at the meeting."

"I was translator," I said, and I felt faint to remember that time. The friar went on but, again, he had thrown my mind back. That was the voyage of misery, when I confirmed for my thick-skulled self that the Castilla were not only cruel and violent men but also liars and crazy. It was during that voyage, too, that Don Christopherens lost his own mind for weeks at a time.

"Cúneo said the cacique spoke in Christian terms about Heaven and Hell, and expressed his belief that good people go to Heaven and bad people go to Hell," Don Bartolomé repeated.

"Cúneo would lie to the Virgin herself, father, with your permission," I actually said. I could not help myself.

"He was a loyal friend to my father," Don Bartolomé responded solemnly. "Though he *was* a rake."

"A perverted man, father, with your permission," I said.

The good friar looked past me for a few moments. He admonished me finally. "You speak with vehemence again, Dieguillo."

"Yes, father," I said. "With your forgiveness, father."

He was right. I insulted him, and I do not mean to do that. But my breast was a sail taut with wind.

"I beg your forgiveness, father. I only meant to say it was not like that. Cúneo did not understand the language and in any case he was not there during that talk between the cacique and the Admiral."

"Where was he?"

"He was exploring, father."

"Exploring what? The coast?"

"Yes," I told him. "The coast." I did not need to tell him that Cúneo was, as my people would say, "emptying his fleshly gourd," all through that evening. Chasing for a place to stick his yuán was always the main occupation of Monsieur Michelle de Cúneo.

"And well then, did the two men discuss the existence of Heaven and Hell?"

"It happened," I said. "But it did not mean what you think it meant."

"Write about it anyway, Dieguillo. It could be very important."

I told him, "That was the time Don Christopherens lost his mind."

The good friar shook his long face. "No wild stories now, Dieguillo. I can take your testimony to the King. I need something new from that time that will help him sympathize with your people."

Eight. *Starting out.*

The problem is: I remember so much more.

The trip to Cuba of Don Bartolomé's question came after our return from Castille, during the Admiral's second voyage and four months into the settling of the new colony of Isabella.

But for Don Bartolomé's insistence, I would not begin my narrative there. My inclination is to start at Guanahani, when we first saw the Admiral. That would be the proper sequence. I would start that first morning, with my father-uncle, Çibanakán, who was the first to see the giant sea gulls, and tell how in the company of six of my kin, I sailed away in the Castilla ships through our small islands of the Bahama, how we guided the Admiral to Cuba, then to Bohío, where he was embraced by Guanacanagari's people and where he left forty men at Fort Navidad.

I saw Castille in my youth. I would write about that next, how I traveled through Spain in 1493. Then I would write about our return, the shock of what we encountered at Fort Navidad. All that and more would come before, in my story, because from the time I met the Admiral to the time we sailed to Cuba and met Bayamo, the cacique who cursed Columbus, it was a year and more.

Now, it is forty years since that morning at Guanahani, when after a night under lock in the hatch of the Santa María, I heard the pilot, Sancho Ruiz, holler the order to pull up anchors and the three caravels hoisted up sails, gliding swiftly as they let the seven of us Guanahani-ti, or as they called us, "Indians," come out on deck just in time to see our beach disappear, our little turtle island of Guanahani become a sliver in the horizon, gone from our eyes.

Nine. *I begin with the return.*

Later in this journal, I will take up the proper order. I want to tell my own stories and I have plenty of paper. But first I will let the good friar guide my pen.

In Castille, the Admiral was received as a hero, but when we arrived again at our shores, that time with seventeen ships and more than one thousand five hundred men, it was not a good moment. The colony Don Christopherens had left behind, Fort Navidad, was destroyed and everyone killed. Trouble brewed.

I remember well those first nightmare days of the new Isabella town, when all Castilla eyes were nervous and distant, weapons always at the ready and quickly used. The Admiral's authority was daily challenged. The Castillian captains and the priest, the buzzard head Buil, disdained him as a mere Genoese. Daily were the fights and contentions among Castillians themselves and against our Indian people.

A simple thing: the taking without permission of a cutlass from a sleeping Christian man. For that I saw the broad ax come down and a fourteen year old Taíno boy hopping and hopping as blood poured from his wrist, the Admiral shrugging his long shoulders, walking the ship's deck in long steps, nodding, "It is the lesson we must teach, Diego. Always understand, I myself have no blood-lust, but the lesson must be sharp to be understood." His hair was still red, that marvelous red hair that had amazed us all. I remember now how I told myself over and over that the bloodletting had its reason: *The Guamiquina knows what he does*, I cried against hope that night, *the Guamiquina knows what to do.*

April 26, 1532

Ten. *A route home denied.*

Columbus was by then my adopted father, this having happened in Barcelona, after his triumphant reception by the Queen. And I still loved him, though it was a love in its final instances. Nevertheless, those first few days sailing, the openness and natural generosity of the sea made my heart soar. Too, Don Christopherens was a man who came alive on a ship. A thing to behold was his certainty of signal from wave and wind and cloud. I admit I sailed happily off with him from Isabella, still as his main interpreter, escaping the troubles of land-locked men.

The hope of my innocence at that time was to once again return home to my island of Guanahaní. I rejoiced in the possibility of return to my own village by paddling home around the Maisi Point of Cuba. That first night, starting out, when I mentioned this wish to the Admiral, he said, "It is possible to do so, Dieguillo." I envisioned rounding Cuba's easternmost point and heading north. Night after night I dreamed myself in a canoe, paddling home those last few suns to arrive at Guanahani in the early morning, where I would make fire for my mother and awaken her gently by stroking the skin of her face.

Sighting Cuban land, our three ships indeed hugged the shore but turned west, not to round the Maisí tip of Cuba and out to my little island of Guanahani. I questioned not the Admiral, but waited; he spoke soon enough. To the officers and crew that very evening he asserted that this land of Cuba, which he renamed first Fernandina and then Juana, was not an island but a peninsula of the mainland of China. He meant to determine this thesis, he said, by exploring the southern coast going west. Don Christopherens got that distant look in his face, a dreaminess, when speaking of Cuba this way. So we sailed around the southwestern point of Cuba, which the Admiral renamed Cape of the Cross.

In my heart I despaired I would never again see my mother, my village or my people. Suddenly I felt the loneliness that would be with me the rest of my life. Yes, a sting-ray jolt was for me that trip to Cuba, that trip that shattered my wonderment about the Admiral, this arrogant man that renamed the world at will, changing the nature of everything, mixing what was ours with what was to be theirs. Yes, that was the moment. My beckoning like a son to this man we believed could cross the barriers to the Spirit World shattered. My heart was as the dried out carapace of the great sea turtle left out in the midday sun.

Eleven. *The trip to Cuba, barbecueing on the beach.*

On the beach in southern Cuba, from the distance, we could see Indian fishermen cooking. Then in front of us, on the open sea, we saw two men in a canoe. They turned out to be brothers and one fished with a net, the other by means of a guaikán, or suckerfish, which fish I am named after. This clever method of my people was unfamiliar to the Castilla on board. It makes use of the powerful circle of suckers on the guaican's head, by which the fish attaches itself to larger fish and even bigger turtles. The fishermen tied the fish's tail with a long, thin bejuco twine and asked us to slow our approach while they pulled in a big turtle.

I talked to the brothers from aboard ship. They gave our ship four large caguama turtles, and invited me to the beach in their canoe. The ship's boat followed us to the shore, where we found other men cooking hundreds of smoked lobsters, yellow-tails, barbecued hutías and iguanas, most of it wrapped in maize husks and stacked in small huts.

The men were of cacique Bayamo's village. Immediately they stated that from there to Baracoa, on the northern coast, and including all the mountain ranges of the region, their cacique and his line of behikes were respected. Their cacique had told them to prepare food for visitors. They said Bayamo was a seer who knew many things. Believing that we must be those expected visitors, they directed us to a place up the coast, a fishing village of a lesser cacique, named Macaca, where we would find Bayamo. They gifted me with many foods for our ships. When the sailors thanked them, they shrugged, and said together, "we'll catch more." Since they had seen me emerge from the caravel's hold, the brothers were sorry to see me go, for they wanted to hear my stories about the hair-faced men who traveled in wooden caves.

Twelve. *Bayamo and Macaca: not a discourse but a curse.*

The next day, I sat next to the Admiral in the row boat going to the shore. The three caravels sat behind us in the thick of the bay. Waiting on the beach, hundreds of men, women and older children surrounded the cacique, an old man, frail but spry, who carried a woven tunic over his shoulder. In one hand he carried a basket of small guayabas. The Admiral spotted him. "Regard thou this Indian his apparel," he said to Captain Juan de la Cosa, his map maker, who sat behind us. I, too, was impressed. The old Cacique of Bayamo watched sternly as his men pulled our boats to shore, then waved us to him. The Admiral stiffened but went to the old man, standing before him a few seconds, then offering his hand. Old Bayamo grasped the hand and held it, peering directly at the much taller Don Christopherens.

Bending slightly toward me, the Admiral said, "Tell him he may kneel and kiss the ring, which is granted me by the Sovereigns of Castille and Aragón, now the united Christian Kingdom ... " but, before I could begin to put that into our language, another old man, the local cacique Macaca, came up and took the Admiral's other hand. The two caciques turned and began walking fast, the multitude closing behind them, and suddenly it was all we could do to keep up, Don Christopherens, myself, captains Herrera and Navarra, a dozen soldiers and sailors, plus the braggart Cúneo, walking for half a league, the soldiers hacking a trail through the greenery, sweating gourds before arriving at a deserted yukaieke of twelve bohíos built in a square.

Their round bohíos were very well made, with tight thatch ties in the roof-poles and bamboo and palm board walls fastened together so sunlight could not penetrate. All had good dimensions and some large ones were forty and fifty feet wide. The square was recently swept. Large woven mats made from palm fronds lay covered with baskets of sweet fruits, pots of cooked corn ears, ñame, boniato soups, barbecued duck, lobster, iguana and a fragrant herbal tea, freshly squeezed with cool mountain-stream water. It all had been left out, smoking and steaming in the empty village, awaiting our arrival. Immediately I felt at home. This was the way it was done among our Guanahani people, to leave food out like that, as if dropped from the sky. Even among small caneys of three or four families, often a family might return from harvesting or fishing and find a meal prepared like that, all warm and freshly made and no one around. As we sat and feasted on the axiaco and casabe, I felt a great homesickness grip my chest.

Thirteen. *The Castilla change everything.*

I promised, good friar, to tell about the meeting and not get too involved in my own story. You say we were like Christians in our ways of worship, that we believed in similar spirits. I will say it is true, that our people had some similar ideas to yours. But another truth is you came from a world other than ours. And that world you brought with you and with it you saw everything that was obvious before.

At Bayamo's open-air batey or plaza, a dance was held. First the young men drummed and sang, then the women and all the children joined in, holding hands in two long rows on both sides of the fire, singing long and melodic areito songs. They gave a beautiful rendition of the areito of Baya-manacoel, which they would, of course, being the Bayamo people. They did this in greater detail than I had heard before or since. Bayamanacoel was the first maker of guanguayo, our sacred cohoba paste, and the areito tells how Bayamanacoel found cohoba the first time, what great trials he suffered to gain its favor and to prepare its powers for creation. Later, in one part of the story, he spits this paste on the back of Deminán, another of our ancestral grandfathers-creators ...

A Taíno such as myself could appreciate this offering, which was ceremonial and spiritual. Truly, I have loved reclining in the wide hammocks of my mother and grandmother, listening to the areitos of our Taínos that can go on and on, night after night and never lack for songs. Bayamo's areito was so intricate, so ancient, that it ended, after almost two hours, where the same areito of other places would begin. Then, four old men and one old women, all wearing the white, woven tunics, joined the great cacique, Bayamo, in reciting ancestral stories for our ears. These doings put through by the old cacique represented a great honor and normally would have been reciprocated with several days of ceremony.

Sitting next to me, the Admiral was impatient to be back on his ship, as night was falling and a bright moon was our only fighting advantage. I knew and informed the Admiral that his turn to speak, as honored guest, would surely come, and thus he waited quietly, observing everyone at the same time that his agonized mind calculated everything. Here, he had been seated by our people in a duho, or ceremonial chair, his back placed against a wide root that protruded, tall as a cathedral wall, from a huge tree that towered over the clearing. Here he was feasted and sung to and offered the hospitality of the village, but in his mind that I know so well, he was engaged in his mission, calculating possession and achievement.

Asked to speak, the Admiral stood. This is what he said, as I remember it. "I am here to claim the lands we stand upon for the Sovereigns of Castille and Aragón, whose loyal subjects you are now become," he began. I stood next to him to interpret and yet consciously moved a bit apart, to establish my own stance before Taíno people.

"We are Christians," he continued, "and we are led by the most Revered Catholic Queen, Our beloved Isabel of Castille, who along with her own sovereign husband, King Fernando, of Aragón, sent us to these lands. If Bayamo wants to be among the good people, who go to Heaven when they die, he and his people should accept what I am telling them. But by our Christian law, once you have heard our doctrine, not to accept it is to be damned eternally, and you would force my armies to war upon you without mercy."

I translated as well as I could the words of the Admiral. My instinct was always to let my people know as clearly as I could the intentions in the Castilla's words, but often they could be so drastic that I had to refrain from giving their full tenor.

Thus, at first, the caciques smiled at each other over the Admiral's words, hearing only favored points. "Tau-ti-taíno," they said, one after another, meaning, "Good, we are the good people, too, the nice-minded people."

The Admiral listened to their words with distant demeanor, until a reference was made to their own land by a young leader, whom Bayamo asked to speak. "This is our island," the man said clearly, "which we share with the Çiboney villages, not far from us down the coast. Our own people, that we understand in our language, extend from here to the small Lucayos and to the Bohío land, to Boríken and Xamayca."

I knew this would cause me trouble, although of course, among our people we have always known Cuba to be an island. All of our pilots who ever guided the Admiral, all, always, referred to Cuba-cubanakan as a land that can be circled by canoe. But when, loudly, I translated the young man's description of Cuba as an island, the Admiral reddened in the face and widened his eyes at me with a terror that frightened me.

Old Bayamo, I could tell, saw the heat of the Admiral and watched intently. The Castilla captains and sailors had also heard me say, "island." I knew looking at the Admiral that he knew I had consciously betrayed his idea. From that moment on, the Admiral always saw me as a potential betrayer of his intentions. Because I did know his intent.

In Barcelona and Seville that previous winter, I sat next to the Admiral at the many dinners given in his honor, and at those, he claimed to have touched the lands of China by sailing west. Thus, he called Cuba, which he renamed Juana, a peninsula of the distant mainland ruled by the Grand Khan. I knew the Sovereigns granted him one in ten of all the wealth generated from lands he discovered and claimed for the Crown. Thus the noblemen who wined and dined him and would finance his return made much of his assertion that Cuba might, indeed, be that main motherland of the rich and vast Mongol Empire, a gold-hued heathen civilization.

Fourteen. *The Admiral is cursed.*

It is true the Admiral felt great pressure in his mind to find the nearest source of gold. He said directly to Cacique Bayamo, "In the most powerful land of Castille, my Queen hurts deeply in her breast with a pain most horrendous. Only one thing can cure her: the shiny metal we call gold." I translated the Spanish "oro" for Bayamo as both "guanin" and "caona," copper and gold in our language. "My Queen, and her King will love dearly any people that can provide them with the shiny metal, and they need much of it to quench their heart's pain," the Admiral said.

Those words I remember distinctly. Since by then I knew how gold is used by the Castilla, what it means to them, I was daunted by his expression. It made everybody wonder just what he meant, and how it could be that the shiny metal might help a sick person, which, interestingly enough, was also our custom. We did not know yet, not even I, the lengths to which the covered men would go to secure the gold.

When Bayamo stood to speak, I also translated his words for the Admiral. Bayamo called the Admiral by a Taíno name, Guamiquina, which means "main chief." He was direct and, again, I remember his words quite well, as they still bounce in my ears.

"Tell the Guamiquina that in these parts we have our kind of people. The good people, Tau-ni-taíno, are peaceful. We share what we have, what the land and the sea give us. As you can see from our many foods, we are a fortunate people. Our spirits are plentiful. Because we are good, our spirits like us. They fortify our plantations. Thus the yuca, thus the maize, the ají, the beans, fruits of the trees, fish, turtles and iguanas. In the sea, in the Kaçi, our eldest Bleeding Mother Moon, guides the women and the snappers ... "

"What spirits is he referring to?" the Admiral interrupted, out loud. His voice was accusatory. Bayamo fell deeply silent and looked surprised. I could tell he had never been interrupted in his life. In our people's ways, an elder is never interrupted, and much less in mid-sentence. Young Taíno faces turned away out of respect for Bayamo, who patiently heard my translation. "It is a natural curiosity for spirited men," I added by way of excuse, although I had no doubt by then that the covered men were not spirit beings.

"What spirits would I speak about?" Bayamo responded. "I speak of the grandmothers and grandfathers, the Taíno who are in us. I speak of no one else. I mean only our old ancestor spirits, the spirit of the sea, the spirit of the mountain, the spirit of our incense and our tobacco, the spirit of our yuca and our corn, those things that forever have helped us ... "

I interpreted. The Admiral responded thus: "This that he says is mistaken. Tell him his faith is misplaced. Tell him he would fare better by accepting our Lord, Jesus Christ, and baptism in the true faith. Then he could travel the road to Heaven and Life Everlasting. Tell him those who do not accept Jesus Christ as Lord and Savior will go to Hell, tell them their souls will roast and burn for ever and ever."

My translation was more gentle and included an apology for the whole interruption.

"Tell him about Hell. He must understand how the punishment works," the Admiral insisted.

I translated. The cacique peered silently at the Admiral. At that moment I saw Don Christopherens rear back slightly, detecting the intensity of the cacique's *goeiça* or living spirit, which emanated that light, hummingbird tremor.

Cacique Bayamo was truly of the elder men of our people, of the ones that spoke to the earth directly, keen with the certainty of our Taíno love and common spirit with the living world.

It is true that the Castilla have reduced us, have just about destroyed us. I admit that our fighting skills could not match their furious thrust. Truly were they decisive and resolute when we, in our trance, in our habitual and cyclical understandings, took forever to decide anything but what our culture dictated, responses so slow that they still hurt. But I know this, the superb among our people, those most steeped in our traditions, were men and women who could spark response in wind and cloud, could converse with plants and trees, could hear the animals speak, could even be heard by snake and caymán, turtle and manatí.

For generations on generations our Taíno were guided by those conversations, held by our elders with the dream-like leaders of the reptile and bird nations, with the leaders of trees, the ceiba and the guásima, with the discernible snake motion of the long fish runs, the passing of the flocks, with the very swell of the sea.

Bayamo himself was of the snake. His neck and loping shoulders on a thin body, his flattened forehead, carefully manipulated from his birth by grandmothers of his line, a practice for precisely such babies in whose reptile eyes could the great mothers feel the cold, penetrating, never forgetting, never ignoring, justice of the snake, who can snatch time from the quickest prey.

Such men and women among our people were extraordinarily powerful. And I can state with certainty that there never was and never will be even one such as those among the covered people, whose very best can forge wide roads out of forest and cross worlds of water and command huge quantities of death and mayhem, but cannot ever hear the adjoining voices, the surrounding and constant conversation from our living world.

Cacique Bayamo began the shaking in Columbus' Christian heart. I saw it, and I was glad to see it, and, now, to remember it. It was in his look, how he transferred to the Admiral's eyes his own body's terrifying inner shaking. Yes, at that very meeting it was that the hummingbird medicine grasped the Admiral's heart.

"We have guided you in our world," the cacique talked on. "So you would not be lost. And now you know us. We are a people that stay on our islands, fishing and visiting, mindful of the present business of our foods, our bohíos, our cunukus and our ceremonies. We have been here for a long time, drinking the same water, eating the same food. Always, in our gatherings, amongst us, we love the children. And our children, in turn, love and respect us. Even our dead, our opias who come through the tree-tops from their Valley of the Dead and have no belly-button, they stay around us and dance with us. We are good, Guamiquina. We don't raid. We never raid, we always build and fish and plant, do for ourselves. In our way, we feed everyone. If a man comes from other islands, and he accepts our peace ways, we take him in, marry him into our people, exchange names with him. In this way, we extend our houses, our bohíos, and give roof to everyone. Our chiefs listen to each other. That way we have grown strong and are growing still on these islands." (I translated "islands" as simply "lands" this time).

"The bad men, Kwaib, thigh-eaters, heart-eaters, from the south and some raiders from the north, are mean-spirited," Bayamo continued. "They raid for women, raid for our young ones. Among them even, some are very, very bad, caniba warrior bands that leave their women on their own islands— the matininos—and raid for the joy of killing, bent on tasting human flesh. My old people said, 'Watch out when you see those uglies coming!' "

The other headmen all laughed, out of habit, at the cacique's joke. As I translated, the Admiral smiled, but very lightly. He liked it that our Taíno had their enemies, and made much of it to the King and Queen. I myself always thought Bayamo and other caciques who said such to the Admiral exaggerated their old enemies' cruelties. However, it appeared Bayamo had someone else's cruelty in mind.

"The giant seagulls that carry you across the ocean, your garments and sand-skin, these things I have heard of," Bayamo continued. "Our brother-cousins from cacique Baracoa's villages, over the mountains on our northern coast, they told us about you. Many things were told, when we met them at our common areito, the dance for Yúcahuguama Bagua Maorocoti, Supreme Spirit. They even said you came from heaven and could fly away. They also said that when you left, you took ten of their people, those you put in a cave hole in your own wooden ship."

Columbus stood up with a bound, as I translated the words. Again, he interrupted. "All people are lost without the knowledge of Christ. Those taken are better because of it."

"He is agitated," I said in Taíno, trying to bridge the minds and minimize the insult. "He is a great Captain, but he is not well."

The Admiral spoke hurriedly. "The light of the Lord has now come to your lands, head man. Innocence cannot save you from eternal torture, the word of God is in your ear now and only the Holy Doctrine will capacitate your people to enter the Kingdom of Heaven . . . "

Bayamo began to talk to himself. I stopped listening to Columbus, who predicated for another full minute, and listened to Bayamo.

"I have a question of yourself, great lord—are you caniba that your giant seagulls eat Taíno people?" Bayamo asked. "Are you a cousin of thigh-eaters who kidnap our people? I ask the question: Are you good or bad? Because if you are bad to my people, you will go to that hell you have mentioned. If you believe every man answers for his deeds after death, then you will not harm those who do not harm you, or you will certainly go to that fire place of hell."

Having said that, the cacique sat down and the Admiral stopped in mid-sentence. The silence left behind by the sound of Bayamo's voice seemed to dumbfound him.

I translated the cacique's words then, and did not tone down the directness, seeking to maximize the impact. But the Admiral had regained his composure. He was not Admiral of the Ocean Sea, Christ-bearer and Grand Navigator, to be without the capability for an answer.

"Tell him, again," the Admiral said, looking to his own captains and twirling his finger to signify a closure to the parley, "that the people taken are meant to serve us and in return are instructed in the true faith of our Catholic Kings."

I translated this as gently as I could. However, the precision for terms of bartering in our language made obvious the faults of the Admiral's proposition.

The old men of Bayamo understood and did not like the Admiral's reasoning. "What if we don't want to be taught?" one asked. "Why this place of burning?" another one asked. "Why is that necessary?"

An old man who was gnarled and had not aged gracefully, like Bayamo, stepped into the circle in front of the cacique. He looked to a line of elderly women, mostly sisters and aunts in Bayamo's line, standing together behind the seated row of men. The women all had a rearing-back look, fixing wary eyes on the Admiral. The old-timer raised his palm and pointed toward the women with his open hand. "Be careful," he said. "When you counsel your cacique, be careful of the hair faces."

I translated bluntly again, and the Admiral smiled bitterly. "He should fear us more," he said plainly to no one. It was not meant for translation.

The old man had stopped. Now Macaca, the village chief, joined him and they went to stand by a tree. I noticed the old man wore a thin belt of caracol shells around his hips and held a small gourd in his hand. Now he took a plug of rolled leaves from the gourd and put it in his mouth. I could tell he was a medicine man, a behike, and that, like his cacique, Bayamo, there was no fear in him.

The cacique, Bayamo, stood again. "Tell my words to the Guamiquina," the cacique said, and I stood by him to hear him better.

"The fire is sacred to us," the cacique said. "We talk with our sacred fire. In fire we think not of death but of life. As for the Spirit World, as I said, our grandparents await us there." The cacique himself nodded at the Admiral, but warily.

Again, I translated his words and, again, the Admiral was taken aback. Momentarily, his face looked flush and his eyes darted about.

"We are going now," he announced, standing, though with a slight wobble. He stared at the cacique, who stared back.

"The fire is good," the old cacique said. I translated.

The Admiral stared at him. "Tell him that fire burns," he said.

Then the curse was pronounced upon him.

The gnarled old man, the behike of Bayamo standing by the women's council, cleared his nose and throat, then coughed into his left palm. Cupping the thick snot with his right hand, he walked between the fire and the Admiral, suddenly showing the gob directly to the Admiral. "With this I will teach you humility," he whispered harshly in Taíno. "The door to your dreams, I close."

The Admiral turned quickly to face him and our soldiers stepped up too.

The old man had no fear in him at all, his palm and fingers slicing through space at the Admiral. "Hell is in your dreams if you, a far-seeing man, commit the deeds that are in your mind," he said.

A soldier drew his sword, sensing the old man's hostility.

"Don't quarrel here," Columbus told the soldier.

With the growing sense of threat, the Admiral regained his composure. He felt the men of Bayamo might overcome our small troop of not quite twenty. "Our business is over here," he said, and ordered Captain Herrera to organize the troop. The soldiers and sailors surrounded the Admiral and as we began to walk, he asked what the old man had said at the end.

"He said to watch your dreams," I said. "It was a kind of farewell gesture."

The guanguayo had power, I knew, particularly for Bayamo's people. Behike men like the gnarled old-timer meant everything they said. For myself, I knew they would not attack us under the circumstances, and indeed, they lit resin torches and thick, rolled tobaccos and led us down to the shore, singing once again. They carried dozens of baskets full of foods for the ships. But the Admiral had been shown a guanguayo, cohoba medicine, teacher of our people, veil of water between the worlds. Don Christopherens moved stridingly, in measured long steps, but even so, walking to the boats he stumbled several times. Later, climbing on ship, he tripped and had to hang by an elbow from a net while sailors hauled him on board.

We sailed on for many more weeks during this journey, the Admiral intent on proving Cuba a peninsula of the mainland. The weeks dragged on and fewer and fewer of his officers believed him. Twice, out of spite, I reminded him of the words of Bayamo's young chief on the island nature of Cuba. He had me flogged the second time—five swift ones from the many-tailed whip. For that I cursed him myself and intoned the guanguayo of the dark over him as we sailed for long weeks among the islands. And it happened that as the weeks rolled on, he slept less and less and I believe that special curse, which he now and forever carried from the people of Bayamanacoel, blocked the doors between his waking and dreaming selves. Truly, the navigation was difficult through the channels of the smaller islands and the Admiral became extremely nervous. Finally he got sick and brittle. And for weeks, in feverish deliriums, he exclaimed how much the Queen would like it that the Indians believed in a Heaven and a Hell, evidence to push the enterprise of their Christianization. "For the use of their labor," he half-sang sometimes, "we will bring them the true Faith!"

I would add, good friar, that from hearing these ravings (which later became law), Cúneo must have picked up the reference to Heaven and Hell, as he helped nurse the Admiral during that voyage.

May 1, 1532

Fifteen. *Hard to explain our Indian religion, even to a good friar.*

Don Bartolomé read my pages of the Admiral's meeting with Bayamo. He shook his head at me. "Cúneo mentioned nothing about a warning or curse. In fact, he said that the cacique wanted to go with the Admiral to visit Castille. He said the Admiral had gone ashore to hear mass when the cacique approached him. And that he was very happy when the Admiral mentioned that he would help the Taíno against raids by Kwaibs."

"No," I said. "What distressed the Admiral that time was how clear the cacique and his behikes were about the fate of our Taíno people."

"It would seem so, from your pages."

"I was there. I saw it. The Admiral was fashioning the idea of the encomienda."

"Yes, I admit that. Your perception of Indian servitude being exchanged or requested for Christianization, that is very good, Dieguillo. And you remember that from the meeting with Cacique Bayamo?"

"Oh yes. He said that even then. And Bayamo knew what it meant. We all did. Even I, as thick-headed as I can be, I finally understood they meant to own us forever. All of us were to be their naboria, or worse, their complete slaves ... "

"A great sadness you must have known."

"Indeed, but that little revenge of the guanguayo, which I confess, father, lifted my Taíno spirit."

"That's witchcraft, Dieguillo, you would persist otherwise?"

"Father, please, trust my character, which you have known. There is no devil in it. The cohoba was at the center of our minds. It was the veil of water for us, it was the passageway between this world in our hands and the one of our memories, in our dreams."

"You still believe in that, Dieguillo? And you, a baptized Christian, and so knowledgeable in our sacraments?"

"This is what I mean. Even now, the Christian owns everything. Even you, the best of Christians, would choke my little space. Let me have a moment with this. Or would thou callest the Inquisition on me for explaining my people's beliefs?"

"Very well. I try to understand you. Proceed and forgive me."

"Understand, they were angered. And they did have a power. In our way. Now, let me finish, father, don't start again. Because they did curse him, directly. And never again would he be as sure of himself. He began losing his way then, after his encounter with Bayamo. By the time we arrived on ship, he looked graven. It was our old medicine, good friar. It was one connection that we Taíno had, a power that existed here even before your word of the Christ and the Supreme God with no mother who begot a man-son with no father. You see, even in that, ours was an opposite way. Our Supreme Being, Yúcahuguama, had a spirit mother but no fathers, no grandfathers."

"You help yourself not with these fancy notions."

"Let me tell you, father. Because, it does not deny your way. It is opposite, yet it is also true. Our behikes used to say, the opposite of everything is also true. What would you say to that thought?"

"Perhaps if you could just answer my question, Dieguillo. I don't want to get lost in too much detail. The thing is, did the cacique believe in a Heaven and a Hell?"

I shook my head.

"But do you not see the importance. It makes your people nearly Christians, even before hearing the gospel. We can argue that the Indian can reach Christ directly, through the clergy, without need of overseers and masters."

I have grown used to his thickheadedness. The friar's cause before the Spanish court has lingered for twenty years to little avail. Our people, those who are not in active rebellion or who like me have received special dispositions, have remained wretched slaves—killed and raped, cut at will. No, I do not care to prove that our people were like Christians before the coming of the first Iberians.

We were not a perfect people; I only have to look in the mirror to prove that. But, I know the truth of what was. So, in my poor health, as I am become nearly a dried up man, my family lost and my heart on the ground, I no longer need to please anyone. I respect the friar, yes, and I am obliged to him for the many gestures he has had with me, but what I saw and heard, I know, and remember.

"He did not mean Heaven and Hell, as you say it," I told him. "Bayamo used the Admiral's own words to warn him to stop stealing our people. Good friar, our world here was very different. We did not just talk of the spirit world as an after-death; it was not a place far-away. We could walk in and out of it, our ancestors danced with us, even as we lived."

"Don't speak of pagan things," he snapped at me. "I won't allow it in my presence."

That was his precise response, and at that moment I felt a nausea from this grease-smelling, thick-headed Spaniard. Truly, sometimes I wish to beat this priest with a club, smash his head like a pineapple.

I stared out my window for a long while. The friar assumed I was in meditation and scribbled away at my desk, copying selected paragraphs from my manuscript. I don't like to displease him. I know we need him and, in fact, I respect him very much. Presently, he wiped his pen, folded his papers and stood up to go.

"You should confess yourself soon, my son," he advised as I lowered my head to receive his blessing.

May 2, 1532

Sixteen. *Enriquillo's conditions and vigilance.*

He came again in the afternoon.

Father Las Casas is dark for a Spaniard. He had the cow pox as a child in Seville and it scarred him. His nose and face are long and he is thin but for a bulge at his belly like the majá snake after swallowing one of our tree muskrats. He sat on a three-legged stool next to my cot and, as always when excitation takes his hold, the bulge of his stomach wiggled. His torso truly resembled the majá's with a meal still alive in his guts.

"Enriquillo is much the topic again at the Government House," he said. "They are obsessed with pacifying him. Another delegation has gone already to King's court about it, even as I would go."

Enriquillo himself will not parley anymore with officials on the island, as troops here have tried to snuff out his hidden camps while pretending peace. Once, shortly after taking to the bush, we met at the ranch of friends. He told me, "On our island all are thieves and liars. If the King is just, as they say, he cannot know what is going on."

Another time, I was sent to him by the Governor General, Don Diego Columbus, son of the Admiral, with an offer of partial amnesty. Then, Enriquillo would not let the Castilla official with me within four leagues of his camp. Even I, who once saved his life, did not visit the main camp myself, though he did greet me properly with a feast at the edge of the Lake of the Encomendador. There I met Ciguayo, his allied chief, as well as the one called Romero.

"Vigilance guides my every step," Enriquillo told me then.

"I trust not a one of them but the good friar, and even he I would hang if I had to." I acknowledged that the good friar and some others among the Dominican and the Franciscan priests were indeed trustworthy, but advised him equally."Learn from the fate of your fathers," I told him. "The Castilla are masters of treachery."

"The King might capitulate now because their campaign to ensnare Enriquillo has absolutely collapsed," Father Las Casas said, today. Again, he told the truth. The island government has fielded ten experienced captains to root out Enriquillo's camps, causing him no end of trouble. Enriquillo retaliated by destroying the encomiendas of the specific captains sent against him, burning several and forcing the other four captains to stay close to their haciendas. I can say without any exaggeration that in the past year, Enriquillo's prestige among our own people and among the Africans here has grown. Since the failure of the last campaign against him, many Spaniards are talking about returning to Spain or migrating to the mainland.

"I am informed the King reasons he risks loosing the island if he does not interfere," said the good friar.

"Enriquillo has never asked for more than the King's intercession," I said.

"Intercession in freeing all Indians," he said. "Fray Remigio, when he saw Enrique in the mountains, reports that among the cacique's demands is an end to the encomienda system in Española."

"He is a true hero," I said, though I suspected the good friar was exaggerating. "It concerns me, father, that he may ask for too much. All-out war from the King will come next if a peace is not reached."

"Not at all," the good friar said. "He must do no less than demand an end to the encomienda."

Seventeen. *The Bible guides Las Casas.*

Tonight, one day later, Father Las Casas stopped by again. He leaves in the morning for the Monastery at La Plata, where meetings to discuss the Enriquillo negotiations are being held. Together we read a chapter from the Old Testament, one in Ecclesiastes where the Good Book tells of "misbegotten gifts," how property and goods obtained immorally are not acceptable to God. He read it out loud after we read it silently and then reminded me of how he released his own Indians in Cuba, in 1514, to begin his work on our behalf.

"The truth of our Bible guided me, Dieguillo," he said. "The Good Book I have given you before. Read it. As you know how to, read the gospels. Read St. Matthew. This you must do every day, on three occasions. Empty your head of the things of behikes. The Devil can control that. You may not think so because you have a love for your people's things, this is natural. But beware that the Devil can control them and you will fall pray. He will damage your soul. He will steal you from us. Fill your head with Christ, my son Dieguillo."

"Yes, father," I agreed, though I hate to be spoken to in this manner. As I wrote before, I am past the point where I have to please anyone. But I said, "It is only that my memories exist, father."

Before he left, Don Bartolomé took my hand. "Resist bad memories," he said, forcefully. "Think of our Holy Trinity, think of our Christ on the Cross."

Folio II

Losing Everything

Thinking of the elders, after my father's death ... First sight of the
Admiral, first greetings ... Meeting Rodrigo, and the Castillas, my turn of
life and leaving Guanahani, my home ... Report to the elders and
pubescence ... The old cohobaneros' vision on the night and morning of
my short farewell ... Last words, for a while ... Enriquillo sends his
messengers, request of cohoba peace pact ... A message and words of
instruction ... A letter to Las Casas ... Useful Castillian things, paper,
horses ... News from Cuba, death of the Guamax rebellion ...
Remembering the elder Guamax ... Jiqui, a warrior, escapes ... Sojourn
in Cuba, along the northern coast, searching for the Great Khan, the curse
of Old Guamax, days of early reverence ... Embassy to Camagüey ...
Carey's doubts and my certainty ... Meeting Baigua, a ni-Taíno of
Camagüeybax, the old ladies call for jaguajiguatu ... Torres reports to
the Admiral, Cuba as mainland ... Çibanakán, my father-uncle, comes on
board ... The old man Guamax, his curse on the Admiral ... Life on
board and learning Castilla ways; out from Punta Maisí, at one with the
Admiral ... Ignoring the feelings of my own people ... Getting closer to
the Admiral ... Even closer to the Admiral ... The good friar returns
from La Plata ... Preparations for his trip to court in Spain ... Jiquí is
captured ... The execution of Jiquí ... Cruelty is the province of the
covered men ... Pressing "the Indian cause" could get Enriquillo
killed ... Las Casas wants to end the Encomienda; I want Enriquillo to
live ... A message for Catalina Díaz, midwife and friend ... A note for
later writing ... Reminding Las Casas of Enriquillo's first cause ... The
townsmen have reasons for peace ... Dissimulated romancing with
Catalina ... Catalina believes in both us and them ... The meeting
ends ... Good-bye to Las Casas, ashamed of my writing ... Breeding my
mare ... Survival in humility ... Our ways were respectful of
reproductive powers ... I do not really feel shame ... Indians tell
Columbus to look elsewhere for women and gold ... Diving for yellow tail
with Rodrigo and Carey ... Çibanakán faces the hammerhead, impressing

45

the sailors ... A generosity of parrots ... Guacanagari, first Taíno
sachem to meet Columbus ... Guacanagari saves the day and provides
the first gold ... The white men's industry is as impressive as their hunger
for gold is immense ... They get more gold from us ... Spirit men remain
behind as we sail off from Fort Navidad ... "Escarmiento"—The fight to
leave a warning ... Sailing out to the great water ...

June 14, 1532

Eighteen. *Thinking of the elders, after my father's death.*

The good friar has been gone ten weeks. Twice in early May he was attacked while walking through the square. Fortunately, Bishop Cisneros, as well as the Governor General, have pressed him into the negotiating embassy to discuss the parley with Enriquillo. For now, he is in the library at the Convent of La Plata, a much more quiet place than this hell-hole of Santo Domingo. Despite our difficulties, on his departure he asked me to continue writing. I took the opportunity to request more paper, but, in all sincerity, I grew weary of the writing. It is only today, after an afternoon watching fluff-clouds dancing through a light blue sky, that the wish to speak arises. The sky carries messages, as does now my pen.

Today I ask my pen: How can I pass on what I have in me but by telling the truth about myself. And I say, reader of my words: Do not think my story more important than another; it is just the only one I know how to tell. Those among my people of whom I have some knowledge, those remarkable among my Guaxeri countrymen, I will try to recount here, so that their names and their deeds might be known.

From a young age I liked the feel of words; always I could make pictures from my eyes to your eyes. I remember cohoba nights that were full of that prettiness, when the chiefs described their old stories, told of our past, how everything came alive again, again and again, our village dreaming in unison, sometimes for days after an areito, sharing their words. I would pick up turns of phrases then, repeat them for my mother, her sisters and for the boys in my group. I was well-named as a boy and often elders would remind me that my being was truly Guaikán—keeping a hold of things, bringing them back with my head, as the guaikán fish will, never letting go. The elders liked me for that willingness of mine to repeat their old things, and in my village I was one of the youngest men ever to participate in the cohoba.

After my father's death, the old men cried for me. They loved me very much, but they revered my father. Many would call me to their backs, as my father had, during the first round of cohoba songs, this for eight nights, and I would, out of my need, hug the backs of my two great uncles, as they sang those beautiful songs I have not heard in forty years. During that time, my father was already drying in the sun, on the small bluff on a hidden bay called the Cove of the Dead. Night after night, following the double snort of the barrel sticks, chief after chief would talk and talk and they would cry to my father for me, telling me again and again his four great deeds, always recalling how our Taíno people came to be. The old people told many stories and sang many songs. With the mind full of words that I have, I never picked up the melodies, but I do remember the stories. I feel grateful for this time with my elders, when they showed me their love and gentleness.

After the nights of cohoba ceremonies full of emotion, the old men prescribed for me eight days of rest. I slept and slept again and I was well-fed, in the spiritual way, by my mother and two aunts. Twice in my dreams, my father visited, once walking the rim of the sky, another time sitting with me, leaving me clear-minded, physically recovered from his death and its condolences. Not two moons later, when the three giant sea gulls of our destiny appeared on the horizon and bearded men covered with cloth first came to our shore, it was natural the old timers would send for me, requesting that I take a group of men to meet them. They could not tell me if I would be in danger or not, they said, because they had never heard of such a thing as the giant seagulls described to them very early that morning.

Nineteen. *First sight of the Admiral, first greetings.*

More than thirty young men, most older than me, followed me down to the shore. I admit I would not call myself a brave man. I have survived enough perils, have been wounded, both in incidents of war and as a slave, but seldom have I dared physical danger if it could be avoided.

We walked toward the shore up and down sand dunes formed behind a line of brush. Gaining height on a dune, I could see the giant gulls were actually huge sails, with men climbed atop long poles while others pulled on long ropes from below. I motioned our men to lay low. "They are something like people," I whispered, as they too preened over the top. Crouching now, we spread across the dune and made our way to the brush line, very near the shore.

Maybe an hour went by and presently we saw three small boats emerge, one from each of the bigger ones. Two men paddled each boat, though curiously, they sat backwards, as they rowed their vessels around the bigger caravels. Rope nets were lowered and other men descended onto the rowing boats. Presently, I remember seeing the Admiral for the first time, at the rudder of the larger row boat, his slender back arched like a Ciguayo bow and that magnificent head of flaming red hair.

Closer and closer they came and then tromped home on our sands. They were not sixty feet away from me. I watched the Admiral directly as his eyes scanned the beach from the boat and saw us. Immediately, two men went to assist him but he ignored them, jumping to the dry sand. All the covered men often looked his way, as if to check their actions. He held a long staff, banners blowing in the breeze.

I am forced to say that the man they later called, "el descubridor," vibrated at that moment. I saw it myself how he held that staff high, such as our own behikes might and intoned a voice for the skies, how he spoke to the heavens in a harsh but resonant language.

We were all stupefied, eyes wide like seashells. "How does one greet such beings," Xiquí, my brother-uncle whispered in my ear. "Where could they be from?"

Çibanakán, my father-uncle, responded, "Perhaps the sky. Perhaps they have arrived from the sky."

It was the Admiral I watched. He was totally clothed, along with six of the others. The rest of them, bare chested, wore short pants and, on their heads, red stocking caps. One man in particular was very hairy, large tuffs covering even his shoulders. All their faces except the Admiral's were hairy too. As he finished his oration, the Admiral handed the staff to two sailors, who jammed it solidly into the sand and then took positions around him, weapons at the ready, as he walked toward our brush.

I must admit something now that still confuses me. As I looked at Don Christopherens the first time, I felt a great glow of warmth, a happiness inside my chest I have never been able to explain, and it drew me out of the brush and onto the beach, pulling a dozen of my men. As if enchanted, we walked toward the Admiral, directly and without fear. Suddenly, the two sailor-soldiers brandished swords, running forward menacingly and we all jumped back. They ran toward us, and we ran, a powerful terror in the calves of our legs. Then they stopped. We stopped and I could hear laughter from them. I spotted their red-haired chief, their Guamiquina, whose palm was raised toward us, and the soldiers now dropped behind him. So I walked toward him again and he came toward us with palm raised as my father-uncle, Çibanakán, properly walked before me to pronounce our people's formal greetings.

June 19, 1532

Twenty. *Meeting Rodrigo, and the Castillas, my turn of life and leaving Guanahani, my home.*

Today, I think of young Rodrigo, and it is indeed a very proper day to think of my dear friend. One of my two twins, born on this day, named Heart of Earth in Taíno, I named Rodrigo in the Castillian, after my good friend. Among the Castillas, I value no one higher than Rodrigo, not even the good friar.

Rodrigo was there on the first day, a young man of fourteen years, kind and soft-spoken. I remember how he came to me, a hawk's bell dangling from his fingers. "Para ti," he said. I responded, "Taíno-ti." And though we spoke different languages, we understood each other immediately. I took the hawk's bell, a great wonder as it would ring when shaken, rather as one of our maracas or gourd rattles, but with a high metallic pitch. Then I cast around to spot one of our men who held a jaba or cord-sack full of fruit. I pulled several guayabas and returned the gift, indicating with my hand that he should crack it and eat. Rodrigo followed my instructions, whereupon Don Christopherens came toward us, and I also offered him a guayaba, cracking it quickly to expose the sweet part, as he extended his hand.

Thus we stared at each other and smiled. More hawk's bells were offered, more guayabas and other fruits were returned. Three men from a coastal village situated around the bend of the cove now joined us. Don Christopherens spoke out loud, locking into our eyes as we crowded around him. Several times Don Christopherens raised his arms toward the sky.

Then my father-uncle, Çibanakán, also spoke. "The spirit men of the skies have arrived," he said. "Tell your communities to bring them food and other gifts." Turning toward me, he said, "We must go and tell our elders. They have instructions for such a day. Where these men come from there is no death. We may be very lucky today."

By instinct I now looked for Rodrigo. I spotted him by the sea brush, urinating. "Para-ti," I called to him in our new language. "Guaikán I am and I go now."

He looked at me in wonder, then pointed to my chest. "Nombre," he asked and, though I did not know the word, I understood him. I said, again, "Guaikán, Guaikán."

He repeated: "Guaikán." Then, he said, "Rodrigo."

I said: "Oligo."

He smiled and nodded his head to affirm my word. He put his hand on my shoulder as I walked away. "Amigo," he said. "Oligo," I said. We laughed.

I looked him up and down. He was all covered with clothes, even his feet were criss-crossed with rope. I caught myself staring and he read my thoughts, grabbing his groin and pointing at mine, again nodding. I laughed, as I had noticed him passing his waters. Our men, of course, went naked. My yuán was free. Everybody, both our men and theirs, stared a great deal that day. Then, while some remained to stare a great deal longer, most of us walked away.

Twenty-One. *Report to the elders and pubescence.*

That night we had a meeting at Old Guanahani village. Everyone, even the oldest of grandmothers came, crowding around the cohoba elders as the inhaling mixture was prepared and the men lined up at the edge of the trees, inserting vomiting spatulas to cleanse themselves.

The old man title holder of Guanahani, whom we called, the Guanahabax, chose the opening song. Appropriately, the song told of the Deminán and his three brothers—the dual set of spiritual twins—our spirit forebears who traveled the clouds, enduring adventures and creating the sea and islands of our world. Yúcahuguama Bagua Maorocoti, Grand Spirit of our sustaining world, was thanked for the creation of the mother of the four brothers, but it was the four, the doers and makers, who were intoned. Significantly, the cohoba was not touched to start. The old men had opted to inhale only after the reports of the greeting on the beach.

Everyone was so greatly excited, waiting in anticipation for the reports, even the food was neglected. The song ended and there was a pause in expectation of what we called in our ceremonies "the little feast," which did not materialize, as the women food-preparers and all their assistants were intent on listening. Aware of the anticipation, the nimble Çibanakán stood, holding his open palm out to the group.

"I will start," he said, as the old men nodded, "to tell of the wondrous day. A Guamiquina has come, I saw today. A Guamiquina and three vessels, full of hair-faced, covered beings. Nothing I have ever seen prepares us for this day. Yet I saw them smile, mostly. They traded gifts with us, and everything they have is wonderful, just wonderfully wonderful. Small rattles, made of guanin, pretty, pretty noise. A cloth, so smooth, I wanted to eat it. A long sharp edge, so sharp and heavy, my cousin Turey was cut in his hand as he tried to hold it."

Everyone looked at Turey, who stared shyly at the ground. A bandage made by the red-haired Guamiquina himself was wrapped around his hand. His old mother, next to him, took the hand and raised it up and Turey smiled.

"The Guamiquina," Çibanakán continued. "He speaks to the sky, and his men murmur with him as he intones orations. It sounded nice, very nice. His hair is red like the inside of a parrot's wing and wavy like the sea. And he has a very quick way of striking fire. Amazing, a click on a click and there is flame, red like his hair."

Something wonderful and strange was happening to me. The sun was low on the horizon, one of those beautiful afternoons, red on the water, red in the sky, the end of a day so full of wonder I could hardly sit. Yet the elders had opened the meeting and it was impolite to fidget. So I sat still, though my heart raced, flapping in my chest like a fish in a canoe and a warming glow that covered my abdomen, my inner thighs, my yuán.

I want to be truthful, so much I have seen and endured since that evening. But that night, after Çibanakán's story was discussed and digested, as my turn came to speak, a great honor considering my age, I felt myself stiffen as I stood and in my chest a heat, an excitement I had never imagined could happen.

I write this because it truthfully happened to me. That very day and moment my body came of age. Everything in my heart and body and in my mind expanded at once. As we are used to among my people, especially in those days, I paid no attention to my nudity, I only felt my heart expand. "I love the new people," I said, quite forcefully. "They are of the sky and of the earth, too. They have wonderful things, and as my father-uncle relates, they think of fire and flame erupts." I admit that I rhapsodized, and with an eloquence I did not know I contained: words of love, excitement, reverence and wonder flowing from my delirious heart. I recalled the oldest of areitos, how they expressed the beauty of our ways, how happy must be the far-gone spirits (everyone, of course, thought of my father), how the wonder of Deminán and his creative hand must have guided the covered men here, how lucky we were. They are friendly, I kept repeating, there is nothing to fear, they smile and bring wonderful gifts and we should love them so very, very much.

Old Guanahabax finally raised his finger, as if to slow me down, and though mildly embarrassed I could only smile, I felt so certain of my words and could see the people's eyes were sparked. When I sat down again, my body had relaxed but I felt incredibly alive, as if for the first time, I was experiencing the world.

After me, others wanted to describe the day, but Guanahabax cut off the speaking. "We have heard the essence," he said, "now the old men will smoke. Then we will snort our cahoba powders. The spirits will advise us. Of one thing I am certain, the life of our people has changed forever."

Only the old men sat in Guanahabax's circle that night. His women assistants brought them the big and small hícaras, the big one brimming with the sacred powder. Twice before I had snorted with them—gestures of sympathy with a bereaved boy. Both times I simply slept and afterward remembered nothing. Guanahabax told me this was proper, as I was not yet a man. "Their messages will come later, in your dreams. All at once, at your age, it would kill you."

Sleep took me in a hammock in my mother's thatch-roofed bohío as I surrendered my hold to the sounds of the cohoba; the wheezing and coughing, the snorting and the hacking, the loud wails and thick laughter and the early morning songs blending with my dream-time thoughts. Once, turning over, I caught glimpse of my mother's gentle face, gazing enchantedly at me. I was the light of my mother's eye. All of my young life, except for times at sea with my father, I always took sleep in my mother's gaze. She would often sing me an old mothers' oration. It went, "I sense your breathing with my eyes, I collect the motion of the distant waves into my ears, blowing my loving breath toward you; I wish you into your dream time peacefully, with all the love of a mother's heart."

The sun was just up when the urge to urinate awoke me. I walked to the brush with such a terribly stiff yuán I could not force it down to piss. I had to nearly hunch over on all fours to direct my spray at the ground.

Some eyes were already watching and company soon gathered to greet the day. But I was sleepy and dived into my hammock once more, barely clutching in my mind the scene of sleeping cohoba elders, curled-up as babies where they had fallen around the fire. A man who had seen me take the dog stance in my morning predicament, walked by. "Sleep, puppy," he teased me.

And I slept. And thus it happened for me, a dream I have always remembered. I dreamt of a rare woman, light of hair and complexion, not on a hammock but on long, white sheets, on a wooden bed, in a cool, moist room, my yuán growing like a yuca, old in my spirit and young in body, and she held me tightly in her sand-colored arms in a place very far away, a place I had to go to, a place of huge caves and her body so appealing, and suddenly the dissolving sensation, full release, sounds and smells of yuca starch popping from the squeezing of the yuca dough in the long squeezing net, what they called the çibucán.

I woke up sticky with the generational water. It was my first time and I understood that the time of turning had come upon me. It was not very strange, as many times I heard the men talk, my brother-cousins and father-uncles, about how it happened to them. Since we come from the earth, they said, it is a natural thing. I felt not strange thus that morning, but oddly weakened, yet agreeable with myself.

Nearby, a group of women did squeeze yuca juice out of a çibucán. I could smell its starch. My mother was among them. She had eight women working in rhythm. As always, I felt respectful of the sight of women's hands squeezing out the yuca's sticky white sap, powerfully poisonous yet a great preserver of food. Across the batey, at the ceremonial fire, several elders huddled, whispering with a sharpness that pulled my gut. I washed at the stream and joined them.

Twenty-two. *The old cohobaneros' vision on the night and morning of my short farewell.*

"I found confusion in our spirit world, nothing was familiar to me, except the wailing of an owl. I heard loud, sharp noises, booming like thunder. I heard strange voices, a strange loud singing and I heard Taínos, men and women, with voices like ours, also wailing," old man Garaboy reported. He was a "hearer." In the cohoba this was his gift. Often he heard old songs, orations, even conversations. Spirit Frogs would talk to him, and snakes and, not long before this day, a grandfather manatí.

Sometimes, Garaboy returned from his cohoba journey with great stories. All day he could tell us tales. He would say, "Only the fish do not speak; only their world is silent." Then he would tell about the pregnant manatí who fooled two hungry sharks, "just a few suns ago," and he would say exactly where this had occurred, on what reef of what cove of our little island. We were always enchanted by his recounting of events from the lives of our relatives in the sea and the forest. "The secret of the pregnant manatí," he would wink. "She stiffens like log in the water. You see, sharks are so easily fooled."

The fish would not talk to Garaboy, so he would not hunt them. He accepted their meat, though sparingly, as gift-food from men he had raised, such as my father. But fish was a being he would not kill because he could not apologize to it in the cohoba. Even in my excitement to go, I felt a great love for old Garaboy, who was so keen and could blend into trees like a flat brown vine.

Sad this morning, old Garaboy spoke little this day of the cohoba night full of wailing. I struggled to appreciate what he had said, holding back my impatience to arrive at the beach, to greet again my friend Rodrigo, the Guamiquina and their many wonderful things. Old man Garaboy looked truly old to me, flabby thin legs that he now crossed, dropping like a sack upon his haunches.

Axeax was even older than Garaboy. He reported his experience next. "I saw a large number of grandfathers," Axeax said. He was a "seer" in the cohoba. "They were crying, too. They scratched at themselves. One stood forward and put on a garment, covering his arms. Then, he put on a garment that covered his legs. I was walking closer when suddenly this man pulled his garments off and threw them at me. He was young but very bony. He had scabs on his face and puss came out of his eyes ... " Axeax stopped in mid-sentence. He cried softly. Lifting an old, wispy hand, he showed that it trembled. "There was much fear in my dream."

Axeax went on at length, repeating his cohoba dream. What he related would scare anyone and touched me to my spine, but I couldn't find a place for it in my reflecting heart, vibrating on that special day with my great recent discoveries, both on the beach and in my hammock. Yes, I was impatient with the old men's stories. They seemed remote compared with a run to the beach and the sight of the marvelous mountain canoes and the many shapes and colors the covered men gave their things. I loved my father's uncles and grandfathers, but I felt at that moment I would have them forever.

Guanahabax felt my impatience and called me to him. "You must stay with us a while this morning," he told me, much to my dismay. Guanahabax knew me the best. He had backed up my mother's midwife when I was born, praying with my father for the strength of my mother and me during several nights. Guanahabax grasped my knee firmly and as always I felt a great deal of love from him. He called on Ayragüex, the third old man who had sniffed cohoba the previous night.

Ayragüex smiled as he pushed a staff into the earth to help himself up before casting it aside. His thin, muscular forearm was extended into a fist, which now made a slow lizard-head bobbing motion. "I saw them fucking," he said. "The new men have white haunches, hairy white haunches. They are spirits, I am certain. But they are the fuckingest spirits." He laughed. "It rains until it stops. They fall on our women like logs. My advice is, nothing sacred should take place today." Ayragüex stopped talking and stood silently a few moments. I lost concentration until I found him staring at my eyes. He moved slightly toward me, whispering with a smile. "Guaikán," Ayragüex stepped up to my ear. He was serious now. "I saw the white skinned woman who touched you last night. She walked through our camp and straight to your hammock."

Guanahabax leaned into me with his shoulder and put his cheek on mine. Even old man Guaraboy moved toward me. They looked determined to do something with me, but Guanahabax spoke. "There are twelve suns of ceremony prescribed for you in the cohoba, if you are to ready yourself. But we can see you are impatient to go. You have all of your life ahead, but not twelve days to give us, not even one."

Guanahabax asked me to wait for him while he went inside his bohío.

I was embarrassed by their directness, even mildly scared, but their knowledge of my intimacy was actually reassuring. I was overwhelmed with the need to run, fast as a panicked iguana, to the shore. Mind you, I had yet no sentiment that I would leave with the Castillas. I didn't know then that I was never to see my uncles again.

Guanahabax came out of his bohío. He put a bundle in my hand, my father's cohoba bundle. "Take this bundle of cohoba, your own spatula and rattle, your gourd and two-pronged sniffer, your feather fans. Remember that cohoba loves you. As you walk, do not turn back. We will speak to your mother and her house. Take our hearts with you. Take our dreams."

A sadness passed over me as I perceived the farewell, but Guanahabax yanked my shoulders and pointed me toward the beach. "No more speeches," he said. "We know there is no more time for Guaikán."

As I walked away, he said, "Go, young son of our beloved Cahobanax! Don't look back. Go to your destiny with the covered men."

I ran and ran and ran with the bundle in my makutí pack. At the beach, relieved to find the ships still there, I noticed little of what was going on. With Rodrigo's help, I snuck in early and hid out in the hold of the Guamiquina's ship. Not only men now, but many of our young women were on the beach, swimming and paddling canoes. By mid-afternoon, half of the Castilla sailors were swimming naked too. I could see them through a porthole near the food bins, where Rodrigo had found me a cubby hole. As Ayragüex said, the "fuckingest spirits." The Castilla kidnapped six of our Guanahani people as they left our shores the next morning, but I was not one of them. Drunk with the pull of adventure, I pressured Rodrigo to hide me—and was the first to go in. No one else can I blame for my captivity, not even Rodrigo. I captured my own self that day, choosing to cast my lot with the Castillas. It was the last free decision of my life, as I now consider it.

August 2, 1532

Twenty-three. *Last words, for a while.*

It now astounds me that I have written the above scenes. I reread these papers and I feel the urge to vomit. I don't want to remember so much, by Yúcahuguama, by Itiba my mother, it hurts. I remember the heart behind the heart now. Once I catch the thread, the words come pouring out. I relive the moments, I see them pass before me, and always, afterwards, I cry. Truly, these should be my last words for a while.

August 3, 1532

Twenty-four. *Enriquillo sends his messengers, request of cohoba peace pact.*

How quickly things change. But twenty-four hours ago, I forsook writing further. Now the heart thumps. That was yesterday morning. Today I am a different man, a man with mission.

It was yesterday, after vespers, I left the convent. Reading these papers in the morning, prior to the last entry, incontrollable pain wracked me all day. Searching for solitude, even death, I walked past the convent gate. I wished to die because I never saw my people again ... because I have seen the destruction of the world ... because I should not have lived so long.

Looking like a manso, a pacified Indian, attired in white shirt and knee-length pants, with my straw hat on, I walked without being noticed down the lane that runs by the convent, cut across a field of grazing cattle and entered woods that immediately climb up a ridge. The ridge overlooks the ocean and the road to the eastern sugar plantations.

When I reached the top, I sat and rested. My leg ached at the knee so, I could hardly open my eyes. All the way I ignored it, punished it, heart and vision darkening deep. Then, I read the clouds a while. They came in soft puffs and calmed me some. "My grandfathers," I said to the directions, "tell me why I should be alive. Why am I not dead, too?" The pain behind my knee I cherished, happy to offer the simple gift of my suffering, though small compared to so much I have seen.

In this island of Española, where finally my days are numbered, how many have I not seen die? Thousands upon thousands, so there is not one in ten, nay, not one in fifty, not one in one hundred, of what there were the first time I came here with the Admiral. Yes, I hate what I have seen. But I will not falter now. Today I do want to tell it, because a young man named Enriquillo is now at large, imposing his own Taíno liberty, and his act gives me life.

Twenty-five. *A message and words of instruction.*

Late evening found me walking toward the docks. The grog of the sailors beckoned me now that the sun was gone. God knows what I might have done had any old sailor from the days of the early voyages spotted me and offered his bottle. Deadly with hurricane eye, I was ready to kill, forthrightly, as I have done twice before—take the Castilla unaware and cut him deep. Such were my thoughts at that moment and, timid as I am, and bent, yet capable

I was of so much damage as I carried my good fishing knife and much Ya, our spirit of movement.

But feeling the ocean close by, I naturally approached it, leaving aside thoughts of the sailors' cantina and went to sit on a rock by the waves. There I sat a while, until the laughter of whores and drunkards disturbed me. Walking west along the shore, leaving the buildings in the dark and searching the line of the sea, I suddenly heard men walking in the sand behind me.

"Tau-ti, Cacique Guaikán, tau caraya guatiao," one said in Taíno. "Good evening, brother Taíno. For you we have been looking."

They were young men of Enriquillo. I answered them in our language, and they came forward. "Guarocuya sends us," the speaker of the two said, using Enriquillo's Taíno name.

I spoke at length with the young ambassador and his fellow runner. The speaker had a long report for me, a speech he had memorized from Enriquillo himself. I was to listen carefully, as they would return to the bush immediately after delivering the speech. As with all our Taíno memorized messages, he spoke in sections.

The young warrior started: "Guarocuya said to tell you that these are his words, though out of my mouth they will come now.

"Our cacique trusts you and respects you. Your gesture with him at the Massacre of Anacaona's Banquet, he remembers, and your many favors over the years."

He paused briefly. "Now I continue," he said.

"A hard campaign has been fought, the cacique of Bahuruku wants you to know. Guided by our own mansos, in the dry season five years ago, Captain San Miguel sniffed out three of our larger camps and destroyed them, killing many of our people. Since then we are much weakened to mount a defense against other major assaults."

He paused again.

"That time, Guarocuya struck back. We moved deeper into the mountains, to the last good places of retreat. Then, did our cacique send our warriors to the enemies' ranches. When the rains started, we followed the Castilla captain home. That night, we burned his ranch and strangled three men who had done the guiding. Many horses we took, many cattle, and weapons, and tools. His bulls and boars, rams and stallions, we decapitated and left to rot. All progenitors he lost, he and three other such captains, all lost their ranches, one by one, destroyed for their aggression against our free villages."

He paused again, briefly.

"Guarocuya said to tell Guaikán these important words: 'We are strong, more than two hundred tested warriors. But camps and even villages we must sustain, and war raids we must withstand as well. A coordinated campaign, such as the Emperor King could unleash, which might all at once send eight or ten fighting squads against our territory, would be difficult to avoid or repel. We depend on surprise and the willingness to punish our tormentors. Thus, we are feared. But, we are mortally threatened if the King's armies should turn fully against our cause."

He paused again. I counted twelve waves lapping at the shore before he continued.

"Many tongues make talk about an embassy from the Emperor King. Our cacique asks, 'Is it only words to roll up time? Or is there sincerity in the wish for peace?

'The King must learn,' he says, 'that the cacique is a man of peace. The King should know the cacique is a man of his word when he says that he would serve the King, who is a fair man, but not the local cahayas, the man-shark captains of the islands. The cacique is a firm man. Negotiations will not happen with island authorities, only with the King's embassy.' "

"I carry these instructions: Five conditions are required, according to our cacique. The safety of the cacique and his chiefs and captains must be the King's first words. The location of our camps and villages he must not inquire. Pardons must be granted for all his people, the Africans among our people included. Good planting land could be offered, for a settlement and gentle peace. Then, if need be, that the cacique should police his own, he wants men among his captains deputized, so arms they can hold, legally."

The young embassador stopped. He walked a few steps into the oncoming waves and I followed him. The three of us stood in the water, our ankles caressed by the waves. He meant to say by that: "The sea mother cleans my next words." It is an old way of ours.

"Now about the good friar, our great protector and your convent companion all these years, the robed man called Las Casas. I am to tell you that he has been in touch, but with disorienting effect. He sends messages suggesting sites for a parley, as such. He sends lists of conditions and offers to come and put up a mass, give us the many sacraments. This is not good. Messengers open paths that soldiers follow. And, for certain, all parleys with Castilla at this moment are death traps. So, the good friar is to know: Deciding where to meet is for later and the site will be chosen by the cacique. And our cacique, who watches over all of us, he says the friar might go to the King's court. This would be good, yes indeed; he should go and report for us, nay demand, for us, that a King's embassy is required for a true parley to take place."

Enriquillo's messenger-warrior stopped abruptly, a final pause.

"As for you, uncle, the cacique asks Guaikán to walk our mountain way.

The steps to peace must be reviewed, he said, and you are requested to remember the time of Guarionex, the way of his peace pact. You are to remember how your old father-in-law conducted his alliance-making areito ceremony. In three new moons, we will come to guide you. And you must let us know when you are ready."

His message delivered, the young Taíno lowered his head to receive my warmest blessing, then they both ran off without another sound.

August 7, 1532

Twenty-six. *A letter to Las Casas.*

I sent a letter today to Father Las Casas. It went with young Silverio, who took my mare. He rides to the monastery at Puerto de Plata to deliver my letter himself. I wrote to the good friar of my contact with "the boy held in the bosom." This is a reference to how I held the boy Enriquillo during the Massacre of Anacaona's Banquet, carrying him to the only safe spot, in Commander Ovando's own tent. His older brother I led by the hand, but a soldier drunk on blood killed him with a sword. I then held the four-year-old Enriquillo to my chest, protecting him as I ran. This story Father Las Casas knows from me.

Twenty-seven. *Useful Castillian things, paper, horses.*

I marvel at the usefulness of paper to carry the message. Young Silverio was brought up manso. I would not wish to trust his memory, much less his ability to hold a secret. The mare, too, is a Castillian thing. I have had her six years. She was a gift of Don Diego, the Admiral's real son, upon his return to Castilla after his time as governor of the island. "For your service to my father during the early years," he told me.

My little mare is a brown, sturdy Andalusian, and has a white face. I call her Cariblanca, in the Castillian. I don't ride her much, for the old leg wound just under my right buttock can be irritated and sends horrendous burning pains down to my knee and up my back. I rent Cariblanca to messengers and occasionally to travelers, but only if they treat her gently.

August 10, 1532

Twenty-eight. *News from Cuba, death of the Guamax rebellion.*

Sad news this week from Cuba. The rebel cacique, Guamax, is dead. A Castilla patrol attacked his main rancho, near Baracoa, on the northeast coast of that island. But the cacique died of an old wound weeks before they broke up his main camp. When they rode into his clearing, Guamax's widows were placing his bones in a funerary basket. They say that for all the running and killing, the two women continued their work until captured inside their bohío.

I heard a version of this story at the dock today from Juan Martín de Ayala, an old sailor of Hojeda's, who now commands his own caravel. He sailed in from Santiago with a boat full of slaves, including some of Guamax's captured men. Ayala said the skull of Guamax was stuck on a spike at the entrance to the Village of Baracoa, as were the severed heads of his chiefs and principal women.

"Our good Carlito (King Charles V) lost his patience with that one," he told a group that gathered later to hear his story at the Pensión Marinera. "Guamax burned our forts to the ground at Sancti Espíritus and Puerto Príncipe. But the King sent new troops, well-heeled with arquebus. Damned Indian faggots were blasted with shot all over that plain. What's left of them are deep in the forest, still running."

I could not call Ayala publicly on his equivocation, so now with pen and paper I will set the record straight. Guamax of Baracoa went to war in 1522, less than two years after Enriquillo took to the bush here in Española. Three years ago, in August of '29, he nearly defeated the Castilla in Cuba, burning down several towns, as Ayala recounted, though Ayala made it sound as if it happened recently. It wasn't the King's soldiers that got Guamax either. It was the smallpox, which got to his large war camps as they moved through the mountains to lay siege on Baracoa and Santiago. They say his warriors and women advisors dropped all around him by the hundreds, nine out of ten of them, over the course of but a few days. Guamax's campaign was destroyed by the pox—that son-of-a-bad-mother disease. Guamax himself was heartbroken by the death that seemed to come in the wind, though his surviving warriors continued to raid.

Ayala and the group discussed Enriquillo next, but I eased away for fear that Ayala or another one from those times of Commander Ovando might remember my actions of then. I owe my peace of recent years to an instinct for evasiveness. Sailors, soldiers and encomendero peons, even some patrones, all hang together in Santo Domingo. They pray at the same church and frequent the same whorehouse. In both, they damn to Hell the good friar, of whom I am a devoted servant, and in both they relish in descriptions of punishments for Enriquillo and his men. Tonight, they will be toasting the death of Guamax.

Twenty-nine. *Remembering the elder Guamax.*

I never met the younger Guamax, though once, at the beginning, I was in his territory of Baracoa. It was with the Admiral, not many days after leaving Guanahani in the ship Santa María. That time, forty years ago, the Guamax who died of recent would have been a crawling boy. Another Guamax, an elder cacique held the title then. We did meet him, and now that I think of it, in a rather peculiar way. While I await the good friar's return, I will take up that tale next, how I sailed to Cuba with Don Christopherens after hiding on his ship at Guanahani, what we did and how we later arrived at this island of La Española, or, in our language, Haití-Bohío or Quisqueya, the big mountain country.

Thirty. *Jiqui, a warrior, escapes.*

Word came today that one of Guamax's warriors among the prisoners sold by Ayala has escaped. His name is Jiqui. He jumped a guard, then bolted for the woods. Two cuadrillas with mastiff hounds took up his trail early this morning.

August 11, 1532

Thirty-one. *Sojourn in Cuba, along the northern coast, searching for the Great Khan, the curse of Old Guamax, days of early reverence.*

I still remember the Yunque of Baracoa, in Cuba—that wide, flat mountain top that can be seen from the bay. I remember the Cuban coast, how thick and lush it was, how big the island felt that first time. The Admiral was very excited. A land more beautiful human eyes have never seen, he said, words I heard him repeat many times later in his discourses with nobles, bishops and powerful merchants of Spain.

In Cuba, we from Guanahani knew Cubanakán, a cacique from the center of the island whose fishermen made the journey, once a year, to Guanahani. And once a year our own men (my father and uncle Çibanakán among them) would reciprocate, visiting also on their shores. They traded woven jenikén ropes produced from maguey grass at Cubanakán for our good fish catchers, hookers and spear points made from the shells of our great caracol beach on the northeast corner of Guanahani. The great Cuban hemp twine, woven from tall savannah grass, was much requested, particularly their long, very fine ropes that made the best reinforcers of fishing nets. In good weather, it took the men six days to make the trip to Cubanakán; in my memory, they never lost anybody during those journeys.

Many times, encouraged by Rodrigo, I mentioned that cacique's name, Cubanakán, and the island's name, Cuba, to Don Christopherens, who wrote it down and had his secretary, Escobedo, write it down comparing the writings to my sounds. Carey, a man of my village and a cousin of mine, was forced on board as we left Guanahani. He was a guaxeri in the fishing with my father, and he guided Captain Pinzón and the Admiral. Carey had made the trip to Cuba for several years.

We sailed into Cuban waters on the thirteenth sun after leaving Guanahani, my home. By the Castilla calendar it was October 27, 1492. I remember it rained all night, drops pounding flat on the decks like frogs falling from trees; the ships hove to, drifting in the bay, and all night rain fell. The morning sky was so clean, the eyes drank from it—the kind of day my elders would have deemed, "swept by Coatriskie," the spirit cemí who, in our Taíno mind, ruled the heavy rains and assisted in the cleansing of the skies.

Cuba was different, from the beginning. The coastal caciques were not forthcoming. As he had done on four other islands, the Admiral landed the ship's boats. He liked the many small and large bays and took boats himself up the wide rivers, but for days the local Taínos fled from him. This excited him even more, as I could tell he had grown tired of the hundreds of people that had swarmed his ships in the smaller islands. When he found two very large and well-carved traveling canoes, one with capacity for over one hundred and fifty people, the Admiral paced and paced and many times showed me, Carey and others a bracelet and a chain made of fine gold. Rodrigo's agile hand signals interpreted for us: *The Guamikina wants to see other great guamikinas. The Guamikina wants to see them wear their gold.*

Thirty-two. *Embassy to Camagüey.*

Carey, though he was resentful for his captivity, which I yet was not, offered to guide the Admiral to Cubanakán's shore. However, the Admiral declined to sail that far west on the Cuban coast, and at a bay near Puerto de Mares, around November 3, decided to send an embassy inland. Both Carey and I were chosen to go on this mission, to assist Luis de Torres, a converted Jew, and Rodrigo de Jerez (a former crusader, not my young friend Rodrigo Gallego), as they led us inland.

Only years later did I learn the reason for our trip inland to Camagüey, but I will state it now. Cubanakán, our cacique brother from Cuba, the great caymán island, was mistaken by the Admiral for the Great Khan, a chief of the Mongol people in the land of China, with whom he wanted to trade. Nothing else interested him that day. The few Indians who had pulled up to trade, mostly canoes from the islands we had passed, he now ignored. "Caona, caona," (gold, gold) he repeated to the dozens of canoes that had now caught up with us. Or he would say, "Turey, turey," another Taíno word, meaning sky, which he at first believed meant gold also. But the Lucayo Taínos offered no caona, only cotton nets, food, fresh water and fruit.

The search for the Great Khan had been planned in Spain, and the Admiral ceremoniously entrusted Torres, the poor converted Jew, with gold samples and types of spices and a letter for the Mongol from King Fernando and Queen Isabel. "I am convinced we are on the mainland, near the cities of Zayto and Quinsay, a hundred leagues more or less distant from one or the other," he told Torres. Instructing him to take no more than five days, the Admiral said, "Find the Great Khan."

Thirty-three. *Carey's doubts and my certainty.*

Carey plotted to leave the Castilla ships as soon as possible. He hoped he could slip away to the forest at Cubanakán village, and later make his way home. But now we were barely on the edge of old Camagüeybax's territories, with whom we had no particular relations. "What do the Castillas want, really?" he despaired, as we walked thin trails south over the coastal hills into Camagüeybax's plains. "They want to see Cubanakán, but won't sail west; now, he sends us here. I do not like this, Guaikán, and I don't understand what you find so curious about them."

It was true. I was still intrigued. I still liked the Castilla. What's more, I believed them to be men-spirits sent by the Spirit of Spirits, first Creator, Yayá, first grandfather to us, in the Castilla's words, "Our Father Who Art in Heaven." The Castilla, I felt, were wonderfully superior and clever and anything they said was bound to be right.

"They have done you no harm, Carey," I argued with my guaxeri.

"They take me against my wish," he responded.

"Don't worry so much," I remember I told him. "We'll all return home safely."

Thirty-four. *Meeting Baigua, a ni-Taíno of Camagüeybax, the old ladies call for jaguajiguatu.*

We walked two days, joined by crowds that reached into the hundreds, arriving at the village of a secondary cacique, one of old Camagüeybax's ni-Taínos by the name of Baigua. Baigua's village was the largest by far that we had encountered and he had been preparing a feast for a day before we arrived. Along the way we had seen small clusters of bohíos, maybe four or five together, but Baigua's yukaieke was made up of more than fifty bohíos, probably a thousand people, and it was where Torres finally decided to stop.

Baigua greeted us with great courtesy, in the open Taíno style. He was the sweetest of caciques, only middle-aged but doted upon by grandchildren and old ladies, and he appeared to have not a care in the world. He had a kind face that stood out for its gentility, even among Taínos. All around his large yukaieke, as far as you could see on a valley of rolling hills, there were planted cunukus (raised beds) of yuca, ñames, potatoes and other types of tubers, much maize, pineapple, herbs and edible grasses, all interwoven with groves of guayaba, mamey, caimitu, anon, guanábana and other fruit and nut trees. The batey or main plaza had been recently swept clean. Around the cacique's central fire, several Taíno ceremonial seats, what we call duhos, were arranged for us.

After exchanging gifts and eating (they served much meat of the delicious yaguasa, the Cuban game duck), Carey let me do the talking. As I was by then accustomed, I conveyed my heartfelt views that the covered men were truly special, sacred, that they had come from the sky in huge canoes with wings like seagulls, and they could guide a ship against the wind. Instructed by Torres, I inquired after the Great Khan. They responded that they knew him but that he lived farther west. I asked, too, after caona, guanin or any other metal, of which they claimed to have none. Torres was obviously disappointed by the second answer but gratified by the first, although, certainly, they only referred to Cubanakán, the Cuban cacique and not the Mongol ruler. Torres showed profound relief when informed that the walk to the "Khan's" towns would take more than fifteen suns, as it excused him from continuing the exploration. With an air of great solemnity, he announced we would spend the night at Baigua's village and return to the ship at first light.

Poor Torres, whom I came to like very much, was a sensitive man, and could read and speak several languages. On ship, he was under constant suspicion for any lapse in his Catholicism, as he was a first-generation converted Jew. He compensated for his fate with a very light foot and quiet demeanor. Among the Castilla men, he was one of the very few who had abstained from laying with our women, making it a point to be at the Admiral's side at all prayers, although he was a man of fine features and liked to gaze nonetheless.

The speeches over, Baigua had large gourds and clay pots of water brought in for us to wash. All the men first and then some of the women smoked large tabacos. Torres was curious about their smoking and they showed him the tobacco plant, our coxibá, sacred offering to the Creator Beings and all cemíes. The older women, who liked the tone of his words, then whispered to the cacique a request that I had anticipated by the manner of our reception. Our own Guanahani people had the same custom whenever, quite infrequently, visitors arrived at our villages.

"Jaguajiguatu," the old women whispered, meaning literally, "fire in the loins," an old right of the housemothers to mix into the village life, and their blood lines, the potential contributions of men visitors. Baigua, gentle chief, was delighted, even enthusiastic at the request, which I explained to Torres as best I could as the older matrons ushered out their selected young women, who commenced to wash and kiss our feet and, in Torres and Jerez's case, to pull and half-carry them into a large bohío, scented by a thick floor of freshly cut pine boughs. I never looked in on them all night, but I laughed with Carey at Torres' ever-weakening admonitions as the women swarmed around him and silently urged from him his traveler's duty to our Taíno grandmothers, ever watchful for their future generations. Jerez, the old slaving hog, needed little prodding, though he was a peculiarly ugly man, short of leg and long of torso, with a little neck. "What good seeds you'll get from Torres, you are losing with the no-neck," Carey jested, in his sardonic way, and we laughed with Baigua's old woman bohío-mother, who wanted the Castilla in the village at least five days, as most of her women were on their cleansing moon, and kept saying, "We've never seen anything like those two, I truly hope some of the girls will take."

August 14, 1532

Thirty-five. *Torres reports to the Admiral, Cuba as mainland.*

Not ten minutes back from Baigua's village, while waiting for Don Christopherens to complete his meal service, Jerez had told the Santa María's pilot, Peralonso Niño, about his night of abandonment. Torres' participation in the overnight adventure came out in the telling and, immediately, several sailors made the most of it. Three men in particular, bad characters from the ship's home port of Palos, made a song about "the converso's hiccups of ecstasy, how the old rabbi must have left something for him to use, after all."

After finishing his dinner, the Admiral came out of his cabin. "Torres!" he called. Torres was before him as the sound faded.

"Did you meet officials of the Khan?"

"No, my Captain."

"What did you see?"

"A very large village, sir, very large."

"And the people?"

"About the same as our guides, sir."

"No slipper shoes, head casks?"

"No, sir, they were all naked as their mothers birthed them sir."

"The way Torres likes them!" someone shouted, from star bow, causing some laughter. It was Clavijo, a nasty character who was one of three convicted criminals granted clemency to join the expedition.

The Admiral would have none of it. "Alguacil!" he ordered, quieting everyone. "Arrest that man."

Clavijo was led down the hatch by three men.

Don Christopherens asked next about geography and the Great Khan's whereabouts. "It's a long way," Torres told him. "Two weeks' journey, maybe more."

"Maybe much more," said the Admiral. "Probably many leagues, wouldn't you say?"

"Probably, my Captain."

"I am convinced this is mainland," Columbus said then. The Admiral was aware that Cuba means "territory" in the Taíno language. "We are at the southern extensions of the Great Khan's dominions," he pronounced. "Cuba of the Great Khan."

Torres, of course, knew better, as did Jerez. Carey and I had even told the Admiral, several times, that Cuba can be rounded by canoe. It is a very large land, indeed, but an island. The Admiral never quite conceded the point. He kept believing it was a mainland, and, as I have written earlier, insisted on it catagorically on the second voyage, as we traveled Cuba's long southern coast.

Thirty-six. *Çibanakán, my father-uncle, comes on board.*

We sailed east from there, as the Admiral decided to round the cape of Cuba at Maisí Point and strike southward to explore the large island of Haití Bohío, now Santo Domingo or Española. Touching points on the coast of Cuba, the ships took in sixteen more Taínos, chosen from the crowds to be kept as captives. This new action disconcerted me. Like our own Guanahani people taken by force, the Cuban Taínos were selected for their strength and physical attractiveness. Of our own men, three had already slipped overboard at appropriate moments, taking rides on the canoes of friend. In one case, the rescuer was none other than my uncle, Çibanakán, who later returned to get me, talked at length with me, and ended up staying. Çibanakán was at the time some forty-five years of age. We made up a story about his wife and children being on board in order to obtain the Admiral's permission. "He should work with you to keep our captives calm," he told me.

Thirty-seven. *The old man Guamax, his curse on the Admiral.*

I promised to tell about the elder Guamax, the old cacique of Baracoa who held that title at the time of the first voyage. I believe he was related to the other great cacique of eastern Cuba, Bayamo, whom we met in the first of my pages.

As the Taíno men and women taken on the Cuban coast increased to twenty or more, the story of the captures spread on land. From coastal promontories, smoke signals telling of sea-borne danger (very black smoke from the resin of the jobo tree) could be seen, and for days after a capture, shore after shore turned up empty. Once our sailors went ashore to search an empty village and found the skull and bones of a grandfather, as customary, resting in a basket near the ceiling of a tall bohío. After the Admiral inspected it and both Carey and I explained its significance, the sailors played with it on the beach, in sight of his hidden relatives, who watched from a hill out of reach. Two sailors tossed the skull around by its long hair, finally discarding it into a river. I remember being sickened by their game. This occurred, I am reasonably certain, near the end of November, 1492. I had been with the Admiral six weeks.

On December 3, as I count suns in my memory, after three days of absolutely contrary wind, the caravels moved east along the coast of northern Cuba, entering small coves as they made their way out of the Baracoa area. That day, as we took final pass of a wide river-mouth, the local ni-Taínos, despite their fear of the Castilla, perceived that we were leaving and several dozen canoes came out. One of our captive Indians, taken days before, pointed out to me an old man wearing a wide headdress. Tall and thin and wrinkled, he directed his young paddlers around the stern of the Santa María, where Columbus was standing. "Tau-ti, Guamax-cacique," I heard a captive man say, next to me, by way of greeting the old man.

The old man who at that time held the title of Guamax pointed directly at the Admiral, took off his headdress and slipped into the water. Kicking against the current, he rubbed himself with sudsy digo herbs all over his body and, when cleansed, swam to just below the Admiral, who looked down at him.

Guamax spoke. "Here I am in the water, a fish in my river. Understand that my words are clean, like my body in this river. Now hear me: My sons and daughters you have in your canoe. I know they have been swallowed. You are to let them go. Those are my children who belong to me. Now, you must respond."

The Admiral understood not a word, and I wasn't much help. I was getting so I could understand the Castilla many of their words and I could interpret their wishes for my people, but Old Guamax's speech shocked me dumb, speaking as it did to the only secret doubt in my immense (at that moment) reverence for the Castilla. "Respond!" the cacique demanded, when the admiral, who perceived the scolding tone, stared at him.

"Do not take them, for I will curse the Guamiquina his red hairs," old man Guamax said. "You will be crazy among our trees and rocks. You will die a fool."

At this moment, another man taken from us, Manaya, yelled back from the boat. "You will be the one that dies, if you threaten the Guamiquina." Manaya took up a sword and a crossbow, showing them to old man Guamax, who was still in the water. "This big knife, it slices a tree in half. This arrow-shooter will pierce the clouds. Don't make the sky-men angry, old cacique."

Old man Guamax made no answer, swimming slowly away and slipping into his canoe. From the canoe, he stared at the stern of the Santa María, then ordered his men to paddle away. I remember Carey standing next to me on the Santa María. He was more trusted now, and had the run of the ship after his trek into Camagüey. Increasingly fearful to be lost among Taíno angered at the loss of their relatives, he had not dared to effect a getaway. At that moment, like many times during those finest days, Carey took my hand in friendship and held it tightly. "I hope you are right about our getting home safely," he said.

August 17, 1532

Thirty-eight. *Life on board and learning Castilla ways; out from Punta Maisí, a tone with the Admiral.*

All us shipboard "Indians," as the Admiral had begun to call our people, were closely watched. No more escapes were to occur. We were to sail to Haití, the Bohío, a major Taíno homeland. Among the captives, and even in me, an intense fear arose, moving now as we were to lands beyond our usual realms. We knew of the Bohío land, of course, as we knew of Boríken and Xamaica and all the many islands in our fecund sea, but we feared the added distance from our home. A fearful outcry now began among three women from the village of Quiribe, across my island from Old Guanahaní village. I had not known them much before this trip and had kept my distance, as they were harsh to strangers, even people from the same island. They wailed about not going home, about their fate to be eaten by our legendary enemies, the Kwaib "thigh eaters/heart eaters" who were known to raid our coasts.

By day's end, the outcry affected the men so that everyone was sad and crying, and the leaders took the job of imploring for their liberty, for canoes to make the trip home, for guarantees of return. "We are heading for the heart-eaters' islands, the thigh-eaters. Bad men who eat other men," our people claimed to the Admiral. I seconded them, though timidly, but the Admiral had made up his mind that we would sail across the (Windward) passage to Bohío and there was nothing to be done.

Thirty-nine. *Ignoring the feelings of my own people.*

I am chagrined now, asking myself what kept me hopeful about the covered men. Yes, many of us were taken forcefully, I would think, but no one has been harmed. It did not seem so to me, in any case, and, then too, I was busy every moment on board ship. I kept with young Rodrigo and often Carey joined us. Among our men, six were learning ship's ropes, and they included three from Guanahaní: Çibanakán, Carey and myself. Those of us on the ropes, or, in my case, often at the Admiral's side with Rodrigo, had little contact, for days at a time, with the huddled group in the holds that came on deck to sit together in the sun and, without task, could only wonder on their fate.

Forty. *Getting closer to the Admiral.*

Rodrigo was grommet, cabin boy, and with my arrival, Castillian instructor. He taught me the daily routines, their timings and sequences and commands, and he taught me to never disturb the Admiral's habits of prayer and dining, so that his mood of fatherly disposition toward young men could be sustained. That was the knack of the early Don Christopherens, I think, that fooled my tender heart. Going through his day, particularly when busy with stellar calculations and the making of knots and sea leagues, the Admiral could be a most happy and pleasing man. The day he saw me keep the ampolleta hourglass for the first time, he worked at his desk, writing and yet noticing my attentiveness. Rodrigo had set me up to the task of turning over the glass as the sand ran out every half hour. I took the shift from three to seven in the afternoon and was strictly attentive throughout my eight spins. "Excellent," Don Christopherens commended, talking to Rodrigo, who came to relieve me. "Your friend has a sharp eye."

Don Christopherens liked chick peas and lentils in soups, took to using our casava bread almost immediately (for mopping his bowl). Near shore, he was always pleased to get a basket of fresh fruit, which I would get for him at least once a day, and often, he would have me sit and look out his small porthole as he wrote and napped, then wrote again. Not often, but occasionally during those first days, in the reverie of long tropical afternoons, he would pull my head to his shoulder and sing me a song or recite a poem or tell me a story from the Bible. He never reached that kind of intimacy with Rodrigo, who served him zealously, but would with me, which endeared me to his instinct and his ways and added to my considerable resolution at the time to champion the covered men's mission to my people.

Even Carey and Çibanakán, who followed my lead but wearied of the experience, could not help but admire the Admiral his way with a ship or any kind of boat. Although we helped him a great deal to navigate our channels and reefs, it was always uncanny the way he could immediately size up shoals and sand banks, depths and winds, and the landfall ahead. Long after I too knew the Castilla were no good at all, I would be startled awake by the certainty of his directions, that quality he had to pull at my heart, to make me want to cling to his back. That certainty of his word during storms and dangerous moments at sea later carried me through my second season of servile stupor with the Castilla; truly, he projected a God of Destiny, a naming God, when his suddenly distant eyes focused on the far point of the horizon.

Forty-one. *Even closer to the Admiral.*

Don Christopherens was quiet and dignified in his personal habits, but
sharp and severe in his judgments. Everything about him was steeped in
his Catholic faith and devotion. The day's prayers, from the morning Salve
Regina to the vespers and its Ave Maria, he led or watched over with intense
attention. He missed nothing having to do with a religious service, how
it was done, who was respectful, penitent or devout. Once, I saw a man
laugh quietly during a mass. Next day, he was worked mercilessly until he
dropped and then set in the filthy bilbowes of the ship for a fortnight. Don
Christopherens was somber in correcting waywardness among Christian
men, and would always turn them over to the worst elements among the
marshall's enforcers for severe punishments.

Those days of his first voyage to our sea, as I knew the Admiral, he never
changed his mind about anything. He was easy to follow and obey. Much
beyond the other covered men, Don Christopherens gathered into himself a
mystical force that seemed to carry him. All the early Castilla captains were
hard-headed and single-minded and would strike out at long distances; they
were tough and mean and powerful. But one had to see the Admiral in his
long mantle on deck in a misty evening to also see his goeiç, his personal
spirit, surrounding him. Even his keenness for gold, which later turned to
virulence, was during those days a detached inquiry, something investigated
but not coveted. At least that was his style. Often he delighted in odd little
things, like cakes of wax, or the smells of particular woods, or the counting
of each and every number of flocks of parrots or doves, such as the ones that
can blacken out the sun of our islands for days.

More than a guaxeri, our word for the common human, even among the
totally uncommon covered men, he was Guamiquina, principal man of the
flaming hair who commanded everything, spirit driven by spirit. I would
look at him standing among his officers and think: Spirit man, what wonders
you must behold. Take me to your spirit lands, take me to your shining cities
of gold. I want to see, I want to hear and smell your world. This was as we
sailed to this island of Santo Domingo for the first time. It didn't yet touch
me how the disturbance of my people had already begun. There percussions
were slight yet, compared to my wonder. And I was clever, too, easily adept
at projecting devotion at his mass. I revered and learned to genuflect before
his crucifix. I quickly learned the Ave Maria, with Rodrigo's tutoring. One
afternoon, standing at the Admiral's side, I joined the singing. He touched
my shoulder proudly, for all the men on ship to see, and next morning he
gave me a long shirt to wear. A few times, with the shirt hanging to my
knees (as did his cape on him), I found myself standing on the poop deck in

the posture and position of the Admiral, watching the horizon. I could feel the shape and power of his spirit at those times, a "greeting of goeiçs," as the old people would say, calming a longing in my own soul.

August 29, 1532

Forty-two. *The good friar returns from La Plata.*

Father Las Casas came in last night. He rode my Cariblanca back to me, having sent young Silverio by ship with several letters to the mainland. The letters were to his Dominican friends in Mexico, who have appealed to the King on behalf of Enriquillo. The good friar is a hurricane of activity, his mind raging. I could tell by the state of my poor Cariblanca, girth swollen and head hanging low to the ground when the friar dismounted in the convent stable. "We must talk," he said, shouldering his own pack. "The final campaign begins."

Forty-three. *Preparations for his trip to court in Spain.*

In my room, by candlelight, the good friar discoursed on his strategy to move court and King on Enriquillo's behalf. It was hours before he stopped reviewing the arguments, and only then did he wonder about the message in my letter: "something about a young boy," he said.

I reminded him about the Massacre of Anacaona's Banquet, how I carried the young Enriquillo. He smiled. Father Las Casas seldom smiles. "God bless you, my son. You did save his life."

But when I told him about the messengers Enriquillo had sent me, he was peeved. "I spent two months trying to contact him! Why did he not answer me?"

I said that Enriquillo could not afford too many contacts.

"Enrique is too independent," he said. "He must work with our groups, we must work together."

Father Las Casas reviewed his strategy. A friendly cardinal has the ear of the Emperor King, who might consent to settle with Enriquillo. Las Casas feels now is the time to go and present the evidence of the encomienda's horrible results and call to the King to settle the injustice once and for all.

"But I have to know what he is going to do," Las Casas complained. "Enriquillo must follow the required steps."

The good friar explained that in 1530, after meeting with the Spanish court and the Emperor King himself, he had returned from Spain to a place in the mainland called Nicaragua, where he met with and delivered an ultimatum to Pizarro, new governor of the Peruvian lands. It was a Royal Decree by Emperor King Carlos V, declaring the Peruvian Indians his vassals, not subject to slavery. Pizarro was shocked, the good friar said. I know this is the reason all the colonists, from Peru to Nicaragua to Mexico, are of one mind in wishing death upon Las Casas.

"The good Queen tried the same in 1502," I reminded him. "It made no difference."

"This King will impose himself, one way or the other. He wants this war here ended."

"The war, yes, but not the encomienda."

"Without pushing, nothing moves."

"At the cost of our young cacique's head?"

Las Casas grimaced at me, in exasperation.

"I can tell you now. Before I came this last time, I was under siege all over the mainland. Pizarro told me, on his way back to Peru, 'What I came here to do is subjugate Indians, work the mines and clear the lands. If I put my sword to their throats, it is for that reason, or there is no reason.' Others said worse. They cursed me as an interloper and have given assassins orders to kill me. It was the new governor of La Española himself, Don Sebastián Ramírez de Fuenleal, who wrote to me from here, asking my involvement in the matter of Enriquillo. Now I can tell you, because the news of an impending embassy is fully known. Tomorrow, I will go meet with the oidores or 'hearing judges.' We will start to set up the covenant and the particulars of the meeting."

I hoped he was right.

"We have them on the run this time," Las Casas said. "If the King will capitulate here, with Enrique, who has a pitiful band, think of what the royal proclamations could mean for the mainland. The encomienda could be ended."

"I am of your group, Don Bartolomé," I reminded him. "But in the matter of Enriquillo, we each know our half."

This much smells: One of the oidores is Juan de Vadillo, a crony and, I think, relative of Pedro de Badillo, the lieutenant governor who had Enriquillo beaten and jailed when he petitioned his court against Valenzuela's attempted rape of Doña Mencía in 1519. Later, Pedro de Badillo commanded a troop of eighty men against Enriquillo, who both led and trailed them around that hard sierra for two months, all the time picking off Badillo's soldiers from ambush. That Badillo got so mad he started to hack his own mansos to death. That Badillo, I will add, though the good friar wants not to hear it, was also cursed with our grossest ceremony, a pure work of well-directed bad medicine. And, he ended up drowned in a shipwreck, his gold-laden ship from twenty years of thievery here sank while sailing home up the Guadalquivir River in Spain.

I trust not these Vadillos or Badillos who hang in with my old tormentor,

Pero López, as well as with the cacique's old master, Andrés Valenzuela; all of them would relish Enriquillo's head. Neither do I trust the King. I am certain Enriquillo will be assassinated, unless we are very careful. Don Bartolomé would save all Indians, but sometimes he is a bit careless about just one.

"Our rebel cacique requests a Taíno peace-pact ceremony at the negotiations," I said. "The way Guarionex used to do them, what we called the opening of hearts or exchange of hearts ceremony."

"Guarionex of La Vega, who was attacked by Bartolomé Colón around 1498?" Las Casas asked. "Who would remember that?"

I nodded, pointing to my own heart. Suddenly, he smiled kindly, again, a rare sight. Thus he recognized my participation in the earliest days, prior to his own arrival here in 1502. He remembered that Guarionex was my cacique by law, as I married his sister Ceyba and lived in his village for more than a year prior to his sad demise more than thirty years ago.

I told the good friar about Enriquillo's conditions. It also occurred to me that my old friend, Rodrigo Gallego, now a captain of the court of Seville, might be assigned to the negotiations. Las Casas agreed to carry my letter to him; then, listening to me more carefully, the good friar nodded at all my suggestions for protecting Enriquillo. He understood that Enriquillo's life was at stake, that he might be assassinated, even as the King's ambassador might come to sit with him.

"Dieguillo," he said, and this is the part of this old priest that I truly love, "We are meant for this moment, you and me. We will gather a crew, all our best people, and help Enriquillo win his freedom."

August 31, 1532

Forty-four. *Jiqui is captured.*

Guamax's young warrior has been caught. Spanish hounds ᵼ
work of the chase and cornered the poor boy yesterday, near a swolleᵼ
His name is Jiqui, same as one of my uncles I left behind at Guanahaᵼ
They have him shackled outside the jail, next to the House of Contracts. His
execution is set for two o'clock this afternoon.

Forty-five. *The execution of Jiqui.*

I write now by candlelight, at the end of a horrible day. This is the
Heaven the Castilla have brought us.

After lunch the good friar and two other monks accompanied me to the
square. The heat was intense today. Nevertheless, they wore their brown
robes and I, too, was dressed, wearing a manso hat low over my eyes.

Many people were out, including the town ladies and their children.
Sailors, soldiers, peons and town merchants crowded about half of the square.
Two local encomienda farms brought all their Indians, over two hundred
men and women.The execution of Jiqui would be a lesson to them. The two
groups sat idle for most of the afternoon, a rest day for their tired bodies,
waiting for a torment dedicated to their minds.

Santo Domingo is a large town now. Two times ten thousand Spaniards,
Indians, African negroes and mestizos live here. There are few "free Indians"
like myself, but there are some. We are the ones with peculiar histories,
given some refuge from the torment of the encomienda by the interest of
high officials. In my case, it was Don Diego Colón himself, my namesake
and the actual son of the Admiral, who freed me from all formal servitude
in 1522. I am ever thankful to him for the act, which allowed me to recover
a measure of my health and no doubt has prolonged my life until now.

The encomienda Indians are pitiful. I walked near to see them fully and
recognized not a one from the old days. As always, they were thin, almost
all. Several men had open sores from whip lashes and saber blows. I saw
only ten children and no old people. They ate casabe and fruit, packed in
among themselves, and many slept in profound stupor before lining up to
witness the prisoner's final torture.

Jiqui stabbed a guard in the leg when he made his getaway. That guard,
leg bandaged, sat immediately behind the planted post, next to the jail, as
two other guards brought Jiqui to the post. The oidores were out with a
rather large group. The bishop was with them.

farthest out. Oidor Suazo, who
...iis, gestured with his hand, and the

...act," said the marshall. "The crime was not
Everyor...then rebel cut a Christian. And why? So he could
is to arran the hills. And why? So he could flee to kill and torture
senteñs, wherever he may go."

...his persuasion of mind and for his aggression against an officer of
...d and King, the young "cannibal" would: 1. be cut across the back of the
calves, 2. be set upon by two mastiff dogs, 3. be raised up above a fire and
slowly roasted until dead.

This happened today. I write it now, only hours afterwards, and I will
tell it now if I must write all night. I saw the cruelty, one more time, and
Las Casas was with me.

There was little in particular about Jiqui. He was young, short in stature
and sinewy. He did not look badly beaten. He had treed himself before the
dogs got to him. As per the formal Spanish custom, he was fed well before
his execution. He was tied chest and face to the thick post, his arms hugging
around it, but I could see his face. His eyes scanned the crowd. The post
itself was of the Xiki tree, a tough wood that will not burn once charred and
hardened. Many poor Taínos have hugged that post before, but Jiqui was
actually named after his death tree.

The wounded guard, whose name was Carrasco, got to do the cutting.
Two men carried his chair to the back of the prisoner and the marshall gave
him a short, razor sharp dagger. Carrasco, a thin, small man with a goat's
beard, held up the dagger and offered the Ave Maria. Then he thanked the
marshall and the principal oidor for the privilege. Leaning over, he then
poked the boy, Jiqui, in one buttock, getting a piece of the skin and slipping
the dagger in a half inch. Jiqui groaned, then Carrasco's dagger scraped
bone and he yelled a loud, "Aiiii!!!"

The crowd gasped and the soldiers and sailors laughed. Among the
guards, several laughed loudly. One yelled to the lined-up Indians, "Hear
the devil yelp, you dogs!"

Carrasco looked up proudly. I could tell he was a nobody among the
guards before this. Smiling, he raised the dagger to the guards, then put
the point at Jiqui's anus..Jiqui gasped and the guards began to titter loudly,
but the marshall barked at Carrasco to, "stay with the sentence." Dutifully,
Carrasco cut the calves then, two deep slits across each, just under the knees.
Blood began to flow. Finished with the calves, Carrasco took a stab at the
thick of one calf and Jiqui yelled again.

I wished he wouldn't yell. It cut into my heart. Searching the crowd, his eyes came to rest on me. I think he could tell I loved him. He was at the age I remembered my twin sons, how I have pictured them since I lost them. But I emphasize that I love all my Taíno, even the ones who have betrayed me. I would kill anyone of them that threatened my Enriquillo, or the cause of our freedom, but I still love them for being mine, and I hold us all to be victims together.

Carrasco was carried away in his chair as two men with dogs on short leashes approached. Mastiffs of war, they sniffed blood excitedly and lunged for Jiqui's bloody calves. The handlers held the dogs up on hind legs inches away from the calves. I wished to yell my love to the boy, but was silent. Next to me, I could tell the good friar was praying. At a signal from the marshall, the mastiffs were allowed close enough to lick the blood with their extended tongues, snarling up on hind feet. At a second signal, they tore in, one on each calf, tearing flesh in sharp bites as Jiqui yelled and yelled and yelled.

The dogs were yanked away when they bit into bone. The two balls of the calves were gone. Two men with hot irons burned into the cavities left by the mastiffs and Jiqui slumped as if dead, but his eyes stayed open. Jiqui was untied and lashed by wrist and ankles to a thick iron bar, which was propped between two Y poles with dry brush gathered underneath. He was washed with water and, as he did move his head, he was made to drink copious amounts of it. Then the fire was started.

All watched intently. Jiqui dangled by hands and feet six feet over the fire. His back blackened slowly, his hair singed and the horrible smell hung like a mist throughout the square. The sun grew intensely hot and you could feel the heat of the fire itself. He groaned for two hours before he expired, but no one left the square. Many Indians, including myself, cried quietly for Jiqui as he burned, and among the women in the slave group I did hear the hummed refrains of our areito song of death, to accompany the separation of the goeiç from the body and the birth of the opia. Poor boy, I felt, how happy he might have been but for the existence of the Castilla on our lands!

I remember Hatuey, who was burned to death and did not utter a sound. I remember the groups of thirteen burned by Ovando after the Massacre of Anacaona's Banquet. Ovando, here on this island, and later Vasco Porcallo de Figueroa, in Cuba, burned us in groups of thirteen to celebrate the Sacred Thirteen of Christ and his twelve apostles.

Father Las Casas himself offered extreme unction to the dying young man. For once, there was no attempt to turn him away, although many in the crowd murmured as they recognized him, and someone did yell, "Leave the heathen his route to hell!" However, no one interfered as the guard himself did not. Suazo, the other oidores and their group waited for the termination of the rite and then walked to the good friar. All nodded and greeted him, somberly but politely. Suazo invited the friar to walk with him a ways, and Las Casas went with him. Following that group, Andrés Valenzuela and Pero López, the former encomenderos of both Enriquillo and me, actually walked together. They stood back and watched as Suazo exchanged words with the good friar and led him away. López's whole group had mean eyes. Several men in their company stood by Jiqui's charred cadaver for a while, one actually poking it with a stick.

Forty-six. *Cruelty is the province of the covered men.*

The Spanish have been so cruel. I say, as a people, they have been very cruel. Never among my people did I ever see that kind of meanness. I admit among the Spanish I have good friends and some of them have been very good to us; but as a group, they have imposed themselves violently. Tonight, Jiqui, charred and twisted, lies in the heap of ashes of the fire that consumed him. I curse them all for that. I curse the soldiers for what they will do as they drink their wine and spirits tonight, which is they will piss all over the charred remains and call on their favorite saints to bless their deed.

I have heard many stories of the thigh-eating Kwaib, how they ate our Taíno people, how they took our women. But in all of my childhood, only once did a strange canoe sail our Guanahani waters, paddled by two men who would have kidnapped a woman. They were discovered in the act, paddled away and were caught within one day by our fishermen. I know of other such incidents, some more violent, among our Caribbean peoples. And, of course, I have witnessed how some of our own caciques attacked others of our peoples, both here and in Cuba, usually in disputes over fishing and planting grounds. But even the worst of those fights, I only saw at the urging and the service of the Castilla. The Taíno caciques seldom went to war against each other anymore by the time the Castilla came. No, all of our hatreds are as a drop in the ocean of Castilla cruelty. Suffering is what they like; even their God-man, who walked among them and spoke with them as another human, they bleed him every day; what they adore is his bleeding heart; in their most sacred ceremony, they drink his blood, again and again, even the young children. Truly, the Christians find salvation in the spilling of blood. They did today to that poor boy what they have done many times. Tonight, as I write, Jiqui's body grease is in my nostrils. I can see yet how his life oozed out of him and hissed on the fire. The Castilla are taking all the fat, from the rivers and mines, from the land, and from our very bodies.

September 1, 1532

Forty-seven. *Pressing "the Indian cause" could get Enriquillo killed.*

Much before the light of morning, I found the monk in our chapel. I knelt next to him and knew that we shared great disgust. In the darkness, brightened faintly by a faint moon, the events of the afternoon seemed a horrible dream. We prayed together for the soul of poor Jiqui, for him and for the many others. I prayed too for my himaguas, my twin boys, that they always be happy and fresh-feeling Taíno, here or in the spirit world. Done with my prayer, I felt like walking, wanting to work a kink out of my leg. The good friar stayed with me, walking behind me, staring blankly and thumbing the pressed-rose beads of a big rosary that dangled from his right hand.

Morning found us facing the ocean, catching the breeze of the outgoing tide. We stood on the promontory that overlooks the coastal road. Mornings like this one, the expansive ocean, palm trees, fruit trees all around, the gentility of our Caribbean islands reveals its imprint on my people. The sea wind speaks to me. It blows me soft kisses from the mother waters; it whispers the hopes of past generations. This wind that parts on my face, cupping my ears, blasting against my chest, my thighs, I can say to this wind, "Treat me well, make me well, carry away my pains, carry away my aches." This wind that came today will do that for me.

I caught my calm; the world once again returned me to myself. I could see the good friar struggling with his pain. His horror stays within and his fury consumes him. He is a good man, but the wind speaks not to him; so on his knees he says his Hail Marys and his Pater Nosters in a strong and steady murmur. The way he closed his eyes and prayed, I could tell he knew not how to talk to the sun, which was coming up strong from the sea at our left. I do not know how to pray without acknowledging the sun, the four winds of the earth, the mother waters. But I have always seen in the priests and monks that they pray through the image of Jesus Christ on the cross, or through a face of the Virgin Mary, in statue or painting. Also, they like to pray indoors, inside the church. Even today, as we moved our service outside, with the sun and sea, with the wind at our faces, he prays to the image of Christ in his mind, nothing else. I have noticed this in all the Christians: they seek not the world in their prayer, but the man-god on the cross.

Walking back to the convent, Las Casas announced his vehement commitment to destroying the Spanish conquistador circles, to achieve the complete renunciation of the encomienda system. He was very forthright and spoke for most of the way. "The time is ripe to line up the pressure," he kept saying. "It is the moment."

His vehemence bothered me. As he leaves soon for the court, I felt again the need to reaffirm the importance of the peace negotiation with Enriquillo.

"This work with Enriquillo must be precise," I said. "His concern is for the safety of his mountain groups."

"They will be safe," he said. "I guarantee it. But these negotiations, at this time, also mean everything to the mainland: for Perú, Guatemala and Nicaragua, for Yucatán and México, even for Borinkén and Cuba. We must push for everything we can. I insist that if we apply all the pressure now, we can overturn the encomienda."

Again, his response bothers me, especially throwing in the two islands, which I could tell was an afterthought. His impatience to overturn the whole colonial system continues. No doubt his concentration is stimulated by witnessing the execution of Jiqui. It bothered me that he could claim to guarantee Enriquillo's safety, as we had just witnessed an execution without hope of influencing the case. I asked him about the attitude of Oidor Suazo and the señores of Santo Domingo. Again, he was casual.

"For one thing, they are loath to finance more military expeditions and even less willing to actually serve on any of them. So they would opt for peace."

"What they did to that boy yesterday is what they would do to Enriquillo," I said.

"What they have done many times in many places," he said.

"But yesterday, condoned by those same authorities, we witnessed ... "

"They are butchering in the mainland like that, Dieguillo. Perú, Nicaragua, Yucatán, the Valley of México. Many hangings and burnings, like the early massacres here. No, we must destroy the encomienda, which is the law and the justification."

The encomienda is what Taíno slavery is called by Spanish law. The encomienda, which started with the early repartimientos or the give-a-ways of Taíno people imposed after the first battles, granted to specific conquistadors the right to use Indians as laborers in the farms and mines, on sea and anywhere. This followed the Admiral's idea that in return for their labor, the Spanish masters would Christianize the Indians. It was an argument that the Queen, who tried to prohibit outright slavery for Indians, could accept.

"Just remember, the encomienda's promise was to teach us Christianity."

"Well, it goes back to that savage Ovando," Las Casas said, seeming to accept my comment. "And he was a man of the church."

"But the idea goes back to Columbus himself," I said.

"The Admiral reasoned it out, but Ovando formalized its structure."

"Yes, we gave our freedom and our lands; in return, you gave us Christ," I said.

"But, Dieguillo. It is not Christianity as it is meant to be lived, as our Lord Jesus taught."

Forty-eight. *Las Casas wants to end the encomienda; I want Enriquillo to live.*

The good friar needed to discourse, as I had piqued his political mind.

I will write down here the good friar's discourse on the institution of the encomienda. I was impatient to review our plan on Enriquillo, but I like what I learned from the priest, who has, among his many documents and books, the Admiral's ship's log of the first voyage, letters from Michelle de Cúneo and Dr. Álvarez Chanca, on the second voyage, and many court documents detailing the history of the dreadful institution.

Las Casas said: "The Admiral had to pay for his excesses in describing the wealth of the Indies. Unable to find sufficient gold, he set about the justification for capturing Indians and selling them as slaves. This is where he clashed with Queen Isabel of Castille.

"When Columbus sent his first Indian slaves to markets in Spain, Queen Isabel denounced the Admiral of the Ocean Sea. 'These are my vassals,' she said. 'Who is Columbus to sell my vassals?' She ordered the Indians freed, though, truthfully, few of them ever made it back to the islands.

"Nevertheless, the Great Discoverer invoked the rights of war and conquest, justifying imposition of Christian sovereignty over heathen peoples. He continued to capture and send Indians to Iberian markets. Because infidel prisoners of war could be sold as slaves, any excuse for war was welcome.

"Queen Isabel pressed for the work of evangelization. And in this she was convinced by Columbus and others that the Indians were 'roamers' who would avoid Christianity unless secured and held to a place. Thus, the conquistadors proposed the 'burden' of granting upon themselves titles to lands and to the Indians that came with the titled land, in order that the Indians could be properly instructed in the Christian faith. To recompense the conquistadors for the burden of Christian instruction, the Indians would be made to work in the farms and in the mines to support the upkeep of the Castillas in their island and to fill up the coffers of the royal court."

What the good friar says is true. The conquistadors' argument about "settling down" the Indians in order to Christianize us was a trick for the

Queen to accept the repartimientos—the parcelling out—of the Taíno population of the island among the early gentry. Afterwards, all notices received
by the court were contradictory and even led to laws to protect my Taíno
people, but their enslavement was just as total and brutal as were the assertions to her majesty by the delegates from the islands that everything was
kind and good for the Indians. Queen Isabel's concern for our people was
to little avail as her health was failing and our islands were so far away from
her.

After Queen Isabel's death in 1504, I say, there was little more to be
done at the court on our behalf. King Ferdinand was disinclined to consider
the fate of heathens. Only the good friar and his allies defended our people.
And to refute him, many calumnies and half-truths were divulged against
us—assertions that we were indolent, could not feed ourselves, that we were
idolaters, that we were sodomites, that we had no law. "Beasts that talk,"
Las Casas said. "That's what they called your Indians."

Las Casas' review of these events and assertions fueled my anger, bringing forth words and curses, arguments and anecdotes, but by late afternoon,
as we took the final uphill trail that would bring us to the rear of the convent,
I was again tired of the polemic and history; I wanted to plan for the survival
of Enriquillo and his people.

"Father," I finally said, "the way my people have died, again and again,
no one knows better than you and I. But what of Guarocuya, how can we
help him."

"That is my point," he responded. "I believe there is room for reform.
I believe we can still turn the encomienda around. Through the righteous
stand of Enriquillo and our Christian faith, our religious orders are building
pressure toward a major investigation ... "

"Father, please," I said, "Enriquillo may want to discuss the encomienda,
but that is the last one of his points. I know his strategy. He is most concerned
over the fate of his people in the Bahuruku, how to bring the war to an end
so he can settle them."

"You must understand, Dieguillo, that this is already beyond Española.
We truly have the religious orders behind us. In Perú, the encomienda is in
a chaos. A new investigation, conducted by the religious ... "

"Father!" I said sharply to him. "If we mix up Enriquillo's needs with
the demands of mainland strategies, we may get him killed."

"That is precisely an Indian problem: thinking too small. Our strategies
must cast a wider net."

"What about the Jeronymites, father, remember that farce?" I said. "What
about the free Indian communities? What happened to them?"

Immediately, I knew I had hurt him. Those two projects of earlier campaigns are dear to his heart. Their demise, through corruption and greed, is a deep wound in him. I am sorry to do it, but there is no other way to get his attention. We walked silently after that, climbing the wooded east side of our convent. Two flocks, one of parrots and one of doves, flocked together overhead, moving through the trees just ahead of us. As we talked, I had not noticed them. But as we settled into our silent walk, slowly the woods surrounded me; I followed the birds, sniffed the lairs of snakes and iguanas, their lairs, noted trees and plantations of fruit. On the way, too, on a knoll, I saw a guásima tree with two identical trunks, beautiful, with equal branches on both sides, almost perfectly resembling each other. I love our forests; I love this world that speaks to me still.

September 6, 1532

Forty-nine. *A message for Catalina Díaz, midwife and friend.*

The past several days I worked on the building crew for the convent of La Merced, which is finishing a wing on its church. I learned to swing a hammer years ago, so they always call me for their building sessions. By good fortune, two mansos who work for Valenzuela were there. Young men of Anacaona's line, they helped carry planks and ran for things. I shared food with them and they conversed with me in Taíno. They agreed to carry a message from me to Catalina Díaz, an old friend who is Valenzuela's senior house servant, and who has helped her nephew Enriquillo before. My message merely stated that I had some baby powders for her, made from the ground-up cranium of manatee. The young men are to let her know I will be at the town meeting in Santo Domingo scheduled for the fifteenth of September, and will have the powder there for her.

Catalina Díaz is a midwife, one of the old-timers who still remembers many of our cures. Even the Spanish ladies go to her with their ailments. She uses the manatee cranium powder in a broth to strengthen the women after childbirth. However, my message was cryptic. With Catalina, whom I have known for more than thirty years, I use the term "baby" when referring to Enriquillo. I mean to ask Catalina to be my ear, referring to Enriquillo. I mean to ask Catalina to be my ear in the Valenzuela household, so she might learn what those vile minds plot against her nephew. Two of Catalina's daughters also serve the household. All three of these women conduct themselves humbly and piously, seldom talking, so that their señores hardly know them to understand and speak the Spanish language, but they do. Among them they are bound to hear most of the talk in the house of Valenzuela.

Fifty. *A note for later writing.*

Rereading my conversation with the good friar, I note my reference to the mission of the Jeronymites and also to his project to set up free Indian communities. I will explain both of these events as they come up in my recollections. I brought them up to him to remind him how his ideas have failed in the past, at other times when he was stronger and hoped for total solutions to our people's misery.

September 15, 1532

Fifty-one. *Reminding Las Casas of Enriquillo's first cause.*

I write this in the late evening. Tonight the grand men of Santo Domingo met at the House of Contracts. The fifteen major sugar cane plantations were represented. Also, the large cattlemen were there, even Bishop Bastidas, reputed to have more than twenty thousand head of cattle in ranches from here to the Bahuruku.

I met the good friar at the convent's gate. More than a dozen monks were already congregated and we started to walk down together. I paired off with Las Casas. "Will you be speaking tonight?" I asked in his ear.

"Yes," he answered.

"Speak please of Enriquillo's cause."

"Of course, I intend to."

"He has always wanted peace, to live in harmony," I said. "He has kept his Catholic sacraments, even in the mountains, fasting his Fridays and even hearing mass whenever possible."

"Do not worry, Dieguillo, we will speak of the cacique's character and of the justice of his cause. But you tell me: Will Enriquillo come to a parley? Can I hold his promise in my hand, that he will come in?"

"Enriquillo trusts you, father," I said. "But can he forget the parley at Anacaona's, Ovando's dirty trick. We must remember, father, how each of the major caciques, one by one, were tricked and killed."

"I will be there to guarantee Enriquillo's safety."

"And your safety, who would guarantee that?"

He shook his head. Las Casas is totally fearless. Always ready for martyrdom, arguments about safety do not quite impress him. But for a chief like Enriquillo, this is pre-eminent. His first loyalty as cacique is precisely for the safe settling of the dispute and the accommodation of his people in their own community.

"It is complicated to guarantee the safety of our people on the Bahuruku. You know they will try to kill him."

"What brutes they would show themselves to be!!"

"Yes, and our young cacique would be dead."

We walked. To impress him again I told him as we neared the House of Contracts, "While you speak, I will try to find out when they intend to kill him."

He vacillated a step and turned to me, as if awakened abruptly. "Strength, father," I reassured him. "I am praying for your success."

Fifty-two. *The townsmen have reasons for peace.*

The House of Contracts is a two-story building. It has a large meeting hall that was crowded with more than eighty people. On the platform, the oidores, with Judge Suazo at the head and Vadillo to his right, looked over the hall. Some thirty or forty servants waited on the street, verandas and stairways of the large government building. Half of them were mansos, half of them negroes. More than twenty of the permanent guard milled about outside, interspersed but not mixing with the servant group. Only four, led by a lieutenant, had stand-up duty, two inside and two outside. The commander of the permanent guard was inside also, sitting in a second row on the platform, behind Suazo.

When Las Casas came up to the door, the lieutenant quickly saluted him and kissed his ring. Immediately, the good friar was ushered toward the raised platform and seated next to the vicar and bishop. All greeted each other graciously, though not one of them respects the other. Las Casas took his seat and I could see his face through the window as he lowered his friar's hood to the shoulders. Then the various señores came in and many, almost all, approached Father Las Casas, offering polite greetings. I found this completely remarkable, because to a man they all hate him deeply, as he has harassed their persons and insulted their endeavors many times.

Of the meeting, I heard the first part, up until the good friar's speech, when Doña Catalina got my attention. After the bishop's blessing, Suazo called the meeting to order, explaining the issues now before the King's court relating to the troubles of the Bahuruku Indians under Cacique Enriquillo. The meeting got started with a recounting of the Enriquillo affair through its thirteen years of hostilities and campaigns. The lesser oidores read testimonies from important people in the island, expressing the wish to settle a peace with Enriquillo. I looked at Valenzuela, Enriquillo's pushed-aside master, who sat silently as even Suazo acknowledged the early grievances of the young cacique. The principal oidor even spoke of some "lack of understanding" shown to Enriquillo when his complaint came to old Vadillo's jurisdiction. The Oidor Vadillo, brother-cousin of the early magistrate, also sat silently.

The commander of the guard reported next. He informed the señores that Enriquillo's fortresses had been attacked by half a dozen well-stocked campaigns. Not one had been successful, he said. The loss of Spanish men was more than two hundred, counting all the campaigns. Several major estates had gone to ruin, pursuing the military destruction of Enriquillo. There was considerable fear that more and more negro slaves would take the cimarron trail and join Enriquillo. "The Indians are very hard to pursue," said the commander. "They eat anything, anywhere, and somehow always manage to survive and keep going. Our troops must be supplied and are not used to the constant climbing. The Bahuruku mountains have many ridges and tall points. The only attack that might succeed would be to penetrate the Bahuruku with fighting squads from at least fourteen directions at once. Such a crusade would be very expensive and even that could fail. Were a major campaign to fail now, I am afraid many Indians and Africans would determine to join the armed camps." Perhaps not too long ago, that commander would have been called down for cowardice and lack of spirit; however, tonight there was considerable approbation in the assemblage. One cattleman said, "Give the cacique his due; bring him to a peace, negotiate with him. We shall give the group a tract and be done with the damnable war."

A merchant man added, "Not only are the armed campaigns ruinous for our townships and estates; while the Indians are in the bush, all merchandising is reduced. Little of consequence travels overland anymore. And even docking ships have been attacked. Our commerce is at times paralyzed by the nuisance assaults. I say as the cattleman from Juan de la Maguana, make peace with the devils and be done with it."

When Judge Suazo introduced Las Casas, he was most generous, crediting the good friar for his steadfast search for a more just treatment of the natural race of the islands. An acquaintance of the rebel cacique in his youth, said Judge Suazo, Las Casas should be recognized for his providential demeanor to make himself available to help secure the peace that is sought. I prayed silently as Las Casas stood to speak that Enriquillo's safety would be at the center of his thoughts and words.

"Many of you no doubt believe the Indian to be inferior to our race," he began, and my heart sank as my mind paid attention. "You are incorrect. The Indians of these islands and over most of the mainland are a race of innocents, pure and gracious people, who had their own beliefs. The original inhabitants you hold now as servants and slaves met us in a state of grace. They have ancient stories, like the Greeks of our ancestry. They are still endowed with that nature. But our own ancestor, Adam, only lasted six hours in that state, before the Lord kicked him out of paradise."

Everybody murmured at once. Las Casas was so brazen, it made me shudder. "Sodomites," I heard a guard say at a nearby window. "That priest is still a puker."

The good friar further demanded that the assembled encomenderos guarantee their Indians sufficient food and other benefits, "if you are not ready to give them up, although that is precisely what you should do if you would respect the doctrine of Jesus Christ." He reminded them, "I have not absolved anyone holding Indians for almost twenty years. Wolves thou shalt not be among these sheep. I believe it is wrong in the eyes of our Lord."

More murmuring was heard, some quite loud. One phrase I agreed with: "Stick to the issue, priest. What about the cacique Enriquillo in the Bahuruku?"

"Peace with Enriquillo, yes. Respect Enriquillo. But free all the Indians, as the King would have them do in Peru and Nicaragua, where he sent word via my own person, to dissolve the encomienda."

From the center row, immediately before the oidores, a rather stout man in a long blue shirt stood and reared his head. He said, "The good friar, as he is called, Protector of the Indians, will forgive a mere writer and servant of the King, if he takes issue with the friar's usual misbegotten logic." It was Oviedo himself, I could tell, as the speaker approached the platform. Gonzalo Fernández de Oviedo, the official historian and enemy of Las Casas—I had heard he was a recent arrival on a caravel from Spain. He went on: "The King, whom I have seen frequently, has not renounced the encomienda, and has in truth congratulated the encomenderos—I heard him say so just this past summer—for the dutiful task of imparting Christian doctrine to Indians. Your information is old, Father Las Casas. Or maybe it simply does not apply to Española."

It was at this moment that Catalina called to me from the street through her daughter Julia, who simply walked by and gained my attention. I was sorry to have to go, as I was both fascinated and chagrined by the widening debate the good friar had aroused. The anti-encomienda talk, as I had anticipated, bothered everybody. I could see the discussion was going to get heated.

Fifty-three. *Dissimulated romancing with Catalina.*

For an extra moment, I watched the clique of Vadillo, Valenzuela and, not far distant, Pero López, the man I hate most in the world. I stared at López that extra moment, thinking quickly in my mind as usual how much I have wanted to kill him. I could see Father Las Casas' face reddening, too, and said a silent prayer for him to stay with Enriquillo's cause. Then, lowering my hat and feigning a bit of a limp to give the appearance of a smallpox-scarred manso Indian, I went looking for Doña Catalina.

The street was quite crowded, but I found my old friend around two right-hand corners, sitting in a group of young women in a crowd of mansos. Catalina wore a long cotton skirt and blouse and, as usual, held a baby in one arm. She was small and thin but wiry and alert. As I found her, she was instructing the baby's young mother, no more than fourteen years old, in the use of an aloe salve for a case of butt-rash. In the moonlight, my eyes watered, as I had not seen her in more than three years.

Catalina had loyal people around her, including several negro girls who challenged me lightly with their eyes. But Catalina jumped up to greet me as I lowered my head to get her blessing.

"Diego," she said, "my old boyfriend."

I had to laugh. I had never been her boyfriend, but it is true she is not ten years older than me, and once, after the Massacre of Anacaona's Banquet, we shared a common adventure. At that time, I still had Ceyba, my wife, and our twin sons, all of whom I hid with Catalina for several months after being pressed into Diego Velázquez' service in 1505. Later, we toiled at the same encomienda, survived it, lost track of each other and re-encountered around 1520, by which time we both had gained a semblance of freedom, I as a monk's servant and she as a house maid in the Valenzuela estate. Time and again, we have seen each other, which I truly enjoy, as she is the closest person I have for a relative; Catalina is a like a mother-aunt to me, or maybe like an older, distant cousin.

Tonight, for this guajira of mine from an earlier life I had a present. She received it graciously. It was the ground manatee brain bone, not for the baby so much, but as our own best cure for side pains, which Catalina and the women she cares for often suffer. She had something for me, too, a good stack of tabacco leaves selected for low aroma and consistent dryness, the kind to be mixed in our cohoba.

Slowly, without any overtness, we walked into the darkness, where we held hands. Nearby, in door frames on both sides of the street, pairs of lovers embraced in the darkness. One man was a guard and it seemed safe to assume that other guards would not disturb couples there.

"We are not a sun's walk from each other," she said. "But I never see you."

"In my moon walk, I see you," I said. "I will always do that for you, and for your line."

The moon walk is a ceremony I acquired through Catalina in the days of our bush run with Ceyba and the boys. Already a midwife to her people, Catalina took Ceyba in and nursed her ailments through that nightmare of violence and persecution. More than once we gave thanks together, and it was during one of those times she taught me the midwife's moon walk, as a thanksgiving to women's medicine and a way to bind our spiritual lines.

"My concern is for your nephew," I said, contemplating that no one else around us would know whom I meant. But I leaned Catalina against the wall, facing me.

"The baby boy is in danger," she whispered. "There is talk of striking him at the first opportunity, at the earliest point of actual contact, before getting to the stage of sitting down together."

"Why early?" I said.

"They would commit the act in the moment of confusion between war and peace. They are certain that he will be drawn out of the Bahuruku this time, maybe into the fields or the lake shore."

"Who would do it?"

"My master's talk is to pay two guards to strike him quick. Valenzuela, as still rightful holder of my nephew's encomienda, would be easily validated to attempt an apprehension or a punishment. Your former holder, Pero López, has made visits to the Valenzuela house."

"And if the King mandates differently? If he mandates a clear peace offering? Such is the good friar's claim."

"You know these señores, Diego. They blaspheme the King his goiter. They believe in cutting off the head, then finding the body. It is true that many are for peace, but only because Enriquillo has proven so costly in war. And they are desperate to quiet the island and attract more ships."

"What you tell me may save the nephew's life," I said.

"I will think of everything I remember and hear everything I can," she said.

She worried that Enriquillo might expose himself prematurely and offered the use of one of her daughters as a go-between that the young cacique could trust. I reminded her such an offer would divulge her relationship to him. Maybe, she said, but if the negotiations were final and conclusive, it would not matter. We all want to help in my family, she said. We would be offended, especially Inez (her own name for Julia), if we could not help in every way we can.

I agreed to set up the deal with Enriquillo and to use her daughter Inez as both courier and message. I mean by this that her actual identity will tell the cacique whether an ambush were expected or not. If an ambush is planned, we would not send Inez, but a Castilla as a messenger.

Fifty-four. *Catalina believes in both us and them.*

Catalina. How good it was to talk to her again. How good to hold her and pretend to be lovers.

We agreed to meet in church at the earliest mass each Sunday. She is a beata, a church matron. Her Catholic vocation has saved her life many times and has given her a certain respect among the Castilla ladies and even the señores. But she has given up nothing of our peoples' beliefs. "I believe what they tell me about the Jesus, but what they say about us, that our cemíes and areitos are the devil's works, that I don't believe," she says. Before we parted, she stroked my right leg, always sore. Her thin hands are strong. She massaged the muscle at the front of the leg, but directed the strength to the back of the thigh, where the Cuban caymán's long tooth dug deep into nerve and muscle, nineteen fateful years ago. When she was done, I stroked the back of her neck and shoulders. "Take bark from the jobo tree," she advised. "Boil it thick and make a jelly. While still warm, rub this jelly into the back of your thighs and calves. If you cannot, I have some. We could meet someday, and I will do this for you."

Fifty-five. *The meeting ends.*

It is late in the evening. I tire now of writing, although I like it more and more. I find I enjoy the telling of actual happenings, and think to preserve these memories for my boys, if they would ever return. This is the hopeful part of me. Catalina is one of my old ones; I have been a fool not to look for her more. She is an ally, a sister, a doctor, a knower of my heart.

The meeting was still going on as I got back to my place by the window. Judge Suazo, principal oidor, was giving the summation. On the platform, Las Casas looked one way and, from his chair on the main floor, Oviedo looked the other way. Suazo pressed the question of peace with Enriquillo and he once again praised Las Casas for enlisting in the endeavor. "The Protector of the Indians is perhaps too persistent in his opinions about the encomienda," Suazo said. "But we all thank him for his involvement now and continue to encourage his assistance in bringing Enriquillo to a negotiating parley." It seemed that despite Las Casas' antagonistic words, the group was more than agreeable to a peace settlement on the Enriquillo war.

"Enriquillo will come in," Las Casas said. "He is a man of peace."

"Yes, a treaty of peace from the King will bring the Carib out," Vadillo responded for the oidores, using the anonymous word, "Carib," that signaled dubious intent. Las Casas simply nodded back. I could see Pero López smiling as he stood to go join the crowd around the oidores.

A toast of wine was made for the oidores and major señores, and the meeting was concluded.

September 20, 1532

Fifty-six. *Good-bye to Las Casas, ashamed of my writing.*

I helped Las Casas embark for the island of San Juan, Borikén in our language, this morning, ferrying his trunks to the docks on the convent wagon. I know he means to go to Spain from there, but dares not announce it beforehand. We spoke while the ship's servants loaded up water and high stacks of freshly baked casabe bread.

All Spanish here eat our casabe bread now, although I remember a time when, except for the Admiral, most of them disdained it, "like eating chalk." If kept dry, the casabe lasts a long time and is good food. Our sacred torts complement any type of meat soup or gravy and will fill your gut, even by themselves. I say they are sacred because to us our main foods were all appreciated in ceremony and, among them, the most appreciated was the yuca, which had its own areito songs and was represented in our principal cemí. I looked around this morning, as the casabe was loaded on ship, and had to remark how much of our Taíno ways the Spanish have taken up. Looking back from the docks, nearly all the Spanish houses, including the tavern, are actually bohíos, walls of palm wood tied together with wet, hard-drying bejuco vines and roofs made of palm thatch. In the interior and along the coasts, the small Spanish settlements all rely on the bohío construction. Many a Spanish fisherman now sails our waters in our Taíno canoe, and lots of them sleep in our hammock. "Temporary matters," Las Casas commented back, cutting my argument. "For all its ills, our Christian civilization will impose itself. It is inevitable. For instance, you don't see thatch-roofed churches or government houses anymore."

"You don't see areitos, either," I said. "Velázquez, for instance, beheaded every behike medicine man he could find."

"The behikes were idolaters," he said. "I disagreed with their execution, but I worked many times to convert them to Christianity."

I felt particularly proud of our Taíno ways this morning. Yesterday afternoon, I prepared Catalina's recipe for jobo bark liniment to rub on my legs, and it greatly lessened the stiffness. I admit, too, that seeing Catalina has rekindled many sentiments. But I did not want to fight with the good friar today, particularly as he was about to board ship, so I held my tongue.

Las Casas cleared his throat. He had a way of doing that when he wanted to change the subject. My reference to the execution of behikes he clearly found discomforting. My "for instance" recalled a particular event from the time of the campaign after the Massacre of Anacaona's Banquet, in 1503, when Diego Velázquez, sent later to conquer Cuba, beheaded two behikes.

Las Casas, before becoming a priest, was a soldier in that campaign and witnessed the murders without objecting.

In front of us, several sailors and dock negroes struggled to load a recently-fixed anchor. "I have read your pages on the discovery and your first look at Cuba," Las Casas said as we walked up the dock to kill a bit of time. "Some of the detail is interesting, but your memory is a bit clouded. For instance, you don't mention the Pinzóns at all, Columbus's other captains. Pinzón left him, you know, took off for Jamaica or God knows where, while the Admiral made his way here to Española."

"But I haven't gotten that far," I protested. "I planned to write something about Pinzón going off like that."

"The other thing is you make them sound so wise and good, I mean your old people."

"Yes, that is how I remember them," I said.

"No doubt, but try to be more true, more realistic. You have to tell the bad with the good."

For some reason I felt his commentary on my writing like a slap on my forehead. I felt exposed and vulnerable to the priest.

"Finally, don't write so much about yourself," he continued. "You embarrass me with your midnight ejaculations ... "

I wanted to run. I had forgotten what I had actually written, and it was something very private as I wrote, but to hear it spoken revolted me. I felt trapped by my words and I didn't like it.

"Writing is very much like confession," Las Casas commented, softening, as I think he could see my chagrin. "But the best writing goes beyond one's own person to describe the sequence of events accurately."

"Yes, I believe in sequence ... " I said.

He admonished me: "The intent of all writing is to discern God's master plan in the life of our Christian nations, regardless of the greed or brutality of our fellow humans beings. It is all right to describe the customs of your people, even as they appear in your own life, Dieguillo, but see these events in the context of our Christian faith. The Devil himself runs your pen otherwise, that same devil that is in the lust of your male blood."

He shocks me much, as I remember the teachings of our behikes, how they spoke of our "male wishes." I remember their true and gentle words. They are so much more clear to me than what the good friar says.

Thankfully, Las Casas changed the subject.

He wanted to know about Guacanagari, the noble. "In thinking about the life of the Admiral," he said, "the Noble Cacique Guacanagari appears to be a worthy counterpart from the Taíno culture ... "

"Guacanagari was a pompous child," I said. "He was not a man of the stature of real ni-Taíno caciques, like Guarionex or Behechio."

"Was he cowardly?"

"Not cowardly so much as very ambitious and politically naive," I said.

"Well, that is the level of discussion I could use from you."

"Guacanagari is next," I said. "As I describe how we made our way from Cuba here to Española, how we met Guacanagari and why the Admiral founded his first colony at Fort Navidad."

"Good," he said. "Tell me about the caciques of that time, how Columbus met them and their first relations."

I promised I would. We were still talking when the call came to board ship. He said this: "One thing to keep in mind. As we know, the Carib were moving north onto the big islands with their raids. Had the Spanish not come, it is possible they would have eaten all of you by now."

I laughed at that one, though bitterly. "No, father," I said, as he walked the plank, basket of fruits in hand. "We Taínos were incorporating both Macorixe and Ciguayo, and even the fierce ones that you call Carib; we were marrying them into our people, our women were teaching them our ways, we were killing them with love."

I got a nervous laugh out of him then, as the plank was pulled up, though I was serious. We Taínos had our diplomacy and our strategy; by our law we lived, and let others live.

September 22, 1532

Fifty-seven. *Breeding my mare.*

It has been five days since I have written. With the good friar at sea on his way to Spain, my life is much quieter. I took time to catch up with my gardens and to have my mare bred. She gives good foals, which are always useful and a source of revenue. The good mare that I have, which I received from my famous namesake, Don Diego Columbus, is a fourteen-hand roan of Andalusian stock. I was lucky to breed her with an Arabian stallion owned by Don Federico Castellanos, a local hidalgo who has extensive cattle ranches. Antoncito, a half-brother of Silverio, provided the entry early last Sunday, after I noticed Cariblanca dripping. I walked her over two pastures and the Arabian paced excitedly with her smell in the air. Antoncito dropped the gate and walked away to hoe a field of yams. The horses pawed and sniffed and didn't take long to consummate the coupling. The Arabian was still on Cariblanca when a huge swarm of bees, thousands and thousands, flew buzzing overhead. We were happy they missed us. Had they swarmed closer to the ground and bumped into us, they would have been quite dangerous.

Fifty-eight. *Survival in humility.*

Soon, I will go to the Bahuruku. Enriquillo will have cohoba ready. I will go there and we will mix it together. Then, according to his behike, we will snort and smoke right then, or wait for a more propitious moment. I prepare now, fasting and concentrating. A route to peace must be found for the baby boy and his camps on the Bahuruku. Enriquillo's people are the last of our free people on this island. Valiant they have been but are yet a small cay in a sea of Castillians. The growing numbers of Spanish will not abate; they are stronger with each passing year. In Cuba, we are more than a dozen strong communities still, scattered here and there in mountain valleys. In Borikén, too, we hide camps in the mountains and in remote coasts. Of course, on my little islands, I hear, we are almost none left. And here in Española, after thirteen years of war, we must find ways for the Castillian (or Spanish as they call themselves more and more) to allow a community, a peaceful camp of Indians. This we cannot do by proposing a political opposition, as Las Casas suggests. We suffer greatly still their dreaded coughs as much as their sword and their fury. They surround us everywhere, and not only Castillians, but others of the covered kind; French and English have I met, Christians also, talking differently but looking the same, doing the same. We Taíno, ni-taíno or guaxeri, will survive meekly, I fear, or none at all.

Fifty-nine. *Our ways were respectful of reproductive powers.*

I find it comical, after listening to the good friar's preponderance of words about the evils of lust, his cryptic references to our Taíno naturalness that, as I revise my cohoba teachings, I recall the instruction to concentrate on the use of my eyes and mind to control the urge of the loins. This, we were told as youngsters, you do by identifying the lustful urge whenever it surfaces and putting it consciously aside. The mind can do that, and it should not be a very difficult thing to do. At least, such was the teaching of my elders. Our people used the mind a lot, not like the covered men, so forcefully, but subtly, in delicate ways. Truthfully, I never saw a passion act among my people that was not intended by all concerned. And, unlike the covered men, too, it was not for its supposed evil that we controlled human passion, but for its power to communicate and create. Our own people went naked, it is true, but this did not promote a tidal wave of lust coupling. People concentrated on their many productive activities rather well.

Even as a little boy, I heard the grown-ups talking of the coupling act as the energy of connection with the spirit world of our ancestors. In the moment of love, if everything lines up, they said, our ancestors on the other side will feed us the spirit of the child to be, the one that will form from the seed in the womb. They said the coupling act itself releases the connective waters between our living world and the spirit world and can create life (and much grief). But, they also taught, and strictly, that the urge of the loins and its act is disrespectful during preparation for prayer ceremonies. Coupling is not a good thing to do when trying to set up ceremonies to *communicate* with the spirit world.

During the special times of ceremonial areitos, and in the cohoba, the behike and caciques, the house mothers and midwives all advised the men and women to abstain; and they did, everyone, without any resistance, as all the people wanted to help out and make sure the ceremonies would go well. Our people understood that the spiritual connection brought on by the coupling act must be carefully guarded at ceremonial times, when the world lines up and the ancestors visit us formally. In our discipline, the men were more directly charged than the women and were instructed as to stages of control. Taíno men were taught to control the desire, when proper, and they could do this for life. The men in fact took pride in doing this, so as not to be led by the yuán in life.

I repeat, the discipline of abstinence was much appreciated in our important activities—in the fishing and the sea, in the facing of the elements or enemies. The urge of the loins, as enjoyable as it is, was not the thing to look for in life. In fact, it is a very poor concentration, as the dead who protect us and breathe us life are made uncomfortable with the heat of lust. There is for instance a great bent for the act of masturbation among the covered men. They do it, they laugh about it, they hide it and they punish it. But as boys, we Taíno were taught not to abuse ourselves but to use the energy to connect, to let our urges and emotions well up, and then on an evening especially tender, to imagine a love for our life before sleep. And this was an invitation to the Good Earth itself, Attabei, to let a human spirit opia visit our living hammock, to join our imagination in the dream world and thus naturally release the pent-up love of our loins.

For Taíno, as you controlled your loins, so you gained spirit as a man and power to communicate with the spirits and cemíes. You were not to let the passions dominate, and neither was strength meant to do violence. This was an understood agreement among our cacique and ni-Taíno families. Gentle treatment of the people by the caciques and by each other was a dominant idea for our people. I believe the discipline Taíno men were taught about our "men's wishes" was very important in making us see more clearly the important things in life and to keep down the wish to do violence.

Women's disciplines were very different. Even their language was different. In sexual adventure, they had more permission, particularly the young girls, who were guided in these matters by their old ladies, all mandated to increase the babies of their households and some of them quite lecherously given to the task. In one special ceremony, we even coupled the opias, or dead spirits, with our living goeiçs, or souls, and even with our living bodies. (You can always tell an opia because the dead have no belly-button.) Yet, even for this one ceremony, fasts from food and coupling were held in preparation, and areitos were dedicated. Pulp of guava was fed to the spirits on those occasions and it was on those nights, dream couplings and other experiences were reported by many people. YaYa, Vital Principle, marrow of life, was called forth by the women elders at that ceremony.

At regular times, the old people would say, it does not really matter what people do. When the spirits rest in their Coaibay, when we the living are left to our own fortune, then permission to copulate was assumed, sometimes very openly, though I must say, among our men the lure was the pleasure of the women. This was pointed out by the old men as a man's best reward, as they said "to make a woman crackle." I never saw angry violations of our women; I never saw and never heard of any among my people prior to the arrival of the covered men.

Father Las Casas would call these notions vehement, but I noticed the Castilla, particularly the early ones without women, were often driven wild by desire when they saw our naked people. They had hot loins lusting for the coupling act, a lust of possession itself that easily turned to blood. They put a lot of words to it, which the Good Friar repeats, but it defined them nonetheless. The Castillas, being dressed, not naked, could not control their minds about it. They saw our women's nakedness and had to have them, mostly by rape. And in their killing, they enjoyed the brutal sexual joke, cutting testicles and breasts and laughing about it. Constantly, they needed enforcers for their laws to control their people. Even among their priests, who are supposed to abstain, very few do. Most fully dressed of Spaniards, many of the priests, go for boys.

Sixty. *I do not really feel shame.*

I am glad to write about all things. Shame I felt when the good friar recalled my words about my night of puberty, but it was mostly surprise. I realize now it is he who was shamed, maybe for his own memories or actions. The Castillas are different from our men in the way they wish so much to hide their nature, from each other and even from themselves. I still call them, "covered men," though I am now also "covered," and I, too, would be shamed of my nudity.

I will be careful to select the good friar's readings from these pages. I will not show him in writing anything that I could not tell him in person. I find the writing hard. It is so much easier to know what to say, face to face. The moment guides our use of words. I tell a thought in the mood and the climate and the uniqueness of a moment, how it carries our heart's secret meanings, to the eyes, to the body and to the goeiç, or soul, to the trees and to the winds that record them.

September 26, 1532

Sixty-one. *Indians tell Columbus to look elsewhere for women, gold.*

I write now about early December, 1492, during the first voyage, just seven weeks after leaving my home of Guanahani with the first Admiral Columbus.

For days we scouted the coast of Bohío, having crossed over from Cuba. In Cuba, after losing several of their own people as captives, the local Taíno had raised the Admiral's expectation for gold. "Caona," they said, pointing to Bohío, this Taíno homeland that would become this luckless Española. "That way, too," they said. "You will find an island inhabited by only women. Matinino, it is called. Women and gold, women and gold to make your heart glad."

Columbus was intense as we left the Cuban coast at Maisi Point to cross the Windward channel. I could say, all the Castilla were intense, very serious, talking only of gold. They believed that inevitably they would find a large mine. At vespers, as the Admiral led the singing, he would invoke a prayer, "Oh, please the Lord, lead me to the source of the gold mines."

The good friar pointed out that Pinzón, captain of the Pinta, had split off with a good wind and sailed part of Bohío's coast on his own. I believe (or I should say, the Admiral believed, since I formed this opinion from his) that Pinzón wanted to be the first to sight the land with the gold. But Pinzón is not important. He rejoined us in due time with nothing of consequence to tell. (This Pinzón made it safely back to Spain, however; he died within days of his arrival, while the Admiral lived to enjoy the glory of his deed.)

Sixty-two. *Diving for yellowtail with Rodrigo and Carey.*

To continue: On the Santa María and the Niña, sailing the coast of Bohío, the days took a happy turn. One morning, drifting east along the coast, the Admiral announced to our people that after exploring Bohío, he would return us to our homes, in Cuba and Guanahani. Suddenly, the Caniba tales were a lot less threatening and even the women relaxed. Suddenly, a red snapper run was all around our ships, the sea red with fish running by the tens of thousands.

I remember Carey, Rodrigo and me diving off the stern of the Santa María into a school of red snappers and yellowtails, how Carey surprised everyone by catching a red snapper with his hand. Carey held his fingers stiff like the head of a spear and, swimming with the fish, suddenly thrust his hand behind the gill of a snapper passing by. He held it up. Several sailors saw him do it and called to others. We were off the coast of what is now Cape Elephant, not far from the Cacique Guacanagari's village.

Sixty-three. *Çibanakán faces the hammerhead, impressing the sailors.*

In the water, hunting in the school of red snapper, which ran by us for hours, two sharks appeared, a small blue and a large hammerhead. Carey and the rest of us left the water. Çibanakán reproached us. "Taíno men don't leave the water because a shark appears."

It was afternoon and the Admiral napped. Two sailors were fishing on orders from Captain Juan Niño. Twice in a row, as they hooked and pulled on snappers, the hammerhead swooped in and sliced off a bite that left only the head on the hook. A crossbowman was summoned, and he shot several arrows at the beasts, hitting the blue shark once but superficially. The blue disappeared, but the hammerhead persisted. A small crowd gathered.

Çibanakán pulled on my arm and I followed him to the captain. Çibanakán wanted to borrow the captain's dagger. With hand signals and the Spanish words "fight" and "shark," Çibanakán indicated he would take care of the beast. I was very impressed by this; the captain was intrigued and gave him the dagger. Çibanakán faced the east, lit and smoked his cigar a few minutes and watched as the hammerhead circled the caravel. Occasionally, the shark would disappear underwater to come up moments later on the opposite side, swimming fast in a circle that widened and tightened as the fishing men hooked new fish. Çibanakán waited for the shark to go by and slipped into the water, swimming out as the shark circled wide, then came around the ship toward him. He held the dagger in one hand (my father had done it with a coral knife) and, I knew from the way he treaded water, he was intent on a maneuver of our fishermen, flipping backwards in the water as a shark rushed to bite, then coming up from underneath to stab its soft belly. It was not easily done and highly dangerous, and he took my breath away because it was one of the four great deeds for which my father was honored.

All the men awake on shift and all of our own people watched intently as the large hammerhead came around and Çibanakán swam calmly in place, dagger in hand. The ugly crab-headed beast was round as a horse, dorsal fin slicing the sea toward my uncle; suddenly, the hammerhead shark darted like a swallow in mid-flight, going out wide on a circle away from the ship, staying on the surface and circling back, and Çibanakán in the water waiting. On the second encounter, the hammerhead came in strong and again suddenly darted, turning sharply away from the large human form half-in half-out of the water. The shark turned and darted away in that great speed of sharks in a panic, sounding to the deep, away from the ship, away from the coast and out to the ocean free. The sailors and all our people cheered. Çibanakán climbed on board nimbly, though I could detect a slight shaking, and gave Captain Niño his dagger back. The sailors continued fishing.

It was already the next night when Carey, laying on a hammock on one side of me, sang out loud enough for Çibanakán, on my other side, to hear: "Çibanakán had a dagger. He was brave. But he didn't have to use it. The shark bolted in fright just to see his face!"

Çibanakán was our elder, but not by so much that we couldn't tease him. Even so, the teasing was also a way of honoring the deed. Tired as I was, I giggled over Carey's jokes half the night. Carey was funny, going on about the hammerhead, how he would report to his spouse about the giant frog that suddenly appeared and what a fright it had given him.

Sixty-four. *A generosity of parrots.*

On December 12, 1492, a Wednesday, one of those dates I still remember from my day-keeping duties on the ampolleta, a young woman wearing a ball of gold encrusted in her nose was captured. Immediately the Admiral was summoned. He ordered her clothed and fed. He gave her many presents and had several of us accompany her inland. "Make friends of her people," he told me, this time sending Rodrigo along, as he was learning our language faster than any other sailor.

The young woman, whose name I remember was Tinima (though I never saw her again), was the daughter of a village cacique. We went with her to a village of a thousand houses, but everyone fled. She went on ahead of us and we got close enough to tell her people that we had come with men of the Skyworld, who had presents for all whom they met. As they listened and lost their fear, they asked what the spirit men wanted, and for lack of an answer I told them "parrots." Within a day, two thousand people had come, bringing great quantities of food and hundreds and hundreds of parrots. It was near there, on December 16, that we first saw Guacanagari, the young chief of the Marién, who they said was also fond of gold. Guacanagari was brought to the beach on a large hammock, carried by four of his naboria, or helpers, and he was surrounded by more than five hundred other men. At his sides, as always, his four elder uncles constantly whispered in his ear. Among his principal people, many wore gold in their ears and noses and in pendants and arm and calf clips and in necklaces.

Sixty-five. *Guacanagari, first Taíno sachem to meet Columbus.*

The Admiral was overjoyed to meet Guacanagari. "But for going naked, he could be a king anywhere in the world," he declared. In fact, Guacanagari was a rare cacique, upon whom several lineages converged. By virtue of his generations, Guacanagari was related to more principal families in the Marién region of Española than any other man. In Taíno ways, this made him a most important person, to whom all would give great care and tenderness, for such a man could be trusted to be most impartial in resolving disputes among his many relatives.

They say much nonsense about Guacanagari these days. Some call him the noble cacique, but Las Casas insists he was a coward who sold his own people out. Oviedo praises him for his friendship with the Admiral. I will say that he was a man in love with his own person. I talked with him myself many times during that first trip and later upon our return from Spain. Guacanagari had no peer among his own people, even though he had done little to deserve his standing. When he met the Admiral, he exuded an immediate love and excitement that touched the Admiral, making him very happy, and, I am ashamed to admit, making me very jealous.

Sixty-six. *Columbus' ship, Santa María, sinks on Christmas night.*

On the night of December 25, 1492, we were set to in a small bay on Guacanagari's coast. Rodrigo and I had fished all afternoon. Schools of yellowtails, mixed in with mullet, sole, hake, pompano were feeding on large beds of shrimp and eel. We hung from ropes at the bow, tied by chest and legs, and speared fish as they went by. Seeing the catch, the Admiral summoned Juan Ruiz de la Peña, a Basque and his best cook on board, who boiled up a large fish soup, complete with rice and lentils and seasoned with salt and chili peppers supplied by Guacanagari's people. All the officers ate together with the Admiral, a rare occasion, and many prayers were said and toasts uttered. Twelve bottles of wine, of sixteen the Admiral had stored, were drunk that night.

After the mass for the Eve of Christ, Columbus sat on a folded sail and talked to all the men, arguing some with Captain Pinzón's brother about the fate of the Pinta, but mostly expounding on the pattern of his own life and his devotion to God's master plan for men on earth. I could understand enough Castillian by then to follow the Admiral's discussion and remember him using the Latin words, "spiritualis intellectus," by which, I have come to know, he meant the understanding of the world and of the seas, which he believed was his God-given gift, the intellect of the Holy Spirit working through him. "I prayed to the most merciful Lord concerning my desire, and he gave me the spirit and intelligence for it," he said to his sailing men and particularly to his captains.

Captain Niño had posed the question of Divine Providence. "How does it come to be that the Plan of Our Lord, Jesus Christ, now on the 1,492nd year of His divine birth, is fulfilled on Earth?" Juan Niño was the Admiral's favorite captain, even during that first voyage. Later he traveled with us throughout Spain. For his question about the fates, the Admiral praised him. The Admiral responded to Juan Niño's question late into the night, drinking much wine. Some of his sentences I have reconstructed from later conversations, but the sense I have of his meanings and topics of that night is more exact, thanks to my conversations with Father las Casas in recent years. It is Las Casas who has given me the Bible to read, as well as many documents from Oviedo, the Admiral and others, all of which have helped me, more and more, understand the thinking of the covered men.

The Admiral said to Niño and the other officers that night, "I believe that the Holy Spirit works among the Christians, Jews and Moslems, and among all men of every faith, not merely among the learned, but also among the uneducated. In my own experience, I have met many times simple villagers who could explain the sky and stars and their movements better than those who paid their money to learn these things." He pointed to Çibanakán and Carey, who had guided him expertly through the islands and keys many days already.

I remember being mesmerized by the tone of his words and what I could understand about what he was saying. Among the white men I have known, only the Admiral ever spoke this way so movingly about himself.

"The Lord proposed that there should be a miracle in this voyage you have taken with me. I tell you that this too is the fulfillment of prophecy. I tell you that it was the Holy Spirit whose marvelous illumination gave me abundant skill in the mariner's art, and whose concern gave me the mental capacity and the manual skill to draft maps and to draw the cities, rivers, mountains, islands and ports, all in their proper places. For thirty years, I searched out and studied all kinds of texts: geographies, histories, chronologies, philosophies and other subjects. With a hand that could be felt, the Lord opened my mind to the fact that it would be possible to sail to here from Spain and he opened my will to the desire to accomplish this project. This is the fire that has burned within me."

All the men were astounded by Columbus that fateful night. The Admiral spoke into the late evening, and most of the officers stayed the whole time. But, he drank a great amount and grew weary and slurred his words. "I also believe that the Holy Spirit reveals future events not only in rational beings, but also discloses them to us through signs in the sky, in the atmosphere and in animals, wherever it pleases him, as was the case with the ox that spoke in Rome in the days of Julius Caesar, and in many other ways too ... "

I listened very intently, trying to catch the words about the Skyworld. I had a running argument with Carey about the spiritual nature of the Castilla, for which idea I had become a main spokesman as we traveled. "I have seen them cut themselves," Carey argued. "They need water, same as us; they eat like humans, they piss and they drop their leavings. They need their sleep. They lie with our women ... "

"A god can lie with a living woman ... "

"Guaicán, you are hard-headed for them!"

Wrapped up in a cotton hammock on the deck next to me, Carey had turned over to sleep when, suddenly, Columbus stood up, catching himself in his indulgence with the wine. "But I will retire now as it is late," he said. He shouted an order for Juan De la Cosa to take over the watch, then went below. In a few minutes, it was very quiet. As he heard the Admiral snore, de la Cosa ordered a young page to take over the wheel and went to sleep himself. I also lay down to sleep, thinking that the night was deadly quiet as we floated on a thick sea that swelled without waves. About four a.m., all the good officers were asleep, the page was also asleep, and the Santa María crashed on the reef, tearing a hole in her underside that sank her.

Sixty-seven. *Guacanagari saves the day and provides the first gold.*

The Admiral was despondent for only a morning. By midday, Guacanagari had more than sixty canoes ferrying cargo, including cannon and anchors, from the wreck and, as is the custom of our people, everything was kept meticulously. The cacique, who wept with Columbus at the sight of the broken Santa María, assigned several large bohíos used for fishing gear and his own canoes to all the cargo, and had many men available to transport the posts and planks from the ship to be stacked on the beach.

Guacanagari had arrived in full court, and soon promised the Admiral he would dress him in a suit of gold. Just days before, he had gifted the Admiral with a mask made of gold. When he gave it to the Admiral, he had asked him to look through the eyes of the mask, to look through the mask of gold. The Admiral did so, looking all around. "I wish I would see only gold through these eyes," he said, which in Taíno translates as "my eyes see or look only for gold." This made Guacanagari very happy, as he thought he had a great deal of gold to give the Admiral, and thus felt power coming into his court from the covered men. On the 28th, he brought the Admiral several chest plates made of thin gold, and he restated his promise to build a full gold suit for the Grand Mariner.

In turn, the Admiral looked more positively on the loss of his ship. "The Lord helps in mysterious ways," he said, "destroying one of my vessels precisely where gold and a natural ally have been found." He decided a fort must be built there, and a group of men were chosen to remain. Because the Santa María had crashed on Christmas Eve, he named the fort, The Nativity, for the birth of the Christ. When we left for Spain, thirty-nine Castilla men stayed behind at the fort, the first colony of the "covered men" to settle in the Taíno islands. The Admiral's final instructions to these men were to search for the source of the gold and to try to get along with the natives. "Everything that has happened was for this purpose," he told them, "that this beginning may be made."

Sixty-eight. *The white men's industry is as impressive as their hunger for gold is immense.*

Those days, I was impressed with the white men's industry. The way they built the fort, mostly of planks and posts from the stranded vessel, was a new wonder for me. I saw another part of the Castilla: how they worked together, how they hammered with nails, sizing up wood with rulers and serrating the wood with an iron that cut right through the widest posts and trunks. So far, I had seen them on ship, tending to the sails and directions, ballast and cleaning of the vessels. This they did well, and they fished and they explored the lands, here and there. But the building was something different. Columbus directed all of it and prayed a great deal, and before our eyes, in days, two large, very strong houses appeared, surrounded by a small stockade.

Those days, the Admiral walked the woods with Guacanagari's old men. He took note of everything, listing the types of woods and plants he saw, calculating distances, rivers and the populations of the many villages. The old men, more than the youngsters like me, had noticed that the Castilla ate a great deal and pursued our women indiscriminately. Through Guacanagari, and using me as interpreter, they offered young women of various bohíos in marriage to the young men of Columbus. The Castilla men scoffed at the idea, which for some reason at the moment did not bother me, although

I knew it would the old caciques, and I did not pass it on to them in my translation.

Explain it now I cannot, even to myself, but I felt at the time it might be right that gods or spirit men from heaven would not take wives among our people on earth. The old councilors of Guacanagari were quicker than me. They did not mind the couplings of hospitality, but got suspicious when not one offer of marriage was accepted. So, they told the Admiral about a great island, three hundred miles southeast that was totally covered in gold. Near this island was another island named Matinino, they said, full of only women, who mate with men but do not tie them down to marriage. The Admiral was very impressed. You should go there, they told him. This part I relayed to him, and he wrote it down. He wrote many things down in his journal and he talked of plans and of places that made little sense to me at the time. "With this gold, I swear our sovereign kings will take back the citadel from the infidel. Jerusalem will belong to Christiandom once again."

Later I will write how in Spain, at banquets in Barcelona and Seville, and even in the new siege-camp town of Santa Fe, near Granada, Columbus, with me at his side, would expound on all the wonders of the Indies, this New World. The great señores would sit me with them and ask the questions often raised by the "discoverer." Is there really much gold? they would ask. Yes, I would respond, some islands are full of it. They liked me and fed me well in Spain, but that was later, after the first trip back and the horrible storms of snow and ice on the Azores where Çibanakán and so many others were lost.

Sixty-nine. *They get more gold from us.*

It has been more than forty years since those first days with Don Christopherens, my adopted covered-man father who pulled me from a home to which I never returned, although it lives in my heart and memory, even today. The good friar will forgive me if my memory jumps from here to there. It is true that I want to follow the sequence of these episodes, but sometimes things make more sense if pulled together—like the thing of the gold, how the Castilla reckoned the worth of this metal in its weight and purity, how it manifested things in their governments and markets. This thing of the gold was of utmost curiosity to us, the Taíno people. We could understand that the Castilla were intent on obtaining gold, but we wondered why they were so very absorbed in its quest. Why, when just a little gold is a great treasure to be cherished in ceremony? Why, when the earth and the sky and the sea provide so well for our peoples? Why, when it is only in the sharing of the bounties that we learn not to fight, that we learn to do our tasks together and appreciate how lucky we are to breathe the same air and feel the same heat?

Guacanagari gave more gold to Columbus than had any other cacique. The Admiral was very happy, and the happier he got, the more gold Guacanagari brought to him. It was the cacique's natural Taíno instinct to supply the Admiral's happiness. Back in the cities of Spain, the Admiral would tell all who listened about the great gold mines, about the docile people who would serve the Spanish, about their fertile valleys, full of gardens and orchards, about the cities of gold of the Great Khan, whom we would find in time, offering a wealth of possibilities, in mining, agriculture and trade.

Seventy. *Spirit men remain behind as we sail off from Fort Navidad.*

Craftily, as he had noticed the Admiral's fondness for me, Guacanagari asked me to stay, but the Admiral would not allow it. The cacique had good reason, because his elder uncles were more and more concerned with the Castilla's penchant for our women, which, even before we left for Spain, had begun to irritate our people. Guacanagari suggested that both Rodrigo and I stay behind to help with the interpreting and, I am sure, to help calm the impulses of the Castilla men. I am glad now the Admiral refused, for I don't think we would be alive today if we had stayed. But at the time, I was saddened, as the Admiral made it clear we would first go to the Castilla country, before returning us to our homes. From my friend Rodrigo's explanation, I could see that the Admiral's destination was completely away from my home island, first east along the coast (where we found the Pinta and Pinzón), then west and north and finally across the great waters, going east. And this is the course I sailed with the Admiral on the Niña, the Pinta following, on January 9, 1493.

One afternoon before we left, the Admiral ordered a lombard shot fired at the remaining carcass of the Santa María. The explosion made Guacanagari's people all drop to the ground; they later marveled at the hole left by the iron ball. The effect was to make Guacanagari more fearful of the Castilla, and more impressed with his new friends, over whom he was quite jealous. Though the Admiral inquired after other great caciques, Guacanagari insisted they were minor people compared to his court, which was the "grandfather of all grandfathers." Once, several canoes full of important elders approached from the nearby island of La Tortuga, wanting to meet the spirit men, but Guacanagari shooed them away, shoving water at them in our customary signal not to land their canoes. Whatever Columbus gave Guacanagari, simple things like a coin, some red, pointed shoes, or a flask of orange rose water, the cacique had his principal men carry on a bed of cotton in their arms, parading down the trails and beaches to show off the gifts. His people put up enormous amounts of food for the Castilla men, who impressed everyone with their great appetites.

The Admiral always saw what was before him but seldom clearly. He thought of Guacanagari as the main king of this Española island, this great bohío of Haití or Santo Domingo, where I now live out my days. Yet, I myself told him of my conversations with Guacanagari's mother, who asserted to me that the Great Bohío land was comprised of six large cacicazgos, or courts, belonging to at least five established cacique lines. Guacanagari was one of them and his territory was called the Marién. However, she insisted, her son lacked volition, and several of the other caciques were stronger and had more territories. I heard from her lips for the first time the names of Guarionex, Caonabó, Guatiguaná, Mayobanex and Bohekio. She asked me to tell a story to the Admiral about the marriage of Caonabó and Anacaona, sister of Behechio. Anacaona had been destined for Guacanagari. However, on arrangement by Guarionex, she refused him and married Caonabó, a very tough Ciguayo chieftain, who frequently had fights with other Taíno caciques. The marriage to Anacaona, of a very strong Taíno line, would bring Caonabó into the Taíno fold. "Of all of them, Guarionex is the thinker," she said. "He straightens up the fights." Guacanagari's elderly mother was an alert woman, and had much to teach us. But it was a complicated story, with too many names, and the Admiral lost interest.

As for Guacanagari, since the fort was in his territory and he had offered to feed them, he persisted in his effort to marry the covered men formally to his young women. He was impressed with their industriousness, too, as well as with their weapons, although the Castilla who stayed behind held themselves above Guacanagari and our people. Yet, they ate together every day while we were there, and this to us Taíno is a sign of good intentions. Sailing away, even as I dreaded the journey across the great water, I was impressed that spirit men were staying among our people. I felt something good would come from it.

Seventy-one. *"Escarmiento"—the fight to leave a warning.*

The first fight happened on the way out. I did not see it, but heard the details from the men who fought it. We headed west on the northern coast of the island, looking to sail for the open sea, when the Admiral decided to put in on a calm beach and caulk the Niña. It was Ciguayo country, and it was not long before we encountered the long-haired, black-faced bow-and-arrow warriors of Mayobanex.

One old man with very long hair was captured in his canoe. I helped the Admiral interrogate him. At that time, the Ciguayo to me were as enemies, maybe the dreaded Canniba of our most horrible tales. Later, I would know them differently. The old man's language was strange to me; I could understand only a few of his words. The Admiral was harsh. He also believed them to be the Canniba of our Taíno nightmares. These Ciguayo, I would learn in time, were partly assimilated into our people. Their fierce appearance and war abilities resulted from their fights with mainland raiding parties. These realities, however, were not the concern of Don Christopherens.

The Admiral released the old man, but the next morning, spotting a group of warriors on the beach, he sent a boat with seven armed soldiers to produce what he called, "un escarmiento," a sort of warning. "This one is for our comrades left behind," he told the men as they boarded. "Show your fighting skills. Leave a memory here of the bite of our steel." Pretending to trade for the Ciguayo's bows and arrows, the soldiers tried to slowly disarm the group on the beach, but the Ciguayo warriors suspected the ruse and became agitated. They left their weapons and approached with ropes to trade for the hawk bells that intrigued them. Then the soldiers attacked, one man slashing at the two nearest warriors with a broadsword. With one blow he cut the buttocks off of one man and with another, half of an arm. A crossbowman quickly fired two arrows, one through a man's chest and the other through a runner's leg. The Ciguayo retreated to shoot their arrows, but the two crossbowmen continued to wound them in their bodies from much greater distance. Nor did any more Ciguayos dare the sharp steel of the three experienced swordsmen who preceded the crossbowmen, swords slicing menacingly through the air. Recognizing they were up against a deadly foe, they took flight into the forest.

Seventy-two. *Sailing out to the great water.*

Just days later, we sailed for a great distance, beginning the monotony of the open ocean. That is the way we left the sea of our reptile islands, and thus ends the narrative of the first voyage of the Admiral, Don Christopherens Columbus, to this world he called "the Indies." Such are my notes as requested by the good friar, Don Bartolomé de Las Casas, at the Monastery of Santo Domingo, about my memories of those early sailing trips and what they meant to me.

Folio III

To Go Forth and to Return

*So much to tell ... Storms at sea and the loss of my father-uncle, among
others ... The traveling priest ... Columbus and the chickpeas ... King
João's bean maps of the Caribbean ... Palm fronds and one less
Indian ... First sight of Spain with Carey ... Laugh and cry—"La
cabra"of the Inquisition ... How Las Casas remembered me ... The
Admiral requests my word ... Rodrigo Gallego becomes our servant ...
Meeting Queen Isabel, who requests my adoption by the Admiral ... A
dinner party in our honor, Rodrigo meets Matilda ... Out with Aragonese
girls in Cataluña ... I find the fair-haired woman of my dream ...
Carey's bout of drinking ... The Admiral is titled and granted ...
Something about Oviedo: he lies about my people ... To Rodrigo's
Gallegos at Otero del Rey ... A run with bulls for San Fermín ...
Rodrigo's home village, visiting the "the dragas" ... Good-bye to Atoya
and Castille ... A country where many are poor and destitute and a few
are very rich ... The romance of Cúneo's mares ... Captain Alonso de
Hojeda, the perfect soldier ... Meeting the "Man-eating" Kwaib, how
tales get started ... Discoverers are saved by an Indian grandmother ...
Perfect proof of Carib perfidy: a castrated boy ... Hojeda draws first
blood, Cúneo is in on the first fight ... Cúneo's treatment of a Kwaib
warrior woman ... Carey responds to Cúneo ... The news on Fort
Navidad ... The story of how Fort Navidad was overrun by Cacique
Caonabó ... The story denied ... Isabela is built, the first metropolis ...
My loss of innocence ... A devilish bout with the grape ... In need of
punishment ... Las Casas reports mixed news ... I must get to the
Bahuruku ... Flogged out of my guilty stupor ...*

October 10, 1532

Seventy-three. *So much to tell.*

I have much to tell, and a good stack of paper left over from the good friar's contribution, so I will continue to write. Rather than disturb the narrative, as I await word from both Enriquillo and Father Las Casas, I will write on about the voyage to Spain, what I saw there and how the Admiral prepared his return trip.

October 12, 1532

Seventy-four. *Storms at sea and the loss of my father-uncle, among others.*

Yesterday afternoon, a late summer storm came up, bringing a rare coolness in the evening vapor. In the early morning I had dreams of Çibanakán, old father-uncle of mine. I felt him hunched over behind me, nearly curled around me as I crawled out from his grasp of death.

On ship, going to Spain with the Admiral, at the onset there were almost a dozen of us Taíno and several Ciguayo, a third as many as the Castilla that had remained at the fort named Navidad. None survived of their colony, and that is a story I will detail in these pages later. While of ours, of the Indians on ship, I can say that only seven survived the voyage. Five died on the way there. Yet others died in Spain.

What killed my Taíno were two terrible ice storms that caught the Niña ship as we entered Portuguese waters. The whole length of that great water ocean we sailed, and pleasantly, to tell the truth. But snow and ice as we had never experienced before took our destiny, with winds that ripped the sails and clashing waves tossing our ship in mid-air, lightning and cold, incredible cold where leather and sail froze and we, most of our Indians, had no clothing. I am certain to have died but for my great father-uncle, Çibanakán.

The storms followed each other by two weeks, February 12 to 16 and March 2 and 3, 1493. The first one started in the early morning with heavy winds and, by afternoon, as the sun set, first a blizzard of snow came, then sheets of ice that froze your feet and fingers. Our people found their best, most secure places on board, but died as the night progressed. The Spanish, even those few that were so inclined, had little time to tend to our needs. They shared little of their clothing, particularly the water-waxed items, and even our own Taíno cotton, gathered from the many islands to show their Monarchs, remained under lock and key. I secured a blanket from the Admiral and called to my uncle, who gathered two more young men under it. I caught the chills badly within minutes of my first soaking, ice forming on my bare skin. I came out of that first storm coughing and shaking badly. Somehow, Çibanakán survived all right that night.

After the first storm passed, Çibanakán nursed me, and Rodrigo strove to secure us food, mostly soggy cassabe and dried fish, a great thing to suck on when you are sick. I never felt so loved as by Çibanakán during those few days. He took on the appearance of my own father, caressing me gently and singing quietly to me. My illness lasted for more than a week, during which the Admiral put in at a port on the island of Santa María of the Azores, and I was lucky for the gift of a chicken, which I ate in a broth. The Admiral departed hurriedly from the small island on February 23, as the Portuguese authorities tried to hold ten of his sailors who had gone ashore to pray. I was too sick to take notice of those events before the ships removed again to the open sea, but I was almost recovered as the tempest picked up again on February 27 and 28.

The second ice storm descended fully upon us on March 2, so violently that two of our men were washed overboard by giant waves. Ice storms were all around us and the decks glistened slippery with ice. Under a ship's boat, Çibanakán curled around me from behind, wrapped in our blanket. He held on to me all night like that, breathing his warm breath on the back of my neck, all night and a day and another night doing that for me, my father-uncle, holding me, keeping my back warm.

On the third day, the sun came out first thing in the morning, a hot ball and wide beam on the water facing from the east and I was still in the arms of Çibanakán, though as I gained consciousness, I felt the stiffness of his embrace. I was cold as the deepest of mountain streams, colder than that, as cold as ice, my feet and hands, my nose and ears. My ears hurt so much, thery were so stiff and cold I could not touch them, though my neck and back had still some warmth. Awakening, I wriggled out of Çibanakán's stiff arms and only a bit of warmth could I feel in him, around the area of his heart. But despite that warm spot, he was stiff from cold, his neck and shoulders, which he had surrendered to the elements, were frozen hard as ironwood.

He was not dead, quite, but there was nothing left in Çibanakán's eyes, his breath was cold vapor. And that next cold night, though I held him all day and evening and Rodrigo tried to feed him broth, Çibanakán died. The next day, the morning was sunny again as we surrendered my noble Çibanakán to the waves.

October 15, 1532

Seventy-five. *The traveling priest.*

Las Casas must be now arriving at Spain. I like it that he is heading in precisely the direction of my narrative, on a ship sailing to Spain, now nearly forty years later. That priest is an indefatigable traveler. That ocean he has crossed at least a dozen times. He has mountains of energy and in his campaigns at court, he causes quite a ruckus. I pray he will be calm and help to soften the King's heart—maybe through the Queen. I hope and pray that he arrives well.

Seventy-six. *Columbus and the chickpeas.*

For the Niña, that first time, the landfall was Portugal. I remember how the Admiral tacked on the coast; I remember the certainty of command he had over his ship and how in the worst of the first storm, while the Niña took each wave in its own angle, he offered a vow to make a pilgrimage and give his thankful prayers at the altar of his favorite Virgin at Santa María de Guadalupe, in Estremadura. One chick pea among many was marked with a cross and put in a sack. Whoever drew it would undertake the fulfillment of the vow, upon return to land, as promised to the Lord in common prayer. And it was Columbus who drew the pea, not once but three out of four times. And it was in the wake of his final vow that the storms abated, and we sighted the Portuguese coast.

I was good by then at the afternoon ditties and could understand most of what the Castilla said. I even sang high the Salve Regina for the Admiral, "Dulcis Virgo Maria," loving and respecting him who had shared his blanket with me during the storms and who had hugged me to him as one after another of my kinsmen had been slipped overboard.

Seventy-seven. *King João's Bean Maps of the Caribbean.*

In Portugal, we were questioned by the monarch himself, King João, who disbelieved the Admiral's news of the discovery of our lands. There was fear he might imprison the Admiral, or even have him killed. Finally, the King took Carey aside and had him draw out with beans a map of our islands. As Carey finished, using several beans for the larger islands and single ones for the smaller ones, the King studied it carefully, then disturbed it. Then he called me over to do the same, which I did, in much the same form as Carey's. This convinced King João, and we went on our way, sailing into the harbor on the Río Tinto at Palos, Spain, on the fifteenth of March, Year of Our Lord, 1493.

Seventy-eight. *Palm Fronds and One Less Indian.*

The Admiral led us into Seville on Palm Sunday (March 31), where a large crowd was gathered. The local people put palm fronds on the road. Having procured a burro, he rode into town surrounded by us seven remaining Indians. Hundreds and hundreds came out to see us, and they sang for him and asked him to speak at every turn. "The man who discovered the Indies," is what they called him in Seville. In Seville, too, we lost another Lucayo, named Bexuco, who, like myself and Carey, had met the Admiral early on. Shaken still by the voyage and unable to swallow the Spanish food, he walked away in his dream. Behuco chose the sleeping death one morning in Seville.

Seventy-nine. *First sight of Spain with Carey.*

The Admiral left Carey and me at a family pensión in Seville during our stay in that city. It was a four-story house by the Gate of the Imágenes, near the cathedral square. Our room was on the third floor and had a window facing the street, and you could see other stone and wooden houses next to each other, and you could hear horse carriages going by on the street below. The room had one small bed that Carey and I shared. The bed came with two warm, woolen blankets, which we learned to appreciate.

I remember that room in the pensión house in Seville, and here at the convent it feels like I am in it again. By that time, Carey was all I had left from my world, and I feel him with me tonight. That night we lay together and huddled to make our bed warm, and for the first time I cried.I cried so hard that Carey started crying too. It was a night of recovery for us, a convalescence. We talked about our time on board, the death of those our people in the storm. By morning, the shock and fright had subsided, but the pain was still with us, and the strangeness.

Everything in the Castilla country was a great marvel to us those first strange days. We saw how people moved in horse-drawn carriages and barges and canal boats, how they lived in houses made of rock and wood, with iron doors, and some with windows of many colorful crystals. We saw barley fields and valleys of wheat, groves of squat olive trees evenly spaced and all the same height, and leagues and leagues of sheep grazing in the plains and meadows. We made our first acquaintance with the wheelbarrow, a marvel of a tool, and of course, we were surprised by the covered people's many uses for oxen and horses and mules. Often Rodrigo or Captain Niño or Luis de Torres explained things to us, how to eat, where to walk on the street, when to stand and when to sit in church. But nothing could have prepared us for what we saw near the cathedral in Seville, the use they had for the goat. This, a Christian scene, we witnessed some days later, after Holy Week had passed.

Eighty. *Laugh and Cry—"La cabra" of the Inquisition.*

Luis de Torres, the converted Jew with whom we had journeyed to Baigua's village in northern Cuba, was assigned to keep company with Carey and me in Seville, where his parents lived. We felt all right with young Torres since sharing his peculiar experience with the eager village women of Baigua.

That morning he led us to breakfast down the street from our pensión, to an inn run by his parents, where he stayed. We ate a meal of lentil soup, bread and a piece of sausage. I remember his parents were darker than most Castillians and they were very quiet.

After eating, Torres led us through a maze of very thin streets, in and out of rows and rows of houses. "I am to show you the cathedral, today," he said. I remember thinking that without him leading the way, I would easily lose my way in those streets. That area of the city was La Judería, the Jewish people's quarters in Seville, where families kept indoors and hung crucifixes near every window.

I had already seen the fear held by Jews for the Spanish authorities when a group of church inquisitors inspected the Niña at the port of Palos. Palos was especially harsh on unconverted Jews, as many had been recently deported from Christiandom through that coastal town. I remember Torres, how he volunteered to pump the filthy ship's hold, just as he saw the group of priests board the Niña. "Don't let them talk to you," he advised me as he disappeared below. "Pretend you don't know the Castillian language." I did as he warned and stood mute near the Admiral as he told the group about his mission on behalf of the Catholic Sovereigns and showed them one of the gold masks Guacanagari had given him. With a knife, he cut pieces of the gold to give them. "This gold of the Indies," he said as they left, happily clutching the gold pieces, "will finance our Christian armies. With its wealth, Their Highnesses will retake Jerusalem."

In Seville, both Carey and I saw more of the Inquisition. Trailing Torres, we passed an arched gateway out of La Judería and out onto a bit broader street, where we turned left and walked two blocks, the street opening into a plaza surrounding the biggest of buildings, a construction of stone that went up into the sky. This was the Cathedral of Seville, a century old and not quite finished when I saw it.

Torres stopped. At one corner of the square, around the side from the main entrance to the church, a crowd gathered. "We'll see what the attraction is today," he said, as others ran past us and I heard someone else say, "Hurry, they're bringing out the goat!"

At the edges of the crowd Carey and I pressed behind Torres, and in brief glimpses I could see a man tied by the arms sitting down on the ground, his legs pulled apart, straddling a post. A stick went under the knees and secured them with rope. Through the crowd I could see the man's very white, bare feet and legs on the stone floor. At the entrance to the cathedral, only a hundred feet away, several monks and the archbishop stood solemnly. They wore pointed white and purple hoods over their heads and faces, indicating the status of the Grand Inquisitors, defenders of the Holy Catholic religion.

I had seen several lashings on board ship and thus I thought this might be occurring. From the look of the man's face, he seemed unbeaten but very frightened. A guard next to the man nodded and a peasant leading a billy-goat by a neck leash made his way through the crowd. He handed the leash to the guard. Then, he unwrapped a cake of honey paste and smeared the condemned man's toes and feet.

I sensed something very bad was going to happen, but could not fathom what. Then he tied the goat within reach of the man's feet and stood back. "Suffer, blasphemer!" he yelled and stepped aside. "Laugh and cry."

"Laugh and cry, blasphemer!" one and two more yelled back from the crowd.

Forty years later, I still fear the memory of this event. I have seen even worse happen to my own people, death accosting us on all sides, but nothing had ever prepared me at that age for watching that goat lick the man's toes, tongue lapping the arches of his feet and the man stretching himself taut, a forced smile breaking his anguished lips as the goat licked and licked and a giggle broke out of his throat. The crowd laughed heartily at the man's giggle.

In my throat I could taste the heavy sausage of my meal, and it is that sensation I remember most of that moment. Because the very next thing, the honey was licked clean and the goat, after licking his lips and looking around, bent down and seized upon a large toe, ripping strips of flesh as the poor devil's shriek in that cathedral square put the shock of ice on my spine. The goat chewed for a hour, taking his time and looking around.

That was "la lengua de cabra," *the goat's tongue,* a favorite punishment among many, meted out in Spain by Inquisitors. It was one of many tools of torture. That luckless peasant, while drunk on wine after a Saturday market, had cursed the Virgin Mary, describing her genitals in a lewd bar song. Several people heard him and reported him to the office of the Grand Inquisitor, who promptly had him arrested. As the peasant did not deny his song, he was sentenced to "laugh and cry" with the goat, who might teach him the difference between solemnity and frivolity. Others, such as heretics and witches, would be burned to death, much as I have described in Jiqui's execution. I saw two of those in Granada, where a man and a woman, she a Moor, were immolated for having raised a question on the identity of Jesus Christ as prophet, rather than as Lord or God. They were flogged and burned, both of them, and before that, the nipples of her breasts were yanked off by a special instrument. The torture session was private, but they announced the torture and the executioner held high the actual iron instrument, and I myself saw the blood on her garment as they went to burn her. I know the institution of the Inquisition well and have discussed it with Father Las Casas and others of the monks many times. They are of various minds about it now, but at that time in Seville and Granada, all the religious backed the Inquisition as the main defense of the Christian faith.

"Laugh and cry!" I remember people in the crowd yelled as the goat ate the man's toes on both feet and licked at the blood for a full hour. "Laugh and cry for all blasphemers! ... Laugh and cry for all Jews and Moors!!"

Remembering la cabra makes my leg twitch even now. I can still see Torres taking our hands and leading us away, and I could tell he was ashamed and worried for us to have heard the taunts at the "judíos."

He took us into the church of the cathedral, a huge cavern, but built by human workers, big as a small mountain, with a door like the entrance to our largest caves. Inside it was dark and cool, and the tap of a boot resounded deeply into the huge space. Every surface of the wall seemed to be handcrafted and led one to look up, and up, craning the neck to follow huge columns, as thick around as three ancient ceiba trees and three or four times as high. All polished stone, it had a clean look, but smelled of must and incense and oils and dead people.

Entering the large central hall, where mass is celebrated, Torres pointed to the altar. "Go kneel and make your prayers," he said to us. "Remember the storm we survived together." Carey and I both prayed, kneeling by that altar. As prayers help me respond to my pained spirit, I asked for the man outside the huge cavern church, whose feet were eaten by a goat and who would undoubtedly die. (Actually, he did not, I now know. He survived the ordeal to join more than two dozen other such men in Seville—the Cabra Men of the Inquisition.) I was very intense in my prayer and have sometimes since wished I had not been so intense about this man, as I have dreamt the event numerous times throughout my life and I have always awakened from those dreams in ice cold horror.

October 20, 1532

Eighty-one. *How Las Casas remembered me.*

Father Las Casas has told me he saw us, "the Indians," that time with the Admiral in Seville. I don't remember him then. My earliest memory of the good friar is from the time he first came to Española, in 1502. Of course, I believe he did see me, as he has described me correctly: at the Admiral's side, a skinny, long-haired young boy handling four cages of parrots. "A boy," Las Casas has told me, "who had an eye for everything."

Eighty-two. *The Admiral requests my words.*

In Seville, at a luncheon sponsored by the Duke of Medina Sidonia, the Admiral requested some words from Carey, as the Indian elder left from Guanahani and also from an even older uncle of Guacanagari. But my fellow Guanahani-ti proved shy in front of an audience, words failing him, and the older uncle, quite frail and having suffered tremendously during the ice storms, said little that was understandable. After Seville, the Admiral had Carey handle the parrots and freed me to speak as he might request. He told me to stay close to him at public appearances and banquets.

Eighty-three. *Rodrigo Gallego becomes our servant.*

In Barcelona, where Queen Isabel of Castilla and King Ferdinand of Aragón, the Catholic Monarchs, held court that season, the crowd was no less excited. We were traveling by royal wagon train now, and even we six Indians had servants. Torres remained with his parents in Seville, but Rodrigo Gallego was still in our party and was assigned by the Admiral to cater to Carey's needs and mine.

"They treat you like kings, and me, a boy of the country, no less a hero, I am your servant," he complained, but mostly in jest. Rodrigo was unlike most of the white men I had ever met. He never minded anything he had to do and was always helpful. Rodrigo was humble by nature, smart and kindly disposed. He was also fifteen years old and, we were finding out, had an itch for adventuresome ladies.

Eighty-four. *Meeting Queen Isabel, who requests my adoption by the Admirals.*

We spent the night on a royal farm on the outskirts of the central city of Cataluña and the next afternoon, the twentieth of April, 1493, flanking the Admiral, who rode horseback with his officers, we entered the Plaza of the Cathedral, crowded with townspeople. King's guards opened the way for us as trumpets sounded. It was sunny but cold, and the Admiral had requested that we Indians strip to the minimum, wear our feathers and hold high our parrots, spices, casabe and several large jars in which fruits from our islands were preserved. I remember that someone suggested the Indians wear a bozal, or muzzle, as they would put on wild animals, and we even tried some on, which, to our relief, did not fit us.

I wondered about this idea, seeing that the cathedral was carved on the outside with beasts, called lions and tigers, that seemed to leap out from the dark stone.

King Fernando and Queen Isabel received us in a small plaza, seated up at one end on a platform that had stone steps leading to it. As the monarchs rose for him and the crowd gasped, Don Christopherens hurried forward to kiss their hands. They blessed him and his whole enterprise, welcomed him and requested he seat himself with them, whereupon the crowd gasped once again. They sat thus a few minutes as a wind picked up the cool of the afternoon and the Queen requested the reception be moved into her Royal Chamber.

Carey and I were quite happy to go into the largest one room and placed ourselves near two large fireplaces that were burning warm. Before even all the seating had been arranged, I noticed the Queen's eye on me and perceived her kind smile. I felt a great deal of love for her at that moment. Later, after all greetings and reports were heard and new honors were bestowed, her page found his way to me, grabbed my arm and pulled me to the edge of her court. "Venid," she signaled with her hand. "Come."

"And this one," she said to Columbus, as I stood before her.

"He's the one who speaks our language," he said.

"What are you called?" she asked me.

"Guaikán is my name," I said, adding as instructed, "Your Majesty."

She smiled, but I could tell she was curious about the name. "It means a kind of fish," I said. She nodded, raising an eyebrow at me. "You're very smart," she said, and I looked down.

"And your home is the Antilles?" she went on.

"Yes, your majesty, the islands."

"Then tell me, what is the most beautiful thing in your homeland?"

"The ocean," I said, "and the face of my mother."

The Queen almost cried. She pulled a silk cloth to daub her eyes and a lady-in-waiting behind her grimaced, clickling her tongue at me. But the next moment, the Queen hugged me and the same lady-in-waiting immediately smiled.

"What a darling child," said the Queen. "You should adopt this boy, Columbus, give him a Christian name. Name him Diego, for your younger brother who accompanies you."

Don Christopherens nodded and put his arm around my shoulders as all rose to sing the *Te Deum* in thanks to God for the successful voyage. The next Sunday, I was baptized Diego Colón, and the Queen had several of her ladies attend. Carey was also baptized, and the rest of my Indians. One was named Fernando de Aragón, after the King, and given to the Monarch's young son, who was chosen as godfather to all of us. This Indian Fernando whom we knew as Atoya, but whose child's name was Ximon, was most unfortunate of all. Years later, when I was enslaved in Cuba during the time of Velázquez, I came to know that the young man was from the region of Bayamo and Macaca, who had cursed the Admiral. Atoya/Ximon, although from the opposite coast of Cuba, was in fact taken captive by Columbus in Guamax's area, where the young man was visiting relatives to attend an areito and a ball game ceremony. The time that old man Guamax came to curse Columbus from the water at the stern of the Santa María, he was complaining about the taking of several captives, but primarily about Ximon, a son of the sister of Macaca, and a very sensitive young boy, destined by his people to become cacique someday. Poor Atoya/Ximon, he was taken from us right away by the prince, Don Juan, who wanted him instructed in the Christian faith.

October 23, 1532

Eighty-five. *A Dinner Party in our honor, Rodrigo meets Matilda.*

There was actually a dinner party in honor of our baptism later that week, a large one, at the house of a Catalán duke, whose name I forget. Of course, our baptism was a minuscule occurrence, a pretext, I believe, for the duke's lavish display of public support as the Catholic Sovereigns presented their new hero of the Ocean Seas. The Queen was in those days nursing the King, who was under rest orders. Only months before, King Ferdinand was stabbed in the neck by a madman, saved, so the legend went, by a thick chain of gold he wore as a collar. The monarchs did not attend, but sent several of their ladies and gentlemen plus many royal dishes to this great party attended by local royalty and landed barons. While the "grandees" ate in the fancy salons, Rodrigo, Carey and I explored the kitchens and the many side salons where various parties had settled themselves to enjoy the feast. Among the younger ladies-in-waiting, a young Matilda Cuesta de Peralta was quite brazen. She and Rodrigo got along quite well, and she teased him that many of the girls talked about Rodrigo "and his Indians." We were the novelty of the season in Barcelona that spring.

Matilda was no noble but a muchacha from one of the families of fancy courtesans kept by high men in King Fernando's side of the court. She had many relatives in Barcelona and it appeared that other women in her family were also courtesans. They were not prostitutes, as I have come to understand the term, and did not have a brothel, such as the one in our docks here in Santo Domingo, but their whole house seemed to ply the trade of entertaining men discreetly.

Eighty-six. *Out with Aragonese girls in Cataluña.*

The girls, who liked to have fun, invited the three of us to drink wine with them at their home on the boardwalk near the municipal docks. As we had our own quarters at the Royal Pensión in the city, no one to report to and nothing in particular to do the next day, we accepted. Everyone else that we knew in town was also celebrating that evening and some were quite drunk, talking and talking, and some of the women tipsy with wine were dancing. Both Carey and I were quite happy to follow Rodrigo and a fourth comrade as they walked down the dusty shoreline streets of Barcelona, looking for the fiesta house.

Rodrigo himself had a bottle of wine, and his friend, Mateo, a local boy who spoke the Catalán language, had two. Carey and I had none, but we were quite willing to drink. "These two Indians are good boys," Rodrigo kept telling Mateo, who understood Castillian. "You should have known their uncle; he faced down a shark in mid-sea."

Matilda and three "cousins" were home, and let us in quickly. Two older women were also home and, after greeting us, made us stand still to be looked at. "So this is what Matilda drags in," one said. "Who's the captain?"

Rodrigo nodded. She looked him in the eye up close. "You can cover these boys?"

"I can," Rodrigo said.

"But these boys are faraway guests of our King and Queen's court. It would honor our grandee's to gift them at least once."

"They're a bit dark and swarthy," she said. "But do they got a pecker like any old boy?"

Rodrigo laughed and pulled out a bag with a thousand maravedies in it. I am sure he did not have much more, but this impressed the older woman, who immediately leaned up against him, fondling his butt in jest. "I'll send you kids up some wine," she said.

Eighty-seven. *I find the fair-haired woman of my dream.*

It was quite a party. The older woman sent a mandolin player along with the wine. I drank a good bit of wine, but Carey drank even more. He was really funny for quite awhile and danced with Matilda and her cousins and Rodrigo and Mateo. That night, I met and talked for a long time with María del Carmen, who was very sweet and curious about me. She drank wine, too; and we both drank together. I talked to her for quite a while about our islands and the storms on the trip and about the King and Queen. She was well impressed and did not hesitate to touch me, and very affectionately. I fell in love with her and we retired early. I am not ashamed to say it, we spent a night of much comfort in each other's embrace, humid and passionate, with a natural timing in our passions that not only overwhelmed me, the novice, but even impressed her, who had considerably more experience. We took to each other like honey and wax. María del Carmen was exceedingly exciting to me, and I went back to her house several times during our stay in Barcelona.

Eighty-eight. *Carey's bout of drinking.*

The next evening after our party, I was off with Don Christopherens to a round table of town burghers, men who would invest in the mining enterprise that the Admiral envisioned for the Indies. It was our first in a round of important meetings, where Don Christopherens formally introduced me to give testimony on the gold, pearls and precious woods in our "Indian" lands. We went to several dozen parties like that over the next few weeks while the Admiral arranged the credits and provisions for our return trip to the "Antilles," as everyone was calling the Taíno islands.

My cousin Carey, however, continued the party through the next day. He and Mateo had become friends while Rodrigo was off in love with Matilda. Through the day, the two young men found a sailors' whore house and, through that evening and subsequent days, drank many bottles of wine. They became a famous duo on brothel row, and the whores celebrated Carey from one end of their street to the other. On the fifth day, Rodrigo came running to get me. Carey is very sick, he informed me, and is vomiting blood. I found him at Matilda's house, on a cot, facing up. There was blood on his shirt and every few minutes he was wracked with dry heaves. His eyes were wild and far inward.

"He can't stop vomiting," one of the older women informed me.

"Leave us, please," I said.

Alone with Carey, I talked to him sweetly in our language. Instinctively I wet a rag and held it to his lips, as we do for the elders at the end of a night of cohoba. I stayed with him all day, gave him lots of water, held him and rubbed his lungs from behind. He coughed up horrible things and then fasted on water. That night, as he was breathing calmly and sleeping soundly, I went to the Admiral about the need to employ Carey in something, and it was decided he would be sent to Seville as a second Indian page for the Queen's Prince Juan during our time in Spain.

Eighty-nine. *The Admiral is titled and granted.*

On May 28, 1493, in a large ceremony, the Catholic Sovereigns granted Don Christopherens Columbus full, perpetual nobility and his own seal. His brother, Don Bartolomé was titled as "Adelantado," a type of forward commander. This was a great day for the Columbus family and everyone acclaimed the act. The Admiral kept me close to him all that day. I was very proud and felt the genial delirium of our great Guamiquina. I was quite conscious that a large fleet was getting together for our return to the islands and men of the highest ranks in Spain were pressing the Admiral to go along. Father Las Casas' own father was among those who went on that second trip. Friends of the Admiral arrived from Genoa and Portugal and Flanders. All of the Spanish court, including many destitute noble families, glued their attention to the Admiral's tales of the islands' wealth. That other Spanish historian, Gonzalo Fernández de Oviedo, who is presently here in Santo Domingo, has told me he was there in Barcelona and saw me with the Admiral as we walked and rode carriages around the city. Several times when I have seen him here in Española, Oviedo has declared this knowledge.

Ninety. *Something about Oviedo: he lies about my people.*

I will say something here about Oviedo, who was and is a gold counter and encomendero that has become a historian. Oviedo is not a friend to us Indians; truly he has put forth many peculiar lies about our Taíno life and mocked our religion many times. It is true that Father Las Casas dismisses our Taíno religion, but at least he defends our capacity to become Christians. Oviedo scoffs at that very idea, accusing us of "wanton heathenism" for having ignored the preaching of the Apostles, whom he says must have come among the Taínos at the time of Jesus Christ. This opinion he bases on the writings of St. Gregory, who claimed the church had preached all over the world the doctrine of redemption. "Indians can't pretend to be ignorant of the Christian faith, as they had news of the evangelical truth," Oviedo says now, and he justifies the encomienda as our fair punishment. He also says that we Indians have rock skulls, so thick the Spanish used to break their swords on our foreheads. That is another of his lies. However, it is true that he was in Barcelona at that time, and the words he remembers me saying ring true to me now. "You talked about rivers of gold and men walking about wearing large plates of gold, who would trade gold for many of our things. You, Diego," he has mocked me several times, "brought more of our people from Castille to this island than anyone I know."

As I think about it now, this despicable man who predicates the enslavement and inferiority of my people, is right to taunt me. And I do take responsibility that I seconded the Admiral in his claims during my stay on the Castilla lands. I got so used to talking up the good things, telling everyone what the Admiral wanted them to hear, that I myself elaborated how much my people would love them and treat them graciously, and feed them, and I know that already in these claims the elements were being gathered for our destruction.

Why did I not see that earlier? Why was I so trusting to continue to believe that the Castilla had our best interests at heart? Why did I not see that as I bragged of my people's gentility, the men of those cities saw not friendly tradesmen and neighbors, but easy servants and slaves; as they heard of gold in our hills, they thought not to go themselves to gather it, but of how to force my people—men, women, children—to dig the gold and take it out for them. Oh, what my people have endured, what suffering and physical reduction for that mining of the gold! I hate to think of how I helped open that door, and even now I feel the need to atone for that and to do what I can to see that our people, however reduced, survive.

November 2, 1532

Ninety-one. *To Rodrigo's Gallegos at Otero del Rey.*

Rodrigo Gallego, our faithful friend, was going home and invited me to go along. He was from Galicia, from the village called Otero del Rey, near Lugo, west of Cataluña across the Basque country to the northwestmost part of Iberia, north even of Portugal, where his own Gallego people lived. The Admiral was done recruiting investors and granted me permission to go for the more than four months of the journey. That was my good-bye to Barcelona, as I would head south to Seville from Galicia. Rodrigo was not to go on the second voyage, but, as he was granted a royal appointment for the Academy of Guards, at the court in Seville, after our visit to his parents, he would accompany me to the Andalusian city. There I was to join the Admiral, Carey and the other travelers.

Leaving María del Carmen was difficult. I had little realized how deeply in love I had become. She was my first love, and, for days as we rode away from Barcelona, I was lonely as a baby possum and I longed for her and cried. I thought of my elders in Guanahaní and I remembered the dream of my puberty night and it was certainly her, María del Carmen, waiting there in my destiny path, coming toward me across the batey, old Ayraguex laughing at how he had seen it, and it was all true.

The trip with Rodrigo took many weeks. He had bought all sorts of provisions for his family, including ax and hoe heads for his father and needles and cloth and iron pots and pans for his mother. We traveled on two horses and led two pack mules, one with our provisions and the other loaded with gifts. We also carried the Queen's seal in a letter of free passage, which proved useful while crossing the country of the Basques, through the low southern hills of the Pyrenees.

Ninety-two. *A run with bulls for San Fermín.*

One of our stops, about halfway to Galicia, found us among the Basques, in a town called Paplón or Amplone. I do remember we arrived there on July 6th of that year, 1493. I remember the day because the Admiral had instructed me to keep a count of my days. He gifted me a pen, which I kept for many years, and two long rolls of paper. Everyday of every week and month I made a mark. I did not yet know how to write or read (my Jewish friend Torres would begin me in that stead later in Seville), but nonetheless, I dutifully made my daily mark. This is why, often, long-distant dates jump before these written memories in the eye inside my mind, certain as the convent calendar.

Pamplón was a crazy place, as cattlemen had driven in their cattle and their vaqueros had money for wine. A ceremonial time it apparently was, too, and a god of the Pamplones, a spirit man they called San Fermín, was on everyone's lips that day. In the early morning, an explosion of cannon or rocket awakened me to see Rodrigo already dressed and hanging out the window.

It was a cool, summer morning, crisp as baked casabe, but everything was confusing for me. The streets of the large village were crowded with people yelling and dancing with their arms around each other's shoulders. Before I could ask who San Fermín might be, so that I might greet him, too, Rodrigo joined in with the crowd, squirting wine out of bags into everyone's mouths. Then the crowd was yelling, "encierro, encierro," meaning *enclosure*, which I also wondered at, and then we were all moving down a very dusty street, the dust so thick I could hardly breathe. Down the street I could make out two big wooden corrals on the edge of an enclosed field, both full of ornery bulls, big and thick as fat manatees, thicker even, and with pointed stakes coming out of their heads and big sacks of balls dangling under their hind legs.

I was carried by the crowd at times, as everyone pressed together, jumping and crowding around the corrals. There was a priest, and some of the cattlemen stood by the gate of the corrals and they, too, were drinking wine. The crowd, all men, was hooting and laughing and the bulls pranced around wild-eyed inside the corrals. Then the priest blessed the bulls with holy water. The crowd quieted and he was very solemn, talking not Castillian but the Basque language, and it made sense suddenly for me that they lived off the balls and production of these great bulls. They were appreciating their food in a way we do also—our yuca and our hutía, our doves and parrots, our iguana and our many fish and turtles, especially the turtles which are so very useful and sacred to us.

What happened next was craziest of all. As the priest ended his blessing, cries of "Viva San Fermín" filled the air and the jumping and hollering all began again. I wondered about this San Fermín, that he might be a bull spirit, and was thus daydreaming when the crowd began running past me and I found myself facing four bulls sniffing an open gate briefly before charging on me like a pack of sharks.

I folded myself into a ball on the hot sand. I pretended to be a turtle, just as I'd been thinking and the bulls stopped short of me again sniffing. Then there was Rodrigo actually hitting one on the snout and running and the whole crowd running and the bulls jumping past me and one stepped on my hand as he charged away.

I always remember that afternoon, nursing my hand and climbing on a fence to watch the bulls running with the crowd from one end of the field to another, and how the men touched the bulls' horns and jumped over them and, finally, how a bull charged into a group of men who fell back on each other. He hooked his horn with a snap of the neck that sent men flying, one torn entirely across the gut so his entrails spilled out.

It was that bull that was left behind in the field as the others were coaxed and herded, with the aid of several steers, back into the corrals. The violent part happened then. A dozen men holding knives and sabers came out. Without hesitation, they charged the bull, who faced them, a bit winded but still defiant. Then they were all over him, cursing and stabbing and cutting at him as he humped and ran with men hanging from his legs and neck, stabbing into him and making him bleed.

Finally, the bull stopped moving. He tried to hook under his own belly as a man gutted at him from underneath. Then the bull's entrails dropped on the man, and he stood still as the man crawled away. Then all the men stabbed at him again and succeeded in pushing him over. A great cry went up from the crowd.

Rodrigo and I watched it together. I thought it way too bloody a ceremony. I wondered about the need of the men to kill the bull so violently, so bloodily. If they love the bulls so much, live off of them and even bless them, why do they fight them in a fury like that?

"Its just a custom," Rodrigo said when I asked him that as we rode west. "All over Spain they fight bulls."

He told me, too, that San Fermín is not a bull spirit, but a man saint, which confused me about it all over again. So I don't know even now what connection they were trying to make, but it was truly repugnant to me. In our way, killing was done quickly, not excitedly if at all possible, and always apologizing, not cursing the being that will feed us.

Ninety-three. *Rodrigo's home village, visiting the "dragas."*

Otero del Rey, Rodrigo's home village, sat on a knoll overlooking a tree-dotted plain which was covered by small and large gardens and scattered sod huts. I saw men and women walking behind oxcarts and leading pack-burros down dusty roads. I saw the valley spread before me and it looked pretty.

As we rounded a hill, across the bottom lands from Rodrigo's family home, the news of our arrival preceded us. Descending an opposite spiraling road, we could see a group of people form and start to walk toward us. They met us half-way through the valley, shouting for Rodrigo and thanking out loud the Virgin Mary, Blessed Mother of God.

Those days were my best in Spain—quiet, listening to Rodrigo telling tales of his travels with Columbus, about whom they had not heard the news yet in Otero del Rey. Of course, the people marveled at me, touched me and pinched me, felt my long hair, fed me many soups and breads, even slaughtered a big pig for me on our second week, which they roasted and which fed us for days.

Rodrigo had four sisters and three brothers, all at home or living in nearby plots. They spoke a language called Gallego, different from the Castillian of Seville, the Basque of Euskera and the Catalán of Barcelona. The brothers, their father and two uncles worked the farms together, planting wheat, lentils, garlic and large fields of cabbage. They also kept pigs, one cow with calf and a flock of chickens. They all worked all day, every day, but, as in our own villages, Rodrigo's people had enough food and water for their families. On Saturday they drove a two-wheel wagon to market and, on Sunday, they gathered at the same plaza to hear mass.

One day I especially remember. Rodrigo helped his father fix a wagon wheel while his mother, Josefa, asked me to carry wide buckets of water for her. She was a small woman, rather wiry, and she was very kind to me, always ready with a broth or the herbal tea they called "cocimiento." I walked with her and one sister up a mountain trail and then down to drop into a thicket of trees where the air was suddenly moist.

"Wait," the mother of Rodrigo said. She had a small bundle of flowers in a bag, and pulled it out. I watched as she knelt down and made a cross on the ground with a stick and then circled it. Then she lay down the flower bundle, thanking dragas for keeping the tree cover of the spring lush and maintaining the water flow. It impressed me that she used that very image, our own circle bisected, cut into the four directions. This was her offering for the dragas, their "little people" guardians of the water spring. On the way back, Josefa said, "Don't tell anyone about my offering to the dragas, but if you must talk about it, talk about it with Rodrigo."

I never did ask Rodrigo about their dragas. It was something private for me, shared by his mother, Josefa, who reminded me of my own mother and her own stories of the higüe, our ancient little beings that live under trees on the shores of our Guanahani lake. My mother, too, offered gifts to the higüe, sometimes tobacco seeds, sometimes food. Often, she would crack a guayaba and other fruits and leave them out for them.

I was sorry to leave Otero del Rey, where I met my friend Rodrigo's family, his mother Josefa and his father Manuel, a country folk who treated me like one more brother in the family. But at least Rodrigo would ride with me as far as Seville, and from that point on, I would be on ship to return to our islands. The fervent hope of my heart during the long days on our way to Andalucía, as we crossed the interminable plains and mountains on horseback, was to open my eyes and see our little cove in Guanahani, see our fishermen paddling their canoes. I would jump overboard and swim, swim to my shore, run to my village and my mother, my uncles and their many bohíos. My urgent need, I remember, was to see them once more and to tell them of my trip and of what happened to the women and our other people who had left on ship, and tell them too of the strange and astonishing things I had seen in the Castilla land and how Çibanakán had died.

Ninety-four. *Good-bye to Atoya, and Castille.*

Once on board at the Port of Cádiz, it was thirty-four days before we sighted Caribbean islands. Carey was with me, and we missed Rodrigo dearly. Three of our Taíno compatriots returned also with us; all except poor Atoya or Ximon, who was given to young Prince Juan, Queen Isabel's son. Atoya, whom Carey got to know quite well, was that nephew of Bayamo's. He appealed that we both go to the Admiral directly with his wish to take the voyage home with us. He cried with us several times as we readied to leave Seville, but the Admiral admonished us not to raise the question. "Inform Don Juan," (as Atoya had been baptized) the Admiral said, "that he now belongs to the Prince of Castille, whom he serves. Tell him he will be educated in Christian ways by the Prince's own mayordomo, and will forever reside in the court of the Prince, who someday might be king." Poor, sad Atoya lasted less than year in Spain, where he died of heartbreak at his lonely fate. Years later, when I heard that Prince Don Juan died after a hunting accident, breaking the heart of the King and Queen, I felt Atoya and his people working their power from the other side.

November 8, 1532

Ninety-five. *A country where many are poor and destitute and a few are very rich.*

That second voyage to our islands opened my eyes and taught me what I had not yet learned about the covered men. I met Cúneo on that trip, and Alonso de Hojeda, Doctor Álvarez Chanca, Father Buil and Pedro Margarit, and many others. Only a very few were kind or generous people in that lot. The majority were nobility, but of the impoverished variety, and there was nothing noble about them. One sailor made up a ditty: "Poor in Seville gets rich in Antille—and always regal in the eye of the Lord." They liked it so much, it was sung on board many of the ships, over and over as we crossed the ocean.

The royal nobility, or the hidalgos, as they called themselves, laughed among themselves and often derided the crew and low-caste artisans and laborers on board. They ordered them around rudely and imposed so many punishments that the ships' captains had to intervene to quell rising hostilities. On one thing, however, all the Castilla agreed: their desire for the gold of the islands. All dreamed of striking it rich and returning to Castille as gran señores, a goal for which they were willing to take amazing risks and to inflict the most horrendous of punishments, particularly on us Indians.

I had a better idea now what the Castilla meant by "rich and poor." I had seen it in their cities and even in their villages. Among some families, you saw some very large houses, with walls around them, called castles, surrounded by stables and barns and fields of herds and crops. These big families mostly raised sheep. They employed or held some peasants, who are their poor people, but don't feed them much. It happens that these poor people don't have enough to eat, yet they are not allowed to use the land freely, even if it may be abandoned. All the land belongs to the King or the barons, or the church, and these vast expanses are not open to the common people.

This I had noticed as we traveled south from Galicia across Estremadura to Seville. Their poor people were everywhere and there was hunger everywhere. In the country villages, those who had land of their own survived better, raised crops and kept their people together. But most of the people had no land of their own or land that they could work and inhabit. In the cities, they had next to nothing, not even food sometimes, and they begged in the streets.

The poor Castillian huts in the cities were crowded together, most often with pigs and chickens, even cows. While walking through those parts of their towns, I often found their stench unbearable, and I was always affected by the wild look on the eyes of so many children, who were scabby and sickly and kept begging and begging from anyone who walked by.

November 9, 1532

Ninety-six. *The romance of Cúneo's mares.*

I have written earlier about Michelle de Cúneo, when I told about Ba-yamo's curse on the Admiral during our later trip to Cuba. Indeed, of that second, and for me final, crossing of the great waters, I remember most indeed the deeds of this great crony of the Admiral. Of great interest, too, is Captain Hojeda, a powerful, brutal man. But first, I will write about Cúneo's mares.

Cúneo, that Genoese dandy, had a great eye for opportunity, and I believe he was the first of the colonists to make a profit on that journey. During the voyage, as an investment for settling in the islands, Cúneo transported two mares on board our ship. By the third week of warm, calm seas, many men on board felt desperate with lust. Cúneo perceived the opportunity and organized matters to make gains on his two mares, initiating a quiet affair that went on for several weeks. I was full of wonder that many of the men on board were comfortable with the use of the mares to pacify themselves, but it appeared to be so; even among those that did not participate, none questioned the arrangement. And Cúneo took in thirty maravedies per session.

A close friend of the Admiral's, Cúneo was the only man I knew who could tell raunchy stories to the Great Mariner. No one else would have dared, but Cúneo had a way of talking Genoese that Don Christopherens appreciated and made him laugh. Even Don Christopherens knew about the "romance of the mares," as Cúneo called it. Many evenings while they dined together in the Admiral's cabin, I heard Don Christopherens laugh as Cúneo regaled him with jokes and his tales of the "romance."

November 14, 1532

Ninety-seven. *Captain Alonso de Hojeda, the perfect soldier.*

We came upon the southern islands, those that guide our way from the mainland, early in November, 1493. The people of those islands were not Taínos, Çiboney nor Ciguayo, but tribes of the Kwaib, the island warriors who raided against us in the northern Caribbean islands.

The Admiral delighted in sighting the new islands and went about naming one after another in his language. He named one after our ship, the Marie Galante, another one Dominica, after his own father, Dominico, and so on. He insisted on doing this, even though I always told him our word for each place, words always more exacting than the Castillian he provided.

Among the men on board that quickly distinguished themselves, Alonso de Hojeda stood out. He was a short man among the Spaniards, but everyone commented on his perfect physical being. I remember in Seville, during an afternoon when Queen Isabel invited local entertainment, it was Hojeda who impressed her. First, he won a ball throwing contest, throwing a rubber ball higher than anyone else. Then he walked on his hands for a full hour, straight as a tree. Then he amazed the court by stringing a rope high from one building to another and walking upon it, back and forth. The Queen gave him special mention and inducted him into the second voyage herself.

Though not a sailor by profession, Hojeda could climb the mast of our ship faster than all the seamen. And he could haul sail, pull rope, take fathom and load anchor in superlative fashion.

He was also quick to fight, and to draw blood. Hojeda saw combat as a captain in the Moorish wars. Cúneo, who had also been a soldier, befriended Hojeda at that time and Hojeda reciprocated, although his obsessive devotion to the Virgin Mary and his severity of character did not allow him to approve of Cúneo's horse enterprise.

Ninety-eight. *Meeting the "man-eating" Kwaib, how tales get started.*

We were anchored in a small cove. Several men had gone ashore days earlier without return. Hojeda went with forty men to hunt the lost party down, but returned without them. The men had vanished in the dense foliage. For days, the Admiral tacked along the shore of the island. Hojeda made several forays. He reported sighting villages and brought back baskets full of bones.

On board, he showed them to the Admiral, who said,"man-eaters," and had Dr. Chanca examine the bones. Dr. Chanca found scrapes and notches on the bones and declared them to be tooth marks. "These bones have been chewed," he said. On another occasion human bones were also found boiling in a pot. This time it was Cúneo who declared the island inhabited by man-eaters. "Write it in your journal," the Admiral told him. "I will write it, too," Dr. Chanca said.

On both of these occasions I remarked to the Admiral that the boiling and the preservation of bones in baskets was more a funerary practice than it was about man-eating, as these were both customs of our own Taíno people as well, and we certainly were not man-eaters. We dried our dead in the sun and the rain, then used shell-tools to scrape the remaining flesh from the bones. The flesh is buried near where the belly-button of the person was originally buried and the bones are either buried, or accommodated in baskets which are kept in the bohíos of those families. These things are considered sacred among our people.

"You are wrong" the Admiral snapped at me. "Guacanagari told me about these people. And your own women cried about them, and your uncle Çibanakán commented on their raids.These *are* the Carib man-eaters!"

I withdrew my observations, but I was not convinced. I always felt that these were mostly old stories and beliefs of our people. Even though some of these practices occurred, the extent of the man-eating was aggrandized. It is true that my own Guanahani island was quite far for such raids, and thus we had less contact with those legendary enemies of the Taíno. But it is also true I have heard stories told in the ancient areitos, both among my Guanahani people and the people from Haití-Bohío, of the ancient blood feuds and how warriors would expect the right to eat a dead enemy's thigh and heart.

It was later, from the elder caciques of Bohío, especially Guarionex, that I heard the other stories, the ones that told about "the change of heart" ceremony. These were tales made up of episodes, each one by one detailing how the old warriors who lived to make war and eat their enemies were convinced they should love the gentle peace ways, how, as the years went by, they would become Taínos, lovers of sea breeze, lovers of the gentle waves and the clean running waters.

I have seen also a canoe of Ciguayo warriors who paddled back from a fight with an enemy's thigh hanging at the bow of their canoe. They would let the meat dry and harden in the sea salt and sun, and then, at special times, those men who had been in the fight would taste of the jerky from the thigh bone, at once honoring the warrior and consuming his flesh, spiritually defeating him.

What I never, ever heard of was anyone cooking up human meat as a daily food, as basic meals for their people and children. Yet, this was the talk among the important Castilla on board the Admiral's ship, some even claiming that the man-eaters would castrate their own boys and fatten them up for the barbacoa. The soldiering men on board began to take out their weapons, sharpen swords, string cross-bows and clean arquebuses.

November 16, 1532

Ninety-nine. *Discoverers are saved by an Indian grandmother.*

An old Kwaib woman whose name I never learned guided our lost party to a promontory from where she estimated night-time fire and day-time smoke signals could be seen by the ships. Those men could easily have been ambushed and eaten by the Kwaib at that time, but they were not. Instead they were fed, and on the second day a sailor on board spotted the smoke signals from shore. Hojeda was dispatched in row boats to fetch the group.

One hundred. *Perfect proof of Carib perfidy: a castrated boy.*

I heard a conversation some days later between Cúneo and the Admiral and some officers and hidalgos about the rules of war during the early crusades and even back in their old-time memory to the Greek and Roman wars. Again the topic of man-eating was discussed, with Columbus and Cúneo explaining that such men were judged among the most abominable of heathens and were legitimately considered slaves. The people now encountered were opposed to my own Taíno people, whom the Admiral said to be peaceable and potential converts to the true faith. But the Kwaib, or Carib, eat people and thus are enemies that should be taken as slaves, he said.

There was much concurrence about the disgusting nature of the practice of the "caniba" and even our own Taíno on board thanked the Admiral for making the distinction between us and the horrible Kwaib who would eat people. I must admit, I felt some relief and even pride at that moment that we had such a standing with the Admiral, even though I did not believe and have never seen where people would eat the meat of humans as a regular meal.

At one island, I forget which one, several young men and women were captured. A young man was wounded and sore in his crotch, causing him great pain. To my eye, the wound was rotted. He had scabs on his thighs and on the edges of his lips, and it was my impression that our dreaded genital illness, the one that is passed through coupling, had taken hold in him. I could not make out his language fully, but he was able to tell me that a Kwaib healer tried to remove one of his swollen testicles, and that had caused him greater pain. The Admiral had Dr. Álvarez Chanca inspect the boy and he noted the partial amputation. "The young man has been castrated," Dr. Chanca declared.

"Why they would do so, I do not know."

"I would assume the purpose was to fatten him up and soften his flesh for the pot," Cúneo said as the Admiral nodded. But they were all unfamiliar yet with our dreadful disease.

Everyone nodded and grimaced, and word spread like fire through the seventeen ships of the armada. In the days that followed, several officers requested permission to inspect the young man. Dr. Chanca insisted at first that the analysis of the castration was speculation, but Cúneo and the Admiral were convinced of its accuracy. Cúneo became a guide to the young man's corner. "They not only castrate these youngsters," he would lecture, "but they eat their own offspring that they engender in the captured women." He would laugh loudly and wink. "They say the flesh of the young boys tastes better than the young girls!"

One hundred one. *Hojeda draws first blood, Cúneo is in on the first fight.*

We were anchored in a cove at the island of Ayay, which the Admiral renamed Holy Cross. Cúneo and Hojeda organized a party to explore inland. They were already in the large row boats when a canoe full of Kwaib rounded the point of the cove and came to a complete standstill in the water, mesmerized by the sight of seventeen Spanish ships and caravels.

"At them, by Santiago!" Hojeda and then Cúneo both shouted. "Get the Caribs!"

They were four men and two women and they showed no particular fear as our men in two row boats, filled with twelve soldiers each, plus the two captains and four rowers, started toward them. As the boats neared, one older warrior in the canoe notched an arrow and shouted at the rowboats to stop and hold their distance. But the oarsmen kept rowing hard and the captains steered at the canoe.

The Kwaib paddled to the side, avoiding the first pass. Two crossbowmen let lose with arrows, wounding one warrior as three men and one woman among the Kwaib also let lose with arrows. The older warrior this time spiked an arrow through one of the Castilla men, who fell to the bottom of the boat. Another soldier caught an arrow in the stomach, but it didn't penetrate far beyond his leather vest.

The Kwaib might have paddled away rapidly as their canoes are faster at paddling than ship's boats, but it didn't seem to cross their minds. I watched from the ship, thinking how our own Taíno people would have taken flight, given the opportunity to survive. Victory for us was many times as simple as surviving to continue pursuing our way of life. Rather than fight head on,

Taínos preferred to retire from the field of action, if at all possible, and let their ires pass.

Not the Kwaib. They liked a good fight. These ones never paddled again, but rather let their canoe drift, lapped toward shore by the waves. Cúneo's rowboat stayed near, menacing and firing arrows at the canoe, but with small effect. As the Kwaib drifted toward a sandbank, still some distance from the shore, Hojeda's rowboat, which had unfurled a sail, and was maneuvering quite rapidly in the cove, managed to ram their canoe, spilling them all in the water. The fight took place within view of many of us at the stern of the Marie Galante.

Treading water, the Kwaib, all except the wounded man, raised themselves out of the water and fired their arrows. The woman warrior was exceptional, a long-legged swimmer, with strong, long arms. As Cúneo's boat approached dead onto hit her in the water, she swam to the side and let go an arrow that traversed an oarsman, doubling him over as the boat passed. But steering the boat, Cúneo turned into her, knocking her over in the water, circling rapidly around to pull her in.

Not far away, Hojeda's crossbowmen fired volley after volley of arrows into two other Kwaib, including another woman; they looked like spiny fish in the water after a while. Hojeda himself decapitated the first wounded man just under the ears as he passed him on the water. However, the old Kwaib warrior, a good shooter and fast swimmer, reached the sand bank. He managed to wound another one of Hojeda's men and was wounded himself with arrows to the legs as the boat approached him. The old warrior jumped into the waves just as Hojeda spiked him through with a lance. Hojeda bore down on the lance with the old man underwater for a couple minutes, then yanked it back forcefully. The Kwaib went limp, but as Hojeda began to turn the boat around, slowly, the old warrior, using only one arm, started swimming away toward shore.

This time, Hojeda overtook the Kwaib easily, using a gaff to hook him and pull him in. Then he had a soldier yank the warrior's head over the edge of the boat while he brandished his sharp cutlass and hacked the neck clean through in two sharp blows.

"Watch the man-eater swim now," I remember the priest, Father Buil, saying on board as Hojeda held up the head for us to see.

November 20, 1532

One hundred two. *Cúneo's treatment of a Kwaib warrior woman.*

One more thing on Cúneo. He showed his woman warrior to the Admiral, who granted her to him as his personal captive. Cúneo pulled the woman to his cabin and tied her down. He came out to urinate, and went in again. Immediately we heard him yell. Then, we could hear thrashing going on inside the room and the high pitched, nearly inaudible screams of the warrior woman. Many men crowded around outside as the sounds of struggle gave way to the dull pounding of the Admiral's great friend into her Kwaib flesh.

Cúneo emerged triumphant and smiling. The men cheered him and envied him. "Better than a mare, boys," he said. "Much better."

One hundred three. *Carey responds to Cúneo.*

Carey and I hated him. I would meet crueler men, more gross and violent than Cúneo, but for some reason I hate him nearly most of all. I hate even the memory of his handsome, arrogant face.

In a fortnight, Cúneo was offering his woman slave out for lease at one hundred marivedies a session. Carey objected. I cautioned him against it, but he insisted on saying something. "The woman is brave," he told Cúneo in front of several men. "Allow her to recover and not be used by so many men."

Without warning, Cúneo delivered a great blow to Carey's face, which felled him against a net. Cúneo, his face very red, put a knife to my countryman's throat. "Don't ever question me, dog," he said. "Or I'll sell you to these men. You might be better than a mare yourself."

He didn't rape Carey, but struck him another hard blow, this time to the chest with the handle of his knife. Carey doubled over in pain.

The rest of the voyage was day by day misery for Carey, constantly taunted, struck and threatened, not only by Cúneo but by several other braggarts on board, including two who really wanted to bugger my poor cousin. Father Buil was another one of them who had that inclination. I kept Carey near me as I served the Admiral and I even inducted him into the ampolleta shifts, but he had become a desperate being, suffocating in the tension of the threats.

I lost him in Borikén, which island we reached on November 19, 1493. One night, while we drifted a mile from the coast, he loaded up on hawk's bells ("for gifts on the way home"), wrapped up a knife he had pilfered from a sailor and announced to me he would swim to shore and take his chances from there. Three women from a group rescued from a Kwaib camp were from Borikén, having been taken by Kwaib weeks before. They had decided to go overboard and swim to shore. Carey was to help them by cutting their ropes, while they promised to speak well for him among their people. I asked him to consider our better opportunity to get home from Bohío, as the Admiral had promised we would round the Maize point of Cuba later and go out to our little islands. But Carey was decided and in the dark of a night without moon, he and the three women slipped overboard. I heard them swim away, my heart praying for love among our Boricua brothers to help get my cousin home. I don't know if he ever made it, and I never saw or heard of Carey again.

November 24, 1532

One hundred four. *The news on Fort Navidad.*

The Admiral was terribly excited as we sailed onto Española's coasts, which we hugged in search of Fort Navidad, the Admiral's first colony on our lands. On board all vessels there was great anticipation. The sea voyage had been difficult on the passengers, the majority of whom had no sailing experience. The talk was of buildings and the uses of woods and how much gold would be secured. I remember hearing long discussions on the carrying capacity of the various vessels, how much gold could each of them safely hold. "Gold makes great ballast" was an often repeated ditty, though it never made it into song.

None had thoughts of farming at that moment, and I certainly don't believe anymore that even one of them had the Christian mission in mind. Father Buil, the ranking cleric, was an ornery, gnarled man. Nothing kind or inspired came out of him, though he talked incessantly, particularly at the Admiral, who heard him out with absent mind. Buil, the buzzard we called him, talked a lot about the Grand Khan, and dreamt of establishing relations for his order of the Benedictines.

It was late November, 1493, when we came upon the Navidad coast. As always, canoes from small fishing villages came out to greet us. The Admiral meant to press on, but for several days the winds strongly disfavored us. I recognized one canoe that circled the Admiral's ship. It had the three-line mark of Guacanagari's cacicazgo. Two of the men seated in it were uncles of the young cacique.

"Taíno-ti, uncles of our great cacique friend," I greeted them as they came within earshot. "Can you see that the covered men from Heaven have returned?"

They nodded at me and paddled close to where I stood on deck. "We are glad to see the double tongue," they said, and fell silent. They asked not for the Guamiquina, and their silence was ominous. I threw them a line of rope that they could hold. The older sub-chief stood in the canoe. "We would speak with the young Taíno two-tongue," he said. "Quietly, let us converse a day ourselves."

I sat in the low hold, the rope in my hand. "A horrible fight has taken place," the elder said, beginning a story that lasted all afternoon and ended with the words: "The covered men left by the Guamiquina are all dead."

One hundred five. *How Fort Navidad was overrun by Cacique Caonabó.*

Here I will relate the story as told by Guacanagari's sub chief, whose name was Guababo and who stood in his canoe as he said these words that are still clear in my memory. Guababo talked all afternoon of a day. Several times he cried. I will write his own words as much as I remember them:

"As we promised the Guamiquina, after you left in the giant canoes, the people of our two villages nearby to Navidad supplied the covered men with food. We had agreed in my village that every day, men and women of my guaxeri would go to the covered men's houses, carrying pack-baskets of fruit and our sweet potatoes, stacks of fresh casabe bread and at least two hand counts of fish or lobster caught that very morning. My village was one of two sworn to feed half of the men, which was the count of my fingers twice. This we performed for fourteen days without incident and were quite willing to continue, and more than that, it was a happiness for us to perform this task for our cacique, Guacanagari.

"My guaxeri group of ten assigned to this task started with the sun, sang areitos to bless the food gathered and even paraded formally through my yucayeque, walking in the four directions of our sacred ritual, which is the design of our villages, before taking the trail to Navidad.

"I say to you now, a ceremony we established to feed the guests of our cacique and this would have lasted right to today. I say, happy we were to take this distinction for our beloved young cacique and our council, on which I too have a seat.

"Now, give me your ears, my relative. On the night of the fifth day, we heard two loud thunders from the camp at Navidad. Scouts were sent and they reported much shouting among the covered men.

"On the sixth day, our guaxeri delivered their foods to the Castilla camp. A man had been killed, they reported back to us. It was the young one we knew as Jácome. His body was layed out in a hut, showing blood and stab wounds, and the covered men had gathered at two ends of the camp. One group called themselves Basques, while the others said they were *true* Castillians.

"On the seventh day, precisely while our guaxeri were at the camp, two men fought suddenly with sharp sabers and one was cut badly in the arm and retreated. The victor, whose name was Pedro Gutiérrez, said, 'Now, I do as I please.'

"Among our guaxeri food suppliers were a mother and a daughter, both healthy women. The father in that family was a fisherman who was one of the suppliers of the food, though he was not a carrier to the camp. The soldier Gutiérrez took both women and had his men hold them. Pointing to the women, he said, 'Daca, Daca,' meaning, *I am*, in our language, but by which he meant, *you are mine*. That done, the women cried out and all my guaxeri ran for home.

"On the eighth day, the woman's husband and his brother went to the camp. Behind them our guaxeri feeders, still carrying their baskets of food, hid in the forest as the two men entered the Castilla camp. To demand his wife and daughter, the husband went to Gutiérrez and pleaded. Without speaking, Gutiérrez stabbed him. Another Castilla cut the brother. The brother ran, but our guaxeri husband dropped and bled and died."

This was the beginning of many horrors, according to the sub-chief. Everyone of the covered men then took women—sisters, daughters and mothers together—and they used them in coitus, and harshly. The men hoarded three or four, even five women each. Husbands and brothers who demanded their families back were cut and stabbed at will in the weeks that followed, and the people were angered.

"No more would we feed the Castilla, and a council was called with Guacanagari," said Guababo, who stood in the canoe, straight as a pole, despite the roll of waves, but trembling slightly all the time. "Our cacique attended. He heard the stories of the killing and cried with us, then he and all his wise ones reminded us of our promise to the Guamiquina. 'They are men from Heaven,' he insisted to us.'Let us continue as before until the Guamiquina returns.'

"In all truth, we tried. Our ways you know, young two-tongue. We ni-taíno tried to forget the atrocity, but none of our people would go near the covered men. The Castilla fought among themselves, again and again, until finally they broke up in three groups, two of which left, one to the Magua of our uncle, Cacique Guarionex, and the other to Maguana, the region of Cacique Caonabó, titled by Taíno but a Ciguayo warrior man, nonetheless, not to be disturbed."

Guababo related that both groups took women and food along the way and cut down any man that objected. Thus, the word spread of their marauding and the chiefs admonished all to stay away from them.

"Their comings and goings we tracked with scouts and runners," Guababo continued. "They were two small groups and they moved fast. Our people are very good at disappearing in the trees, but some were still surprised in their daily chores. Without warning, then, more and more the covered men attacked and killed the Taíno men, took the women and chased off the children. We heard the stories as our runners returned, telling of each incident. Caught with gold on his neck, they tortured an old man, gouging his eyes when he could not turn up more gold.

"Three moons passed and our cacique received a messenger from the Ciguayo cacique, Caonabó, announcing a visit. Caonabó, who I say is a Ciguayo and only by marriage a Taíno, only now learning our ways, soon himself arrived at our own cacique's village. He demanded to know who these men were that were doing such terrible things to his people. Soon, he said, his many warriors would destroy these men.

"Our beloved Guacanagari argued with Caonabó against attacking the Castilla. Caonabó told him, 'Cousin: if you are host to these people, why are they so mean to my own? As for you, man-boy, you are a little thing. Cousin, understand, the deed is for me to do.'

"Two more moons passed. It is known that one group of the Castilla went through the country of Guarionex, then in time, it passed as well into Caonabó's villages. We did not hear from Guarionex, our revered grandfather, until much later, but then we learned that he had gone in retreat over the news of the Castilla and that, like Guacanagari, he ordered his warriors to avoid contact with the roamers. Over these news of covered men, seven days twice, Guarionex fasted, and he cried many times at his runners' descriptions of the covered men."

At that point, standing in his canoe, the old sub-chief cried, too. And as I write now, I, too, cry, remembering the jolt of his tale upon my eager ears. It was the most horrible thing he was telling me, not the many abuses Guababo's people had suffered, which already in my mind I felt would be remedied by the Admiral's presence, but I feared I was about to hear of a retaliation, of an ill deed committed against Castilla men by our island people and that shook me to the bone.

"By his cacique's permission, Caonabó's fighters took down the Castilla covered men," the sub-chief said. "By ones and by twos, arrows they shot into them, and from behind trees, they clubbed them. When most had suffered wounds, and other Castilla panicked, our warriors rushed them and finished them off."

"Were they all killed?" I asked, in our common tongue.

"Every one, yes. Then to Navidad Caonabó came and he burned the fort. The Castilla rushed to the sea, swinging swords, as foolishly they fled into the waters, where they were no match for Caonabó's men."

One hundred six. *The story denied.*

At the end of the tale, the elders would not stay. They would come back later, they said, with presents for the Admiral.

That evening (November 27), they did return and they greeted the Admiral by candlelight, seeking out his face in the dark. They talked a long time as I waited anxiously for the story of the killings to emerge, but it did not. Instead, the Admiral was told by the uncles that the Navidad Fort was still well, reporting a few deaths due to illness and nothing else. They gave a gift of gold to Don Christopherens: two gold masks of beautiful workmanship, for which they took back, and happily, a dozen hawk's bells.

They were out of sight in their canoes when I told the Admiral the truth of the situation, how Caonabó and others had killed off all thirty-nine Castilla left behind. He yelled at me, "Liar!" And he was much angered, calling me a dog and a braggart, loudly, and I believe he might have struck me, but the shriek in his own voice stopped him. Fatigued of mind, he was already in a long season that would take him into the next September, the first full cycle of Castilla inhabitation in our islands.

He got earfuls now each day from the large number of men on board the ships, crowded and indisposed those many weeks. The heady boasting of great wealth to come, easy servants and nubile maidens, bragging lies of Barcelona and Seville would now catch up with him (and me). There were complaints and accusations already. They were quiet yet, murmurs, but they were constant.

I slept outside Don Christopheren's cabin door that evening. I heard him cry, and that's when I knew that he knew. Next morning, we came upon the site of Fort Navidad. Bodies were found, first two, then eleven, even more later. The fort was burned to the ground, no notes or messages of any kind left behind.

Numbly, over the charred ground, the Admiral walked. Then he directed a search for gold, digging out the well now covered with stones and turning over other likely sites as well. But no gold was found. "Damned barbarians!" was a favorite expression, spat often from those days on.

I remember Father Buil. All were angry at the deed of violence, but Father Buil was maniacal. Face contorted, he walked to and fro. "They should hang for killing Christians, they should burn," he demanded, but he did not bury his people, a strange act I never understood.

The Admiral led us away to a place up the coast where he would found a new town, which he called Isabela in honor of the Queen. For eight days we fought contrary winds before landing the armada (a word I would come to understand) at his chosen site.

One hundred seven. *Isabela is built, the first metropolis.*

I remember now the building of Isabela, where I learned to pound nails and size up planks. I remember Columbus talking again with Guacanagari, how his people still helped the Castilla build and how they marveled at the cows and pigs, chickens, sheep and horses that came off the ships. I remember Father Buil crying for blood and Hojeda angered, and how everybody in that first town seemed irritated all the time. They were angry at our ni-Taíno, whom they were, for the moment, obliged to respect; they insulted our guaxeri, their lack of building skills; they quickly abused our naboria, assuming a complete superiority toward our simpler cousins; they were angry at our trees, which were so big and hard to cut. They prayed to the Virgin Mary and the Holy Infant, Jesus; they prayed to the Holy Trinity; they prayed to the Pope and the Queen and the King. But right from that moment, as they fixed their corrals and their mills, as they planted new seeds brought over from their world, they cursed everything ours. They cursed at our insects, they cursed at our foods, they blasphemed our spirits and cemíes, they even cursed at the mother sea.

A deep sadness settled over my spirit as we built Isabela, one I had held at bay, I realize now, even since the intimations of my father-uncles that first night at Guanahani, what the cohoba had shown them. All we Indians could see, for one thing, the Castilla were building Isabela on a pestilent swamp, where no good water was to be had. For all their mountains of knowledge, we were learning that the covered men are often blind to the simplest, most obvious things. Any simple naboria can tell you a village must be built near good water.

My elders' words came back to me often at that time, and I so much wanted to see them and my mother again. I had already a terrible agitation in my belly, and then our heat made the Castilla's wine go sour. As the covered men built their houses, our guaxeri, by order of Guacanagari, brought them gourds full of juices from dozens of varieties of fruit that grew all around, wonderful juices not to be found anywhere in Spain. But the Castilla cursed them, nonetheless, and many sipped obstinately on their rancid wine. The darkest of clouds was gathering, I could tell, a temper of ire in the back of the eyes, the casabe-colored men were so hard. Such was my feeling in that first season of colony, as their first houses were built and the plans were drawn, right at the Admiral's table, for the settling of Castilla towns on our Taíno lands.

January 6, 1533

One hundred eight. *My loss of innocence.*

It has been three weeks since I have picked up this pen, this pen I hold that opens forth so much hurt, arousing memories of a more innocent time, of my own elders and what happened to them. I sit to write and the mere act provides picture after picture, as in those paintings that I saw at the Cathedral of Seville, Christ being flogged, Christ being stabbed, Christ bleeding in the agony of crucifixion. I remember real crucifixions; I remember beheadings upon beheadings; I remember wanton injuries to child and mother, wanton, wanton, the boot of the soldier applied to the neck, the torch of the Inquisition to the pyre of Taíno. But of all that my mind can hold, I most dread the memory of my own innocence, my Taíno goodwill upon which I have gathered so much hatred.

One hundred nine. *A devilish bout with the grape.*

The result of memories brought on by this task of writing, plus a touch of deviltry ... An incident occurred on New Year's eve. It has cost me dearly with the monks and even puts in jeopardy how much I can do in the Enriquillo negotiations. I am so bothered with myself, I will write it here, as confession.

In agony I had finished writing on Carey and my elders when Fray Remigio offered a bottle, an error in judgment for both he and me. We passed a bottle of wine back and forth, the young monk and I, as we weeded my patch of onions and peas. We drank the wine in the late afternoon as the sun cooked my brain. By dinner time, a holiday affair that day, I was deep in my spine, or I should say, my spleen. For one thing, I sat at the abbot's table without care, waiting as the younger monks served me. As wine was passed, I drank one glass and then another. His Eminence, Abbot Enrique Mendoza, sat at the head chair. He is a calm man, old and a bit frail for his many duties, although he walks steadily through his day and his sharp eye misses little.

"Master Diego has had his pleasure in the wine today," he said, with a glance at Fray Remigio, who immediately felt the scrutiny.

"My mind is clear, Your Eminence," I said. "Fear not unreason from this humble guaxeri." It was true: I had just entered that place that wine can bring you where everything gets starkly clear. It had been a long time, nearly five years since the last time I succumbed, although I admit I have had my long days of inebriation.

"I fear not," the Abbot said. "Tonight is the eve of the New Year. We shall eat well and enjoy good company. Among others, the Judge Oidor Suazo himself will soon join us and I believe he brings along that noted intellect, Don Gonzalo, who I am sure will prove highly entertaining."

A worse combination could not have been joined by the devil himself. Don Gonzalo, of course, was Oviedo. I felt my whole body stiffen, anticipation and loathing quickly stirring my senses.

"Fernández de Oviedo y Valdés," I said with loose tongue, pronouncing fully the Castillian sounds I have learned too well. "It is a good thing Don Bartolomé is not present."

Several monks laughed a bit too heartily and the Abbot smiled, mischievously, knowing Don Bartolomé and Oviedo are bitter enemies. Abbot Mendoza has a sense of strategy. He supports the positions of Don Bartolomé, but the two men are often at odds on daily matters. The good friar's reputation and authority can at times suffocate all other volition, and the old Abbot is often overshadowed by Las Casas. So, in his absence, the Abbot courts the same high office-holders of Santo Domingo, including Suazo, who have approached the good friar.

Minutes later, Oidor Suazo and Oviedo were the first guests to arrive. Oviedo recognized me at once. I remained in my chair as he took his seat and in his face I could see some wonderment at my presence at the table. "Our great Admiral's Dieguillo-boy has grown into quite the personage," he said. "Now he sits as a guest of abbots."

"Properly, sir," I responded. "It is you who are my guests, as the islands are my natural home."

Food and wine were presented promptly by monks, who hurried in the silence following my remark. But I was feeling good. Besides, custom was on my side. Governor Diego Columbus himself it was, legitimate son of the Admiral and former governor of the Española Island, who in his father's own memory granted me the right to join a Castillian table, sitting me near him many times at official gatherings in the final weeks before leaving his governorship.

"The Indian is a notable one," Suazo joined in, as always speaking of Indians only in the third person. "Truly, he can say he was with the first Admiral, may his grand soul rest in eternal peace."

"Thank you, sir," I replied, reminding them, "It was by order of the Columbus family that I have this privilege. ... "

"Very well, Dieguillo," the Abbot interrupted me. But I continued.

" ... To sit in the company of such esteemed intellect and authority as the present company."

The meal began quietly at that juncture, and I was silent as the young monks who were serving plates of fish, fowl and pork, rice and beans scurried about. I knew a reproach was likely from the Abbot if I persisted and, although my nerve to push the conversation was taut, I naturally backed off. In my mind I have been contemplating the work ahead with Enriquillo and the good friar and have wanted to avoid, now most of all times, any public altercation.

In my silence, as always with a guaxeri like me, I was totally ignored. Perhaps I am that good at dissimulation by now, after years of surviving by blending into my own trance. But it was not hard, really, as the company quite readily ceased to see me altogether, even the Abbot. Thus I continued sipping.

As they do on this island on New Year's Eve, other gentlemen dropped by, and the table grew to more than ten important men. Only I, and young Silverio who was helping to serve dinner, were Indians in the room. The convent cook had prepared four large brazos gitanos, a common sweet cake of Valencia. The Abbot turned over the wine cellar key to the serving monks, who kept pouring. The company conversed about many subjects, from the preparations for planting new sugar cane to the variety of accommodations and experiences during the ocean passage, but finally, as always, their conversation ranged to the life of the people who had been encountered on our islands, how they did this or that, subjects acutely painful to me.

Of course, Oviedo dominated in this regard. He liked speaking about my people, as he is also writing a history of the Indies, talking of Taínos and ni-Taínos, this cacique and that one, about villages of the large islands and of the Lucayas, speaking even of my long-lost home of Guanahani. I sipped as he explained who we were and how we acted in the times before the Castilla. For nearly two hours, the wine, rather than excite me to violence, distanced me from Oviedo's words.

At one point, while drinking steadily, Oviedo talked about the marriages of my people and how they were accustomed to making love. He went on and on, as I had heard him years before (and precisely at the table of Don Diego Columbus, the second Admiral) about the caciques having many wives and how upon a cacique's death, sometimes one or more wives would be buried with him.

Everyone laughed. "A hard lot on wives," said an hacendado sitting to my left. "Of course, the Indians did many barbaric things."

I twisted inside myself, not because what he said about cacique wives was totally untrue, but because in my mind it was not cause for such ridicule. In my mind, the Castilla did much more barbaric things. "It is of interest," I said, "that more often than not, a wife's devotion and love compelled her voluntary journey to the spirit valley, what we call Coabay."

"Even so, a barbaric custom it is," Oviedo answered quickly.

"Yet, I wonder if a Christian lady would ever consider doing so, that is, out of devotion?"

I got a laugh out of most of the men, including Oidor Suazo.

"The Indian is clever," said the Oidor.

"So observed the most revered Queen Isabel, the Catholic, at Barcelona, when she met me in 1493," I said.

I realized I was being boorish to speak so much, interjecting myself like this, but as I sat in my chair and looked upon their persons, they all became smaller and smaller and I felt the superiority of my knowledge.

"The Dieguillo is clever," said the Abbot, "but tonight his tongue rides the nectar of the vine. He forgets our Spanish ladies, whole convents of nuns, are devoted to the one true Lord."

I raised my glass to him with a nod, both of indifference and mockery. But it was a table gesture I had seen in the nobility, and it ingratiated me somewhat (or so I thought) to the group.

Oviedo continued more calmly now about our abilities. "It is true that here and there a clever Indian is found. Witness our natural companion this evening. But, overall, the Indians were a sorry lot before our coming. Most were imbeciles, made by nature to serve."

About our holy people, he said, "Blindly, the Indians believed their witch-men, whom they called behikes, who fooled everyone by babbling with their little cemí idols. Of course, our priests discovered immediately an assistant of the brujo who would hide behind the altar of the cemí and emit sounds so as to frighten the people."

Oviedo lifted his wine glass and pretended to hide behind it, making phantasmal sounds, then feigning a witch's voice: "I am your master, give me your tribute!"

He might have gotten applause for his drama, but at that very moment I interceded. "We never had tribute; it was always exchange, trade."

It was my mistake. He had had enough of me. Quietly, a blotchy redness flushed Oviedo's oval face. "Idolaters!" he spat. "The true Indians from those days worshiped images of the Devil himself!"

"Never mind this diablillo know-it-all," the Abbot interfered, to calm him down. He looked at me sternly, then turned with a smile to Oviedo.

"I understand from Don Bartolomé that they were an abstaining people about coitus," the Abbot goaded him deftly by way of deviating his anger.

Oviedo snapped forward. "Nonsense. They did as snakes, wrapped up under the leg, men with women, men with men. Anti-natura, in the wrong hole!"

I gestured to speak and spilled my glass of wine.

"Diego might consider a retreat," Abbot said quietly.

I shook my head and he did not insist. "Father Las Casas is a truthful man," I said. "Of all Castilla, he understands our people best."

"Only in going after gold did they abstain," Oviedo said loudly, talking over me as if to ignore me. He glanced around the table and laughed loudly at the group. "Did you know that? Before going to gather gold, the Indian abstained from coitus. It was the only time. Every other time they plugged everything in sight, mothers excluded." He laughed again. "But they abstained when they went after gold. Ha, and Las Casas, the Great Defender says the Indians didn't put value on gold!"

Of course, he was all wrong, but for the moment, my head swirled and my heart raced. Twice my elbow slipped on the table as I tried to keep a silent composure. The love I do feel for the good friar was suddenly high in my breast, mixing in with the many other emotions.

Oviedo spoke on of sodomy now, in a torrent of words that pierced me deeply, although he avoided my face. "Repulsion and shame," he kept repeating, calling our people "irredeemable liars, lazy, dumb, a people who would rather kill themselves than work hard. The pestilence," he said,"was only to be thanked for wiping nine out of ten Indians off of the Caribbean islands.

"It was divine intervention directly worked to deny a place on the Earth to such savage and bestial peoples, abominable and vicious. It fits them well and it is most convenient the frightful sentence carried out against them by an eternal and sovereign God!"

My head in a fog, his words pierced my breast again and again. It was another half hour before my mind calmed enough to formulate words. This is where the wine lifts all caution.

"Only the blacks of Africa are more bestial than were our own natives," Oviedo was claiming, recalling Governor Diego Columbus' acts of swift violence in 1522 while suppressing a slave rebellion in his own sugar mill. Then he made a mistake, as he wound down to stop. "Your own benefactor, Dieguillo," he said, pointing at me. "He hung them by the dozens, including many Indians who joined in."

"The second Admiral, who saved my life twice, was only a man," I retorted. "And a Castilla."

I saw young Silverio jump in a corner. He was the only other Indian in the room.

The Abbot sized me up. As I only held him in check with the potential for greater scandal, I continued quickly, by way of explanation. "In the case of the negro rebellion, exactly ten years ago, the second Admiral acted swiftly and brutally, it is true. More than twenty blacks had gotten away and word was spreading to other sugar mills. He sought to ... "

"Everyone knows he feared a general rebellion," Oviedo had caught my challenge. "But why do you say, a Castilla, by what meaning?"

"The way of your punishment has been to hang and burn our elders," I said. "Or is this strange to your learned ears?"

"Only rebellious ones," Oidor Suazo intervened. I think he tried to change the conversation. "What say you, Don Gonzalo, of the efforts to deal with Enriquillo?"

"If done properly, he would be hanged," Oviedo replied quickly, looking at me, and spoke slowly. "He is a brigand, Indian or not, and has committed acts of theft and cruel violence."

"He fights only for a justice denied him," I said.

"He is an outlaw, a rebel and a murderer, regardless of ... "

I interrupted. "He is a man of conviction, not a fingery gold-counter!"

Oviedo stood, making as if to reach for his dagger. "This Indian must go," he yelled. "I will not tolerate this insult."

Oviedo, now turned historian, came to these islands to count the King's gold. Everyone knows that, and there are many stories on the depths of his pockets. Two monks stepped behind him, I think to prevent violence, as he stood erectly facing me, hand on the hilt of his dagger.

"Las Casas knows these things," I said, with deadly calm. "He writes the truth about us."

The Abbot stood. "Dieguillo must retire," he said as Oviedo, facing me, yelled, "Las Casas is another lying fool!"

I stood, too, wanting to insult him again, but more words were not forthcoming. I was ready to kill that Oviedo, to yank out his lying tongue. Leaning on the table, my hand clasped a serving knife, a gesture noticed by the Abbot. "Go at once, Dieguillo," he commanded. "You are dangerously close to illegality. Do not threaten an officer of the King."

Thus did I retire to my cloistered cell in the early hours of this new year, marking now 1,533 since the birth of the Christ.

January 10, 1533

One hundred ten. *In need of punishment.*

My body felt a wretch for two days after contention with the bottle. Only Fray Remigio, the Franciscan, and young Silverio visited my room, and then briefly after meals. I ate steadily from their offerings, but as my body recovered, my mind and heart bemoaned my thoughtless indiscretion.

Now I am ashamed, not because of the insult to Oviedo, who is an old whore full of calumnies, but because my own stupidity allowed such a scandal. I hate to think I gave Enriquillo away, and precisely to the wrong people. Nothing did I hear from Oidor Suazo nor, of course, form that "intellect" about the need for "peace" with Enriquillo, although they pronounce such thoughts in their more public gestures. It is not a good moment to lose my anonymity.

With the knotted rope the convent keeps for such a purpose, I will ask Fray Remigio to flagellate me. I will ask him to strike me hard, make me bleed from the shoulders and suffer. I am such a fool, and I have always been such a fool. And how can I change now, but through more pain? I must concentrate my mind on the task before me, which is to ensure that Enriquillo lives, that his movement is not crushed just as he would make a peace.

January 10, 1533

One hundred eleven. *Las Casas reports mixed news.*

As if to torment my agitation, a letter arrives from las Casas, but full of troublesome news—all the more reason provided me for the painful remedy I have dictated for my soul.

The good friar met with the Empress, as King Charles was not yet back in his Iberian court. Long dialogues, he reports, but the Empress was not well disposed. As of July, 1532, she commissioned a captain to press the war on Enriquillo, annihilate him once and for all. His name is Barrionuevo and, according to the friar, he and more than two hundred soldiers will have left for our island by my receipt of the letter. The friar will also return now.

He writes: "I demanded from the Empress Isabel of Portugal, wife of King Carlos I, an adequate plan for a peace in Española based on the principle of just treatment," he writes. "She called me a meddler and referred to over a dozen documents of complaint against my person, several authored or seconded by the Oidor Suazo, of late so endearing with me.

"What to make of all this I am not sure, except that a strong position at the court is that Enriquillo should be invited to come here, on an embassy from which he will not return. I am more worried than always now, noting the Empress' response. I believe the King is more disposed to establish a peace, but he is tending to his German dominions and is not expected for several more weeks."

One bit of good news: My old friend Rodrigo Gallego is to make the voyage as an officer of the guard. He is now a captain and well-regarded. His application to join the mission was easily accepted. The good friar reports long conversations with Rodrigo, who professed himself a sympathizer these many years to the plight of our Taíno people. I am very happy about this news that I will see my friend, missing from my life since our tearful farewell in Seville in 1493.

"Seize the initiative to negotiate on our own with Enriquillo," writes Las Casas. "The island hidalgos have the stealth for a devious assassination, but I don't believe they have the courage for more campaigns in the Bahuruku, which describes the Empress's plan. Assist the baby boy (here he employs my code) to design a careful negotiation. A captain and a soldier, Barrionuevo nevertheless carries secondary instructions to recognize Enriquillo's original complaints. I expect, if our efforts are rewarded, that he will go empowered to grant pardons if peace can be achieved.

"As you receive this letter, I will be on board a returning ship. Please be very careful and strategic, as the moment comes for definitive action to make gains at the end of this fourteen-year old affair. I have raised the encomienda as a point of discussion. Yes, it angers everyone anew to discuss this sin we all share, but it must be raised, again and again, until justice is done.

"My friend, I remember seeing you those many years ago, not far from where I now write these words, your skinny young frame and quick smile and the wonderful parrots you handled. I hope you are well and commend you to keep writing, keep writing. What you have to say about those early days is, I believe, of great importance."

One hundred twelve. *I must get to the Bahuruku.*

Now I sit and ponder, hoping my lunatic indiscretion with Oviedo and the Oidor will have minor repercussion. The monks, I know, are watching me more carefully. Most are sympathizers of the good friar's mission, but I fear their constant curiosity for my expressions on the cacique. So they watch me, wondering, and I wonder, too, is there a traitor among them? And how can I leave here without notice? How can I get to the Bahuruku to talk to Enriquillo, which I clearly must do, and not give him away? I am such a magnus fool for what I have done, and at such a wrongful moment!

One hundred thirteen. *Flogged out of my guilty stupor.*

Finally I am flogged. Fray Remigio understood my request and gracefully backed me up without word, administering my torture faithfully and quietly, assisting me to my cot as on the fortieth stroke I crumbled from the pain. I intoned a prayer when I awakened and for two days I have forced my arms and shoulders to move, causing a dismay through my neck and head that has made me wretch anew. Such is the power, though, even in my stupidity, that one day later, an opportunity arises. I feel the strength of the spirits in this, a prayer returned. The sugar mill near San Juan de la Maguana constructs a new milling building and has called for carpenters. I will go there and set a message out for the baby boy.

Folio IV

A Visit to the Rebel Camps

Francisco Pedro, Yoruba friend ... Two weeks later, sugar mill story ...
A new day begins ... In the free Taíno territory ... Greetings by
Enriquillo and Doña Mencía, council of captains ... Younger captains'
proposals for raids to procure arms and munitions and tools ... Touring
the camp, the young men ... The capture of Caonabó ... Lessons for the
boy-warriors ... The Castilla dance for gold ... Caonabó serves notice
on Fuerte Tomás ... Blood not spilled, but a chopped hand ...
Discussions in the evening ... Caonabó's deception by Hojeda ...
Nobody liked the story ... San Miguel's deception ... Seeking a path to
peace, Enriquillo ... Looking for the behike ... Early cohobas with
Guarionex ... Fasting and old stories of Taínos ... Peace-pact ways of
Guarionex ... Friar Pané, the busybody priest that got many good people
killed ... A Castilla army readies for battle ... Maniocatex riles up a
war ... Pané riles up a cacique's yukaieke ... The Battle of
Christiandom over the Heathens ... Guarionex is prisoner ...
Guarionex is released, Guacanagari disappears ... A Taíno offer on the
land. The first Castilla rebellion: Roldán attacks the Admiral ... I take a
bride, Ceiba ... Making a family, home days ... Enriquillo's camp is like
the old yukaiekes ... The old man knew so much ... Death spirits that
open sores in our faces ... Roldán and the first Indian repartimiento ...
Guarionex retreats to the mountains ... Guarionex falls, and
Mayobanex ... Castilla swarm the island ... Surrounded by young
Taíno, education for peace ... A song comes to me ... Going to meet
the medicine ...

One hundred fourteen. *Francisco Pedro, Yoruba friend.*

I write tonight from a small bohío near San Juan de la Maguana, where I have come with young Silverio. The bohío belongs to a free Negro named Francisco Pedro, who served with me in the encomienda of Pero López before that singular son of a she-dog lost his Maguana holdings, during the time of the Admiral Diego, and returned to Santo Domingo. Francisco Pedro is a good friend who, like myself, has benefitted greatly from the friendship of the second Admiral and that of Father Las Casas. He is a lucky Negro just as I am a lucky Indian to come out alive from inside the nightmare of the past forty years. He was one of the first Yoruba negroes brought over by Antonio de Torres, before the time of Nicolás de Ovando in 1502.

When I was encomended in 1514, along with Enriquillo and his father, already Francisco Pedro, whom I call by his common apodeme of Yoruba, was an older man. Today he fixed us herbal tea and cooked a hen in onions and rice and boiled yuca for us, and he seems as agile as in those days. He still calls me boy, although I am certainly not that anymore. "You better rest a day and be ready to work when you go over to that Solana's sugar mill. You are now used to that soft life of the convent, dusting altars and cooking for priests. But at the mill they work you, even a freeman, sixteen straight hours, with a one hour stop after mid-day."

He is right, of course. The life of the sugar mill is the worst now. And he is too polite to say, Indians don't work the cane or sugar-grind anymore. All that has gone to Negroes in the last ten years, the strongest arms for the cane cutters, and the biggest ones to work the grinding machine. Wielding the machete in a field of cane, spiny slivers by the millions falling on your face and sweaty neck, burning sun of the harvest torching your head is about the hardest work a man can do on this island, now that the gold mines are nearly exhausted. Almost all cane cutters are Negroes now. Many Negroes are like us in build, but many more than us are big and muscled heftily and those are put to work inside the mill, where the machinery is huge and heavy and everything is hot to the touch. "The Castilla treated Indians as if you were wild game," Francisco Pedro told me today, "but they treat us Negroes like beasts of burden."

Tomorrow I will ride into the Spanish village of Vera Paz, what used to be the main yukaieke of old Cacique Bohekio, here in the province of Xaragua. I am to go to the sugar mill and cattle ranches of Don Diego Solana and his wife, Doña María de Arana, where a new mill building for squeeze-grinding sugar cane is to be built. Solana is probably the biggest cattleman on this side of the island, with more than twenty thousand head of cattle, thirty Spanish foremen, three dozen Indian peons and more than one hundred African slaves. Most of the plain from Santo Domingo to the foothills of Bahuruku is crowded already with cattle, sheep and sugar cane. It is hard to believe how much everything has changed. I count forty years since the first Castilla settlement on these parts, and it is amazing how the sugar cane sea of deep green has spread. Sugar cane tastes sweet enough, but it burns the land and feeds nothing but ships going to Castilla. Not even animals or birds does the sugar cane feed; no animal does it feed except for the plague rat that came over in their own ships. And that one not even the maja snake eats. The sugar feeds not even the men of the sugar boilers. At the refineries, the Negroes near the boilers are forced to wear muzzles so they cannot open their mouths to swallow even a bit of its product.

Silverio rides a yellow gelding I rented from the Abbot, who was pleased to see me off. "The work will do you good, Dieguillo," he said, although he warned me not to go near Oviedo's cattle ranch near San Juan de la Maguana. Of course, I intend doing no such thing, as my mission here is to work two weeks at carpentry on Solana's mill, while Silverio rides on to the Bahuruku. I am trusting with this delicate mission young Silverio, who is mostly a resourceful lad, precisely from the people of Guarionex. Interestingly, he worries not about the danger presented by the Governor's cuadrillas, but wonders if Enriquillo's warriors might not lynch him, which deed they have carried out at various times against suspected manso informers. "I can avoid the Castilla, Don Diego," he assures me. "But I fear the guaxeri of the Cacique."

I prepare for him tonight a note, waxed over and wrapped inside the sheath of his machete; the note will deliver him and be delivered to the baby boy. Meanwhile I will write not during my stay at Solana's sugar mill, but instead will hide my writing things away here with Francisco Pedro, whom nobody bothers, while I fulfill my obligation in that stiffling atmosphere. When I find myself at the Taíno camps, at our free places on the Bahuruku, where my people are still maintaining themselves, there I will write again.

One hundred fifteen. *Two weeks later, sugar mill story.*

Once again tonight at Francisco Pedro's bohío, I take up the pen. Two weeks exactly have passed and later this morning I will ride my white face mare to the old Camin River where it enters the plain. Word from Silverio already awaited me here, delivered two days ago by a mounted guaxeri of Enriquillo's. It indicated the place of my entrance to the free country.

I make only two quick notes before departure. One is how excited I am to be near the baby boy. The daring ride of his messenger, who was chased by two Spanish squads before slipping free, warms my heart.

The second note is this: At Salana's hacienda, which is on the foothills of this plain, I saw the remains of the irrigation canals used years ago by Bohekio's gardens. This dry plain, rich in soil but poor in water, required an intricate plan from that thoughtful cacique's forebearers, who turned out large quantities of yuca, yams, corn and beans.

I heard a foreman from Asturias berate an African man at the hacienda. "Negro estúpido!" he yelled, as the Negro led a wagon of water pulled by oxen. The trail was rough and the Negro, who led the oxen by way of a nose ring, kept tripping, jerking on the oxen's nose so that it bled. The foreman let fly the whip, three, four times, at the poor negro man's shoulders. Their activity was to transport a huge barrel of water, carried by oxcart to moisten the soil of the vegetable gardens. As the blows stopped, the Negro recovered his composure to lead the oxen, but then the wagon wheel itself became stuck as the road's edge collapsed. I was walking by with tow planks of wood keeping my head low. That's when I saw the old canal under the dry-cracked lode. It was the old irrigation canal my good Taíno brethren used forty years ago to water all of this beautiful plain, turning a dry valley, year by year, into mountains of food. Typical maguacokio, I thought, beating someone else in frustration when the solution to his problem is right under his feet!

One hundred sixteen. *A new day begins.*

Tired I am tonight, exhausted and agonized by my cramping leg, after a journey through iguana trails, down rivers and up buttes. But I am found, I say, and I write this in the bright night of a circle moon. I am here, I say. I am laying up in a hammock, in the yukaieke of the Cacique Guarocuya (my baby boy Enriquillo), surrounded by the constant din of the forest.

I saw him already; he was there at the water's edge to greet me with Doña Mencía, as always, at his side. They are so young and yet their manner so grave, so beautifully calm. I am entirely content to see them, to be here, to write these words—incredibly, wonderfully—by moonlight. Now the coquí, our tree frog, barks in his quick rasp and the whole forest chirps back. I note it happily. Near me, also on a hammock, young Silverio sleeps, breathing in tandem with the night.

Silverio helped guide me here. He came in the company of a young warrior from this camp, a tall thin man named Cao, after the black crow of our islands. He claims descendancy from Hatuey's people of the old Guahaba province, just north of here. I could see they were good friends already. In only three weeks with Enriquillo's men, young Silverio has lost the nervousness that has characterized him for me. I met the two by a huge ceiba tree that grows in a place of large boulders, where the river turns west and enters the plain. We rode upriver a while, then it got thick and they let their horses go.

I left the whiteface in a meadow. With the help of the guaxeris, I made a corral surrounding a heavy salt stone. The corral is closed off by the river on one end at the other by a thick brush and a post fence hidden behind trees. I expect she will be all right there. We then walked for six days, the going so rough at times, I wondered if we would criss-cross the Bahuruku's thirty leagues of length along the coast and twenty-five leagues of width inland before getting somewhere. We followed the river up rugged peaks and through brush so thick we had to crawl on hands and knees. Then, slowly we made our way down the valley called Cayobani to the shores of the big lake called Aybaguanex. Cao located his canoe, hidden in the brush, and we paddled off, trailing a line and a wide basket weighed down to scrape bottom, which caught about three dozen hand-sized xaiba crabs. The line caught one large fish I did not recognize, but which Cao said was good eating.

Enriquillo and Mencía waited at the waters' edge. It brought tears to my eyes to see them in white cotton garments surrounded by captains and guaxeri, and to hear the sweet words of our language, "Caraya tao, cacique Guaikán, welcome to our home."

It was late afternoon. We drank a pineapple drink, ate guayabas and small sweet plantains, but no hot food as there were yet another four hours to walk. It was this walk, brisk and totally uphill to a plateau, that crimped my leg and layed me out.

One hundred seventeen. *In the free Taíno territory.*

I now see part of their yukaieke, eight wide bohíos set back on the open plateau, silhouetted by moon shadows. I smell the smoke of the braziers, where fish and pig and crab are barbecueing, and I can hear the soft murmuring of guaxeris as they prepare the food and they greet and feed the out posted warriors coming in from their guard. Tomorrow I will see the place by sunlight, and the enchantment will, I am sure, dissipate. A war camp it is, after all. But now as I struggle with my tired eyes and fight the pain of my caymán-bitten leg, I feel with certainty the reason for my being alive. Thanks be it to the Yucahuguamá-Bagua-Maorocoti, first powers, Lord Spirit of the Yuca Beings, Spirit of the Sea, Male Spirit without Grandfathers of Woman Only Born; it is in you, the Three Combined Into One, who still breathe life into our Taíno nostrils; thanks be it to Itiba Coahubaba, Ancient Bleeding

Mother, Mother of Deminán, Leader of the Four Brothers, remembered creators of our Taíno world. Please be with us, all the greatnesses; thanks to all the cemís you have empowered, Xán-Xán, please be with us, yes, all, and thanks to you, yes, again,yes, and again and again, yes. Xán, Xán Katú, Xán Xán Katú.

One hundred eighteen. *Greeting by Enriquillo and Doña Mencía, council of captains.*

Three days have passed since I touched this pen, three days full of life I have spent with the men and women of this place. Now, on a clear day, I will make notes.

The morning after my last entry, I awoke with the sun already mid-sky. A boy watched over me as I opened my eyes. He peered to make certain I was awake, then ran to tell. I was up and stretching when Enriquillo and Doña Mencía walked up. He brought water in a bowl and she a white cloth. I washed and then we went to where they had food for me. Enriquillo was immediately busy with two men, and Doña Mencía indicated a meeting was starting that morning. As I ate, one by one, nine captains arrived. They all took a drink and sat around the fire.

I recognized none of them. Five were clearly of Taíno or Ciguayo stock, three were mixed Indian with Castillian, and one Indian mixed with African. They all dressed like Enriquillo: in greyish white cotton pants to just below the knee, no shirt, their corazas spread out at their sides. Corazas are suits and vests made by rows of thick, tightly woven chord. All nine captains carried sword and lance, three held crossbows and two were armed with archebus. One by one, they all bowed their heads to be touched by Enriquillo or Mencía before taking their seats.

I will tell first about the young cacique. Barely over thirty years old and already a fighting leader for fifteen years, Enriquillo has the old Taíno look, with a long, broken nose, long black hair, lean body with a broad chest and taut calves. Enriquillo is taller than most Indians. He wears wrapped leather sandals made of manatí hide and braids his hair in one lone strand down the center of his bare back. He too protects himself with coraza, and has two pages who carry extra swords for him. His eyes are stone black and deep, with a brightness in their gaze that touches the soul. He seldom smiles, never laughs, but speaks in a low tone, gentle but firm, a concentrated mindfulness I have seldom seen before in any of our people. It has been ten years or more since I saw the Enriquillo. Once was in the second year of his struggle, when I carried to him a message. He looked more then like the "guinea hen" he had been nicknamed after. His eyes scurried and didn't fix. He spoke to me then, our first time together in several years, with great distance, openly but tersely, even haughtily. He had the attitude of the free stallion toward the tamed donkey. The haughtiness is totally gone now. The eyes fix, intensely, and he is calm. All the captains hold him in great esteem and some revere him immensely. His two pages, thin young men, complain that he seldom sleeps but nightly leads them around his camp's perimeters and sometimes even out to other lookouts, weapons always at the ready. In the Indian Bahuruku, Enriquillo is gavilán (big hawk), the final judge. His word, trusted by all, often becomes law.

Doña Mencía is his reason for being, his open love, and his greatest ally. In our old saying, "the men are the jawbone; the women are the backbone." Thus with Doña Mencía, who takes care of everything. Never does Enriquillo's return find Doña Mencía asleep. This she would never allow, in her words: "He watches over all of us; I watch over him and what he does." Everything is ready always, because of her. She runs the whole food line, organizing harvests and food preparation at the camp and at far-off cunukus, where stashes of food are kept. Her stashes have saved many a cut-off Indian chased by Spanish cuadrillas, many a camp discovered and scattered via insufficient vigilance. Standing with her feet wide apart, legs straight, hand on a hip, usually with a baby or small child from one of her young women, the look of Doña Mencía penetrates. Regal is her demeanor as she points with her chin or lips for guaxeri to pick up or bring food, instructing messengers to other camps, crew leaders to their fields. She is a constant source of direction and information.

Doña Mencía wields a machete with total dexterity, and I was told yesterday by one captain, Romero, that she has wiped blood from it after combat. She wears pants, too, cut at the knee. A cloth wrapped around her torso covers her breasts. She likes a shawl, too, in her evening repose, when the elders talk and smoke. There is nothing extravagant about Doña Mencía, but she commands naturally, clearly of ni-Taíno line. In her face Doña Mencía is slightly round, rather like her grandmother, the well-loved cacica, Anacaona. She is well-rounded of breast and buttock, also, again, like the revered cacica of this old Xaraguá province, who was a most imposing woman.

The meeting of captains the morning of day before yesterday was little about my visit, as they are all active warriors with many responsibilities and important points to discuss. Enriquillo introduced me briefly. "An uncle I have in my camp, whom you now see," he said. "He is one of our caciques, who saved my father's life and my own, many years ago. Though he lives with the friars, as I once did, he is Taíno." He lit a small white pipe with tobacco and had me smoke first, a sign of respect, then rolled tobaccos were passed around to the captain and to Doña Mencía and other principal women, who sat in the second circle backing their men.

Done with his smoke, Enriquillo spoke to everyone. "All of you are my nephews, your children are my grand children," he said. "Always treat each other well and help each other." "Xán, Xán Katú," the captains returned, in agreement. The warrior captains, with the women of their families, then greeted Enriquillo and called him grandfather. Everybody brought presents, which Enriquillo promptly offered to the visitor: baskets of fruit and casabe, stacks of tobacco leaves, a good rope, a hammock, a cake of wax for light, a large clear conch full of live cocuyos, the firefly of our islands. These were all put at my feet, as guest of Enriquillo. Doña Mencía later bundled the gifts up in the hammock and had them carried here to my bohío across the clearing from her own. (The cocuyos, or fireflies, I let go a few each night in my bohío, where they cut back and forth, hunting mosquitoes by the hundreds.)

Of the captains, three are from other main camps and six run separate cunukus or garden camps. There are four main camp areas, spread out in the Bahuruku over several days' walking distance. They also have hidden gardens and fruit orchards. Warrior groups on raids emerge from the thick and rugged mountains in places far from the home camps. Usually, a major action is preceded by the taking of several horses, somewhere in the vicinity, which are used in raiding haciendas or towns, holding up travelers and particularly in helping outrun Spanish squads, or cuadrillas, which take their toll.

One hundred nineteen. *Younger captains' proposals for raids to procure arms and munitions and tools.*

The main purpose of that morning's meeting was a request by three of the captains to carry out expeditions near San Juan la Maguana. They spoke in favor of a "lightning" raid on a ranch in the nearby foothills, where they could apprehend ax handles, iron hoes and saws for planking wood; they spoke of a place where they could gain more powder and shot for their arquebus, maybe even a small piece of artillery.

The two younger captains spoke directly and stood together firmly, yet their manner was quiet and deferential to the cacique, who did not respond at first, but invited more reasoning from the raid's proponents and the opinion of the others. As the captains discussed the proposals, groups of guaxeri walked by and topped briefly, but this was clearly a captains' meeting and no one offered them seats, so they went about their business.

The wizened captain named Tamayo, who commands four dozen men, reasoned for the younger captains. "My cacique," he said, "everything that makes us stronger in our fighting, I favor always, so my opinion will be obvious. In full sincerity, hear it then for what it is.

"The Castilla press on us with more and more frequency. There is talk of a big attack, from several sides, as they have done before. We need better fortifications, gunpowder and, I think, a piece or two of artillery, for which they would respect us that much more."

This Tamayo is a tough fighter who has led most of the rebels' excursions into the plain and all recent raids on ranches. The Castilla fear him most of all, as he gives no quarter and expects none. Recently, after a skirmish, he captured two Spanish soldiers. One, an older man, cut the gut of Tamayo's lieutenant, named Antonín, who later died from the wound. Tamayo ordered his men to hang the Spaniard.

The other prisoner was a sixteen-year-old Castilla lad. Tamayo pitied him and spared his life, but he ordered the boy's sword hand cut off. When the young man offered his left hand, the warrior who captured him complained, as he had seen him fight with the right. The young man begged and cried. "Don't petition us, you lucky boy," Tamayo told him."You are fortunate that, because of your age, I don't hang you."

Of the other captains, one more sided with Tamayo,while the rest nodded to Enriquillo to speak their mind for them. The young cacique stood to speak. He took in his hand a black, caoba-wood cane. These will be his exact words, translated into the Castillian: "Tamayo, my captain," Enriquillo began; the use of a personal name indicated some tension within him. "I am very happy that you are with us. You are a strong warrior and a defender of our people, and I greet you. Remember our history in these mountains, which we entered separately and yet on similar grounds. I am very happy now that it has been two years since we have joined forces, as I have sought that for many years previous to our mutual pact, when you agreed to come under my cacicazgo.

"Now, hear my words. In all my time in the Bahuruku, since the year of 1519, I have been the advocate of our quiet withdrawal, fighting as we had to, but with constant vigilance. This, as you know, has been my strategy. Defensive vigilance, survival and, always, retaliation. Not attack, but retaliation. Thus, my young men and women are trained early to run, fight, plant and harvest, recognize the herbs, fish and catch birds and pigs and iguanas, all on their own. Thus, many times the Castilla have tired of hunting us, as we seem to them to live on air and feed on tree leaves and, as they say, on lizards. As they tire of hunting us and will run out of food and wind, I have sometimes punished them, and hard. Thus, the time of the seventy we trapped in a cave, before you came to us; thus, the time I punished the

Castilla captain, San Miguel, for his malignant attack on our camp in 1528, when I followed him home and burned his ranch.

"Open wide your ears, my nephews, only twice in thirteen years have they caught us unawares, and those only because of traitors, because careless warriors led them to us, giddy with the triumph of raids on the coast. Let me say, yes, I have gone out to take them on their own grounds, to teach them that their own homes will not be spared. But I seek not from them, I do not descend the mountain just to irritate them, just to steal from them.

"Since those first days, when we defeated Valenzuela and his men with sticks and short knives, killing two of his dreaded foremen, we have sought to disengage, to build our own small ranches in the hidden valleys of the Bahuruku. Never have the Castilla wished to fight us on our grounds and as we have left the forefront of their memories, passing from their eyes unnoticed like soft winds, for years at a time, they forgot us and so we built our lives.

"Nephews, continue to widen your ears.

"I am not saying they do not want us. They want us very much. Ten hard captains they have sent against us. Each and every one has been routed by our warriors. We have fought like cats gone to the wild, which is what we are, cats and dogs gone to the manigua; and, yes, hawks, hawks who have grown claws and teeth and even talons; we have made carapaces for ourselves, see, like the turtle, and even the thunder stick we now use. I will fight to the death and I sleep not my nights in my vigilance, but I will remind you, it is our quiet watch and, of course, our willingness to fight when pressed that keeps our peoples here alive. Raids only scare the Castilla into action, into wishing to murder us and press our families into slavery.

"Now, I repeat my observation. As we go about, quietly constructing our camps, we have what we need, and they do forget us for a time. But, as some of our captains continue to raid and kill, so do Castilla angers grow. They take up pesos and set squads actively against us. I remind you captains of this reality, and ask you to temper your excursions. Think not just of your strongest arms, think of your weak ones, your children and old people, your women caring for your homes.

"You hang much with warriors, Tamayo. Spend more time with the women and the children, the old men. Listen to them. Let them tell you their fears, and their hopes."

The captains listened carefully and even Tamayo nodded. After a time all looked to Romero, Enriquillo's brother-cousin on his mother's side, a genial man who is their main "spider" or "web maker" man. It was Romero who brought Tamayo into Enriquillo's circle. He is short and stocky, with a face that cannot stop smiling.

"I love you all," he began to speak. "Taíno-ti, my fellow cousins. The words have been good and should not wound. Love each other, captains. Respect our Cacique, who has guided our survival these many years. We have never defeated the Castilla but our mountains have. Their own thirst and exhaustion, their fear of our thick brush and darkened forests, these are the things that have defeated them. They cannot fight us if they must hunt us among these peaks. But they are many, many. And if enough of them came for us, they would find us, and they would kill us all.

"Relatives, where is our Ciguayo comrade? Where our great brother, Hernandillo, the One-eye, whose great singing we enjoyed so much?"

Romero never quit smiling though he shed a long tear before squatting back on his flat duho. The two captains he mentioned had been killed in recent raids. I had met the Ciguayo, that other time, and was touched to hear of his demise. The One-eye, Hernandillo, I knew only by reputation.

Next, I was called on by Enriquillo to express my thoughts. I did this by informing the captains of my message from the good friar that, indeed, if peace could not be struck, the King himself would order total war on the Bahuruku. The words of the young cacique had warmed me, confirming the veracity of my own instinct for preserving his hard-won jurisdiction. I told the captains they had good friends among the friars and that the important men of Santo Domingo were tired of the war, so it was possible they could make a peace while keeping their freedom. "Some want to hang and burn you all; others would bring an end to the hostility and let you settle once and for all," I told the group. The rest of my words I gave to Tamayo: "The cut-off hand of the young man has been much seen in Santo Domingo, and has stirred up hornets," I said to him. "But, since there was cruelty in the kindness and kindness in the cruelty, it has them confused."

Tamayo, whose face carries three large scars and one ear cut by half, smiled uneasily at my words, and Enrique invited them to smoke again, closing the circle with these words: "I seek the trail that allows us our survival. War is not the trail itself, but only the horse we have been forced to ride. My captains, I am still on that horse, but I prefer to walk. Our people have been walkers, and we will live by walking, even if, for now, we must ride the horse."

January 30, 1533

One hundred twenty. *Touring the camp, the young men.*

We eat well. There is plenty of corn, peppers and tomatoes, lots of casabe and many fruits, always a bit of meat. The yuca plots, I have learned, must be protected by young boys against packs of wild pigs, which have multiplied all over the island. A good job for the boys, they learn to shoot a straight arrow and bring in extra meat.

Enriquillo has liked my words. Yesterday again, as I was writing, he honored me with a visit. "Come uncle," he said, "let's walk."

I quickly finished my last entry, where I write about Tamayo's request. Enrique asked what I was writing so intently.

"I write the early stories of Columbus," I said. "And also some of what happens as I go every day."

He was leading me down a thin trail though a dark woods and suddenly stopped.

"Do you write about me?" he asked.

"I have," I admitted. Her cleared his throat and looked away, giving a moment of thought to this information, then continued walking.

We came up on a clearing where groups of boys were jousting. Enriquillo hurried. "Come see the boys," he said.

Some thirty boys and young men practiced with various arms in the open area, under instructions of two older guaxeri. The boys used sticks as lances and swords, pairing off in twos and fours, sparring and thrusting, feigning and swinging at each other with more than enough ferocity. As we watched, one boy caught a stick behind the ear and nearly passed out. "Take a rest," Enriquillo told them. Then he had a lesson for them, showing the boys how to take out a man on horseback bearing down on them. He asked me to put a young boy on my shoulders and charge him as he stood his ground with a long stick.

"Squat down into a ball, and as the horse approaches, spring up. This will make him rear back," he said. "Then jab at the face, first of the horse, then of the rider. One-two, one-two. If you face him and fight him, you are faster on your feet by jumping to and fro, jabbing, jabbing with your lance. But never turn your back on a horse unless you can make the bush. In open savannah, he will ride you down and lance your back."

The boys listened attentively. Enriquillo is incredibly agile, rolling on his back to land on his feet, back and forth as he demonstrated in front of me, jabbing his stick nearly into my face, but never touching me. The demonstration over, he had the boys sit. He queried them on their dexterity with the crossbow, the spear throw and their force and accuracy with rocks. "Always be alert," he reminded them. "Walk our trails, go on watch to the coast. Learn to see and smell the Castilla and his manso Indians and Negroes. Spot his track and sign. Never trust that Castilla man. He feigns friendship, then captures you."

The young men were quite enraptured. Enrique described torture for them. The yanking of the fingernails, the slow burning of the feet and underarms—what the Castilla will do to make them tell where the camps are located. "Can you resist such a torture? Would such a pain make you betray your grandparents?"

The young men all agreed they would die before betraying anything. "Live it then, boys," Enriquillo said. "Be alert, but don't go look for trouble. Defend us. Help your mothers and grandmothers. Always help the women. Listen to these old guaxeri who would teach you, and never forget you are Taíno."

What I loved were the faces on the boys, who smiled so hopefully, so lovingly, even as they trained for war. They are still Taíno, young men of noble sentiment, who can be aroused by the love of grandparents. And I could see Enriquillo's strength, its origin in that same feeling, that warm, loving attitude that was foundation and center pole of our Taíno hearts, our strength in spirit. My people have been so beautiful and their reduction so brutal. What joy in my heart to be in this camp! What joy to see our survival yet in the light of our boy-men's black, deep eyes. Now I feel we are not dead men walking, like so many of our people encomendados to the haciendas; no, not here in the Bahuruku where the Taíno still walks alive and free.

Enriquillo asked me to tell them a story. Of course, I wanted to back him up with his people, to have my own words serve the cause of his dignity and his survival. I thought of Caonabó and I thought of Guarionex, two of the great caciques of the early conquest, who they were, what they tried to do, how they fell. I settled on the story of Caonabó, to illustrate both our valor and the deviousness of the Castilla, whom we then called "the covered men.

One hundred twenty one. *The Capture of Caonabó.*

Not far from where I write, just down the mountains some five leagues, near where that so-called savant, Gonzalo Fernández de Oviedo, now owns a large sugar estate with more than sixty encomendado Indians and many more enslaved negroes, Caonabó, our first warrior against the Castilla, was deviously captured. He was taken in his own village by that captain of the Admiral, Alonso de Hojeda, of whom I have written in earlier pages, when telling of his attack on the Carib canoe, as we sailed on the return voyage from Castilla lands. It was precisely that Hojeda, a great devotee of the Virgen María, who drew first blood on both Carib and Taíno. And it was he who captured Caonabó.

On this island, the first cut Hojeda made was in a village of Guarionex's territory, where the noses of two caciques he himself left hanging on their faces like the split breast of our mountain dove. Not only that, then he ordered their ears cut, top half sliced completely off, again on both caciques. These wounds I witnessed myself later, and so I told the Taíno boy-men, whose eyes focused beyond my person to imagine the scene.

What I told them happened in 1494, even as the town of Isabela was constructed. Remember in my story how we landed at Navidad, the first fort left here by the Admiral. We found all Castilla here dead, punished by Caonabó, cacique of Maguana, of whom I was sure some of the young men were descended.

The young people's faces were a wonder of curiosity and I pledged to instruct them on their history as much as my memory allowed. Then, to my bigger joy, four of the young men, two of the young women, two of the older women and three of the captains can read. They approached me last night and asked me to write it, so they could read it to the others after I am gone.

These stories in my memory, of Caonabó and the Admiral and the first season of the Castilla, I told them over several days and nights, starting with the young men in the clearing and continuing later in the evenings, the circle growing each night.

Today my mind and imagination are strong and I feel charged in my heart with my people's mandate to do this for them, their spoken request that makes me shiver in my determination to write these truths, as I pledged before, so that no matter what is forgotten, our inheritors, our people of the stones, like my young men and women of the xiba mountain, will remember.

March 6, 1533

One hundred and twenty two. *Lessons for the boy-warriors.*

The young people knew parts of the history after the fall of Xaraguá to Ovando, in the year of 1503, more or less. They knew a lot about Ovando— Nicolás de Ovando, not to be confused with Gonzalo Fernández de Oviedo, with whom I quarreled on New Year's Eve. Ovando was a knight commander and a priest who came to the islands with 2500 men. A cold and mean man, he conducted the worst of all massacres, the one against our Queen of Peace, Anacaona. Many of Enriquillo's people are from her line, so the young people knew more of their Xaragua region, here in the southwestern side of the island and of the fate of their revered cacica grandmother.

But of Caonabó, who was her first husband, of Guacanagari, of Guarionex, of the Ciguayo Mayobanex and the other old caciques from other parts of the island, they knew virtually nothing. Of our sister island, Borikén, they knew nothing. Of the largest of our islands, Cuba, they knew very little, only the story of Hatuey. Of the Admiral and the first conquistadors, two boys still believed they had been spirits (my own lie persisting these many years).

When I goaded the group for their ideas, nearly all the young men believed we had started the first wars, that we, Taínos, had attacked the Castilla first. About Caonabó, one said he had heard that he had desired to eat Castilla meat. This bothered me very much, even though the boys laughed heartily at the image of Caonabó chewing on a Castilla thigh.

Caonabó, I told them, whose name means "lord of the gold," was a very special man, a Ciguayo, part Kwaib, yes, from Guadalupe, but one who had come to Bohío as a boy and settled with three older brothers in the land of the Ciguayo cacique, Mayobanex. No, Caonabó, as I see it clearly, was a great man of our people, a defender who saw quickly, much before I did, the darkness hidden in the covered people's desperation for the shiny light of gold. "It was really about the gold," I told the boys. "This is what commands their thoughts."

And I told them, too. "Xán, Xán, yes. Believe, yes, that your ancestors fought over the women in our families, our mothers and grandmothers, sisters and wives and daughters. But it was not jealousy. We were not that way. It was because of what I saw with my own eyes, how they raped our mothers and sisters, and butchered the grandmothers."

I could see the boys all stir, realizing what they had not yet learned.

This Española, our Bohío, this Quisqueya island was a central point of the Taíno people, I told the boys. Here our people came to parley, here is where the great caciques talked and sang for days. They came from

Borikén, from Cuba, from Xamayca, even from my little islands farther to the east. Seamen chiefs of Taíno, the ni-Taíno and their relations met and knew each other and shared the knowledge of their ancestors. Here in the great Bohío, our great and first house is found, in the caves at Cacibajagua and at Amayauna, where the ancestors, good and bad, guided by the wish to bathe in the streams, emerged from the earth, from the long tunnel of our mother.

We Taíno were a large people, with many learned ones among us, I told the boys. Our people knew how to do everything we needed to live well and happy. We were on these big islands a long time and knew our places of respect and prayer, where we gathered to remember our ancient stories. The Cuban caciques were the best traders, in ropes and in good conch; in Borikén, they held the best ball games; in Xamayca, where many Macorixe settled before our Taíno, they knew archery and there was interest about the bow and arrow among our other Taínos. "Remember that your peoples had possession of these lands at one time. Just that will make your thinking stronger," I told them.

To the east, I told the boys, past Boriken, the Kwaib raiders still inhabit the little islands. Before Castilla arrived, only Kwaib raiders came to our shores to bother us. Truly, they were fearsome, but they hurt us not that much, compared to what would come. Raids came and went for a very long time, generations upon generations and yet our Taíno multiplied and grew stronger. And of the Kwaib, many also settled on the northwest coast of this island. These were the Ciguayo territories, which were a kind of defense and entry point for Kwaib people that tired of raiding and intermarried with our people, especially through Guarionex, who formed the most clever alliances.

The young boy who became Caonabó was one of those and he proved an able defender against Kwaib raids from other islands. In time he became well known not only among the Ciguayos, who were mixed descendants of Taíno and Kwaib, but also among the pure line Taíno caciques, like Guarionex, Guacanagari (who greeted Columbus) and Bohekio, the brother of Anacaona.

Caonabó was fearless and feared. For years he warred on all sides, yes on many sides, as he not only defended our island shores against Kwaib raids, but as often he disputed over land with the villages of Guarionex and Guanacagari, giving battle fiercely against them and raising the level of turbulence.

Here in Bohío, when I arrived with the Admiral, there were five chieftain ship lines, each with many village and village-cluster chiefs. They knew each other, spoke a common language, and shared many common memories of the clear lineages of careful intermarriages. On the other side were the Cuban cacicazgos, Taíno as well, and their simpler, older relatives, the Çiboney. In Borikén, under one main Cacique, Agüeybana, they were the people of the ball game, of which I remember tales, even in my home islands, of how in Borikén, large valleys were covered with ball courts, where caciques in grand ways hosted dozens of competing villages and clans and some of my own people had gone, in years past, to the Borikén ball games. Then we had people of our own talk in Xamayca, too, and they were quite belligerent, even against each other. And of course there were the smaller outer islands like my own Guanahani and we were the same people. But the origin island was always this one of Bohío, our home, where the origin caves remain, where our Taíno gold veins were born.

The old caciques of that time, Bohekio and Guarionex, together held ceremonies and put through many doings for their peoples. These oldest areitos of the Taínos, kept among the grandmother-guided lineal-breeding sachem families and among the behikes and some of the learned guaxeri of the clans of the ni-taíno lines, were the laws by which our villages were sustained, so that fighting could be kept to a minimum and that wars would never destroy the mother lines. There was mutual recognition among all the main caciques, both Taíno and Ciguayo, including Guacanagari, Bohekio, Guarionex, Caonabó, Cotubanamax and Mayobanex. They had respect for each other's place in our island world, and it was balanced.

Yes, of course, sometimes they fought, but these were men who considered it a victory when the big shark can be deviated while the canoe paddles away without notice. So a fight might be decided most of the time by one combat. A good whack might sprawl a man on the ground, and the old men would throw up their hands and call a halt to the fight, call for the peace talks. Inevitably, despite their mutual irritations, the guaxeri groups peace-pacted. This was a common custom, to call in the old caciques who valued harmonious relations. Of these, Guarionex was the grand old man. Others, like Bohekio, whose line was quite strong, had the prestige, but not the art. Guacanagari, first friend and ally of the Admiral, was much younger. He was gifted with the most clear genealogies and was about equally considered with Bohekio, but Guacanagari, the bosom friend of Columbus, was a mere child compared to Guarionex.

I told the boys that the two prominent caciques here in Bohio were Guarionex, who was the cacique of peace, using the laws of reason about safety and sustenance of the yukaieke, and using also the art of the gift, in provoking peace offerings; and Caonabó, who was decisive in war and excelled at leading warriors in fighting.

What made Caonabó and his brothers fierce was training by a Kwaib father who prepared them for war, even as they learned to walk. From two years of age, the boy was made to run, endure hits, eat raw fish and meat, made to swim long distances and always he was urged to fight fiercely. Caonabó endured the Kwaib boyhood discipline. But he was named and taught also by his mother, a woman of Taíno line through Guarionex, and she, before her death, saw him named Caonabó, Lord of the Living Ancestor, the Place of Gold.

Guarionex was a holder of the most ancient areitos of our people, and through them, he became a great strategic thinker. The peace-pact areitos were central to his knowledge. Guarionex's power, even more than that of Bohekio and Guacanagari, was based on the refinement of the areitos he and his male and female societies could sing. Guarionex was a gifted singer, whose sweet, lilting song could melt any Indian heart.

Guarionex's areitos came from the second cycle of Deminán stories, in the original tellings, which Guarionex's people remembered in disciplined fashion. At the time that the Admiral reached our shores, Guarionex was fashioning the system of alliances that were to ensure the Taíno people's life in the whole of Bohío. The success of his life's vision, he professed in his areitos, could guarantee generations of peaceful existence for our island peoples. As his vision of prolonged survival required not only strategy, but also the best defenses against the raiding Kwaib that he could secure, Guarionex had engaged Caonabó, channeling the fierceness of the warrior chief to protect the Taíno future.

It happened some ten years before the coming of the Castilla. Bohecio's sister Anacaona inherited the caciquedom of Maguana, with its main village in the valley of the gold, Bonao, ancestral entrail of our island. Gold, as you must know (but the young people didn't quite know it, I realized), is the residue of the spirits of our ancestors. It is not to be disturbed. In those days, Bonao was a territory guarded and respected as a most spiritual place.

Guarionex planned it all. It culminated his vision and life's work. He offered Anacaona, the "flower of the gold," to the young Caonabó ("keeper of the gold") in marriage. Anacaona, who was a trained peace queen, royal in all her lines as her brother Bohekio, gifted in the poetry that calms hearts and leader in the carving and spinning arts, was a lovely woman, and would make Taíno out of the Ciguayo's children. Thus it was done, a marriage peace pact. Thus Caonabó was brought in to the sister caciquedoms by the old peace-pact maker, Guarionex, who taught him the areitos of the ancestors and assigned him to guard with his fierceness the sanctity of the Bonao. All this, I told the boys, is part of your old history, of the time before their coming, when our world could be understood in our own minds, when the currents of our own migrations, settlements, wars and alliances had their own dictates and interpretations. The Taíno were a people who thought of peace, and among them, of the generation of caciques when the Castilla arrived, Guarionex sought peace the most. He was a true Taíno. And among them was the fighting defender, too, Caonabó the Ciguayo, who supported their peaceful, respectful ways with his truculent character and his iron wood arm.

One hundred twenty three. *The Castilla dance for gold.*

Caonabó acted quickly, I told them, when the Castilla imposed their presence on our people. It was he who first said, enough, when the forty covered men left behind here from the wreck of the Santa María took to killing and raping and stealing. Not one of our women did a Castillian ask for in marriage, not one mother or father was consulted, no one's recognition sought, but by rape their relations began. Not once, after months, did any honoring of the Taíno families take place. So it was that Caonabó, as I have written before, our first defender, told his men to arm for battle and led the parties that hunted down and killed all the left-behinds.

The boys hollered in delight and I waited for them to quiet down.

But the Admiral returned, and I with him, and of Castilla came many more, I continued. They settled a town, Isabela, the first one. And immediately the clamor among the Castilla was for the death of Caonabó. Occupied with pressing matters, the Admiral did not hurry to vengeance. I helped in this by reminding him of the many misdeeds against our people committed by the left-behinds, and I believe my words helped tame the Admiral's potential for revenge, which, in any case, was overshadowed by his organizing of the first gold mining expedition. For this purpose, he ordered Hojeda and others of his trusted captains out into the territories, admonishing them with strict instructions (as he had left with the forty of Navidad) to"treat the natives well," taking nothing but food and gold and giving many presents.

Thus, in January of 1494, I was sent by the Admiral to translate for Hojeda as he crossed over the coastal cordillera and south into the Magua plain, later called the Royal Plain. This territory of Guarionex was famous for its leagues and leagues of cunuku gardens. With Hojeda, we came to the foothills of the sierra of Cibao, on the edge of Caonabó's territory of Maguana. There, reverently, shyly, our own people pointed out gold dust and gold nuggets to the Castilla in the rocky crevices of rivers.

This is where for the first time I saw the Castilla dance for the gold. And, yes, dance they did, laughing and splashing each other and hopping around, screeching like parrots and several even linking arms on shoulders and hopping together in what they call a "jota," a dance of King Ferdinand's country, which looked to many of us Taíno then something like our own areito and confused us that maybe a thanksgiving was offered. And it was, but it was not a thanksgiving for the gold, it was giving thanks for finding the gold, for being led to the gold, that they meant to take out of there and trade for other things, it was not our caona but their "oro," that could transform their life. That was why they danced and sang.

Even this behavior on their part no longer surprised me, I said to the boys.

I remember the report from Hojeda to Columbus at Isabela days later. The hidalgos present did not quite dance, but paced and spoke in high glee, and joyfully a column was organized, commanded by the Admiral himself, which would take formal possession of the gold streams and build a fort. This was truly the beginning of the end, I feel now, for by this action was announced the taking of all that is precious to us. I must confess, too, at that time, I understood enough of the covered men's passion for the yellow metal—the vibrating of our ancient souls, our people said, could be felt in the streams and places of gold—that I accepted the Admiral's decisions as inevitable and questioned them not.

I remember the cinching of horses and porters, the dressing of the soldiers, banners unfurled, the Admiral and troops anointed to the field of battle by Father Buil, armor on all shoulders and chests. But there was no war that time, only the long, fatiguing march through thin trails in the heat of our Caribbean month of first rains. Coming fully into the villages of the Magua, the Admiral had lombards fired and scrolled pronouncements read in Latin, and all our people were once more astounded by the covered men and offered them great quantities of food, which they hardly touched at first, and helped them cross rivers and carried their packs and even sang for them. Thus a fort called Santo Tomás was built, beginning on March 15, 1494, and some twenty of the best miners, guarded by a squadron of more than thirty soldiers with arquebuses, were left behind to commence mining operations, under Captain Pedro Margaritte, whose report I later heard.

Twelve suns passed, and I returned with the Admiral to Isabela to witness, incredibly, the appearance of a little town with more than a hundred houses and bohíos for over a thousand Castilla and several hundred Indians. Only twelve suns, and I was horrified to witness the creation of a little piece of Seville or Barcelona or any Castilla town, without the cathedral yet, but with cows and pigs and men living with each other inside houses. With slop all over the place and the men stinking so violently, the new town was already pestilent.

There was insult and accusation in the air. Those Castilla men who were not sick with fevers and vomit or famine were in active opposition to the Admiral. These included the priest, Buil, and most of the so-called nobility, who resented the forced labor imposed by the Admiral on all able-bodied men, regardless of nobility or rank. Father Buil, whose shouts and insults against the Admiral I heard again and again, was the leader of the disrespect. Don Chirstopherens was perturbed and agitated by all this; only by his invocation against mutiny and rebellion and his imposition of lashings for the mildest insubordination was his command maintained.

One hundred twenty four. *Caonabó serves notice on Fuerte Tomás.*

Cacique Caonabó, aware that the covered men were walking his territory again, requested to know if they were accompanied by women this time. Informed that they were men alone, he inquired as to their treatment of the local people, which, at first, was not abusive. (Pedro Margarite was one of those few Castilla that were touched by the message in our natural kindness and was adamant that his men not impose upon our people.)

For a few days, Caonabó watched as the covered men built the fort. Then, on the fourth day, a crew of miners went to the richest river and began to extract gold. This the cacique found intriguing, as the very activity was meaningful and sacred to our people.

Remember, I told the gathered group, the caona for us was the bright light of the sun made matter through us, the humans; remember what the old people said, in those places, even without cohoba, you can feel the emanations of the earth; there, the breath of our ancestors mixes with ours. Our ancestors stayed with us and would not be dissipated if the places were prayed over and often resin-smoked.

I must note my surprise to see how many of the young people awakened to my words. Even Enriquillo, who was after all educated by priests, grew up at a distance from that knowledge. Thus, over the past few days that I have been talking now, the group has grown, including even more and more young women.

I have told them a teaching of our old behikes who believed that the best of ancestor spirits rested and were reflected in the gold. Blessed with much light in life, these "good minded ones," these most Taíno of our people, do not fully depart the earth at death, but deposit their spirit in the gold, adding ever so slightly to its creation in the rocky crevices of brooks, there to keep cool and to be gathered and fashioned to our likeness and to reflect our ancestors in the light of the areito fire at all-night ceremonies. We go to the sun when we die, the old people said—the spirit that is in us in death travels to the bright yellow father of the cloudless sky. As our flesh dries in the wind, our spirit is released and returns to the sun. Thus the shiny metal was respected and loved and what was made of it—masks and chest (heart) pieces and belts and ankle braces—all had a purpose and a connection. The gathering of gold was reserved for the most serious of ni-Taíno among our people, and always they abstained from sexual relations twenty days before going to gather it.

The gold taking bothered Caonabó enough, but then on the seventh day, a walking group of five miners came upon two of our girls bathing and captured them, making use of them repeatedly and with desperation. This Caonabó was told by one of the girls who could do so, for the other one was sick with vomit almost immediately and later bled from her insides and died. Caonabó gathered warriors and descended on the miners, demanding that they leave and threatening to burn the fort and kill everyone. Margarite sent out three men who half-ran to Isabela and were pushed around by the warriors but were sent back unharmed.

Thus started the second war between Castilla and our people, just as the Admiral prepared to sail on to Cuba. Those were indeed dark days; dozens and dozens died. Everyone complained to Columbus: "Where is the gold that was like rocks on the beaches?" Father Buil taunted him: "Where are the friendly native servants that will do all our bidding?"

The Admiral wanted to escape the tumult. He was a man of the ocean and thrived in long silences. The future of his enterprise, he felt, lay in Cuba, which he intended to prove a mainland, the outreaches of oriental empires. Discovery of a mainland on this second and misbegotten voyage would indeed make the trip worthwhile, at once achieving hegemony of the promising mainlands and rekindling support for his explorations. Thus, the Admiral entrusted Hojeda and Captain Margarite with orders to pacify the island, organize for a war of conquest, and warn our people, using terror first of all. While he did that, I must admit, I happily loaded his three new caravels.

That was the time I thought I would go home. What was happening in Española mattered little to me at that moment; I was only a thirteen-year-old, and I was going home. War was next; I knew it. Caonabó would be attacked, Caonabó, whom I feared as much then as I have come to respect and love his memory. Truthfully, I wanted to miss it; I wanted to go home. At that time, my fervent anxiety was to return to my home island of Guanahani to see my kinsmen, my mother, be again in my bohío.

I remember Hojeda organizing three hundred infantry and thirty mounted Castilla and twenty-eight mastiffs and eight hundred men of Guacanagari. Guacanagari always allied with the Admiral. Hojeda lined up the troops and marched them, ran them in phalanges and squared them into squadrons. "Do you know what phalanges are?" I asked the growing group of youngsters and adults. A phalange is the pointed attack formation of the Castilla, also called the "wedge." From Hojeda it was I first heard those terms, as he was organizing the Castillas for war. He requested me from the Admiral, as translator, but was refused. Thus, busy with preparations for sailing, I was happily spared the bloody campaign of requerimiento, a conquest by announcement and massacre, which, after all required little interpreting.

"Understand," I told the circle of young people, and the many guaxeri and captains who had joined in, "I have lived in this Española island longer than your cacique has years, but I am not from here. I had my home on the Guanahani, one of the cays. I was a fisherman with my father and uncles when Columbus took me." (Here I fibbed, to simplify the story.)

"Did you ever return home?" a young man asked, impolitely.

"No, I never did arrive at my bohío, not ever again," I said.

(Maybe now, in the passage to Spain of some ship, by paying a captain plenty, I could go to my old island. I care not to. No one is there anymore. All my own people were hunted down for slaves, sold into encomiendas, a few here, most in San Juan Bautista or in Cuba. No one lives anymore in my old island or my old village; all is empty.)

I had not finished my tale that first afternoon before the boys were needed in other activities. I was thanked by them formally and made to promise to continue my story during the evenings, for which Enriquillo offered his bohío. Here and there, over these past weeks, I have responded to requests for my interpretation of events and, in this vein, I find the words to write it down.

One hundred twenty five. *Blood not spilled, then a chopped hand.*

Thus it continues.

Armed groups went out against Caonabó. But even Captain Hojeda, who hunted and killed well, could locate him not, neither in ambush nor in frontal assault. Nevertheless, Hojeda moved his troops around the country, looking for the first incident, as the "pacification" had begun.

On the Vega, Hojeda encountered Indian humor, which he rewarded with blood. Two Castillas had requested rides across a river on Indian shoulders, trusting their clothes to porters. Halfway in the river, they were dumped by their young carriers and left naked. Watching the naked casabe-butts swim and hop to the other side delighted the young Taíno men, and for days the village laughed itself to sleep with the vision of the hairy Castilla enjoying a river bath.

Hojeda stormed the village and took two minor caciques. This is where the noses were slit down the middle and the ears of the two caciques were sliced in half, a deed of which I was informed by Indian runners within a day of its occurrence. Oh, the blood, one said in my ear, and scurried off. Other Castilla arrived on their heels with caciques tied about the neck and pulled, the same way they pull now the Negroes coming off the African ships. The Admiral glumly studied two of these caciques and one of their guaxeri and ordered: "Decapitate them. In two days."

But we were ready with our voyage to Cuba, and I had not the need to look. In my mind every day and night I hugged my mother and lay in my hammock, hearing her songs. Many relatives of the doomed who pleaded came to beg the Guamiquina, as they called the Admiral. "Please, don't kill our fathers, please don't kill my cacique."

They spoke in my ear, too, and the night before the execution, as the Admiral readied for bed, I brought him fruit. "The people here would cooperate more if their women were not violated and the cruelties could stop," I told him.

"The men are sentenced, Dieguillo."

"Consider the sentence, my admiral. Noses have been split for the mere dumping of a pompous ass." I knew the Admiral enough to intuit he did not like the dumped hidalgo and I got the slightest smile out of him, but he answered: "I can not underestimate the element of respect. An Indian must not challenge the dignity of an hidalgo."

"Even so, my señor, consider the balance. A well-deserved bath against two with slit noses and ears. Their warriors, even now, want to make peace. They want no war with you. They fear, they even love, you."

Finally, he released the two men, after all their sub-caciques and ni-Taínos pledged perpetual tribute to his jurisdiction.

Those days, we were ready to sail, but we went nowhere as the winds proved contrary. The Admiral ordained a round of masses. These were about finished and the prevailing winds shifted in our favor. At that time a "thief" was caught with great excitement. A young Taíno man had stolen a cutlass. He was brought in tied by the hands. The Admiral, impatient to go, was petitioned to grant the maximum sentence against the thief, that is, the chopping off of his hand.

I remember the young boy. He was my same age. They tied him to a post at the docks. "Why do they do this?" he asked me as I brought on board the last of the fresh casabe torts. "I took the blade only to cut a few vines. Before, they took my pendant, and this man whose big knife I took even gave me a name. Why can't they just let me go?"

I wondered what response to give him when I heard the Admiral. "Dieguillo, get away!" he shouted. "Leave the thief alone."

The Admiral of the Ocean Sea was busy with instructions for everyone. There were ships to be dispatched for Spain, final instructions to his war captains ("Reduce all resistance to the King's dominion"), instructions on what to build and what crops to put in. The boy sat in the sun and cried, knowing what his punishment would be. "We are not a thieving people," he said a few times. "Like all my people, a simple reed I will respect."

The ax came down as we pulled away, the Admiral witnessing it from the poop deck. I meant to miss the moment, working below deck and burying my gaze for minutes at a time. It was fate itself that forced me to look out a small hole, precisely to see the arching blade and hear it hit, the boy crying like a caught sea gull as tears popped into my eyes to join his running blood.

One hundred twenty six. *Discussions in the evening.*

"What makes them that mean?" It was Enriquillo speaking. "So many things like that they have done to our people."

This meeting was during an evening at the cacique's bohío. For three straight nights I had told stories, many more even than I can write. Most of the captains, including Tamayo, and many guaxeri come to listen. Cao, my first guide of the trip, was there and, I noticed, he was seated behind Tamayo. I spoke of the chopped hand because of Tamayo, to help put him at ease with my words over his recent deed. I want to be closer to this warrior captain. It is important that Tamayo accept Enriquillo's orders to stop raiding. Ill-timed violence could destroy all chance of negotiation. I looked to Tamayo and nodded the palaver over to him, which he recognized.

"I believe the gold makes them crazy," Tamayo said after a few minutes. "That is truly their god. Gold is more important to them than their own people."

"That is what Hatuey said when he fled over to the Cubans," Romero added. " 'The Castilla worship only one God, his name is Gold,' he told them."

"I heard that story as a child," Enriquillo added in. "How Hatuey was burned at the stake."

"Yes," Tamayo continued "That story was also in my ears. Everybody told that story some years ago, even the priests. It impressed me very much how he knew that about the gold. I was told that he even put together a new ceremony, which he introduced at villages in Cuba. He would lead them to the top of the mountains overlooking the sea, carrying their baskets with all their things made of gold. The behikes would sing death and farewell songs, offering their spirits back to the waters, a way of refuge. Hatuey would sing an areito, asking the winds to hold the Castilla back, and they would throw all the gold into the deep waters."

"Hatuey was caught by mastiff dogs," Enriquillo said.

"I was there when he was burned," I told them. "At the place called Yara, near Bayamo, Cuba. But we are getting ahead of my story, Hatuey's death was in 1512, or so. I was telling you about things that happened at the very beginning, the war against Caonabó, in the year of 1494."

"And Guarionex," Enriquillo added. "They were the old caciques then. Big men. Because Hatuey was a lesser cacique here on this island. He was respected, but he was not as important as Caonabó, Bohekio or Guarionex. And, it is true, his story comes later, when he fled from here a year after Anacaona's Massacre," Enriquillo said.

"Yes, maybe about two years after the massacre, around 1504 or 1505," I said, noticing Doña Mencía, who looked away at the mention of Anacaona, her own mother's mother, and the memory of her sad demise. "But what I was referring to, the early wars, happened against Caonabó and Guarionex."

Enriquillo stood. There were upwards of sixty or more people surrounding the elders' circle where my stories are being heard. He looked over the group. "Tonight many of our people have come," he said. "It is a risk of assemblage I do not often allow. We are nevertheless well guarded by warriors at all corners.

"My elder, Guaikán, sitting here with us, gifts us with his memory. He makes me very proud to be Taíno tonight. You, our younger ears, hear his tale, as he would tell it to you; he knows your four generations. He speaks of the generation before our own, the generation of Caonabó and Guarionex, Guacanagari and Bohekio, and Anacaona, those first ones to meet the Castilla. And before it is over, we will hear of Caicicú, who was of a generation before that. Guaikán knows that story, too. His own generation comes next, and then ours, of Mencía and myself, and Tamayo. Then comes you. So, these stories are your stories. You will do well to remember them, and listen to what your elder says."

Finally, in truly regal manner, Enriquillo turned to me. "Ni-Taíno Guaikán, our questions have taken you away from your story path. But since it is late and some must travel before they sleep, perhaps you could finish with the story of Caonabó, how he was betrayed and caught by gold, and of his final moment. Of course, the next time, we would like to continue, with the story of Guarionex and even hear about Hatuey."

So, I finished that evening's round of stories with the Capture of Caonabó, a memory I dedicated to my young guide, Cao, who had been true and ensured my safety into camp.

One hundred twenty seven. *Caonabó's deception by Hojeda.*

Caonabó was a warrior's warrior. His own father was a Carib war captain and his father's own grandfather was the first in his line to settle on this Bohío island. I was gone on our trip to Cuba when his capture happened, but I heard the story from Caonabó himself.

Caonabó was caught by gold, treacherously. Hojeda chased him several times after raids near Isabela but had not dared battle the old cacique in his own territory.

Hojeda was on his own and he was clever. He did the one thing Caonabó did not expect: he lied to him. Hojeda sent Canoabó a message that the Admiral wanted peace with him and was requesting the cacique come to visit. He wanted to give him the bell at the church of Isabela, he told him, the bell that rang so loudly and that he said was heard directly by the Great Spirit. Caonabó would not come, but, wondering on the bell and its meanings, instead invited Hojeda to visit him. The intrepid Hojeda took nine men on horseback to see the cacique, knowing he would be received in peace. Caonabó said he was suddenly encouraged by the Castilla's friendly approach.

Over the next few days, the cacique took a genuine liking to Hojeda, who was quite the diplomat and full of acrobatic and juggling tricks. Hojeda's men were on their best behavior and pretended to respect Caonabó's court. They talked about customs and visions, but mostly they talked about gold. They both respected the gold, though for very different reasons. Hojeda had brought a set of handcuffs made of a shiny bronze, the metal we call guanín. These shiny handcuffs were not caona but a fine metal that is also cherished by our people. "They are very special," Hojeda told the cacique, "meant only for a great king." A few times, Hojeda let Caonabó handle the intriguing contraption, even locking one handcuff onto the cacique's wrist and using the other side to hold around the forearm, but always releasing the cacique before suspicion could arise. Caonabó wondered as to the shape of the cuffs, but did not connect their purpose. He was reassured by Hojeda's references to their "sacred" nature, certain that no one would invoke the spirits deceitfully. Deep in his own territory, Caonabó was completely relaxed. For one thing, Hojeda, at that time, was still quite a correct man and forbade his men from abusing the women.

One day, the Castilla captain solemnly proffered to gift the cacique with the bronze handcuffs. Hojeda said he had had a dream the night before, that prescribed a ritual bath in the Taíno custom. The cacique, at ease in his own country, agreed. Hojeda led the cacique to a stream where the ni-Taíno bathed themselves. Both men entered the water and conversed through an interpreter. Hojeda by then had learned some of our Taíno protocol. He spoke of cleanliness of body and spirit, the sacredness of the digo, our own Taíno sudsy herb. Then he spoke of a horse ceremony that would properly honor Caonabó, who agreed to let Hojeda honor him after the bath. The Castilla captain seated the cacique behind him on his horse, then ceremoniously placed the handcuffs on him. The cacique, happy and very confident about his Castilla friend, complied with all the requests. Suddenly, the shiny handcuffs secured his second wrist and the Castilla were all mounted around him, two lances to his neck and quickly rode away with Caonabó a prisoner in his own land, in chains and on his way to Isabela.

One hundred twenty eight. *Nobody liked the story.*

Neither young nor old liked this story, how it ended for Caonabó. It was too easy. He was too fierce to fall so easily. Some even complained about the evil of pretending friendship in the cacique's home bohío, only to betray him.

"Learn," Enriquillo told the group, after I sat down. "In such a maneuver our fiercest cacique fell, he was the guardian of our ancestors. Think how easily we can fall, ourselves, if we trust the white man."

One hundred twenty nine. *San Miguel's deception.*

Tamayo felt compelled to speak up. "We are clever now in ways our fathers were not," he said. "Like the time with San Miguel, when his troops went for the gold."

San Miguel was the captain who pressed Enriquillo into moving his camps deeper in the Bahuruku. San Miguel's Indian trackers uncovered Enriquillo's main camps one time, in1527. The Castilla attacked constantly and overran them. "Do you know of that episode?" Tamayo asked me.

A little, I indicated by showing half a finger. I was unclear about the sequence of events, except that a substantial bullion of gold, worth more than twenty thousand pesos, was recovered by the Castilla at the time.

"San Miguel was hurting us," Tamayo told me. "We were hard pressed to fight off so many well-directed attacks. They were hurting us to the gut. At one moment, I remember our fighters were scattered wide and we did not know who was lost and who had survived. So, they had us by the throat, the only time ever. It was then, when I believed all was lost, our cacique thought to request a parley and began negotiations. You should have seen it, elder. He met San Miguel on the twin peaks, which are only twenty feet across from each other, but separated by a deep abyss." Tamayo turned to Enriquillo. "But please tell us, yourself," he said.

Enriquillo smiled thinly. Tamayo's and everyone's mood suddenly lightened, even at this slightest signal from the revered cacique.

"We fooled San Miguel," Enriquillo said. "As we talked, for two and then four weeks, our camps moved farther up the mountains. Still, San Miguel massed his troops to bear down on our trails, and he had good guides. He negotiated harshly and mandated a date for my capitulation. So, we hurried to move our camps, and we searched for a way to break his strength."

I could hear loud whispers in the group. "The gold," a captain said.

"Yes, the gold," Enriquillo repeated loudly. "We had gold from a raid years before, a bullion taken in 1519 from a Castilla convoy traveling by trail to Santo Domingo. It was gold from the mainland, not from here. I always kept that gold, never spent any of it. In truth, I did not want it and even punished the captain who led that raid. Yet, the gold saved us, for in the morning of August 4, 1528, when San Miguel came to take me in, his guides found instead five piles of gold, neatly stacked.

"We were already in retreat, moving fast to cover our trails and disappear. The gold gave them pause. San Miguel ordered three captains to follow us, but they found ways to discuss the orders and never chased us. They quarreled about how to distribute the bullion; to which I heard San Miguel had immediately proclaimed his own captaincy's ten percent. That claim, plus the King's twenty percent and other formal claims, kept the troops near the gold.

Not one squad chased after us. They watched each other closely as they transported the bullion down the mountain. For two years, I later heard, San Miguel's captains sued each other over their claims to shares in the gold."

There was a lot of nodding and the cacique was silent.

"Our cacique fooled them," Tamayo spoke. "And later we punished them, even San Miguel. We burned his ranch house, we killed all his bulls, we beheaded every one of his stallion studs, every one of his boars and his rams. And we hung or strangled every manso guide that ever trailed us. Every one."

One hundred thirty. *Seeking a path to peace, Enriquillo.*

Enriquillo knows he can't win in the long run. Yesterday morning we walked his perimeter and he was very measured and determined. He started twice to talk, but ran out of words. "It happens like that," he said. "My thoughts of the future stop coming. I have fortified my ears and eyes over the years. I do not think so much but feel for danger. I am the hawk in the tree, watching. I am the caguayo lizard, scouting the outer trees, spotting the flocks of shiny blackbirds that would eat the egg of my young ... "

He had started by saying that he thought it best to settle for a peace, that it was better not to push the Castilla if the King actually sought peace. "I consider that I would bring my men in," he said. "I tell my warriors that the reason we are here is not to make war but to ensure the survival of our people. My warriors, you see, are trained for war. I demand a vigilance from them that is complete. We have put up a world here, in these mountains. Our hunters and guards are instructed, as in our Taíno times, to take seed pouches into the woods, to propagate the guayaba, the anón, the caimitu and the mamey; thus we have orchards in the forest whose location only we know. Preparation for survival from battle, the assurance that we will be attacked in our villages has been our constant idea. So, we have plantations, deep in the forest."

We walked in silence for a very long time, his two pages trailing behind us. Again later, as we circled back, he tried to talk. He complained that he still had to teach constant vigilance to his people. "Our Taíno are still too trusting of the white man. Our men sometimes will walk the savannah and run into woodcutters, or cattle boys, white, Indian and Negro, gift them with foods and establish talk. This happens so often I have been forced to threaten with execution any such act," he said. "Survival this way, I know making war, I know. But I see not how we go if peace is possible, I just don't know ... "

No more words came to him and he walked rapidly a long time. Suddenly, Enriquillo froze. A pig could be heard in the forest. I watched him stalk the pig with only a short, thick stick in his hand. As the pig fed, so Enrique moved in. As the pig froze to listen, he, too, froze. Truly he is very keen; his face and eyes have the quality of a hawk, although his movements were those of the majá snake, his body blending in smooth motion, positioning to fix on the feeding pig. Suddenly, Enriquillo darted and threw the stick, the pig yelping loudly as he circled butt-first around a broken front leg. The pages made the kill, gutted him quickly, wrapping the tripe around a stick. Tucking the carcass into a macouti backpack, they carried him to camp.

One hundred thirty one. *Looking for the behike.*

Seeking talk of the future, then, we circled back to Enrique's bohío, where we found Doña Mencía directing four men, two of them full African Negroes, in the structuring of a new cook-house. "We should convene our behike, Baiguanex, and see what we can do," Enrique told her, after they had kissed. The men also greeted us cordially and Enriquillo gave them his kill for their evening meal.

Doña Mencía accompanied us around the camp. She and Enrique held hands and, then, she also held my hand as we walked. I was curious about the behike, Baiguanex, whom I had not met. Nearing the hut of Baiguanex, some distance from the main camp, Enrique cooed like the mourning dove and, without stopping for an answer, walked up a slope to the bohío.

"Enter my home, which is your home, cacique," a voice said from inside the circular, thatch-roofed bohío.

We entered to the left and sat down in a circle as he instructed. The behike was younger than me but I felt seriousness in the way of his deep composure. From the rafters of his bohío he had various herbs drying and he had a small white pipe that he loaded with tobacco, lit and passed to Enrique, Doña Mencía and myself. He took his pipe back when we had smoked, reloaded it and smoked long and hard by himself, filling the hut in spiraling fumes.

"I know I will hear questions today," he said. "I know too that the words carried to my cacique's ear by the elder Guaikán will change our world." I had met the behike. On an earlier evening, after one of my talks, I spotted him among the listeners, his eyes looking a bit beyond me. I noticed that all the young men requested his blessing, touching their foreheads with his hand and that he conducted himself simply. What he said about my "words" changing their world touched me, as it described my history with the Castilla and their entrance into our world.

"A change is certainly coming," Enriquillo said. "What we have protected here, with our vigilance and our lives, would now accommodate itself in their Castilla laws."

The behike looked past me, then focused on me, in a cross-eyed look. "Guaikán has much story," he said. "But where does his trail lead us, cacique? That is one question."

"I think of our survival behike," I said, quickly. I accept my own pain at the fate of my people and I am aware of my own particular failures these past forty years, but I accept no other man's impugnation about them. "I am at calm with my grandparents," I told him. "The earth of this island is now mine. I have buried love here, and blood. This young cacique of ours," I said, "his life I held in my arms."

Enriquillo confirmed it. "He pulled me from the massacre at our great clan mother's," he said, and Doña Mencía held my hand and began to cry quietly.

The behike lost all reservation. He looked me straight in the eyes, and I had confirmation myself that he was very old inside, and that he had been trained properly.

"I apologize to my elder," he said. "I am not worthy to run ceremony for you, but should wait for yours."

"I am pleased to accept your guidance, behike," I said. "You have the hand, I am sure, for what needs to be done."

Baiguanex had no Castilla name and knew only a few of their words. He had lived with his grandparents in the Bahuruku from before the rebellion, hiding in a deep valley and living the old way. He was alone by the time Enriquillo had left for the mountains, and he had tracked Enriquillo's people for weeks before making contact.

"My parents died in the famine of Guarionex," he has told me since. "They sent me ahead with my father's father and his two wives into these hills. My grandfather was a cohobero, who left me two cemís, the Sleeper, which is a warrior spirit, and the Baibrama, which is at the center of my altar, the yuca-maker who can reach Yucahu Bagua Maocoroti, the one who can thus give answers to our human questions."

"My father too was a cohobero," I said.

"I can tell," he said.

"Guaikán worked the peace-pacts with Guarionex," Enriquillo said to the young behike. "He knew the generation we missed."

"They all died," the behike said. "But they still can help us."

"We are going to talk to the Castilla," Doña Mencía said. "We are going to make the peace."

"Then their help we need very much," the behike said, reaching behind to touch his cohoba bundle and gazing deep into my eyes.

One hundred thirty two. *Early Cohobas with Guarionex.*

Twice during my years with Guarionex I partook of the cohoba. Once, it was early on, shortly after the Battle of La Vega, when he sent runners to get me. This was months after my return with the Admiral from the Cuban voyage. With Caonabó in chains, a calm of sorts had been worked out but it was not peace. Guarionex was troubled. Early understandings he had assumed from the Castilla were not forthcoming. Instead, a great battle had taken place, not directly against his villages, but many of his people, including his own son and hundreds more, had been slain or taken prisoner. Many lesser caciques were beheaded. He himself had been taken and nearly executed before his brothers petitioned the Admiral and his soldier brother, Bartolomé, with great offers of tribute.

One hundred and thirty three. *Fasting and old stories of Taínos.*

I have been fasting now for four days while the behike prepares cohoba snuff for me, making his prayers and burning for me. This is the outcome of our meeting with him. I am to snuff cohoba on behalf of Enrique, whose keen senses are too protected to partake of cohoba's dream world.

I know cohoba will be a difficult ordeal for me. It has been a long time and I carry too much life, too many convoluted thoughts. Cohoba respects not the twists of a mind, but attaches to the cool-headed, sincere intent, for it cannot avoid opening the trails of memory, leading the sight spirit into your dream world of blended time, where so much is possible. Already, the memories of earlier ceremonies reminded me of the deepest pain, makes me cry just to think about her, my Ceiba, mother of my twins. Of all my loves and relatives, I have had her memory buried from my sight, a pain so deep it makes me sleep.

"I am your relative by marriage," I told the young behike, today. "Guarionex and his principal wife, Ainaicua, became my second family, his young sister, Ceiba, was my wife. We joined together in 1497."

"I remember my grandfather's mention of them, but vaguely," Baiguanex said. "When I was very young, a little boy, he talked of areitos at Guarionex's main village. He said food there was always plentiful and there was always much singing."

"Yes, Guarionex handled both food and areito with mastery," I said. "His ni-Taínos held the oldest of our songs and dances. They were truly beautiful ceremonies and the Ciguayos and even Caribs themselves coveted those songs and teachings. Guarionex was best at using the teachings as exchanges to develop his permanent relationships between Taíno and Ciguayo villages. But when he tried his mastery with the Castilla, it all went the wrong way."

"With the pale-faced men everything is contrary," the behike said. Since he is of Guarionex's line, I am glad to tell him this story, although I never met him or his family in those days.

Guarionex was tall among our people and quite stately. He was already an elder when I met him, and he moved slowly. His hair was very long and his wives would braid it for him so that it reached his knees. They said that as a young man he had wrapped an enemy's neck in that braid, holding the man for capture.

Even then, they said, Guarionex sang peace songs to the Kwaib raider as he held him.

Today, his great-nephew behike worked the fire for me, he purified me with smoke (I gave him the tobacco leaves Catalina gifted me) and heard my dreams. The behike is quick to grasp the way to go with a thing. He told me, "In the humility of your hunger, consider this: What makes them do what they do, why are they the way they are?" He said then "Remember well and tell your stories of Guarionex, and later we will call him and see what he can tell us."

One hundred thirty four. *Peace-pact ways of Guarionex.*

Tonight, on the third full day of fast (only water am I allowed), I close my eyes and think of Guarionex and his times. I think of the peace pacts, how they were working. I think of the love and respect my people were instructed to carry for each other.

The main value of the peace pacts was to share the soil, share the bounties of the yuca and maize and other harvest cycles. This was the basis of our law. The world had so much for our people in those days, in the way we made our lives. We had great fishing, much fowl, iguana, manatí and hutía, great tubers, great fruits, grasses and herbs and, always, the wish for peace.

I state without hesitation: Our Taíno ways sought peace. We did fight sometimes, but briefly and with small consequence. Our people simply had not the wish to war. This is why I say: prior to the Castilla, Guarionex was defeating the Kwaib raiders with love, with food and with our good ceremonies, which they loved to receive, and, most of all, with our good sister-women, making marriages that would bind.

The Kwaib raiders, Carib or caniba, as they might be called by the Castilla, and sometimes the Ciguayos, the mixed people, and even the migrating Macorixes, who were great archers, all of them could be mean and hard, but truly, they admired the peaceful, prosperous way of the Taínos. Many a Kwaib captured among our people, and married in, found himself intrigued by our name for ourselves, Taíno, "those of the good," and by our elders' argument for happy human existence based on good heart and dutiful mind. Honesty and generosity amongst a clan or a village, and even with strangers, were greatly valued by our old ones. Thieves and liars were quickly purged among our people. Truly, a skinny reed across the door of a bohío was all the fortification needed against theft. Not all of us always lived up to those ancient ways, but it is true that these beliefs caressed our people's minds from childhood and most of our people accepted the truth that good treatment begot good treatment. It was disrespectful and impolite to deny or to offend other people. The Kwaib could see the thinking in that, whenever they were broken out of their predatory track, and Guarionex, following the prophecy of his own grandfather, Caicijú, made it his life's vision to intermarry them with the main cacicazgos of the Bohío island. Guarionex was a great man, I say.

It was Guarionex who, over the objections of the timid Guacanagari, worked through the marriage of Caonabó, the Ciguayo, with Anacaona, a queen of exemplary Taíno line. It was Guarionex who gifted the other Ciguayo cacique, Mayobanex, with two important areitos, something the Ciguayo treasured and never forgot. It was Guarionex who was working intermarriages between that same Mayobanex and Cotubanamá, the Taíno cacique of Higüey. It was Guarionex who offered Columbus to take in a simpleton friar named Román Pané, who was assigned, as the Admiral put it, "to gather Taíno stories and to impart the true Christian beliefs."

One hundred and thirty five. *Friar Pané, el terco, the busybody priest that got many good people killed.*

I would tell here about the cohoba ritual, how Guarionex ran them, but it does not feel right to do so yet.

Yesterday afternoon they accosted me, many young men who gathered from several camps. "We respect that you are fasting, but your stories we would gladly hear." So, I told them about Pané and how he introduced the gospel of the Holy Trinity to our lands, the Christian evangelism Friar Las Casas talks about with such great affirmation.

Father Pané came to the islands with the toughest Columbus brother, Bartolomé, the Adelantado (Forward Commander), who arrived in Española shortly after our departure for Cuba. A man of action and well titled, Bartolomé Columbus imposed rigid controls on behalf of the Admiral. He fixed on Guarionex's obvious prestige among all caciques on the island and was equally preoccupied by the open rebellion of a Castilla captain named Francisco Roldán, Don Christopheren's choice for mayor of the Isabela town and a thoroughly soured man. While pursuing the truculent Roldán, who earlier "confiscated" many horses and cattle from the royal ranch, it was the Adelantado's own idea to place the little friar, Pané, in the village of cacique Guarionex to see what he could find out.

Pané had an obvious facility for learning our language, and commanded the ear of the Adelantado, much the same as did I the Admiral's ear. He was a real pouter, though, always silently angry and vindictive about something or other. Both Don Christopherens and the Adelantado gave Pané instructions. The Admiral asked him to gather stories of our ancients, and he did write a small book that Las Casas has shown me. However, for the Adelantado, Pané provided military information. He reported on the movements of warrior groups and the general opinions of the caciques, particularly Guarionex, about the Castilla.

As we were just now back from the trip to the southern coast of Cuba, during which the Admiral's health deteriorated, I was still close to him. For weeks after the curse of Bayamo and Macaca, as we sailed the many cays and bays of southern Cuba, he caught not a good sleep, reaching points of exhaustion and a clairvoyance truly astounding. At times I saw him stand on deck in bedclothes, slight from lack of food, a constant vomit in his condition, red hair flaming up like fire. More than once, as blackened clouds of the Caribbean came out of nowhere at him, snapping their thunders, I saw the head of our giant snake mother, Iguanaboina, wide as a storm cloud and as blackish grey, its eyes flashing on Columbus's neck and shoulders, hissing and hissing, and I knew he would never recover from our old men's curses. He did slowly get his health back, but his spirit never returned to him, and he was increasingly a vacant man, even as his intellect continued to command him. For five months, while I helped nurse the Admiral's bouts of delirium after our return to Isabela, Pané was assigned to live with Guarionex.

Monthly, Pané returned to inform his patrons. Often these sessions occurred at the Admiral's bedside. Guarionex had installed the friar in his own bohío, where he learned some Taíno language, conversed with elders, both men and women, and wrote down some things he was told about our areitos and old stories. When he would come back to report to the Columbus brothers, he complained about having to live in dirt "with Indians," who were all miserable beings, except for his own servant who fiercely accepted the Word of God.

I remember Pané's reports, how he mocked everything. Pané particularly vilified the mother of Guarionex, an old clan woman who could see into his eyes and disliked him intensely, as he constantly denigrated the Taíno food (when she fed him iguana soup, he spit it out) and scoffed at her reverence for the cemís in her home. I state further here that it was Pané who was responsible, out of his own vindictiveness, for starting the first war on Guarionex.

One hundred thirty six. *A Castilla army readies for battle.*

Truly, Guarionex's sub-chiefs all wanted war on the Castilla, but the old cacique held out for his peace pacting, accommodating Pané and accepting the imposition of the gold tribute, even though its terms were brutal. Caonabó's old villages were fully under tribute at that time. Guacanagari, as principal ally of the Admiral, provided food from his villages and over a thousand healthy men to the Adelantado, who immediately set them to train for war. Under Hojeda and others, these Indian troops of Guacanagari quickly learned the use of the phalange as a tactic of attack, they learned to wield cutlass and sword and were goaded and trained to attack a body of enemies fiercely, with full anger and intent to kill. "Blood is good," they were told. "Cut deep and leave no life." The captains had under them now a well-organized force of four to seven hundred seasoned Castilla troops, including several mobile pieces of field artillery, eighty men with arquebuses, eighty mounted cavalry and about twenty mastiffs commanded by a troupe of eight efficient handlers. The Indian troops were trained to follow Castilla squads in frontal attacks.

Guarionex worked to keep the peace, but Caonabó's three brothers gathered an army, intent on freeing their powerful sibling, who was in chains. The prominent question among Indians that season was: "Why do the Castilla continue to stay? Will they ever return to their lands?" For long months no ships entered or departed from the harbor at Isabela, a place of continual pestilence, and the injuries to Indians continued to mount.

It was during this time that a young man named Díaz, who fled punishment after stabbing a sailor in a knife-fight, was taken in by Doña Catalina's people, from the southern coast. They had a large, well-fed settlement on the banks of the wide Ozama river, which flowed into a beautiful and calm bay on the most protected coast of the island. Díaz and three companions married sisters of a local cacique and learned to appreciate the qualities of the site for a true Castilla city. It turned out that the stabbed sailor recovered, so Díaz went to the Adelantado, Don Bartolomé Columbus, who forgave them their transgression. Doña Catalina's people had found him, he proclaimed, the perfect site for a prosperous city. Thus did the Adelantado set out to establish the port and city of Santo Domingo, the present capital of this Española island. This was terrible news to the central island caciques, who for the first time fully appreciated the permanency of the Castilla on the Bohío island.

One hundred and thirty seven. *Maniocatex riles up a war.*

Maniocatex, second brother of Caoanbó, called together representatives of the major caciques of the island, both Ciguayo and Taínos. Bohekio sent several ni-Taínos, as did Cotubanama. Guarionex came in person, in the company of Mayobanex, a Ciguayo. Over three hundred lesser caciques also attended.

Maniocatex called the caciques to support him in a major battle against the Castilla. "Give me men, let your men come to my army, and we will march on them and together push them to the sea. They have taken my brother, they have taken our mothers and daughters, they are killing our people and abusing us without respite."

Guarionex asked for time. "The Castilla have many desires. Let us try to satisfy them, as we have all our enemies. There are only so many of them. Remember, too, they are very good at killing and will do us much harm if unleashed against us."

Maniocatex formed an army of nearly ten thousand men. Many caciques who joined him brought whole villages to camp on the Vega. Guarionex was impressed, but he cautioned against a frontal war.

One hundred and thirty eight. *Pané riles up the cacique's yukaieke.*

In those days Pané was in Guarionex's village all the time, living in the cacique's own bohío. He had the disgusting habit of asking for the old stories, taking notes as the storyteller humored him and, afterward, arguing with the elder storyteller, declaring the stories "nonsense" and "devil stories" and always invoking the biblical story of Jesus for the listeners.

It was these "dialogs" with Pané that most bothered Guarionex, for Pané never deviated from his opinion about our most sacred tales. One day, insulted, Guarionex left a session abruptly and spoke harshly to a gathered group against the Christian efforts to indoctrinate his people. "They are thick-headed," he said. Next day, several of his young men took the message to heart and brought down a large Castilla cross that had overlooked his village.

Friar Pané was incensed. He went to the old chief and demanded to know how Guarionex could reconcile such an action with the fact that he himself had invited the Catechism of his children and grandchildren. "We learn from you, but you care not to learn from us," Guarionex told him. As Guarionex was increasingly called out to the growing camp of fighters, Pané attempted to organize against him in his own village. He was challenged in this by the cacique's mother and nephews, who finally ran the nitwit priest out.

The Admiral heard Pané's angry report and, despite his slowly recovering corpus, implored his brother to let him lead the troops into the imminent engagement. On March 25, 1495, they dressed the troops for battle, which the Admiral named, "The Battle of Christendom over Heathenism."

"Crosses have been dumped on the Vega ground," the Admiral himself exhorted the war captains. "We have just cause to battle and, by Santiago, the Lord is on our side." He ordered the Marshall of Troops to read the law on war slaves. This was another of the Torres brothers, from the converso family in Seville. The Queen's law stipulated that natives of these Antillian islands, like others in Africa and elsewhere, could be enslaved, if taken as a result of war or to prohibit cannibalism and other abominable heathen practices.

The Castilla army marched in two formations toward the Vega. Upon reaching a plain they called The Hope, the Admiral ordered a fort built that he called Magdalena. "Crusaders are we in these far lands," the Admiral told the captains. "The infidel has declared his deviltry. It is not just ignorance, my fierce captains, the savages now repulse Our Savior and a lesson must stamped on the land."

Maniocatex organized the battle for the Taínos, but nevertheless it was up to Guarionex, as senior cacique, to confront the enemy first. Ritually, Guarionex deployed his men in one long row, and behind them, Maniocatex and other caciques led their own men. They were all there but had made no real plan and assumed their superior numbers would suffice to convince the Castilla to sue for peace. I was told that Guarionex said to his ni-Taínos, as he watched the Castilla troops approach, "If they agree to a peace, blood may be unnecessary." Just then, the arquebus units and the artillery pieces fired all at once on a wide pattern, some eighty detonations of the shouldered weapons plus the two midget cannons that spewed forth all manner of shrapnel. Nearly one hundred Indians fell dead or wounded. The carnage amazed and froze everyone. Guarionex would later tell me he saw the eyes of death in a cloud behind the Castilla and that he was left without thought at the sight of the totally severed torso of his own second son. The cavalry and mastiff handlers waited nearly two minutes for a second volley that dropped another hundred Indians and panicked everyone else, caciques and everybody running this way and that as the mastiffs and the cavalry charged among them at will, in complete killing discipline.

I stood at the Admiral's side, holding the handle on a dagger, but surrounded by his private guard of twelve men, while the Adelantado and eighty others on horseback charged the mass of running Indians, hacking and stabbing with swords and short, sturdy spikes propped against their saddles, piercing back after fleeing back.

Not all Taínos ran. Many were fearless, watching and trying to grapple with the soldier formations, trying to wound them with our spears and clubs, but the Castilla and, yes, their Indian troops, advanced swinging heavy, sharp swords of steel. Three, four, five, I think as many as twenty major discharges were directed against the Indian mass, now divided in two or three groups, with the cross-bows shooting volley after volley and the dogs chasing and tearing at the many trying to escape. I saw how it was done. Truly we were chased in place, denied the opportunity to regroup and kept moving by sheer terror so that large groups ran and ran into each other and in circles while the Castilla cut large swathes into them.

One hundred thirty nine. *The Battle of Christiandom over the Heathens.*

The Battle of Christiandom turned into a long afternoon of gore. More than a thousand bodies were counted when the killing was done. Two dozen Castilla were wounded seriously and twelve died in the battle and, for that, dozens of prisoners were made to run gauntlets and other revenges. Two expert swordsmen delighted the company for a while in a contest to see who could cut the most prisoners completely in half with a single blow. The champion at this sport sliced eight men in half before having to repeat a stroke. The women seized were all raped, some repeatedly and very violently, then herded together with the children.

As the fight subsided, the Admiral was still worked up. "Punish the heathen!" he charged, several times, not once flinching from the inflicted punishments. I saw him use a dagger twice, both times on badly wounded Indians, severing the spinal cord at the base of the neck, waiting the second time for his brother to witness the act. "I shall put him out of his misery," Don Christopherens said. "A Christian crusader can take pride in the painful spilling of heathen flood," Bartolomé replied.

Seven hundred and sixty Taíno people were made prisoner that day, of which five hundred were later sent for sale at the slave market of Seville. A second large battle was fought weeks later as the Castilla troops cornered Maniocatex, who was captured and his villages scourged. The Admiral delighted in the combats against our mesmerized caciques. As infidels taken in war can be sold into slavery by law, he now had a cargo that he could legally send to market.

One hundred forty. *Guarionex is prisoner.*

Guarionex was taken prisoner. I went to see him with the Admiral. "Why did you force us to kill your people," the Admiral asked, and I translated.

"It wasn't my idea," Guarionex said truthfully.

"You ordered the dumping of a Holy Cross."

"No, that wasn't my idea either."

"Pané informs me you spoke against our Christ."

"I only wondered why you don't listen to what we have to say. I felt you were disrespectful to us. My young men were angered and dumped the cross."

"Which ones?"

"All four died yesterday."

"You forced us to attack," the Admiral said.

"I have seen your arms before. I wanted not this war," Guarionex said. "But even I did not expect you could kill so many so fast. It was frightful seeing so much blood at once."

"Our Father in Heaven makes us strong," the Admiral told him.

One hundred forty one. *Guarionex is released, Guacanagari disappears.*

Many came to request the freedom of Guarionex and, finally, the Admiral gave in, but he imposed a large gold tribute upon the cacique, and his people.For the wise cacique it was to be a full calabash of gold dust per month. Most everyone else was charged with amounts of half an ounce to one ounce every three months. That first tribute system for gold was very rigid, not only with Guarionex but with Maniocatex and Caonabó's people, and,more and more, even Guacanagari's villages were called upon to provide tribute, not escaping from the harsh punishments imposed upon failure to provide. The tribute for gold worked like this: you brought in your assigned quota of gold and received a wooden pendant on a string, to be worn about the neck. Any Castilla could check any Indian under tribute. Any Indian caught without the proper pendant could be punished, either by whip or by the cutting of fingers, hands or ears.

Now even Guacanagari, the Admiral's "noble cacique," who saved him in his time of trouble, was pushed about and called "dog." His own guaxeri, now trained as soldiers of Castilla, imposed upon him his gold tribute, which they themselves would collect, fiercely aggressive toward him. During those days, it was that Guacanagari walked into the forest one morning and was never seen again.

One hundred forty two. *A Taíno offer on the land.*

Guarionex was astonished that so many of his people were maimed. He had so much gold to gather that his guaxeri would give their portions to him to turn in and they took the punishment meant for him. Guarionex decided to take cohoba at that time, and he received an instruction which he followed.

Guarionex was to organize all of his planting guaxeri, a very impressive group that involved some of the best Taíno farmers. He brought together the guaxeris of the yuca, of the maize, of the peppers and the fruit orchards. They would make a pilgrimage, Guarionex informed them, to the Adelantado's farm. I was in camp with the Adelantado when a runner came in from Guarionex, manifesting the peaceful intentions of the gathered group. The Admiral came at once, with his own troop. I remember thinking there might be another battle and was horrified, but indeed a quiet parley was the occasion.

Guarionex lined up his best gardeners, his orchard keepers, and thousands who came behind them, planting sticks in hand and seed pouches around their necks. The whole group sat on its haunches as the parley began and Guarionex beseeched the Admiral and the Adelantado to consider his offer, which was to plant a huge sea of conucos, with yuca, boniato and other tubers, with peppers and plantains, maize and beans. He would work plantations that would run the width of the island from the northern to southern coast, the cacique said, more than eighty leagues by thirty leagues square. "Never will you want from hunger," he promised. "You and your children we will feed, here and in your Castilla lands. So much food we will grow that you may never feel a threat to your existence. Happy, like us, you will be. Make the villages, keep your animals, cut the trees and build huge boats, bring your women. Yes, we will feed them all, as we have done before, but plentifully, and we will plant and plant, and make casabe for you, and fish for you, and present it to the Castilla with good heart and with consistency."

Guarionex's own words this day mixed in with a well-known speech among our areitos, one orated during the establishment of a new fire or village. It is called the speech of the naboria, and it was designed, in our own protocols, to invite a newcomer tribe to settle peacefully, as was happening with the Ciguayo in Española. For enticement, the naboria speech offered agricultural assistance, even labor. This was the oldest of areitos, used even by the earliest Guanahatabey, in western Cuba, when greeting with fruits and roots and conch fish the first Çiboney to come on their beaches. It was used by the Çiboney with our own arrival, as Taíno, in their eastern shores, many generations ago. It is the gentle way of the naboria, our ancient serving cousin, which was our own human way to cope with power and the migrations of warrior groups.

The Columbus brothers, including Diego Columbus, the sibling, who came along with Don Christopherens on the second trip, listened to the great cacique's offer, spoken in grand gestures and meant to cover the needs of generations. For a few minutes, they were entranced. "He is a smart old man," Don Bartolomé whispered. Guarionex finished by assuring the brothers that his men were most enthusiastic about the offer and he looked at the Admiral directly.

The Admiral laughed. "But what could he want," he said, "in return for his food."

"There is something," the cacique responded. "Stop the gold tribute, which is maiming my people. We cannot meet it in any case and it seems without sense to cause so much injury and death of people. We are trying, señores," said the grizzled cacique, "but there is not that much gold to be gathered."

I translated Guarionex's offer as generously as possible. It made sense to me, as the Castilla colonies were in fact suffering from constant hunger and making food is what Taínos could do best. Relief provisions had not arrived from the motherland for the Castilla, and production in our own villages was greatly diminished by the comings and goings and incessant terror of Castilla squads. Famine had materialized in the areas most affected by violence. I could see that Guarionex's gesture spoke to our ancient Taíno idea to always offer food and gifts as a way to peaceful relations.

With sneers and short laughs, the Columbus brothers dismissed Guarionex's idea. I knew their mood and expected as much, as all afternoon I had heard them discuss the operations of gold mines (a bigger sifting pan seemed a good idea), and the upcoming trip by Don Christopherens to represent the long-term reality to the Monarchs. "Thank the Great Cacique for his generous offer, Dieguillo," he said. "Tell him we will certainly receive his men to work many conucos. However, as to the mines, we offer a better idea." Bartolomé explained: "This is our wish. The great cacique is to redouble his efforts to mine for the gold. Identify new streams and mines to work on. By all means, plant more and more, but bring the gold without manufacturing fanciful excuses. Failure to do so will be to force harsher punishments on his people." For good measure, the Adelantado demanded the cacique take back the friar Pané into his village to continue his work of conversion.

"The Cacique will not be heard," I told Guarionex in our language, when I was certain his offer was not considered. "I am sorry, for it makes sense to provide for the food supply." I even told him how honored I felt to spend time with him and to help him make the offer.

Guarionex left in full dejection, but looked at me warmly as he left. I approached him and he put his hand on my arm. "I appreciate your attempts to help us. Come and see me, I will tell you my stories."

Later, the caciques, with Guarionex conducting them, refused for two seasons to plant extra yuca, thinking thus they would starve out the covered men. Just when the plan might have succeeded, a convoy of provisions arrived from Spain, the Castilla were replenished and the guaxeri of Guarionex faced famine and much sickness on their second season without a yuca crop.

One hundred forty three. *The first Castilla rebellion: Roldán attacks the Admiral.*

By this time, 1496 or 97, Francisco Roldán, the former mayor of Isabela, was in open rebellion against the Adelantado. With a hundred Castilla under him, this fascineroso, or torrid one, as Columbus called him, moved constantly from the Vega Real to the Xaraguá region, making excursions into Bonao to commandeer gold and to Isabela to steal horses and cattle. Roldán made pacts, after his own manner, with several caciques, camping out with them, marrying himself and his men into several cacicazgos. The caciques listened with interest to his call for ending the tribute system and to his threat to kill the Columbus brothers, but then recoiled at the treatment received from his own desperadoes.

During one of these runs, Roldán himself and another captain took over Guarionex's village and twice raped his younger wife, Bema. As Guarionex pondered starting a second war on all Castilla, his mother's helpers once again ran the persistent Pané off and took hold of all the church items left in a small chapel the friar had built. For lack of a better approach, they buried the religious items in a recently planted field of yuca, a field assigned to the ceremony of the three-cornered cemí, the Yucahuguamá, planted thus with the new tuber field, prayed for and watered by urine to call forth early germination.

Pané was mortified and cried for the Admiral about the great sacrilege. Demanding swift punishment for the perpetrators, he identified six men who took part in the act. They were six nephews of Guarionex.

The Adelantado ordered the six men captured. Then he burned them at the stake.

I visited Guarionex during that time. He cried in fury and agony at the punishment of the young men, having also lost his own son at the Battle of La Vega. Despite my being in the service of the Admiral and the Adelantado, Guarionex and I talked a great deal. I commiserated with him about his poor young men and he accepted me without hesitation as a fellow Taíno seeking also for a way out of the horror that had befallen us. It was then he asked me to stay with him awhile, calling me a nephew and introducing me to his youngest sister, Ceiba, in consideration of marriage.

One hundred forty four. *I take a bride, Ceiba.*

I had met Ceiba twice, we had even spoken, and neither of us had qualms about meeting again during a couples' dance arranged by the cacique. The Adelantado Columbus was in the vicinity, chasing after Roldán, when Guarionex's offer to me was made public. For his own reasons, the Adelantado encouraged me to stick close to the old cacique, whom he still considered potentially dangerous. With our route opened by Guarionex, and Ceiba in agreement, I quickly began the arrangement for a marriage ceremony by moving a hammock into my new wife's bohío.

This was the beginning of the best part of my miserable life. For nearly a year the Castilla busied themselves with the building of new forts, starting new mines and moving the main metropolis of Española to the new site of Santo Domingo, on the southern coast. The Adelantado chased Roldán and his two hundred men around the Xaraguá area (not far from where I write), while the Admiral embarked for Castille to combat accusations by the rebel's friends, including Father Buil and Captain Pedro Margarite, that the "Genoese tyrants" were committing atrocities against Castillian and Indian alike. A respite of sorts, short but sweet, was the gift of those days for me.

One hundred forty five. *Making a family, home days.*

It is only now, experiencing as I am the freedom of this rebel camp, that I fully appreciate those days with Ceiba in the old court of Guarionex, those blissful few months of a season of relative peace, when Guarionex put through areito after areito, singing from his great repertoire of hundreds and hundreds of story songs and ceremonial chants, recalling the ancient prophecies and teachings with me.

Ceiba and I liked each other too. She was a mature woman, slightly older than me. In our second month, a full wedding ceremony was arranged and Guarionex had a new bohío built to house the new couple. In our custom, a nuptial bohío like this must be built all in one day, with many people working. That day was a great celebration, with many joyful elements, all the more heartfelt as the times were certainly harsh and the people had already much to mourn. But the people of her yukaieke loved Ceiba a great deal and they accepted me as a possible factor in relieving the great burdens imposed upon them. And it did happen, once, that I turned away a band of four Castilla who wounded a guaxeri of Guarionex and were intent on settling forcefully in the village. The Adelantado, I lied to them in perfect Castillian, had given strict orders, under penalty of death, that Castilla soldiers stay out of Guarionex's village.

Ceiba and Catalina's people were friendly and frequent visitors. Thus a large group came with Catalina to the wedding. Catalina, a cousin of Anacaona's and older by ten years than Ceiba, led her young cousins in singing Moon songs. In the early evening, she gifted us a fortune-telling, looking to our destiny as a couple, a fertility search with manatí bone games that always came out two. Everyone nodded as this was considered good fortune, and the elders all reminded me of it months later when our twin boys were born. Catalina, bless her heart, came to help with the birth.

One hundred forty six. *Enriquillo's camp is like the old yukaiekes.*

I am glad to be here. This camp reminds me of those days when we went for months not seeing even one Castilla and we could take the time, every day, to be Taíno. Ceiba and I put in a conuco all our own, even planting tobacco and herbs. We worked together every day, bathed at the stream twice a day and coupled excessively, day after day, wherever and whenever we wanted. She was wide of shoulder and hip, a strong woman who could work and work in the sun and who made love with certainty, grabbing a man firmly and opening herself in full trust, and she was so easy and so wonderful to love. For those months, as her belly grew and we continued to sneak around like mice in the corn, I became a poet in the style of old Guarionex and my grandfathers of childhood, full of thoughts for our little family and for our village and formulating thoughts of peace and words of love for Ceiba, and words of reason and harmony for the Castilla, feeling in love strong enough to carry impacts of importance.

One hundred forty seven. *The old man knew so much.*

I sat with Guarionex and I heard him many times ponder the future. I grew to love the old man and, through him, was once again touched with the beauty and the reason of our Taíno customs. Guarionex knew it all. He was one of the very few, even in the best of times, who could remember the songs for all the areitos, all of the origin stories, the traditions and safekeeping practices for each and all of our cemí helpers. About the medicines, he knew their ceremonies and could check and instruct behikes and medicine women who regulated such things. But his interest was the peace pact, for which he could draw on a great repertoire of memories.

Peace-pacting was a strong tradition in Guarionex's court, and he was often drawn to help resolve fights between caciques. With me he talked much about these things, and together we wondered about the motivations of Castilla, why they settled on Taíno lands and what accommodations might yet be made with them so that our people could survive.

One hundred forty eight. *Death spirits that open sores in our faces.*

It happened, too, that with the spread of Castilla settlements, new illnesses grew among our people. There were constant deaths in villages where once the occasion was relatively rare. Every day now, many people were dying and many others laid up on hammocks, very hot and wretching and unable to eat, ears and noses running liquid and in many cases, open sores formed on our peoples' faces and bodies

Guarionex pondered out loud on all this. Through the cohoba I experienced with him then, I did see my elders (though I could not talk to them), and I remember that they gestured for me to not come near them, but to stay where I was and open my ears and eyes wide. I saw my old men of Guanahani and my father's mother, who waved at me, clasping her hands with two thumbs raised. I had not experienced the cohoba long enough to know what to do within my trance, nor how to move about nor how to bring forth sound. I had no real skills, although I felt at ease with it and in the morning my body felt clean and my mind clear.

Guarionex was powerful in cohoba and could communicate with his grandparents and especially with his great-grandfather, Caicijú, a behike of renowned power whose cohoba vision of three generations earlier Guarionex shared with me.

"Caiciju fasted six days," Guarionex told me. "Every night he took cohoba and dreamed. Three nights he received sorrowful messages for one or another of his relatives. Then, even animals reported to him stories of future hardships. One night, Vital Force Supreme Spirit, Yucahu Bagua Maocoroti, the one without grandfather of grandmother born, He who is Creator of our sea and islands, creator of all fish and of our Taíno people, Ancient Waves of Our Ocean, spoke to him. He took Caicijú out of himself and into the bright day sky past a thin cloud cover. Caicijú told later that he re-entered our world through the clouds to see our crab-like island. On the ground, he moved through his known haunts. A man spirit, not Yucahu, he said, showed him his third generation on this earth, not free, as was his own, but enslaved, chained and lashed, dying of hunger. He saw "covered men," he said, who came from the east and rode four-legged beasts full of fury.

"Caicijú asked himself, how can this be? Who could do such a thing? He thought of the Carib, their pesky raids, but that didn't make sense, as they seldom settled for long and, even then, more often than not, were taken in by our people.

"Of course, whom it was I know now," Guarionex told me. "The Castilla it is whom he was shown by Yucahu Bagua Maocoroti; the covered men were carried to us by his own great spirit vision, on the waves of his own mother sea."

One hundred forty nine. *Roldán and the first Indian repartimiento.*

One day in early spring, 1498, some six months after our twins were born, Guarionex came to our bohío, which was nearly a mile from his main village and a quieter place. He was distraught. His men had been severely punished in recent weeks. "So much blood, I cannot sleep."

And then, he had heard something worse. The Adelantado sent an offer to Roldán. The rebellious mayor and his men would receive land grants from Columbus, including whole villages of peaceful Indians. Roldán and his men would be installed as captains over caciques. Guarionex asked me to check this information for him, and I did by spending some days in the Adelantado's company. (I took a wide cape of parrot feathers to him from Guarionex.)

One hundred fifty. *Guarionex retreats to the mountains.*

Don Bartolomé confirmed the offer to Roldán. It was true, the yukaiekes were to be split off and Roldán would receive land and many Indians. Francisco Roldán, who led the first rebellion against the Columbus brothers' central authority on the islands, was a troubled man, quarrelsome. At times, he took up the Indian cause, demanding an end to the tribute system. And this way, here and there, Roldán enlisted caciques in plots against the Admiral. Thus, at one moment, Guarionex himself threw his lot into a battle at Concepción, where his warriors wiped out nearly a whole garrison.

The problem was Roldán's men had no morals. They relied on the guax-eri for food, but constantly abused the women. Roldán sought our alliance against the Admiral, but just the same demanded complete subservience from us. After one such campaign, I have written, Roldán raped Guarionex's second wife. Now, the Admiral, whom Roldán insulted a hundred times, was to give him as gifts our lands and people. It was the final act for Guarionex.

"I see Castilla fight, son against father." (He meant Roldán versus the Admiral.) "They would kill each other, and in that fight, each of them seduce us to be of each their ally. But, no matter with whom we elect to stand, they each of them, in the end, despise us and disdain our place. Our friendship ceremonies, our guatiaos, the change of faces and exchange, our areitos we have sung them, it all amounts to nothing. They are a people who live in constant shame."

Guarionex would start to speak slowly, but the words soon pounded out of his mouth in stark blows. "I know his weapons can blow men apart. He commands the fury hurricane, and it does horrify. But beyond the fear of death, what I truly fear, is the way they are. How certain of their destiny are these covered men, and yet how willingly they have lied to our caciques. This covered man sees not my eyes. He sees not this world. He is not a god, that is certain, but he is not a human like our people are human."

Guarionex was agitated by his growing perception. "I will withdraw from my territories," Guarionex said. "The Admiral cannot just give away my people like so many fish in a canoe."

That day, Guarionex asked Ceiba and me to take his mother's clan house under our care, hoping they could avoid direct persecution as he went to war. Ceiba and I agreed to make a village for over one hundred people, and Guarionex asked the people to accept me as cacique. As his sister's husband, I could take this place, according to our ancient tradition, since she held the actual cacique line and not him. Of course, in calmer times, she and her sisters would raise one of their boys to be cacique, rather than choose one of their own husbands. As the Adelantado had granted me, with Don Christopheren's permission, a tract of land, then I settled my new relatives into a formal cacicazgo.

Days later, the old man moved his main villages into Cacique Mayobanex's territory, who had offered to protect him from Castilla attack. Mayobanex was Ciguayo, a strong warrior and elder. He greatly esteemed Guarionex's superior knowledge of our ceremonies and stories. Weeks passed and then Guarionex started a war that raged for several months. Guarionex and Mayobanex both led warriors and raided with impunity. Many ambushes of Castilla took place during that time and it wasn't always clear who had the upper hand. Divided as he was by the attacks from Roldán's men and the various Indian skirmishes, the Adelantado Bartolomé Columbus strung out his forces, until accommodations with Roldán allowed him time to pursue the Indian chiefs.

One hundred fifty one. *Guarionex falls, and Mayobanex.*

I told the story last night to the young men (and captains) in Enriquillo's circle, of how Guarionex and Mayobanex, a Ciguayo and a Taíno, stood together and were destroyed together. I told them of the character of the Adelantado, who chased them mercilessly, finally cornering each of the old men in their turn and alienating their jurisdictions. Poor Guarionex was chained and placed in isolation in Santo Domingo. Nearly three years he languished before being sold into slavery. His only luck was to die enroute, no longer a cacique but not yet a slave.

One hundred fifty two. *Castilla swarm the island.*

The Castilla were beginning to swarm the island by then. The central plain was nearly pacified. Santo Domingo and the other Castilla forts grew. I hear Las Casas tell that some three hundred repartimientos, or early encomiendas, were already granted by 1500, including many ranches and mines and large fincas. I do remember that they cleared roads for their oxen wagons and horses, and they traveled in groups between towns. At that time, I did all I could to hold Ceiba's yukaieke together, feeding and protecting her old people and our growing twin boys. We had settled into the valley granted to me by Don Christopherens, a remote conuco, away from the traveled roads, and we went nearly undetected for five years.

Many of our people did what they could during that time to hide away in remote places. Three of the five main cacicazgos, the Taíno big houses, and one Ciguayo, had been annexed or destroyed by the Castilla. Guacanagari was absorbed. Caonabó, Guarionex and Mayobanex were taken down. Only two provinces, Higüey and Xaraguá, on the eastern and western ends of the island, retained their own jurisdiction. Neither had gold to offer, yet each paid substantial tribute, in casabe and fish, in woven cotton and the labor of artisans. Only later did I travel to Higüey, so I never met its cacique, Cotubanamá, though I often met people from their region in Santo Domingo, when they came to deliver their goods. I had more contact during this time with Bohekio and his sister Anacaona, widow of Caonabó, who maintained their Taíno cacicazgo intact, this in the province of Xaraguá, which surrounds these Bahuruku mountains. They were very calm, people, just as my own little village was calm and it seemed for a few short seasons that peace might return and a common ground could be reached with the Castilla towns. Of course, Ovando, the Knight Commander, had yet to come.

One hundred fifty three. *Surrounded by young Taíno, education for peace.*

Speaking to their young Taíno minds last night, surrounded by friendly forces, I felt incredibly light. I am light, anyway from my fast and my mind is light, too, like dew on a spider's web. I move in a flow and the warriors notice. The behike, whom they greatly respect, is constantly with me, and Enriquillo signals approval at every turn. He likes my stories and attitude, and I am conscious of returning his new message to his fighting people. I must educate them at every turn, prepare them for a possible peace. For fifteen years Enriquillo has taught them to abhor and kill Castilla, to kill especially manso Indians like me, who have always been the greater threat. Now he needs them to appreciate an end to hostilities, if such should come. For this, he even interrupts his vigilance; he produces me as his voice. Sometimes, as I speak, I feel his face on my own, the weight and the tension of his brow in my eyes.

One hundred fifty four. *A song comes to me.*

This afternoon, on the sixth day of my fast, I write. Tonight we snort cohoba. Day by day, the behike, often with Enriquillo in attendance, sits me facing west, looking away from the sun, a circle of yuca and conch shell dust drawn around me. He gives me water but nothing else. I sit with my back to the morning sun, respecting his power. I thank this mountain site, thanking too the ancestors who would pay attention. When the sun hits my face directly from above, the behike opens my circle of protection by brushing aside a line of the yuca and shell dust, inviting my hand and step.

"Maybe you cannot sing," he said before, as he noticed my silence. "Make the noise, hum it, if you remember it."

This morning, as the dew steamed away, a song came to me. The mist was still around us. The behike burned the lightest bit of tabanacu incense and the smoke rose in little puffs that dissipated before reaching the forest canopy. It was the puffs of smoke as I watched them that recalled the touch of that old wooden drum of Guarionex, which he beat many times singing cohoba songs for me. Suddenly, in my ears I picked up a song that went on and on, repeating itself and branching out and I could hear in it voices that had not lived for many years. What a good sound it was, how pleasing and warm to the memory!

One hundred fifty five. *Going to meet the medicine.*

I make final notes and prepare my mind. Afterwards I will not write but prepare my return to the convent in Santo Domingo. I will write more there. For now, I can say that my mind is very calm and that I feel as complete as I have in years. I am convinced of the life that exists beyond our awakened earth, the resounding mind that accompanies our waking days and the many spaces and folds in its world. My father is there, I can tell. My father is with me. Nearly every day, here and there, I sense him. I see him in my dream and I smell the sweat of his back on first awakening.

Today, walking through the woods from the behike's, I felt the ground rise and fall in waves beneath my steps, soft earth supporting my body with her heat. Everything smelled green. The world was green-smelling as I walked lightly, so lightly over the earth.

It was then I felt them all around. I felt warm winds embrace me, even dance around me in the woods, walking so lightly, walking in the weakness of no food, of hunger denied and then ignored, removed. So light I was, I felt, the water as I drink it travel through me in clean rushes, a coolness in my thighs. So light, I feel I could see them already, even in the light, knowing that the cohoba was being prepared, greeting me in their shy way as I walked. For them, the earth said to me: Remembered son, I clean your feet with my dew, as with your step you caress my back.

My father told me: Never rush the first medicine. Even your certain medicine, never take it on the first pass. So, I asked the earth, I intoned: On you, beautiful earth, why is there so much suffering for my people? I asked, too: And, will there be survival for the good Taíno?

Folio V

Cohoba Dreams

*Two weeks later, at the Convent in Santo Domingo ... Journey with
cohoba, a returning memory ... The cohoba journey ... Message of the
cohoba, a way to guard the survival ... I conduct a strange ceremony ...
At the convent, las Casas returns ... I ask Catalina to help me ... In the
woods with Catalina ... At my old yukaieke in the lower Magua
country ... With cohoba again, with Ceiba ... Finding love with
Catalina ... Barrionuevo has arrived ... Tempering the Good Friar ...
I hate telling a lie, but ... The good friar confesses a deed of his
youth ... Las Casas goes again ... In the memory: Velázquez presses me
into service ... The route to Xaraguá, with Velazquez ... The Massacre
of Anacaona's Banquet ... The killing begins, Enriquillo in my arms ...
Encounter with Manazas at the stream ... Suspected in the killing ...
My village becomes an encomienda ...*

One hundred fifty six. *Two weeks later, at the Convent in Santo Domingo.*

Quietly I have returned to the friars' cloister. No one questions my long delay at the sugar mill, although I know that there are whispers about me. They wonder about young Silverio, who decided to stay and become a warrior guaxeri among his people. About him, I have said that he stayed to work as a carpenter's apprentice on a second Maguana sugar mill.

No one has raised any question about the way I look and act. I have decided to speak to no one, directing but very brief words to Father Remigio, who took up the care of my poor, mangy mare and announced my deep "retirum" to silent prayer the morning of my return.

Truly they think of me as another monk. And though I have never taken vows of any kind, I could run a high mass, a baptism, a confirmation, a marriage and even the extreme unction. Now I protect myself by retiring into prayerful sacrifice, and they must respect it. No one speaks to me directly. I put on their hooded mantle, I emerge only in the quiet moments and spend much time in the chapel, kneeling for my faith.

One hundred fifty seven. *Journey with cohoba, a returning memory.*

I entered the Coaibay in my trance. I saw my elders again. Smitten I am by the cohoba messengers, and I walk everyday, all day and all night, in the company of that recent memory.

Baiguanex and Enriquillo assisted me. Light already from my long fast, I was led by them to the fire. Behind a western peak, the day's sun sprayed its final signals. Light I was of body, but not weak inside, not in my heart nor in my mind. The moment was alive as in my childhood days. My eyes were not so weak that I could not see with precise clarity. Baiguanex had out for me a long, low duho seat. I sat in the recline of its curve. "Close your eyes, uncle," the behike instructed, and I did.

Baiguanex said, "Prepare to leave our world of human senses. Prepare in darkness now as the cacique and I will smoke you with sacred tobacco, as Doña Mencía prepares your tea and cleans your spatula. Prepare in the darkness of your own mind, human being. Share the darkness, little guaxeri, as we clear the spirits of animal and tree, shrub and herb and we open the very place where we are sitting. Yes, our little uncle, keep your eyes closed. Here, drink from this güira gourd the juice that will fully cleanse you. But don't open your eyes while I prepare the snuff of cohoba in your bowl, stay in the darkness from which you will travel, yes, yes."

I sat in darkness and remembered the words of Guanahabax, our old man of my home island. "Remember all your days that cohoba loves you," he said. "It will always welcome you. Xán, Xán Katú."

All these years later, and I still have my own spatula. I lost the feather fans, the two-pronged sniffer, I lost the rattle and broke my gourd, all years and years ago. Somehow, the spatula I never lost. It was my father's spatula, made of hard, smooth coral, and I always managed to keep it. I drank freely from the cleansing tea, filled my gut to its busting, then asked to "face the woods." Eyes closed, I was guided by my assistants. The tea caused my belly to expand. Situated, then, I heard, "Give it back, now, uncle," and I used the spatula to cause a sudden torrent of vomit, long and dark to flow out of my body. I staggered and my assistants held me up, then guided me back to my reclining seat.

"Prep are to travel," Baiguanex said, approaching me. "I will now load my caximba," he said. "It has two blow holes that I will place at your nostrils. Then, as I was taught, I will blow the cohoba dust into your head. And you will be released."

I heard him stand up then. He offered the loaded cacimba to the four directions. He sang the song of Deminán and the four sky walkers, the ones without fathers. He sang the areito of Attabei, the Ancient Bleeding Mother. Then he invoked his two cemís, Baibrama, to guide me, and the Jumper, a helper, to instruct Opiyelguobirán—dog guardian of the Coaybay—to not molest or attack me but to receive me, and later, release me. In a few moments the behike said, "Are you ready, uncle?" I nodded, then felt the cacimba le an into my nostrils. "Blow," I whispered to my guide. "Push off my slippery canoe gently from this shore."

One hundred fifty eight. *The cohoba journey.*

There was light, and transference was immediate. I held the sneeze, then felt my body give, then succumb. Then it was midday, clear as sunlight, and I sat on a dock made of two long tree trunks tied together with bejucos; they jutted out into a cove. The cove was on the mouth of a river and many canoes paddled out to sea. In the cove some canoes were latched to each other as people talked. Two men in a canoe glided up to the dock. They were old and naked, brown wrinkled skin hanging from thin arms and faces with missing teeth and alert eyes. "Boy," one said to me, "we have a full canoe, but you can't come with us." I looked and saw that their canoe was not full, but actually upside down. And now they paddled away, chuckling to themselves at my surprise.

Now I was chopping wood. I was by myself. I had a Spanish ax and I had a log against which to chop. I was making firewood for cooking for Ceiba. I was in my wood lot, near the bohío we kept in the valley of Guarionex. I was chopping by myself and I could hear the twins calling to each other. I could not see them, but I could hear their voices near by. "Good Wind," said Heart of Earth, "come see my worms. I have many of them in a pool." And Good Wind replied in that high pretty voice he had as a little boy. "Let's go fish the river, my jimagua twin."

Then I was alone again in the same place, but there was no sound at all. Then I felt a group of men approach through the woods, eight or ten of them, Taíno guaxeri of the old generation, all hardy and straight-standing. Without sound, I could tell they meant for me to drop the ax and go with them. They walked and I fell in line as they moved fast through the woods. They ran in the old manner, single file at a half-trot for hours. This is the way the men liked to travel in the old days: They formed a line, put a singer at its head and trotted to the next destination. And there I was for hours, it seemed, trotting behind a pair of legs and hair tail spinning in the wind and running. Once the singing started, it went on and on. Among many voices I heard Baiguanex, and I knew, briefly, he was working with me from the living world.

Then we were at the bottom of a rocky mountain. The man before me pointed out a small trail and I was alone again, walking that trail up the hill that suddenly opened to a plateau. I heard a dog snarl behind me, turned quickly and saw only a rustle in the grass. Then he was ahead of me, the cemí, Opiyelguobirán, guardian dog of Coaibay. Suddenly, I could do nothing, could not move as his mere gaze captured my movement. Opiyelguobirán sat just as his cemí depicted: on his haunches, with front legs extended. He was small and he was big, so big at moments I felt just his nostril could take me up in a breath. Suddenly the songs caught up with me, the sweet running songs and then the ones of Guarionex and the ones of my father and even the death song of Çibanakán, long imbedded in my ear from the time of his freezing. Hearing Çibanakán's song, Opiyelguiobirán began to diminish in size. Then, quite small, he wagged his tail, tended his head for me to pat and darted away.

Sunshine appeared. In a wide field I saw multitudes. There were Taíno people all over the plateau and I could hear talking and I could smell roasting casabe bread and corn. An old man I did not recognize came up beside me. "We can smell the food," he said, wistfully. "But we cannot eat it."

He moved on and then Guarionex was there, and my father behind him, and the other old men of our cohoba circle in Guanahani. It was all men, and they circled around me, then began to walk me up the hill.

"We welcome you, beloved," old Guanabanex said, and I heard my father singing softly behind him. I could see ahead of us the entrance to a cave, a dark hole in the side of the mountain, maybe three feet wide.

"This is the way we come," the old man said, crawling in. "Now, let's enter."

Inside we could stand. Sabananiobabo, Lord of the Jobos (dead men turned to trees), guarded the entrance from inside. He is an old man with grave eyes. He greeted us and walked next to me. Suddenly, from above, large flocks of bats dislodged and flew around us. Sabananiobabo waved them away. The last flier of the flock was not a bat but an owl, which circled once and flew off. Sabananiobabo sat the others in a circle, but took me aside. "Come look at the owl's reminder," he said. "You have something here that he retrieved for you."

Then in front of us, near a stream, there was a hut. He pointed through the door. Inside I saw a long log bench, with two men sitting on it. One was the soldier, Manazas, a hefty Extremaduran; the other was the foreman, Moisés, thin and slight. They didn't look up, neither of them, their necks hanging low. I recognized their bodies and faces. They were the two men I had killed.

"I can do nothing with them, so they will wait, until you meet them at your proper time," Sabananiobabo said.

The cave was large and open, very old and musty, humid, almost cold. Now, both women and men walked through as I sat in the men's circle. I saw the cohoba twins float by, crying, yet watching everything and reminding me of the meaning of cohoba: the opening to the other self. They reminded me, too, of my own boys, gone from me now these many years.

My father now sat to my left in the circle. "They still live, both of them," he answered my silent question. I was totally happy and dared not inquire further about them.

"And your mother ... ," he said. "She is all right, here, in the Coaibay."

Happy to know that much, I inquired no more about her either. He said nothing more, but sang his canoeing song for me. "Glide in this cloud of a sea," he sang. "Carry my son ahead of me, carry my son ahead of me ... " And for a long while I leaned into my father's back, smelling the sweat of his neck, listening to his favorite song.

Then I was in the circle of men, and I was very young, a boy in a circle of elders. I knew I was receiving instructions. "Protect the baby boy," one man said. It was Cai'ciju, great grandfather of Guarionex, who was also there. There was also my second father, Çibanakán, and my grandmother, and my uncle Jiqui, and my brother-cousin, Carey, all among the many faces in the circle of cohoba. I had no need to greet them directly, but they had come and I had come, so we were all now here together again. Guarionex sat next to me, real as anything, and now as I write in this Christian convent, I close my eyes and see him next to me still, as in a waking dream.

My cohoba didn't last much longer. I remember only snatches after that. Most of it was sitting in that circle, hearing the songs, and Guarionex, who whispered in my ear. "The Castilla need us no more," he said. "That I know."

He also said, "Between the Castilla and their gains of gold, the baby boy now stands. They would make a peace, finally, and leave him more or less alone."

He said too, "A warrior of the Castilla who has killed must be opened again. Sing a song of words in his ears. Clean his eyes. Clear his throat. He must hear and he must give the baby boy respite ... "

He said too: "Our own warrior man-killers, they too must be cleansed. Thus humans we would be again, and so could be our poor people who remember, our poor people that have struggled. Taíno they all must be again, Guaikán of the living sea. Taíno they must be before the torrent waters of white and black faces wash the mountain current of our native blood, before all that remains of us is the depth of our black eyes and the love in our living bones."

And I remember clearly, he said, "For those who would kill him, put gold in their path. Even revenge they will ignore for gold." He repeated, several times, "So that our people can survive, put gold before their enemies and useful purpose before the eyes of our friends."

One hundred fifty nine. *Message of the cohoba, a way to guard the survival.*

I sat with Enriquillo and the behike for two days. I fed on bits of casabe and dried fish and drank the juice of guayaba and other fruits of our trees. Everything of my cohoba they would know and interpret, and I told them everything I could.

"The ones who would murder you," I said to Enriquillo, after hearing Guarionex's message, ... "we should guide them to the gold. We can put in their path a few bars of the bullion that you have left, and knock them into our trap."

This was agreeable although the details remained shadowy. I mentioned Valenzuela and Pero López as likely culprits, among others. And I prepared a written message for López, an invitation for him and Valenzuela to meet and exchange gold bullion for a pardon and good terms for Enriquillo. I suggested the use of the good friar as ago-between, to confirm the gold exchange and the manner of the pardon. This too was agreeable.

I wrote the message with the point of a fishing hook on leaves of the copei tree. This broad leaf will maintain such an inscription forever. I saw it used by Captain Hojeda early on in the conquest; he would fool our people often by sending messages to others in ways that appeared divination to us.

I talked with Doña Mencía about Catalina Díaz and her daughter Julia, who work on the Valenzuela estate. If the would-be murderers could be deviated, and a real peace were possible, I promised that Julia would deliver the message.

Enriquillo himself took me to my horse, crossing the lake accompanied by eight canoes. I felt very connected to the young cacique, and loved everything about him. We found my poor mare, Cariblanca, quite molested by red ants during my absence. She was a bit wild and it took me an hour to calm her down. "The good friar gets full of ants like that," Enriquillo commented. Then he instructed me with great certainty: "I do not want him near the peace negotiations. Later, to guarantee the safe passage to our new community, yes. Then he would be useful. But not now, not for this mission of the peace pact, when calm must be at the center of our discussions."

I took this as an order from him.

Cacique that he is, Enriquillo then listed for me the core of his negotiating conditions: "I must have four things. One, the embassy must come from the King himself, no one from the island will I speak through. Two, the King must guarantee full pardons and freemen status for all our people here. Three, he must guarantee land and our own community. Four, the law should deputize my captains to guard the peace and manage the arrest of future runaways. Thus, we will keep our weapons and our power to travel the roads."

One hundred sixty. *I conduct a strange ceremony.*

I did the old peace-pact orations with the captains, during my final days. The behike had our pine tree resin shaped in candles for me, and I the set up the alter as Guarionex had shown me. Then I called on the fiercest warriors to come into my discipline that I carry from those times.

Tamayo was the hardest, but even he believed in me when I knelt him down facing the fire of the resin and its smoke, and I asked him to feel it in his chest. I implored him then to open up the throat, the ears, try to use the eyes, deliciously, to love the world again, what he might see or sense of being alive.

Tamayo's mother had been disembowel, his father burned alive. In reprisal, these past few years, he had killed much. "I have liked it," he said, his voice quavering. I asked him to cry if he must and he did. He cried vigorously. Tamayo has been very hurt. "You've made me cry, uncle," he said, after the ceremony. "I hope peace is truly our new way. Because war will be harder now."

I worked on young Cao, who, to my dismay, had killed almost a dozen times. Of all of them, it was young Cao who surprised me the most, as he truly had killed without bother and had no remorse to clear away.

Astin the Lucumí, a veteran from the rebellion of enslaved Africans at Don Diego Columbus' sugar mills in 1522, was another hard one. He helped hang many whites during that rebellion, even one or two who were friends. "Ever since, I have killed Castilla," he said. "By myself, more than thirty men." So much hatred came quickly out of the men that I became concerned lest they surrender their fighting spirit too soon. One plan I could not get out of my mind: the capture and just punishment of Valenzuela and the monster, Pero López. Tamayo it was, I felt, that must set the trap for Valenzuela and Pero López. In the midst of my doings with them, I was suddenly certain I wanted Tamayo and his most experienced killers to do that job. Tamayo and Cao and the Lucumí, I knew, would kill Valenzuela, would kill Pero López.

I enlisted Tamayo for the ambush of Valenzuela and Pero López then and on his own he picked Cao, Astin and three others to go along. I would lure the men to their trap, where they expected gold. The rest was left open, although Tamayo hated Valenzuela immensely, and I knew in my heart, survival was not likely for our former masters. Such talk provided a strange ending to a "change of heart" ceremony, and Enriquillo avoided having to accept the plan. I did feel twisted behind my eyes, and I noticed later the behike disappeared to the woods without saying good-bye.

One hundred sixty one. *At the convent, Las Casas returns.*

Las Casas is back. He returned quietly, the day before yesterday, on a busy morning when four other ships came in.From my high window, I saw him enter the convent, hiding under a cape. The next evening, Fray Remigio came for me. "The good friar wants to see you."

We met in his main room. Fray Remigio quietly withdrew after ushering me in. Las Casas sat in darkness, by the window. "Do not look upon me," he said. "I may or may not be here yet."

He would go out this evening, and he intended the next day to come in overland, as if from La Plata, he said, to dissimulate his comings and goings.

"That way, maybe I was in Spain, maybe I was not, but on the mainland, or in Cuba."

"I am happy not to see you again," I said, following his logic. The logic was not strange, considering that assassins have tried to kill the good friar. He ignored my remark.

"I have had your letter," I informed him. "The news of Barrionuevo has reached the baby boy, who is willing to entertain a real peace."

"Excellent," Las Casas said. "It is of great importance that I carry word of the rebellious cacique myself. I must have an exact idea of his demands when Captain Barrionuevo arrives."

"Enriquillo has formulated his own plan on this," I said, feeling guarded about the priest's willingness to command the negotiations with Enriquillo.

"The final crisis for Enriquillo is upon us," he pressed on. "Barrionuevo arrives in days. I have things set up so that the results of Enriquillo's treaty with Barrionuevo will be taken immediately to Spain, where several others are ready to carry our demand."

"What demand, father?"

"The abolishment of the encomienda, of course."

I was quiet and decided not to oppose him. The good friar is like that; once a goal enters his mind, he does not deviate. I was glad for the clarity of Enriquillo's final instruction to me. I love the good friar, but at that moment I decided myself how to deviate him, by subterfuge, from attending the negotiations. This I write with some shame: At that moment I decided to enlist him in the trap set for Valenzuela and Pero Lopéz. In the midst of a peace-pact mission, I cannot get out of my mind and heart the face of Pero Lopéz the day he took my son and sold him; and I cannot get out of my mind my joy at the sight of his face when Tamayo corners him. I thirst for the justice coming toward me in this arrangement.

"Enriquillo has communicated this to me," I said. "He would conduct two negotiations, good friar. One is with the King's ambassador, Captain Barrionuevo. The other one is with Valenzuela, his former encomendero. The second one is the dangerous one."

"Valenzuela will have to adapt to the King's capitulation, of course."

"There is danger he would destroy the negotiations, by killing or capturing Enriquillo himself. Such an occurrence, remember, would save the King the embarrassment of making a treaty with the Indian bandit, as Oviedo calls the cacique."

Las Casas said immediately, "How can we shield the cacique?"

"A message must be carried to Valenzuela, from Enriquillo, just as Enriquillo makes contact with Barrionuevo. The message will call Valenzuela and his men in a deviant chase, away from the real negotiations."

"At any time, whatever Enriquillo needs, I will do. This message I will deliver, if need be, before I leave for the negotiations."

"I am certain it will soon be time to do so," I said. Then I cleared my throat, taking my time.

"I have some notes for you," I said, still clearing my throat. I gave him a stack of written pages. "They are about the early days of Bartolomé Columbus and Guarionex."

"The Battle of la Vega?"

"It's in there."

"And Pané?"

"He too is in there, how he went to live with Guarionex."

"I have his little book," the friar said. "I got it in Seville. Martyr de Anglería had a copy made by Pané himself. It is a wonderful recollection of your old tales. I am certainly glad he noted all that."

"He didn't learn that much," I said. "Though he always had his nose in somebody's armpit."

The good friar laughed. He was happy to be back and to get the pages. I slipped away before he could deliver me with instructions. I knew for certain then he would attempt to represent Enriquillo and he believed he was empowered to do so. That could wreck everything. I needed time to lay out my plan and have things ready for when Barrionuevo arrived.

One hundred sixty two. *I ask Catalina to help me.*

Today I sought Catalina. For the fourth day, on awakening, she was in my mind's eye. I sent her a message to meet me at the back of the church. I reached from the bench behind her and put a bundle next to her. It was cohoba and tobacco. "The baby boy is well," I whispered. She grunted lightly.

"I must visit the old place, where Ceiba is resting. I must talk with her, in the cohoba."

"I can help you," Catalina answered. "I will say a birth has come up."

"I am afraid I would stay in the other side, if there's no one to remind me."

"Yes, I will excuse myself and go with you."

One hundred sixty three. *In the woods with Catalina.*

We went by way of deep woods, walking north for four days. We wanted to see no one and we talked little. Mostly she walked ahead of me and set a brisk pace. At night she rubbed my thigh forcefully for a long time with her liniment and strong thin fingers. Then, in silence, she made her own sleep in her own hammock. Twice I hunted hutía, which we roasted at night and ate with casabe torts carried in macoutíes looped to our foreheads. On the way, we gathered fruit and other things to eat. In 1533, I can write that it is still possible to find the old orchards, and even old conucos where the herbs and nut crops planted by Taíno farmers forty and fifty years ago still come up and can be harvested.

One hundred sixty four. *At my old yukaieke in the lower Magua country.*

Our third morning out, I stood in the place where once I had chopped wood with a Spanish ax. It was my first time back. The clearing was mostly overgrown, but I did find my old ax handle and I found the center post to our old bohío. Catalina found things too, which she bundled and put away without showing me.

I propped the old post up between two low parted branches on a huge ceiba tree, then lay my back against it. Catalina prepared the cohoba and made fire. In this ceremony, she would also take the cohoba snuff, but only to thank her spirit helpers and Attabai, Great Bleeding Mother, with whom, as a midwife, she is particularly related. Catalina had a double cacimba that she loaded. It went both ways, placing the snuffers into both of our nostrils at once, so we could blow each other's load at the same time. "I have not much powder in mine, so I will come out first," she said. "Do what you must and return, set your mind to return. Listen for my song, and I will bring you out."

One hundred sixty five. *With cohoba again, with Ceiba.*

That is how we did it, two days ago. And it worked for me just as I had hoped. We sat in darkness a good while. The night was early, warm and dry. We blew together, then separated. Once again I took the trail, only this time I got there on my own. This time, too, the dog walked at my side. "Beloved son," he told me with his mind as he trotted. "This will not be hard."

We came to a plateau again. Then, it was not a plateau but my old little valley and I was walking near the brook. Near the water, on a rock I remembered, Ceiba was sitting. She looked only at the water, but her body was happy to see me. We had no need for greetings.

"I was told they are alive, both of them," I told her without speaking.

The light of her spirit body emanated and I could see it. She turned my way so I could see her face, but still she did not look upon me. "One went south and one went north," I said. "They are both well and there are children."

"You are a good guaxeri, my husband, to come to me this way."

"I want you to rest. Go home to Coaibay, where the elders will surround you."

"I should not have left you, but I could not live without my Good Wind."

"They are still on earth; I cannot know more."

"Thank you, my husband. I will go join my parents now. As for you, accompany yourself, make a nest for your days ahead."

Ceiba walked away, following the current of the brook. I felt very complete and greatly satisfied. I felt tremendous peace, even in her lonely walk. I felt all my pain suddenly lift and tears began to pour from my eyes, purging my heart and lifting the pressure from my shoulders. Then suddenly, my right leg, crocodile-bitten all these years, felt strong and had bounce, and I began to run as I turned from the stream to the flat field of the plateau, jumping and hopping and with each step bouncing higher and higher and there I was jumping about my old, little valley, bouncing from clearing to clearing. And suddenly, below me, seeing my curled-up body, a shiver in my lightning spirit, I began to bounce higher and higher and I was going away and I wanted to go away and I could feel the tremendous harmony of my breath and of all Taíno memory, all Taíno goodness, all the ancestors, all of our beautiful knowledge, all of the seas and valleys of our spirit domains and I heard her singing.

> *In the path of flesh and blood you walk,*
> *Come and join me, man alive, come and join me.*
> *Your mission is done, your celestial steps complete,*
> *Come and see me, man alive, come and chew and come and swallow.*
> *Come and join me in the light, man alive, come and sleep.*

Over and over, I heard the song and I didn't resist it. I let it call me down and lull me, and I followed it back until I felt the heat of the fire, and I remembered that I was alive.

One hundred sixty six. *Finding love with Catalina.*

Catalina had fixed our hammocks. I slept until mid-morning. She was already up and had prepared a tea and a plate of fruit for me. After I ate, she led me to the stream. "Bathe," she said, handing me a crunched up ball of digo root with which to lather.

I entered the stream and bathed. Then I swam against the current a good while. Catalina sat by and watched me. "Work your leg against the water," she said. She, too, had bathed and now wore a skirt, but nothing over her breasts. Neither her nakedness nor mine bothered us. We bathed naked for several hours, occasionally walking along the shore and picking fruits and nuts for the journey. The nuts made a good paste that Catalina put in a gourd. I found a tree full of honey combs, and we sweetened the nut paste; it was very good. It was like the old days. Ceiba and I would do this, too, gather foods with her aunts and uncles, all of us naked in the old way, without a care about it.

That evening, we slept again and in the false light of dawn, I caught sight of Catalina's eyes gazing on me. I motioned her to come, and she came to lay in the crook of my arm in my hammock. We felt easy with each other, and soon she lifted her leg over my thigh and, lizardly, I hooked myself into her hold. I felt her slightest tremor, and didn't move at all. She hugged me with her deepest love and I was ironwood for her, holding fast. Catalina sighed softly and leaned down. She leaned down hard and held on so tightly it hurt. Then she caught, as we say, "the rhythm of the hammock," and we took the long ride together.

We walked back in silence, but full of love. Now, she walked behind me, watching me. That night, we stopped to rest and again, in the night, she came over. In the morning, she cooked for us as I greeted the sun and the four directions. Then we walked again, and she followed me and I could feel the warmth of her eyes, and I could fell her womans's heart envelop me. It had been many years, and it was as obvious as frogs croaking at the clouds before the rain that Catalina's was the love I needed to call warriors to peace.

One hundred sixty seven. *Barrionuevo has arrived.*

Barrionuevo, the King's embassador, has arrived. Yesterday morning, as I sat down to write, this was the shout of the town. Still at that very moment, full of words and tears of joy, I was ready to pour my heart upon the page. Four days I have been back, four days without Catalina, and I am as lonesome as a manatí pup; I, sour man with a hide like leather and a heart full of scars, I love a woman again.

But Barrionuevo has arrived. Time speeds up. The town has gone crazy with criers and rumors, the cathedral's bell rings, and the archbishop and mayor have invited the town's señores to a public meeting tomorrow. Las Casas himself has been summoned twice this afternoon, and official discussions have begun.

Barrionuevo brings two hundred men, including Captain Rodrigo Gallego, my old friend. I saw Rodrigo; however, I will wait to visit, as he is posted across town in the house of a señor named Quesada. This Quesada is quick to see deviousness in little acts and might suspect my motives. Rodrigo looked portly and quite tall. His face jowls down but still it is kind, as it was when I knew him. Rodrigo commands a troop of seventy-five men, and he is second captain under Barrionuevo. I saw him line up his men and lead them to Quesada's inn and horse stables, where they will bivouac. Something warmed inside me to see old Rodrigo, a friendship reawakened from those old days.

One hundred sixty eight. *Tempering the good friar.*

Barrionuevo is housed in special rooms at the House of Contracts, where Oidor Suazo is providing grandly for him. Las Casas goes back and forth from the convent to the House to consult with Barrionuevo. He went for a late lunch, then returned to rest and ponder. Later, he was invited to a late dinner, where he is now. After his nap, he summoned me and I put his clothes out as he bathed. He has a small tub and a sponge, with which he wipes himself off, stepping in and out of the small tub.

"They now know I am their best mediator to Enriquillo," he said. "The hook is in."

"I am glad they listen to you, father."

"The oidores know I am the one that can talk to Enriquillo. So, they are attuned to my every word," he replied. "You can be sure we will gain wide concessions."

I cannot tell the good father, I cannot even intimate to him that his argument for the negotiations centering on the abolishment of the encomienda has already been dismissed, and that he himself is not desired at the treaty-making. I must not confront him, but deviate his mind and his feet from the path of the Bahuruku parley.

"You will remember this Barrionuevo," the good friar told me as I helped him into his robes. "He was a soldier under Velázquez in the war against Guahaba and Xaraguá, around 1504, 1506."

I remember not Barrionuevo but I remember Diego Velázquez, conquistador and first governor of Cuba. I remember him very well and I remember the campaigns against Anacaona of Xaraguá and Hatuey of Guahaba. Eight

years before his mandate to conquer Cuba in 1511, Diego Velázquez commanded troops under that master of assassins, Knight Commander Ovando,
here in Santo Domingo. It was Velázquez who actually ordered the torching
of Anacaona's eighty caciques at the Banquet Massacre, in 1503. The same
Velázquez hunted down our people afterwards and caused the enslavement
of my own family. In 1511, Velázquez took me to Cuba, where he again
"gave" me into servitude. I can say I remember Velázquez very well and I
know what the soldiers did under Velázquez.

"Before the Massacre of Anacaona and the war against Xaraguá," Las
Casas went on. "Barrionuevo commanded troops against cacique Cotubanamá,
in Higüey. Afterwards, around 1508, he went on to the conquest of San Juan
Bautista (Borikén), with Ponce de León."

"Many took part and were brutal at that time, father," I said.

"He is a much older man now," the good friar responded, staring directly
at my eyes. "Barrionuevo is forthright about his mission."

Las Casas said this curtly, staring at my eyes until, out of respect, I
looked away. My remark, we both knew, recalled his own involvement in
the slaving wars back then. He himself committed acts against Taínos at
that time that now make him suffer with remorse. Knowing the good friar
for many years, I know that spiking his heart is the only way to keep his
attention. I very much want to keep his attention.

"Forgive my opinion, father?"

"Be kind, Dieguillo."

"I would stress to Barrionuevo that a pardon with dignity for Enriquillo
and his people would be an acceptable route. Enriquillo desires most of all
peace with freedom."

"The King instructed Barrionuevo to make a quick peace or a total war."

"Total war would be disastrous," I said. "And a quick peace is possible,
if we don't press for too much."

"I think his position is stronger than you think," he responded. "I tell
Barrionuevo that a new military campaign would be costly. If it were to fail,
and if Enriquillo appeared victorious, and multiplied his forces with Indians
and Africans, the Spanish could very well lose the island."

"A war would be disastrous for us, father," I insisted. "According to
Enriquillo, there is not much area left to retreat to. They could not sustain
multiple attacks ... "

"Well, but Barrionuevo, as the King's special envoy, can agree on principle to abolish the encomienda."

"One thing at a time. The encomienda as a main negotiating point could
delay the impulse too long. It could raise opposition and lead to the war."

"The moment is ripe now, and such a pronouncement, from right here in the Indies, would mean much more. At this moment, Dieguillo, if we plan this right, Barrionuevo will accept this. A royal decree just now, on the eve of a major peace—think of it, Dieguillo, it is the only justice possible for the Indian people."

The good father being resolute, I took the route of deviation. "As you say, father, it is all strategy. 'Everything in its time.' So I would add: Please let Enriquillo make that demand, let him demand the end of the encomienda himself. And if Barrionuevo balks at it, then you step up, for you must know you will be right there, at Enriquillo's side. He asked me himself to tell you. At his side." Las Casas looked relieved and alert. I smiled upon him, making my lie complete. For the first time in the twenty years I have known him, I have control over his volition, and it takes a lie. The Good Friar wants very much to be at the center of this event. I thought as we spoke: I truly have his attention now.

"Let Enriquillo lead the discussion," I pressed on, pulling now on the priest's heartfelt wish to help our people. "Let him approach as the sovereign cacique that he is. He deserves this moment." "Absolutely," Las Casas said. "I will sit at his side as a supporter, but he will lead the talking. Barrionuevo must see him as his equal." "Excellent," I said.

"When he mentions the encomienda and demands a Royal Decree, I will be there to support him, to throw the weight of my church behind him."

"At the parley, father, please. At the right moment. This is very important to Enriquillo."

"Yes, of course. I will wait for his demand, then support it."

One hundred sixty nine. *I hate telling a lie, but.*

I hate telling a lie. But the father, blessed protector, would endanger our lives with his love of our cause. No, he is too agitated and too controversial here on the islands to represent Enriquillo's interest. In fact, he will not get there. The baby boy himself spoke about the need to maintain the peaceful mind, keep humble so as not to block the path of peace.

I will ask Las Casas to certify the existence of more gold bullion and Enriquillo's offer to have a special gesture with Valenzuela. This will happen soon. He will carry the word to Valenzuela for us, I am certain, in order to deviate them from the negotiations. Then, to Las Casas I will assign a guaxeri guide, who will pretend to lose his way and keep the good friar himself from the parley site. I do this now without hesitation, although I know it can confuse my goeíç to be this way. Valenzuela and Pero López

I thus send one wrong way. And the good friar, too, will follow another wrong trail. With this I hope to keep clear our thin path to peace.

One hundred seventy. *The good friar confesses a deed of his youth.*

Again I saw him tonight. It was a long, difficult day for both him and me. I write here again how sorry I am to lie to him. I do hate to lie to this great man that trusts my word.

Las Casas paced slowly several times around his room. He was puff-eyed like an owl from lack of sleep. I prepared his cot. Finally, he sat down. "We spoke much about Ovando," he said. "Gonzalo Fernandez ... Oviedo was there. He knows it all, as usual. The gold-counter is writing a book about the Indies and he read some parts to Barrionuevo and the assembled gentlemen. It was all I could do not to fight him. He speaks of Knight Commander Nicolás de Ovando and his times as the 'years of civility' on the island. He claims Ovando established good government and stimulated a true economy here. Ovando is his big hero."

"What did you say, father?"

"I held my tongue, the bastards."

"I thank you for your silent indignation."

"Ovando massacred coldly," he said. "He calculated everything about his ways of terror."

The friar was deeply upset. He breathed heavily and rubbed his temples.

"Ovando watched it with arithmetic," I said. "He counted the dead, like logger captains count felled trees."

"What violence we have shown your people," he said harshly. "I wretch at the thought of it."

"You have done your best, Don Bartolomé. No one ... "

"I, too, have killed men of your race. Dieguillo, I even took slaves, several times, and sold them, I accepted an encomienda ... "

"You don't have to confess to me, father," I said. "I am pitiful before you."

"Tonight you are my confessor, Dieguillo," he said. "You who remember those days."

He had fought as a soldier, and had once led a cannon crew, during the round-up of caciques after Anacaona's Massacre. During a skirmish, he held the igniting ember on the cannon when a Taíno group of about fifteen people approached. "We had fought all day," he said. "They had only wooden weapons and there was no fight left in them. There were men and women and I knew they would not attack. Yet, the fury was part of me. I had the urge. I bade our crew prepare to fire. I looked at the group of poor Indians and lit the fuse. I remember the blast was of a furnace exploding toward them. Of fifteen, six fell dead, cut to pieces, and then everything was still. I can see the faces of the ones left standing, how surprised they looked."

"I know what carnage looks like," I said.

"Oh, Lord in Heaven, forgive me," he said, and knelt. I touched his head. I felt mildly sick.

"On behalf of your people, Dieguillo, forgive me."

I could forgive him, too, even though it was precisely during those campaigns I lost my own free village and even my family. "You have saved more than a hundred times six of our people, father, and many more, since that time. A devil's act in your youth does not define your destiny. You did not cause the wars, nor did you command your own place in the circumstances. As for the dead," I told him, "in our way, we believe they will be waiting for you when you pass on to the Spirit World. There you will have to explain yourself to them." "Forgive me now, Dieguillo," he said. "So I may be absolved that horrible task."

"I forgive you, father," I said. "And I pray for you that they, too, will forgive you."

One hundred seventy one. *Las Casas goes again.*

Today early again, Las Casas went over for meetings. I caught him by the big wooden doors shortly after the seven o'clock mass as he left the convent. "Remember that Enriquillo is a peaceful man," I repeated to him. "Barrionuevo can trust his intentions to settle a community with his captains, to farm and raise cattle and be good neighbors."

Las Casas nodded. "Friend and brother, we are in good accord," he said. "We will free many Indians with this one."

One hundred seventy two. *In the memory: Velázquez presses me into service.*

In the morning, I sent Father Remigio with a note for Rodrigo Gallego, inviting his visit to the convent tomorrow. I ate at mid-morning and then took a nap, having stayed up writing last night. I dreamt vividly during my nap and now I write my dream.

I saw Manazas in my dream, just as I saw him in the cohoba, sitting, looking away from me. Manazas was a big man, a soldier's soldier. He wore plated armor and he carried two swords. I killed Manazas at the Massacre of Anacaona, in the late afternoon, after ten hours of mayhem and carnage, when the Taíno men had retreated and Ovando was counting the dead.

That was in 1504, or thereabouts. I say that truly because, even though my duty on the ship's ampolleta fixed in me the breaks of daily time, those later years have blended for me one on another. Those were my seasons of peace, my only ones since I left home. That was when my world was ruled by Ceiba, my cacique queen that could run a yukaieke of a hundred and forty relatives with the precision of nature itself. That was when I saw my two boys, who are still *alive*, who are still alive, that was when I saw them grow and sprout, those two skinny reeds forming out calf and butt, strong little chests, running and jumping in the grass. That was the time when the Castilla forgot about me and my little village, and for almost five years we tended our cunukus and gathered our honey and fished in several abundant streams. We grew pigs even then, in those early years, and hutía was still abundant—and yaguasa duck and iguana and majá—and, as always in our lands, there was abundant fruit. Perhaps this is what Enriquillo's camp recalls for me most of all: those peaceful seasons for me before I met Las Casas, between the time Guarionex left us in 1498 and the time in 1503 when Captain Diego Velázquez and a hundred of his Castilla troops, with more than three hundred Indian mansos, came into my little valley looking for me.

Velázquez carried a letter from the Admiral's son, Don Diego Columbus, pressing me into service as interpreter and guide. At the end of my service, which was mandatory in any case, I would receive a horse, the letter said.

I left with Velázquez within the hour, apprehensive anew of the many soldier's eyes that had gazed upon my valley. Avarice was the expression in those faces for the pretty gardens and the layout of the streams and the able-bodied Taínos in my yukaieke. I remember Ceiba's eyes that would not cry in my presence. The twins played behind her in our bohío, and I saw only flashes of them as I walked away.

One hundred seventy three. *The route to Xaraguá with Velázquez.*

"We travel south and west to Xaraguá," Velázquez informed me, as we camped for the evening. "Anacaona is to greet us. The Knight Commander, Nicolás de Ovando, and his army, are to visit her villages soon."

Of the major seats of Taíno authority on the islands, Xaraguá was the only one left. Bohekio, its distinguished old cacique, had died, but his sister, Anacaona, who held several clan lines in her own person and who was the highest ranking ni-Taína, commanded increasing respect. Anacaona, who was Doña Mencía's direct-line grandmother, was quite a woman. Tall, beautiful and regal, she was in her late thirties and had boundless energies for every sort of activity. With the demise of the great cacicazgos of Caonabó, Guarionex and Guacanagari, and the death of her brother, Bohekio, the court of Anacaona became, more and more, the gathering place for the island's younger caciques and elder guaxeris.

Of the island's sachem women and their families, from which the caciques were chosen, Anacaona was queen. Beyond holding nearly all hereditary lines, Anacaona herself sponsored many areitos and organized societies of singers and dancers. She had been an intimate of Guarionex and had married Caonabó, and she had been the forbidden love of Guacanagari. She was Ya-ya Grandmother, and all of our Taíno people gave her great respect. Moreover, adept agriculturists were her guaxeri. They had an ingenious system of irrigation that distributed large volumes of water from the verdant hills to their much-drier plains. In Xaraguá, they brought up huge quantities of yuca and produced mountains of casabe torts, also much corn and peppers and several varieties of beans and several varieties of tomatoes. For their feasts, Anacaona's guaxeri produced many combinations of foods, recited poetry, put up jousting contests, huge ball games, acrobatics and other things.

Along the way to Xaraguá, Velázquez, who rode a red Andalusian gelding, spoke to me in ways that inspired some hope for a positive meeting with Anacaona. Velázquez was already forty-years old by then, but he was lean and tough and very vigorous. "Xaraguá is well-organized," he said. "The people are productive, and Anacaona wants peace, it would seem."

"My captain," I said, always repeating a Castilla's words back to him, "this Taíno queen would make peace with the Castilla, and her people produce many beautiful things."

"I have seen her gifts to the Adelantado, Don Bartolomé Columbus."

"The Xaraguanes have paid much tribute," I said.

"They have no gold," he said. "But I am told they are fine artesans, that they can build good boats and homes and they can feed a mighty number of people."

Then, without another word, he rode off. That was on our way to Anacaona's main batey, her court of Xaraguá.

Later, as we approached her villages and the Xaraguá men spotted us and began to trail us, I hoped some friendship could be maintained. Maybe, I thought, the Castilla will see the productivity of the Xaraguanes and allow them to continue with their own cunukus and villages.

One hundred seventy four. *The Massacre of Anacaona's Banquet.*

I will write about the massacre here, because of course I was wrong to hope. The Knight Commander joined forces with our troop at the Yaqui River, just at the entrance to Xaraguá province. More than three hundred Castilla soldiers and some seven hundred Indians, more than a thousand combined troops, formed companies and marched into Xaraguá. I should have known the Knight Commander planned a wicked thing, but at that moment only the officers knew. The Indians were not told until just before the deed.

Anacaona's main village was squarely set, following the four directions. In the center, a large batey, or plaza, opened quite wide. The visit began with song and ceremony, with a feast and a dance and with the highest of expectations among our people that the Castilla might still learn, after all. Anacaona feasted everyone. She had foods prepared for weeks of feasting, and some eighty caciques gathered to celebrate areitos with her and to see what the Castilla might plan for them. She distributed our thousand men, ten or twenty to each bohío, for the cacique families to feed and host. She assigned to our herd of seventy horses a large pasture with water that Castilla soldiers secured and guarded.

The Knight Commander Ovando was an austere man of the church, lean and cold, with a very big face and head. He wore long robes, even on horseback, and he forgot nothing, ever. When two years before Bobadilla took the three Columbus brothers, including the Admiral himself, to Spain in chains, accused of excessive violence, corruption and other abuses of power, it was Ovando, a count, who was the King's selection to clean up the mess. Ovando was a man of great authority and inquisitorial character.

That fateful morning, I sat with Commander Ovando and his captains as they met with Anacaona and several of her caciques in front of Ovando's caney. This was a large palm structure given to him by the cacica, where I myself had hung my hammock at the Commander's instruction. At a second caney, almost as large, built across a corridor, the Commander ordered a cross put up.

I knew I needn't interpret for Anacaona, since she spoke more than a bit of Castillian by then, but she did not reveal her capacity, and I did not either. However, I felt a great tension, despite the diplomatic talk and many gifts being exchanged. Anacaona sat next to Ovando, her voluptuous breasts barely covered by a black Spanish shawl, a gift of the Adelantado Bartolomé Columbus, in earlier years. The Commander looked away as he spoke to her, even as he gave her gifts of combs, mirrors and small looms, but Anacaona was wonderful to look at. Not only was her body fully endowed, a woman of proportion, she was endowed with a masterful energy, a vibrant, continuous motion. The urge to hold and envelop her hung around Anacaona like a warm mist.

Anacaona's diplomacy, I could tell, agitated the Knight Commander. A natural consequence of her energy was that she approached principal men with both her mind and her body and had thus known several of the commanders that had come her way. Thus she had tempered the excesses of both the Adelantado, Don Bartolome Columbus, and of his mortal enemy, Francisco Roldán. Don Bartolomé was honest with her, but it was precisely Roldán who denounced her to Ovando as treacherous and rebellious.

On Ovando's first night in, after a late meal and some wine, Anacona enveloped him in her fog and led him across the yard nearly to her hammock, where suddenly the Commander declined her invitation curtly, walking rapidly away, eyes widened and red-streaked. Everyone saw the move, caciques and officers, and Ovando made his blood-furious plan. I heard him say in the late evening, "A rebellion is in the offing here. The filthy slut won't let things be."

"Her people will follow her, Commander," Velázquez, who was nearby, said.

"She is in need of a Christian example," Ovando replied.

One hundred seventy five. *The killing begins, Enriquillo in my arms.*

When, after lunch the next day, he told her he would celebrate a mass for her many chiefs, I interpreted Ovando's words to the cacica, and thought to myself how simple and easy everything might turn out. First he would show them a parade of horses, then he would celebrate a mass. He loved their souls, he said, and would endeavor to show them the way to everlasting life. Yes, I thought that maybe I was seeing Christian love for our people. Tribute would be exacted, no doubt, but possibly softened by the mission of the sacred sacraments. Among the horses, a bay gelding was trained to dance on his hind legs, to bow and curtsy. He did this to sounds from a flute. It was quite gracious. All seventy of Ovando's horsemen were mounted when Ovando requested the Indian chiefs of the region to join him inside his second caney. About eighty caciques went inside, and I was to follow when Ovando held my arm back. "Stay with me," he said. He then grabbed a golden crucifix that hung from his neck.

Suddenly, the captains jumped into action and the caciques were surrounded in the big caney. Velázquez seized Anacaona, looped a rope around her wrists and tied them behind her back, and then brought her out. Led away by two soldiers, she stopped in her tracks where I stood with the Commander. "What have we done to you?" she cried to him. "We received you with song. We have offered you everything!"

"You are as soiled as a mud snake," Commander Ovando said calmly to her. "By authority of Church and King, I will hang you for your sins against nature."

Holding lances and swords at the ready, a hundred soldiers and another hundred manso Indians surrounded the captive caciques. "Prisoners you are," a captain said, instructing ten men to tie up the caciques. "Submit, or we will burn your queen," he told them. A dozen other soldiers held flaming torches, and many others piled dry branches around the palm and thatch building. When most of the caciques had been tied up inside, the soldiers exited and tightened up around the building. "Fire to the devils," Velázquez cried on a nod from the Knight Commander. All around, the caney was lit and a fire roared in minutes.There was much groaning and coughing. A few men tried to break through the cane walls but the soldiers sliced and poked at them as they did, then pushed them back on the burning pyre.

Guaxeris and the few remaining caciques not at the banquet but around the yukaieke began to come over, inquiring about the fire and commotion. They met a quadrant with lines of horses, bowmen and arquebus shooters. Then four companies of swordsmen were signaled to rampage. Great mayhem broke lose, hundreds of people running, then circling back and attacking with rocks and lances, clubs and daggers.

I stood by the Commander, frozen. He had ordered a crossbow and, after several shots, spiked an arrow into an Indian's neck. Ovando had a guard of twenty around him, half mounted, half on the ground. Suddenly he mounted his own horse. "Commander," I said, fearing for my life to be left alone, with battle raging all around me. He looked at me and took off his red shoulder cape, then hollered to the troops all around us. "Do not harm Diego Colón, who is protected by my cape." Several captains and soldiers repeated the order and many Castilla looked my way in mid-fight. Then Ovando was gone, mounted and with his lance set to his stirrup, out to run Indians through.

The guaxeri of Anacaona fought well. They attacked fearlessly, trying to get to their burning caciques and more than once the Spanish horsemen had to retreat. Many horses were killed and more than fifty Castilla soldiers. I moved little from Ovando's assigned caney, as the Castilla in battle often went berserk, killing even manso Indians like me.

Once, after several hours, I was suddenly alone, the battle having moved on to a field at the edge of the village. Venturing out, I turned and found myself facing a wounded Taíno, a minor cacique with a deep cut in his shoulder. I helped him back to the Commander's caney and dressed his wound. This was Enriquillo's father, who died months later from his wounds. Suffering horribly, he told me about his two boys who were hiding in a grove of fruit trees about a hundred yards away. The soldiers had almost found them, so he had jumped out to draw them away. He took a sword blow, but distracted the soldiers and kept running. "Please get my boys, guaxeri," he said. "Bring them here before the maguacokios kill them."

I could see the tree grove through the door of the caney. Small groups of Indians still confronted soldiers in the distance, but around the bohíos the fighting was dying down. Wearing the Commander's red cape I walked rapidly to the grove of trees. "Come boys," I whispered as I came near. "Follow me to your Guarao, your father."

The boys came out and took my hands. Just then, three Castilla swordsmen came around a corner of a bohío. "Who goes?" they challenged me. "Under orders of the Knight Commander," I lied, walking away. "I am to care for these boys."

"The Knight Commander has skewered half a dozen like that," a big soldier said. He had huge hands and forearms. Manazas (Big Hands) was his nickname. "Don't you know that nits make lice?"

He walked behind me, on my left, his sword in hand. The two boys and I hurried, but now the other two men ran around my right, to cut me off. They were mostly playing, those two, but I lost sight of Manazas, who was not. Then I heard the swoosh and the sword clearing by, and the boy on my left dropped, both legs cut off at the knee.

"And fuck the cunt of your mother to hell," Manazas said, threatening to strike me. I huddled down under the cape, pulling both boys under me, although the one struck was quickly dying.

"Enough, Manazas," one soldier said. "The Commander ordered safe passage for this son of a dog." Manazas put the point of his sword under my ear, then pulled away. "A turd on this guy," he said.

The boy was already dead as the four swordsmen walked away. The other one I picked up in my arms and held to my breast. I ran with him to the Commander's caney, where his father hid behind bails of cotton.

That boy, then five years old, was Enriquillo. It was his older brother, Nicosa, whose legs Manazas sliced off.

In the late afternoon, the Knight Commander returned. He was weary and sore, having taken severe hits by stones and sticks on his body. He had one elbow the size of a pineapple. As I helped him undress and hang his hammock, I explained to Ovando about the wounded father and his son, how they were good people and had volunteered to come under my command.

"Let them rest in the corner," he said, as he lay down, "so they won't be counted among the slaves."

One hundred seventy six. *Encounter with Manazas at the stream.*

In the fainting sunlight, I noticed myself caked with blood and thought to wash in a nearby stream. On the way out, I spotted several daggers in the Knight Commander's sword case and, on impulse, pulled one out, and tied it to a cord under my shirt and the Commander's red cape that I still wore.

Outside, some soldiers made small fires as others piled the dead in rows at the center plaza. Indians not captured had retreated across the wide savannah to a nearby forest. Captives were crammed into bohíos, threatened with death and cut on the slightest pretext.

I carried a jug and told the guards, "The Commander requires water." Then I walked down the maze of bohíos to a small hill circled by a brook. I followed the brook a few minutes into the grove of trees, in the darkening woods, to a small, deep pool. I took my cape and shirt off, folded the dagger into my clothes and was about to enter the pool, when I heard a crashing through the trees and retreated with my things behind a bush.

It was a Castilla soldier. I watched his big shadow as he took off his helmet and chain link shirt and breeches.Then I could see quite clearly it was Manazas. He stood by a tree to piss, then took his pants off. He was naked but for long socks. Then, he was on his knees, leaning at the water's edge, splashing his face and scrubbing his hands and forearms that glistened in the receding light. I was naked too, and it was not even a thought but a silent command I felt in my chest and thighs, and in two bounces I was on his back and straddling his waist like a horse I spiked the dagger deep into his lower back, right along the spine.

"Cabrón," he jumped up. "Indio de mierda," he yelled spinning around once and twice, but my legs were strong and I held onto his hair and the hilt of the dagger that was deep in him. His hair smelled of rancid olive oil. I felt his hand come up behind me and grab my shoulder, and I twisted the dagger hard as I could and scraped it through the bony column and felt his back snap. He dropped to his knees and I fell off, rolling to the side. I could see him leaning on his elbows, trying to look up.

"Man of the Devil," I told him, as his head drooped. "I have killed you." And I had. His one elbow gave and then the other. I jumped on his back again, pulled the dagger out and carefully placed the point at the base of the neck, as I had seen the Spanish captains do. Then I drove it in. Manazas gurgled and vomited and defecated and his body went totally limp at the edge of the pool.

I washed hurriedly, dressed, and came out of the woods with a full jug of water. The light of the sun made faint effort to guide my steps. I felt the cool of the woods recede. I felt very good and I felt very hurt, out of balance. I felt a great release in my breast, but a clog was coming up in my throat that I would cough up for days.

One hundred seventy seven. *Suspected in the killing.*

Soldiers found Manazas' corpse early the next morning. Some remembered my encounter with him, and others remembered my going for water the previous evening. I had put away the dagger unnoticed and stayed in the caney all day, but they came to accuse me. "Son of a dog," one of Manazas' squad told me. "Manazas should have killed you. You put the blade to our capo from behind."

"I am incapable of such a deed," I said to the Knight commander, Nicolás de Ovando, whose side I dared not leave. "Besides, I carry no sword."

"It is true, he is unarmed, and has served me loyally," Ovando told the men, who desisted upon his word.

Captain Velázquez believed against me. He kept me in service until the main villages of Anacaona were secured, then released me with these words. "Castilla blood stains your hand, Dieguillo. But for the Knight Commander's piety your eyes would be the shit of worms now. So take not glee in your freedom, a debt you owe my Lord and King."

One hundred seventy eight. *My village becomes an encomienda.*

That was in 1503. I returned home but within six months. My little yukaieke was run over by new settlers and soldiers, veterans of the campaigns against Higüey granted their own lands. The next year, Queen Isabel called for hearings on the dreadful massacres, then died. Ovando held the requested hearing, where his own captains testified to the guilt of Anacaona in planning an insurrection. No one paid attention. New ships were arriving by the week. Before long, I heard say, twelve thousand Castilla populated the island, and some three hundred hacendados held very large estates of gold mines, sugar cane and cattle. They had founded seventeen townships and the great hunt for Indian servants and slaves was on. Those taken in war were to be slaves.

But all were counted and tagged or branded and assigned to encomiendas large and small. Every soldier, every newcomer, brigand or noble, demanded his Indians to command and work.

In mid 1505, our whole yukaieke became an encomienda for Juan de Pastrana, a Christian man who died suddenly one night, having worked us for a horrible year that cost us forty-two people. I was branded in the shoulder, yet I might have traded freedom for my early services when, in 1506, the Admiral of the Ocean Sea, Don Christopherens Columbus, died in Spain. His brothers and sons still owned property and political office on Española, but they had many problems, not much real power and no time for me. It was then that Pero López de Mesa bargained with Knight Commander Ovando for the rest of us, and Ovando parceled us out to that son of a great whore. Our encomienda to Pero López appears in the books, when such were formalized by Pasamonte in 1514. Although by then we were not even any longer under Pero López, the book shows my assignment, with fifteen persons, and Ceiba's, under the name of María de Luna, with fifty-eight others. But truly, not six years later, even before it was recorded, I had not one of my village people, not Ceiba, not my boys, not anybody—all dead or lost. But for that bastard, Pero López, I might still have some family; damn him to hell and to rot in the swamps for his wretched deeds!

Folio VI

The First Good Treaty

*Death remains ... Morning feeling ... More gold for the Castilla ...
Rodrigo comes and hears my tale ... I arrange with Rodrigo to guard
Enriquillo's safety ... On the King's vessel ... Conversation with
Barrionuevo, his campaign in Borikén ... Barrionuevo has questions
about Enriquillo ... Picking at my wound ... Hatuey, "Certainty of Sun
in the Sky," our great hero ... The spirits are all around us ... Another
conversation with Barrionuevo ... Continuing to work with
Barrionuevo ... Opening the path ... Making connection, the change of
heart ... Cruelties of Vasco Porcallo ... Caymán-hunting days ... One
areito remembered ... Another gold trap ... Happiness to be in thick of
events ... Catalina becomes my wife ... Going to the Bahuruku
again ... Deminán and the guanguayo turtle create the islands ...
Warriors who would be husbands ... Catalina stays with Mencía ... At
the enchanted falls ... More cohoba revelations ... Details of
contact ... A hint of reversal ... Guarocuya does a hawk dance, he takes
me out ... The behike explains ... Tamayo's report ... My paper runs
short ... Staying away from the peace making ... Feeling the good
friar ... Last of the paper on the ship ... Indians as dignitaries ...
All that I can fit ...*

One hundred seventy nine. *Death remains.*

Today I woke up tired. I wrote late into the night and didn't dream but turned over and over. If I lay still, my heart thumped brusquely in my chest, bringing a tremor to my limbs. I was not made for killing, and even the memory of my act, and of my second such act, later, in Cuba, when I killed "Skinny" Moisés, put shivers in my bones.

"Death stays with the man who kills," Guarionex used to say. I know what he meant. He did not mean the spirit of the dead will haunt you, or that death itself will take you prematurely. He meant that the cold breath of death will be there to stunt the things that you give life to, to sour your human communion with the earth.

One hundred eighty. *Morning feeling.*

I reread last night's entry. This is true, too: writing these memories helps lift the weight of my spirit. More and more and more, I like what it does. Oh, but to have the time and paper to write it all, everything, now that my memory has fully awakened. I fear not the night, for I will never be alone. The little voices speak to me, the little souls of my dead people that say: remember it all, Guaikán.

One hundred eighty one. *More gold for the Castilla.*

Time is now for the gold to be shown, according to our strategy. Today I send Fray Remigio to Valenzuela. He will carry the message from Enriquillo, the one written in the broad leaves of the copei tree. I send with him also one of two small gold bars I obtained from Enriquillo.

At his mountain yukaieke, Enriquillo told me, "Use these gold bars, the last ones I have left. This is the gold they love, that shines beautifully and is heavy."

"I see its light," I told him. "and it is beautiful."

"They will follow the gold," he said. "It is a certain thing."

The gold bar should convince the would-be assassins.The message tells them of the trail they will be shown. We will lead Valenzuela and Pero López and one Vadillo cousin to the gold. Thus, they will travel away from the place of negotiations. Thus, we will protect the baby boy.

One hundred eighty two. *Rodrigo comes and hears my tale.*

This afternoon, Rodrigo came, my friend of the days of the Santa María. He has grown stout these past forty years and has a full beard, and his head is balding, but in his smile I see the boy I knew.

"Guaikán," he said, embracing me. "My boyhood friend." We sat near the garden, under a tall guásima tree.

"When Friar Las Casas delivered your letter, I was very happy," he said. "I knew that, if chosen, I would come."

"There are but few of us left, Rodrigo," I said. "You remember the hundreds of villages, all over the islands?"

He nodded. "I forget not Guacanagari and the kindness of his people. I remember that time like a beautiful dream.Your people seemed so peaceful to me, the way they lived."

"We have nothing left of all that," I said. "But for the young man in the bush that you are here to pacify."

"I have heard the stories, through Las Casas and others," he said. "It saddens me what has occurred to the good Taínos."

Again, I think that Rodrigo is the only truly pure one I ever met among the Christians. He is a man of pure motive. I have lived long enough to confirm that this is a rare thing among the "covered men."

"Enriquillo, he is the only one we have left," I repeated, looking at Rodrigo's sincere eyes.

"Yes," he said. "And I believe we can settle with him. In fact, we have to resolve the hostilities. Total war will follow the failure of peace."

A young monk served us tea. Rodrigo was impressed and winked at me. "They treat me well," I said. "My place here is on a grant from the second admiral, Don Diego Columbus,who recognized my service to his father."

We talked of the first Admiral, my adopted father, whom I had seen a final time in 1500, when Bobadilla accused him of corruption and took him back to Spain in chains.

"I saw him not much later in Seville," Rodrigo said, "when the Queen reinstated him and before he embarked on his fourth and final voyage."

"He stranded himself in Xamayca that time."

"Around 1504," he said.

"Yes," I said. "Knight Commander Ovando was governor then. Ovando would not rescue him. He left the Admiral stranded for months. They say around here that voyage broke his health."

"I remember the news of his death, in 1506," Rodrigo said. "Meager was his funeral." He shook his balding head. "Ay, Guaikán, it has been a whole lifetime for us since then. By 1506, I had three children of my own."

"I had two," I said. "Twins."

"Boys?"

"Yes, boys," I said.

He wanted to know my story, everything about it, from the time of our tearful farewell in Seville, in 1493, to the very present. His own children were grown, he said, with their own families, and he was a grandfather twelve times. I told him about my boys and what happened to my wife, Ceiba.

"In 1509, just after first rain, they took one my boys. Good Wind. He was eleven. They sold him to become a pearl diver. I never saw him again." My words quickly watered his eyes.

"Captain Hojeda set up an operation at Cumaná, on the mainland, where large beds of pearls were found. Pero López, a man who still lives, owned my encomienda then. My boy could dive well and Pero López realized it. One afternoon, while I planted a field, he took my Good Wind away."

"That presents a tremendous disgust," Rodrigo said. "Agh, what horrible disgust!"

I told him about Ceiba, how she fainted, again and again. Good Wind had understood immediately. This is what hurt her so much. His mind was always so keen and clear. "Tell my father I am gone," he told her. Then he put up both his thumbs next to each other and told Heart of Earth, his brother. "This is us. At night I will look at my thumbs and think of you."

He was gone two weeks when Ceiba took the hyen, the poisonous juice of our yuca and lived three days in mortal pain. "I am sorry, my husband, my son," she said, to me and to Heart of Earth. "I can no longer live."

Rodrigo looked away from me. "She was heartbroken," he said. "She died of a broken heart."

I thought of Ceiba in my cohoba dream, how lucky I was to have seen her. But this is only mine to know.

"And the boy?" Rodrigo asked.

"I heard years later, from a sailor. Ten months my boy dived for pearls. Then, once, he dived and never surfaced."

"I am sorry," he said.

"I believe he escaped," I said. "I don't know how, but I believe he escaped. He swam underwater somehow, and escaped into the great forest."

"I pray that it is so," Rodrigo said. "And the other?"

I told him that story, too, how Heart of Earth and I went to Cuba with Velázquez, in 1511, how we lived the conquest there, which was the very worst, how my boy left with Ponce de León on his voyage to explore the coast of La Florida, how he never returned.

"And his fate?"

"He lives, this I know, but nothing else."

"So he stayed in the Florida land?" "Yes."

"And you believe he is alive?"

"With certainty." I caught his eyes, which without knowing how, understood the depth of my certainty.

"I am disgusted by my countrymen, old friend," Rodrigo stood up suddenly, going nowhere. "The thought of their deeds sickens my heart."

"Dominus dedit, Dominus abstulit; sit nomen Domini benedictum," I said, to calm his spirit. "The Lord giveth and the Lord taketh away. Blessed be the name of the Lord."

One hundred eighty three. *I arrange with Rodrigo to guard Enriquillo's safety.*

I am thankful for the presence of my friend. He stayed late into the night and I told him many things. On our last few weeks together in Seville, after I had learned the Castillian language thoroughly, it was the same. He liked to hear my stories then, too. I talked to him today about Ovando and the Massacre of Anacaona's Banquet, and about how I carried the Enriquillo boy after his brother was killed.

"So you know the young man?"

"Like a son."

"Will he make peace?"

"If these monsters don't kill him first."

He promised to help in any way possible. I told him about the assassination attempt we expected and gave him the names to watch for among Valenzuela's and Pero López' henchmen, particularly that of Francisco Hernández, Valenzuela's foreman, who will go along on Barrionuevo's ship.

"Barrionuevo is encouraged to go in search of Enriquillo," he said. "We are to sail along the southern coast. I can bring you along as an interpreter."

"I will go," I said, suddenly my heart racing. I know now this is the why of Rodrigo. That is the ship for me to be on at this moment.

"We take few troops, as a true peace will be proposed, but enough to curtail the scabby rats that would kill the cacique. If Enriquillo will react as you say, and everything goes all right, there should be no need for war."

Everything I have arranged via Rodrigo, including the use of Julia (Catalina's daughter, Inés), as intermediary to Enriquillo from Barrionuevo. The two women will meet me at Yakimo. Rodrigo and I achieve a loyal understanding without need of promises. We leave in a week on board commander Barrionuevo's ship. I also have made final arrangements for the misguidance of Friar Las Casas, who is to go the wrong way, north; and of the chief plotters against our baby boy, the heartless and the greedy triad, who will go the wrong way, south, deep into the wrong peninsula. Remigio takes the good friar one way while Cao and Silverio make the rendezvous with Valenzuela and Pero López. May the good father forgive me for my deceit; may the three walking murderers, especially that walking dead man, Pero López de Mera, meet the fate they fully deserve.

May 8, 1533

One hundred eighty four. *On the King's vessel.*

I write today on board the ship called *El Imperial*, which is the King's very own vessel. We sail west along the southern coast. Thirty-five soldiers and sixteen Indians, including myself. I have brought a few sheets of paper to make these notes, although the bulk of my pages I have left in my room at the convent. I have grown fond of the pages I have written, and read them over and over, despite the sadness they often bring me. Truly, life has improved for me. Catalina is in route to meet me and Rodrigo, my boyhood friend, is with me; we face the sea-breeze together again. On the ocean now, we head toward Enriquillo's mountains and my thoughts clear.

May 10, 1533

One hundred eighty five. *Conversation with Barrionuevo, his campaign in Borikén.*

Knowing who I am and wanting to converse of the early days, Barrionuevo called for me today. We sat in his cabin, where the roll of the ship is little felt.

"I remember hearing of you during the campaign for Higüey, but I don't think I ever saw you."

"I was under Captain Velázquez then."

"And you served the first Admiral in his first voyage?"

"Yes, and in the second."

"And you were in Cuba, too, with Velázquez?"

"Yes," I told him.

"And San Juan Bautista, were you ever there?"

"Borikén, in our language," I said, and he nodded, recognizing the word. "Yes, I was there, but briefly, once, with Ponce de Leon. I was encomended to Pero López de Mesa, here in Española, during that time, but he lent me out, first to Ponce and then to Velázquez."

"I fought in San Juan Bautista, Puerto Rico," Barrionuevo said. "A difficult campaign, that one."

He spoke about Agüeybanax, the main cacique of Borikén, who led a war against the Castilla.

"Our soldiers were real men in those days," Barrionuevo said. "Sleeping on the ground with rocks for pillows, swords at the ready, not like the dressed up darlings in Santo Domingo."

"Yes," I agreed. "They were very tough."

"Even so, Agüeybanax gave us a good fight. He defeated Sotomayor and killed eighty of his men. And around the island, his warriors that time killed maybe seventy or eighty more of our men." "I remember the dog, Becerrillo," I said. "He went on the same ship as I."

Barrionuevo laughed out loud. "Yes, the dog. I had forgotten that dog."

It was that awful dog, I believe, not the soldiers, that defeated Agüeybanax. He was a war mastiff, big as a pony and with jaws that could snap a man's leg. In Borikén, when that war started, I saw two of our Indian men gutted out in but a few seconds by Becerrillo. This was the sport of Ponce, who favored that sort of spectacle. A great laugh he caused once, when he let the Becerrillo loose against an old Indian woman, made to run for the purpose of being torn to pieces. As the dog approached her, the old woman sat down. She said in our language, "Big dog, do not kill me, I mean you no harm."

The Becerrillo sniffed at her but did not bite. Instead, he lifted his leg and pissed on her.

I told the story to Barrionuevo. I always tell that story to make the old Castilla captains laugh, and it always gets a rise out of them, how an old woman's terror ended in dog piss. Barrionuevo laughed. I knew he would.

"That dog was a wonder of nature," Barrionuevo said. "Never has there been such an animal again."

"He had not a chance to breed," I reminded him and he nodded. That was another story. Having gifted Barrionuevo his laugh at the expense of an old woman of my own kind, now I wanted to interject on our behalf. "Becerrillo was executed by a poisoned arrow."

"A Carib war party murdered him," Barrionuevo offered.

A raid was mounted just to kill the awful beast and did succeed in putting a poison arrow into him. And they were not Carib but our own Taíno men from the lesser islands who killed him. But I let the error pass. The Castilla have always confused our different Indian peoples.

"Those were some grand days, eh, my friend?" Barrionuevo said, as he walked away.

I am glad for his gesture of friendship, but I disagree. Those were horrible, confusing days. In Borikén, our Taíno still believed the Castilla to be spirit people, men who knew not death. Agüeybanax, a fearless cacique, could not get his men to fight such beings. One of his caciques, Urayoán, ordered his men to drown a young Castilla, named Salcedo, just to see if he could die. Three days Urayoán waited before declaring Salcedo dead. Then he went to war. That was on the Guarabo river, as I remember it.

One hundred eighty six. *Barrionuevo has questions about Enriquillo.*

Barrionuevo listened out my story, then commandeered the conversation. "But the cacique, Enriquillo, he knows the Castilla can die."

I nodded. "There has been much killing, on all sides, to prove it."

"I quarrel none with that fact," Barrionuevo offered. "But I have a question for you. Enriquillo takes to the bush in 1519. I understand his reasons—the rape of his woman and the ill-treatment at the encomienda. But why then, and why him? Such abuse was common, after all."

"Everything else failed for him," I said. "With your forgiveness, even the schemes of the good friar Las Casas, bringing the Jeronomyte fathers to abolish the encomienda ... "

"Those friars were bribed. They ended up owning Indians themselves," Barrionuevo said.

"That is what I mean. Enriquillo could see no other recourse. He tried to bring his case to the court. He even understood the Queen's laws protecting the family"

"I hear he carries himself with dignity."

"Yes, a very serious man."

"From Anacaona's people?"

"His father was a lesser ni-Taíno and a good man. He died of his wound later, but Enriquillo's yukaieke survived the massacre. On my own recommendation, Enriquillo himself went to the Franciscans, who instructed him in Christianity and the law."

Barrionuevo is short and rotund of belly. He has a wide, very white face that exudes determination.

"He sounds like a man of his word, from all I've heard. If he wants, he could make peace this time," he said. "His case is acceptable if he would seek a pardon and pacify his people."

I was gratified to hear Captain Barrionuevo express himself thus. Enriquillo has wanted no more. And he knows this is the last chance for peace.

"It is the general feeling right now to make a peace," Barrionuevo said. "The King has much to administrate already. Here, few of your Indians are left, but in Yucatán and Mexico, Nicaragua and Perú, they are many, many. And the Africans are expensive to bring over. The talk, even in Santo Domingo, is to secure a way that will not destroy the laborer or slave. What is sought is a long-term prosperity. After all, if Enriquillo can carry on such a war here, what might not happen on the mainland?"

"The young cacique is not a man of threats," I said. "A good approach by a man of your honesty ... "

"Of course, if not by peace, the killing will be total when we press on. The Queen herself said, 'No quarter for the treasonous ... ' "

"A man has only so much killing in him," I said, angling for his own sentiment.

"For me it is so," Barrionuevo let on, opening his heart to me in a way that feeds my hope.

May 16, 1533

One hundred eighty seven. *Picking at my wound.*

Today I write in Rodrigo's small room, as our ship sails slowly against a strong current. We sail along the coast and soon will be at Yakimo, a port near the foothills of the Bahuruku. There I will disembark and seek the baby boy, to make proper arrangements for a parley. I feel totally engaged in this peacemaking now, my concentration deviates not and it feels I have everything in motion.

I think of many things today. I think of my other son, Heart of Earth, who went with me under Velázquez. I think of Ponce de León, the conqueror of Borikén, who later went to Cuba. I think of Las Casas, who was there too. I think, too, of that awful monster of nature, Vasco Porcallo de Figueroa, who settled Camagüey, in Cuba, as his own private kingdom, fornicating and killing our people at will.

Barrionuevo's casual reference to the lack of Indians left in these islands, referring directly to my own Taíno people, picks at my wound. Yes, it is true what he says, but I am deeply chagrined and would say this: Everywhere there has been death around me these past forty years, everywhere in my world. We had no pestilence here and we were healthy, healthy. The evil came with them; it did.

One hundred eighty eight. *Hatuey, "Certainty of Sun in the Sky," our great hero.*

There is so much to tell and by this mist of sea that surrounds me right now I will leave as much of it as I can, speak the names and write the deeds of the dead, impolite though it may be to do so, jarring, in our Indian way, as a badly-sung areito.

The fight went to Cuba with Hatuey, a great hero of my race. Hatuey, who fought Velázquez in retreat after the Massacre of Anacaona, and who moved his people in canoes to Cuba. He settled near Maisí point and he warned his hosts: "The Christians have but one god, and that is the shiny metal they call gold. They must have it, and they will kill and maim anyone in the way of its possession."

Hatuey took the Cuban ni-Taínos to the top of a mountain that overlooked the ocean. He was greatly respected, even in Cuba, and when he asked them to bring all their gold ornaments, most people did so willingly. They had already heard the tales and felt the cruelty of the Castilla in Cuba. Boricuas had traveled to their island and Castilla slavers, beginning with the Admiral himself, had many times taken captives away. Guamax, the elder, as I have written, and later Bayamo, cursed all "covered men/floating cave dwellers" during the first voyage days. ...

Hatuey, ni-Taíno cacique, was a grave and valiant man. The Cuban caciques, as I heard it several times during my years in Cuba, gathered around him and many old people touched his hand to their own heads. The substance of his words were still a fresh memory among our cousins there.

Hatuey told them: "Our people have things in common, but not so with the 'covered men,' not so. They covet much and they are so small inside in their covetousness.

"They know many things, but they dismiss their dreams; they try not to think about them. Invited to cohoba, they hate it, then go on to kill our behikes and cemíes." He instructed that the gold be put in baskets. Together, many people, hundreds and hundreds of principal people, went up to promontories by the ocean and over fast running river,sang, prayed, danced and tossed their baskets of gold to the waters.

Velázquez landed in Cuba in 1511 and within weeks his men had engaged Hatuey several times. With much arquebus, they forced the cacique's retreat over the coastal mountains.After one brief combat, two mastiff dogs cornered Hatuey on a rocky ledge. He was by then in the territory of old Bayamo,who had spoken so vigorously with the Admiral, twenty years earlier. At a place called Yara, the soldiers tied him to a stake and gathered dry brush, preparing to burn him alive. I tried to dissuade Velázquez from the deed by reminding him that Hatuey had a wide following, but Velázquez paid me no mind. "A lesson we will teach with this immolation," he said, and ordered all captured Taínos to witness the act.

Hatuey looked gravely on, humming his death song. He begged not for his life, but a priest approached him and with me interpreting, offered up words that recalled and continued that other dialog, so many years ago. (I say we have places on these magical islands that make us repeat ourselves, places where time turns in a circle and the land reclaims its own intelligence from us humans, generation after generation.)

"You ought to seek the baptism from me, Hatuey," the young priest said to the grave cacique, "so that you may be saved."

Hatuey looked at him not, but towards the sky, at the hot wide sun that dominated the day. Such was the meaning of his name, Hatuey, "Certainty of Sun in the Sky."

"I offer you baptism, savage man," the priest repeated.

Hatuey answered loudly, so the other Indians could hear. "And what will it get me, your little water?"

All ears were glued to his words. Not only the Indians but also Velázquez leaned forward to hear what Hatuey might say.

"It will open for you the gates of Heaven, and life everlasting," the priest responded. "Without it you are condemned to the Hell of eternal fire."

Hatuey thought a while, looking at the Sun and never at the priest. Finally, he asked, "And the Castilla, upon death, where do they go?"

"If baptized and repentful, they go to Heaven," the priest replied.

"I do not want to be with such mean people," said Hatuey, loudly. "Baptize me not. I prefer to go to Hell."

The priest walked away, shaking his head. I watched the face of Veláquez, that queer man who later killed his own wife. I had to laugh to myself, he was so absolutely chagrined. Watching Hatuey, too, I saw the slightest trace of grin on his face, which never wavered again. He burned alive for two hours and never cried out, but stared at the sun while his strength held and then, as he drooped, he gazed upon Velázquez and me, eyes open, even in death, that light grin still visible on his darkening lips.

May 19, 1533

One hundred eighty nine. *The spirits are all around us.*

I am filled with longing for my boys today, as we sail along these shores. Surrounded by Castilla am I, soldiers and sailors, but even with Rodrigo, as warm a friend as can be had, and often at my side, I am alone with the little voices. On board, no action is required of me; I sit long hours looking back at the wake of our ship on the water, wondering. Visions I see in the foam of our waves, faces of our people in the fluff of clouds. Thousands upon tens of thousands were we, uncounted and replenished as the cloudly flocks of doves and parrots that fill our skies. And now we are but handfuls, here and there a group of huts, the rest in encomiendas. Month by month entire ships full of Africans are brought over to replace us. We of the islands, we Taíno, now blend into the white and the black and our language is little heard.

We were not weak, truly, nor stupid. Our mothers taught us well. Taíno women bore children firmly, prepared sustenance, sang with the heart of the generations so our ancestors surrounded us, sharing the trance of the living. Remembered in the breeze, the spirits of our dead we breathed into our very bosoms. Adventurous and hardy, our men met the sea with full hearts. We feared not hurricane, we welcomed wind and rain.

Out of our very winds, Castilla have sucked the life, their very breath has made us die by the thousands. This have I seen: our people dropping one upon another, circling blindly like leaves in a storm. The worst was in 1519, just as the baby boy struck his blow for freedom. Though already cut by more than half, we were many even then. In 1519, we dropped and dropped. It is one thing to see the blood run and the body die; it is quite another to see the living spirit suddenly depart from dozens and dozens and hundreds and thousands of people at once and see no wound, no reason, no fault.

May 21, 1533

One hundred ninety. *Another conversation with Barrionuevo.*

I spent time with Barrionuevo today again. We talked about Cuba. It turns out Barrionuevo once knew Vasco Porcallo de Figueroa, the young conquistador I was given to by Velázquez.

"We called Porcallo the ram," Barrionuevo laughed. "He was a small man, but so brusque and decisive in his actions, everybody feared him."

"He was another Hojeda," I said. "But without the physical grace."

"I did not know Captain Hojeda."

"Hojeda was quite good-looking, in the Castilla manner. Fair-haired and perfectly-proportioned in his chest and limbs."

"Vasco was not."

"He was a ram, a mounting ram," I said.

We both laughed. In fact, Vasco Porcallo did look like a ram, with irascible, curling sideburns and a compact head and neck. He even walked fast, with head lowered.

I was very happy that Barrionuevo liked me and could share a joke with me. He has his tender part, this Barrionuevo, but he is also an old soldier, one of the old guard, conquistador, capable of complete impunity.

Barrionuevo has said, in my presence, "I am instructed to make peace with Enriquillo, but lacking that, upon my word, the wrath of the monarch himself, ruler of the greatest power on this earth, will be mobilized against him. And then, the two hundred or so men I bring, and the authorization that I also bring, to enlist into my brigades two hundred more men right here, these numbers will only be as one tenth the number that I can without reserve count upon from the royal guard, the best of our lion-hearted, whom I will deputize and enlist and I will myself lead this war to this fugitive cacique, and I will burn all of the mountains if need be."

So today I told him stories all afternoon, and I laughed with Barrionuevo about the characters in the "old days," the lion-hearted of whom he speaks that are as heroic and comical to him as they are despicable to me.

May 23, 1533

One hundred ninety one. *Continuing to work with Barrionuevo.*

Rodrigo, too, helps me. He dines with the Knight Captain each evening, a function to which I am disallowed, as they discuss logistical and potential military needs. But I know he speaks of me to Barrionuevo, and dispels the doubt the captain may carry still about my sincerity. I had some thought of this most intimate of missions as I boarded ship, but now it is obvious. Barrionuevo is the man to be near, and I am in the right place, by Rodrigo's grace, to feel his goeíç.

Today, in the afternoon, as Barrionuevo scanned the coast by long-glass, I lay in a hammock and watched, face hidden behind the lace of the net. He searched the coast with his glass in a concentrated stance, but saw nothing of what he sought—no sign of smoke or light or movement of any kind that could point to contact with the rebel camps. I watched and watched him, then quit watching but felt my gut and chest move in his direction, taking measure of his time so I knew exactly when he was about to quit, anticipating the moment when he took down the long-glass and looked my way. My head I lifted at that very second, looking to the coast in my own concentration. This brought him over.

"The search for this cacique of yours could be tedious," he said.

"He seeks not yet for us, my captain," I said. "After I disembark at Port Yakimo, I will initiate various messages to Enriquillo's camp."

"I will find him on the coast, and I will deliver the Queen's message to him," he said, and I was silent. Barrioneuvo was not interested in my participation at the negotiations; he merely liked my information.

After a while, he said, "The thing of the ram made me laugh."

Barrionuevo likes joviality, which is the way to reach him. Barrionuevo was making obvious his enjoyment of my tongue. Vasco Porcallo, whom I served for nearly two years in the Camagüey region, was indeed a comical (and despicable) apparition.

"He was every bit a ram," I said "He even hopped rapidly about from one place to the next." To humor his mood, I told Barrionuevo how Porcallo would take the Cuban girls, one after another, sometimes as many as eight or ten in a single day.

"Most often he did it from behind, like a ram," I teased. "And sometimes standing up against a post."

This got a boisterous laugh out of Barrionuevo, who said, "Dieguillo Colón, you nasty old-timer, you are a rascal to remember these things!"

One hundred ninety two. *Opening the path.*

My tongue not only humors but measures Barrionuevo. Today, in his light-hearted nostalgia, I found a path to his mood and put in my pitch. Since in a few days I will leave him to travel ahead by land to the hills of the Bahuruku, I am glad to reach him.

One hundred ninety three. *Making connection, the change of heart.*

As he formally left me, Barrionuevo patted my back. "You have survived a great deal, Dieguillo," he said. Immediately, I sought and captured his eyes. "So have you, my captain," I responded and he nodded. I said then, "And so has Enriquillo, who is a decent and brave man, a man who wants nothing more than the peace of the land for his relatives and other Indians."

"Is this totally so?" he inquired and, yes, I felt trust for my answer in his interrogation.

"Totally, my captain. Show this cacique but few soldiers, yet go to his lair. He is a fair man and will not attack an offer to parley. Then, do not threaten violence, but show him the Queen's message and capitulate with him in clear language. Pardon issued, he would settle in a quiet farm somewhere and your Indian war will be over forever on this island."

I looked into his eyes without fear or bashfulness, and I knew at that moment that peace was possible with this man, a real peace for our remaining Taínos, with a settlement on land, pride and authority and even a community for Enriquillo and Mencía's people. "By the love of the Baby Jesus, by the purity of the Holy Mother Mary," I said. "A great war captain could by an act of peace redeem the years of horror on this island with a measure of just finality."

"I will do my best," he said, and I believe he means it.

May 25, 1533

One hundred ninety four. *Cruelties of Vasco Porcallo.*

This afternoon Barrionuevo and Rodrigo Gallego talk alone. I am very lucky to have Rodrigo here at this important moment.

I will write about my time with Vasco Porcallo, the man-ram of our joking, who put my remaining son and me to work mining gold at the swampy rivulets near the new town of Sancti Spiritus. Those days in Cuba repeated the events in Española, but much more quickly. This time the Castilla arrived in larger numbers, always well stocked and with a clear strategy to subjugate our people quickly. In their attacks and raids to take slaves, they chased them from their villages and cunukus all over eastern Cuba, so that two and more planting seasons were entirely missed. Famine ensued among the Cuban Taíno.

Vasco, a young man of twenty then, was granted a huge estate, spawning cattle and sheep and pigs and many planted fields. His foremen organized gangs of gold panners and rakers into regular squads, working long, long days with little food and the constant sting of the whip and the whap of the "planazo," a blow with the edge of the cutlass or machete that easily turned bloody. Vasco ran his encomienda severely. As his raiders took many men prisoners, he would feed them not, but worked them for weeks until they dropped. Sometimes, a few were allowed to go after fruit, when in season. Once, several men made a pact to assuage their desperate hunger pangs by copiously eating dirt. They knew of course, that this would kill them. Vasco was personally insulted. He rescued the men by forcing large quantities of oil and water down their throats, then tied them to posts. If they could eat dirt, he said, perhaps they could eat something else. Then, he cut the testicles off the three men and made each eat his own. The act was so horrifying to the people that suicides stopped. For actions such as that Velázquez hailed Porcallo a "great encomienda administrator."

The obdurate Porcallo was among the most emulated of the conquistador class. And, yes, he was an untiring fornicator who, day after day for thirty years passed over our women and spawned hundreds of mestizos. Porcallo was not without plan, however, as he conceived of peopling the region with his new race, the power from his own loins adapted to the land as the offspring of the indigenous women. He had an accomplice and even a teacher in the old cacique of the savannah, Camagüeybax, who arranged many of these couplings and provided young maidens for the man-ram. Once I tried to scold the old cacique, but he refused to be admonished. "War is useless against war-driven people. To pacify them with their own desires is our only protection and our only survival," he told me. Porcallo put up women who gave him children in their own bohíos, and he kept going back to them. Later, he went on to import artisan and even noble families from Spain to marry his first generations.

I hated it, all the fornicating and begetting without lineage, without any sort of guidance from the elder mothers. But having lived another twenty years, I know now that mere survival is our only possible victory. And I do wonder now if Camagüeybax was right. The region of Camagüey is today peopled by our mixed race, and guaxiro is a term often employed to describe our survival in the loins of Taíno women, seeded by Castilla men. What matters, Camagüeybax would say, is that our old people's eyes and ears, our expressions survive in the generations, and not just die away.

Some people say that every mestizo means one less Indian. Others say that inside each mestizo an Indian survives to come through.

May 26, 1533

One hundred ninety five. *Caymán-hunting days.*

My boy and I were fortunate, saved from the killing hunger by the extra food provided through the meat of caymán, which danger I was after some weeks assigned to eradicate by hunting. I was given an old arquebus, dagger and lance and fashioned for myself several long bejuco ropes. Heart of Earth was not allowed to hunt with me, but stayed in the gold panning. I fed him much caymán that year, and he lived on it. I also used oils from the caymán on him, to rub his water-wrinkled skin that turned to blackened leather on his arms and shoulders. Thus I saved my boy from the open sores that killed many of our miners.

I also met Las Casas at that time. His own encomienda was not far away, on the Arimao River, and I was borrowed by his partner to eliminate a reptile on that waterway, a giant beast that had taken a servant boy as he filled casks with water.

I hunted that monster on canoe, by the light of the moon, and saw him one night leave the water to stalk a young calf. Knowing his hunting area, I cleared all animals away but a young calf we tied in a field not far from the river. With eight men I waited six nights and then the giant caymán left the water. We surrounded the beast and we stuck a long pole into his snapping mouth. Killing him was easy after that. Las Casas was quite happy, and that night we conversed until the early hours. He was changing his mind about then on the keeping of our people as slaves, and not much later he gave up his own encomienda to take up the campaign for our freedom, a cause he has never relinquished.

I hunted large caymán by the dozen for nearly a year and was never hurt. Then, once, while bathing in a quiet little pool, clear as glass and with nothing in sight, a puny caymán not three feet long snuck in on me and bit my leg. He was so small I walked out with him hanging from my thigh and ran him through with a knife, but the damage was done. His long tooth pierced me to the bone, just above the knee, the wound festering to high fever until I lost track of all time. It was Las Casas who nursed me, upon hearing of the case, and even in my sickness I was worried twice as Heart of Earth took sick himself from the constant panning in cold, dirty water, and I was certain he would die.

I recovered first. Las Casas, who was friendly with Velázquez, obtained my son for me. I nursed Heart of Earth myself, feeding him honey paste and fruits, rubbing him down with caymán oil and wet digo compresses and smoothing out the ridges in his now scaly skin.

Around that time, Ponce de León, who resided in Borikén, heard the tales of the Fountain of Youth, said to be found at Bimini or on the coast of La Florida. He would mount an expedition to find it. Word of this was heard all around, even in Cuba, where a group of volunteers agreed to join. A complex tradition among my people was this story of the Fountain of Youth, referring as it did to our own Taíno movement to the smaller islands (my own Guanahani among them) and the settlement of new villages. Thus the youthfulness it promised referred to the founding of new communities and the rekindling of sacred cemís, not the rejuvenation of old men. But the Castilla took it as enchantment and set out to find an actual foundation.

Heart of Earth, who had recovered, thanks to the good friar, wanted to go along on Ponce's expedition. A young man of fifteen years, he would leave for the port of San Germán with the Castilla volunteers, reasoning thus to me: "Father of my days," he said "Let us go, if allowed. No life is there for us here. I would go and see our days before us. With luck, we might see our people at Guanahani, and maybe find a spot of earth and a people of our copper color who will uphold us."

I myself applied to the expedition, but Velázquez would not permit my going. The young man, yes, he said, after all, he offered everything I could, plus youth. Reluctant was I to see my son go, but no true argument against it came to me. Thus, he embarked with Ponce, and I know from later testimony that he did land at Guanahani, where he might have seen my people, and onward they sailed to Bimini and La Florida. On a Florida beach, Heart of Earth one day went out to chop a palm tree, I was later informed, and disappeared; I hope, I pray, he walks among our own Taíno people, who previously settled in those parts.

May 27, 1533

One hundred ninety six. *One areito remembered.*

I cannot help thinking at this moment about my twins, how they looked together layed out on the hammock just after birth. It turns my mind to the songs of the double twins, in our origin stories: Deminán, first ancestor, and his three ximaguá brothers. Many round dances were sung throughout the villages of the Taínos for these four beings. Episode after episode was sung, the cycle starting the evening after first rain, and running, night after night, through the wet season.

Of woman born without male ancestor were these four brothers, who are the four winds, who brought powers from the other world—they who walked the rim of the sky. Said one areito song, "in the world where heat does not exist, the eyes, coldest of human organs, can create." I think of it today, as I lay and write in a hammock that hangs low behind the captain's cabin. We are clipping fast toward Yakimo and this well-made shop, the King's own, has the grace of a giant dolphin. There is nothing like the swing of a hammock on a gentle ocean.

Our areitos said, this world of humans is of the heart, the belly and the groin. Mind exists, and spirit, but in little proportion to the other three. In the world before ours that the dead endeavor to reach and in which they are forever in, mind and spirit are nearly all. There is some heart, very little gut, and no groin, no link to the rudeness of procreation, no hope of the fleshful love, nor the command of touch necessary to its generation. Yet, in the mind is everything, in the spirit of the other self, the other me, the opposite, in that link is where movement originates, and the spark of existence.

A pondering people were our Taíno on the measure and the breadth of our existence. Origins we had, and creators, generations of creators. Before ever I heard of Adam and Eve, ancestors of the Castilla or of the Jesus from Nazareth, from a place beyond Iberia, in the Kingdom of Judea, whom all Christians venerate, though his own people betrayed him, before all of that, we had the Sky-Walking Brothers, and before them Yucahu and, even before that, YaYa and Atabey and so much more . . .

Deminán was first among the brothers, and many of our songs told the tales of his intelligence, his beautiful looks. Deminán could swim where there was no water, and while his younger three brothers were being born, his laboring mother told him, "Search out ways of creating a world where Taínos can live, a sea and a bracelet of islands, all manner of fish, the action and heart of man, the mind and love of woman, a language, and, best of all, the cohoba and the tobacco to make the link complete. All the forces necessary are in you path," his mother told Deminán. She said to him, "Spirit beings you will find in your path who hold the needed medicines and powers, but know not how to use their gifts to spark the world into being. That is you. Your are the next creator," she told him.

Yúcahuguama Bagua Maorocoti, first force yuca giver-sea-provider-of woman born without grandfathers, already existed and had accomplished his main labor on the heated earth. Birthed by Atabey, along with his brother, Guacar, they had been formed by their mother out of the invisible elements of space. Atabey, ancient bleeding mother, brought the life-giving powers to earth. She sucked the wind into herself, churned it into her spiritual waters and birthed twin boys. They were the best and the worst, natural harmony and natural chaos. Yucahu, the harmony, continued to create the earth, and the sun and the moon he brought out of their origin caves. All this Yucahu accomplished before. He had accomplished beauty on his mother's instructions. But his brother Guacar, in his own nature, sought only ugliness; he created what his brother did not: all manner of disintegration, turbulent storm, pests, diseases, aggressive fish (shark), poison sea jellies, pain itself and, of course, death.

But that was a time much before, and even then a race of human beings was already coming out of caves and forming out of trees and manatí and out of the heart of palm. Some paddled in the spirit waters, but blindly and lost, and needed to be taught. All were guarded from the sun, which was fierce. All this his mother, who died as the fourth brother emerged, told Deminán. Now, he must walk the clouds and follow his wishes, his curiosities, and it would be all right, he would accomplish the rest.

So, Deminán traveled and his impulse was certain.

It so happened that a spirit named YaYa was the ultimate father. He lived with his wife in a bohío that was the beginning and the end of the road. His own first son, who had a great gift, YaYa had killed. Yayael was the son. He was now bones in a basket hanging from the rafters, in the western-most corner of the bohío. One day his bones, caressed in his mother's hands, became fish, and both father and mother ate happily. Now with his wife, YaYa went to his cunuku, where a patch of spirit corn needed cleaning.

Deminán, walking the rim of the sky, saw YaYa's empty bohío. He knew he should respect a strange bohío, but on impulse approached and entered. His three brothers only waited at the door.

Deminán moved carelessly through YaYa's bohío. Spotting the basket, he climbed at the rafters without thinking. Suddenly, the brothers whispered, "YaYa is coming." Deminán lunged for the basket and toppled it. Out came mountains of water, heavens of wet water; long, heavy fish tumbled out, all manner of sea life, an immense volume of life-giving water world. YaYa approached his bohío angrily; he felt his son, whom he loved above all else, desecrated by a simpleton. Deminán fled, trailed by his brothers, and, the song says, all four were suddenly consumed by a hunger that craved casabe, smelled casabe—crisp-roasted tort of the yuca root, sustainer of Taíno life. This, just as the waters of the earth were teeming with life.

June 2, 1533

One hundred ninety seven. *Another gold trap.*

Soon, maybe by late this afternoon, we land. After a night of drifting in the open sea, a pilot who well knows the coast indicated a shadow like a darkened eye on the line of land. "That is Yakimo," he said. "We can be there in half a day, if the wind holds."

I talked again to Rodrigo. Barrionuevo approves the arrest of two guards on board, Valenzuela's men who mean to strike at Enriquillo at the earliest opportunity. They will be taken at the port of entry, handcuffed and turned over to the local marshalls in Yakimo with six-month sentences. The charge, admittedly trumped up, will be transactions in gold without authorization. This, set up with the last piece of gold from the cacique.

One hundred ninety eight. *Happiness to be in thick of events.*

After so many cloistered years, I am living grandly these days, a purposeful happiness in my heart. I am relishing my intense participation in the effort for Enriquillo. Suddenly that old gift (or curse) of mine, to arrive at places of central action, to be in the midst of men who must converse, I feel it working for me. Something in my soul tells me I am the one to carry out this function, and I am enthusiastic to join the two men and put them through an old-time, Taíno peace pact. Even the song of the guatiao, our exchange of names ceremony, I have been singing to these lonely waves. I feel I am ready to fulfill this destiny and, through this work, if successful, to salvage from this life my shame that I carry for having introduced, so many times the Castilla to our people. Shaking off the life of the monks, I feel more than ever my life is clear before me and I am my own man.

Catalina is to meet me at Yakimo and, right at this moment, the wind in my ears whispers the music of another areito, also of the four brothers, about the time the men lost the women and how Deminán helped us. Why is it when I think of her the music of my childhood resounds in the wind? I long for Catalina so deeply right now, I want so much to be in her presence. And here I am again, after all these years, riding on the royal ship of the King of Spain, towards an Indian cacicazgo, a sovereign and a people. The wind holds.

June 6, 1533

One hundred ninety nine. *Catalina becomes my wife.*

Out again in the bush, down old trails and small carreta roads. Catalina is with me, and Silverio, both with good mounts. I have my Cariblanca. Today, the three of us rode the coastal savannah to these first foothills. We are resting tonight under the perfect canopy of two huge ceiba trees, where we made a small fire and hung our things. The horses we have tethered in a pasture of tall grass nearby.

Catalina met me at the dock, dressed like a white lady. Silverio acted the servant and holding the three horses at a distance. Her daughter, Inés, known to the Castilla as Julia, came along. I introduced the two women to Barrionuevo and Rodrigo. I used the phrase, "my betrothed," when introducing Catalina, and both men bowed deeply for her. Her daughter Julia stayed under the protection of both men, who vouched for her well-being. Julia will act as a guide to Enriquillo's camp, when they spot a sign to follow from the ship.

Catalina becomes my wife now, setting my hammock next to hers at night, prescribing my tea and even tasting my food. I love to have it so. There is nothing I would not do for the Catalina now, nothing. As a teacher and midwife I have appreciated her and, now as my wife, her way I will make easier. Catalina is still full of spark in the daytime, but she is a bony bird at night, slight to settle in the curl of my arm and chest. I am complete once again in my time, called to the active life by this great occasion. Suddenly there is Catalina, again, the same and yet this time a different Catalina, ready to have me and give me life. Oh, I am full of happiness and optimism as we ride into the hills of Enriquillo's country.

(Difficult it will be to write long here. I've only ten sheets of paper left and little time. Nevertheless, I will continue to make notes.)

Two hundred. *Going to the Bahuruku again.*

Where the plain breaks into bush and begins to climb sharply, eight young guaxeri made rendezvous with us. I recognized only one man, but Silverio knew several by name and talked our old language to them without hesitation. They are severe about moving rapidly to meet with Enriquillo.

Two hundred one. *Deminán and the guanguayo turtle create the islands.*

At night, the warriors are polite, but cautious. They are particularly impressed with Catalina, who shows them how to improve on a good balm for cuts and bites from the bark of the jagua tree. Now she hums areito music late into the Bahuruku night. The eight warriors crowd around her, listening.

I finish here another Deminán story, the one where he again accosts the bohío of a holy spirit man, requesting casabe to eat. The old man spirit spits a gob of cohoba on Deminán's back. A swollen hump forms on his back and he loses strength. Lying down on a sliver of sandy beach, in the middle of the vast ocean, Deminán takes deadly sick. Using a coral knife, one of his brothers lances the swollen hump. Out of his back comes one and other turtles, out of his back slide out longer reptiles and swim out to sea. Where they surface from under the waters, the heat of the sun petrifies them, forming the islands, big and small, mountain ranges all over our Taíno sea. Thus were our lands created.

Two hundred two. *Warriors who would be husbands.*

On the trail, I talk openly with Catalina and Silverio about our mission to Enriquillo. The young men warriors listen. I talk about our old Taíno peace pacts, and Catalina confirms my description. A leader of the warriors says, "Our cacique maintains we will marry, all, and settle down to farm with our wives. Is that possible? Do you think so?"

"Yes," I tell him. "If the peace can be arranged, it will be a very different life."

"I can help boys get matched up with your own women," Catalina said. "when the peace is made, we will work on that problem."

The young men smiled all around. "Anything you need, great mother," one said, humorously, but not in jest. "Only look my way."

Two hundred three. *Catalina stays with Mencía.*

Mencía received us at the water's edge. She led a troupe of twenty men and her three women assistants. Everyone was very tense.

Enriquillo was with the young behike. They were in cohoba. Tamayo was also gone, along with Cao and six other captains. Mencía was in charge of everything at the camp, which had been reduced. I did not discuss with her Tamayo's mission, which I put out of my mind.

"We prepare a great lot these past few weeks," she told me. "It is confusing because we build new hidden camps, as precaution against sudden raids, yet I tell my young people a peace may take place, that we may get our own farms. It is confusing for the men who might now think of peace yet still we prepare for war."

At their main camp, Mencía and her women received Catalina formally, singing an old areito about the creation of the Moon for her. Catalina, who knew Mencía as a child, offered to stay with her while I go to Enriquillo. "I want to help my niece," she said. "You go see what you can do for the baby boy."

Two hundred four. *At the enchanted falls.*

Silverio brought me here. We arrived at midday. There is a little falls just at the entrance to a cave facing the ocean. A gentle trail leads to it from the forest behind it, but facing out from the cave to the sea is jagged rock straight down to the hard-breaking waves. At the entrance, a pool is formed on clear white stone from a cascading spring of fresh water. The cascade flushes a mist that cools the day. We sat down a while and Silverio cooed like a dove. Finally, Baiguanex came out.

"Guaicán, uncle, I see you again," he said, but heavily, not his usual light sing-song greeting.

"behike," I responded. "I find you in a place of beauty."

"We are in the enchantment now," he said, again seriously.

"And how is our serene cacique?" I asked.

Baiguanex asked us into the cave, which smelled of cohoba mixture and old fires. At the rear of the cave an opening from the top let the sun shine in. Enriquillo lay curled beneath a sheet, his lower body in the sunshine. The Cacique slept with abandon, his breath pulling and blowing in long rhythmic aspirations. "Three nights he has been in cohoba," Baiguanex said.

Baiguanex led me to a ledge at the cave's entrance.

Two hundred five. *More cohoba revelations.*

I smoked with Baiguanex. He grew his own and rolled tabacos like an old Cuban. We faced the ocean and he would not look at me.

"The cacique is tired. His young body has lived in perpetual alertness."

"It is good to see him rest."

"Cohoba forced him. For two nights he saw nothing, heard nothing. They filled his mind with night and collapsed him. On the third day, I fed him. He ate a casabe tort and drank fresh water from this well. Then I gave him a piece of roasted iguana. He sprung to life like a gray-tailed hawk. At noon, he danced for me, low on the ground, pecking at the earth. That night, two evenings ago, they talked to him.They thanked him for what he has done and they gave him permission on his new path."

Baiguanex scratched his back against the rock, watching the ocean. "Then, last night, he saw the ocean, and a Spanish ship, coming toward him. It was coming from Spain, for him. The ship, they told him, has the answer he desires."

"Barrionuevo's ship," I said.

Baiguanex looked up, but past me. "And then this morning, this morning early, as he napped again, I saw the ship. Right our there. The Spanish ship of his cohoba vision."

"A long one, with three main sails?"

"Yes. And a second one, a coastal launch with one sail."

"Exactly. Barrionuevo's ship. You actually saw it."

The behike nodded. "That much I think is good," he said.

Two hundred six. *Details of contact.*

Enriquillo awakened an hour later. He called the behike, who brought him water and a casabe tort. Then he came out to the pool and greeted me with eyes deep set, holding a dream.

"I am to meet the Castillian captain," he said. "Have you prepared a way?"

I gave him the details of the contact with Barrionuevo, how I sailed with him, how Catalina's daughter, Julia, would be sent by Barrionuevo's guides.

"And is this captain from the King?" he asked.

"He is that," I said. "Even the ship he commands is the King's own."

"Can he enforce the King's law?"

"Yes, cacique, he can."

"Your path crosses with my cohoba, uncle," he said then. "I need your heart's eye on this man."

"Barrionuevo I felt in my being," I told him. "I believe he would be true to his word."

"We will guide him in then. Wherever he lands, we will have men chopping wood, calling attention to themselves. They will bring him to the edge of our lake. Julia can be sent for me from there. I will send Romero to set up the parley. I will come down myself when this captain is settled on our lake."

Two hundred seven. *A hint of reversal.*

"I am ready to help with all that," I said. "I have rehearsed the songs of Guarionex. We can make a peaceful moment . . . "

But Enriquillo looked up and I felt Baiguanex behind me.

Baiguanex touched my shoulder silently.

"I should tell you, Guaikán," Enriquillo said, for the first time ever calling my own name to me. "Many runners have come, from dozens of families, maybe hundreds, who want to join us if a peace is made. Now, this peace will be a very complex thing for this cacique."

"Do you doubt that peace can be made, cacique?" I asked.

"No, but I know I won't live long enough to see it survive."

Two hundred eight. *Guarocuya does a hawk dance, he takes me out.*

The Guarocuya boy danced at noon again. He is a hawk when he dances, pure hawk spirit and motion. Baiguanex beat the drum and Enriquillo twirled left and right, first one leg, then the other, twirling and looking, pecking at the ground and swooping. I could see the hawk mind in his eyes that no longer would focus. Then, he slept.

When he awoke, he called me to him. "Uncle, everything is set," he said. "I will meet this Barrionuevo. I am ready for peace, if he is and if the King's word he carries. If so, I will make peace with the sovereigns and see what of our people can be settled, that at least a town of us could survive, a place we can gather our survivors.

"A town may be too big a project," I said. "But at least your band here could get a farm. There is talk of a farm at Azua."

"We will have a town," he said calmly and with total assurance. "The Indians on the island, the ones of us from here and the ones like you and so many others brought here from the islands and from the mainland, all will come to our free land."

"If the cacique says so," I said.

"Yes. Even the Africans, the ones that came to us in '22, after the rebellion of the slaves on the second Admiral's sugar mill. They must have a place in this town. So will you and Catalina."

"It is a dream of mine to live among the Taíno again," I said, though in my heart, at the moment, I did not believe it. I have thought more on a pardon for Enriquillo. What the cacique now envisioned implied the end of the encomienda in Española.

"Possibly Barrionuevo is not authorized for suggesting a community scheme, or a refuge for Indians. This is what Las Casas throws at them and arouses their anger."

"Las Casas is accusatory and he angers everyone. But he was right to push for abolishing the encomienda."

I nodded, thinking briefly of the good friar, where he might be at that very minute. I thought of Tamayo, too, and Valenzuela and Pero López. Agitation and cross purposes were in my mind suddenly, where before I felt the medicine to make the peace pact.

"With careful words, I am sure, you opened my path to this new captain," Enriquillo said. "This means that twice you have saved me, uncle. I thank you. Our people thank you twice."

The words had a finality to them I did not like.

"There is more to be done," I said. "The negotiation is ahead, and the settlement ... "

"My message is clear, uncle," he said, in that way of Enriquillo, with that sense of knowing exactly the road to follow. "Your part of the task is done."

I felt very old suddenly. I felt his truth, that my part was done. I felt maybe my life was done.

"My cacique," I said, feebly. "I know Barrionuevo now. Even his main guard is an old friend of mine, Rodrigo Gallego ... "

"The cohoba says no. Your path is blocked now."

And I felt exactly that way, blocked. I had felt greatly needed, central, and, now, I was out of the events I had been fashioning. Over and over I had prepared for the pact, reflecting on the ways taught to me by Guarionex, thinking the words aloud.

"Forgive me, Enrique," I tried one more time. "I need to continue in the making of this ... "

"It can not be," he said, and walked back into the cave.

Two hundred nine. *The behike explains.*

I sat at the outside of the cave, looking out to the ocean. Silverio readied our things to lead me back to Mencía's camp. Baiguanex came to say farewell, bringing two tabacos for me.

"We follow the old ways here," he said. "The priests will never know it, not even the one they call good friar, but this great cacique of ours is guided by the cohoba. The time you came and were in cohoba with us, you also helped us see the past and the future. You have brought much, Guaikán, but the spirits don't want you near it now. The cohoba says: Take the edge now, not the point."

"I have done no wrong, behike," I said.

"No wrong," he said. "But you have worked too long in the devious mind of the covered men."

"I have learned to spin a web of scheme," I said. "I know that. But I do it for this purpose ... "

"It is complicated, Guaikán, and we appreciate you. But you are not to come. Your heart is not right in this cycle. Now is time for you to smooth and comb your mind," Baiguanex said. "Pray for this peace and go home. The cacique will take the words from here."

I bowed, took his hand and put it to my head. "Tau-ti, Baiguanex," I said to this young man, then got up to leave.

"When you get back to her camp," he instructed "ask Mencía to send for Tamayo, who has been by here already. He has something to tell you."

(My supply of paper is running low. I have so much I want to write. And even back at the convent, I have but a few more sheets stashed away.)

Two hundred ten. *Tamayo's report.*

Mencía sent for Tamayo. Cao came with him. Both men were cordial but formal. Tamayo was sterner than usual.

"I thank you for your clever scheme, Guaikán," Tamayo began, and I understood completely why I could not be a peacemaker this season, why, as Baiguanex said, my "heart is not right."

"The piece of gold led the pale ones to us like the flower calls the hummingbird," Tamayo said.

I looked away. He would have to tell me his report, and I would have to hear it, just now. In my anticipation I felt deeply chagrined. I took Tamayo and Cao and we walked up a nearby hill. We smoked the two cigars of Baiguanex.

Tamayo waited. When he told me, he relished the telling. He had killed for me, and I would have me hear it all. I will write this about it: Pero López died quickly. He begged not for his life, and they were kind to him. They didn't stretch him up, but put him on a horse. His neck snapped in the fall. (It is true, I could not resist feeling satisfaction when I heard it. The behike is right, I receive this death gladly in my heart.)

Valenzuela and his servant managed to break free, Tamayo said. They grabbed weapons and put up a strong fight. Cao himself was cut in the face before both men were run through with lances and daggers and Cao wrestled the servant down and cut his throat.

"Valenzuela lived the whole night," Tamayo said. "He cried for water all night."

The old war captain grinned at me. He has scars on both cheeks and an eyelid that dangles from an old wound. "The Castilla dog was gut wounded but didn't bleed much," he said. "He dried out quickly. You should have heard him cry for water."

The remark sickened me slightly. I have seen Valenzuela many times. I could see the scene before my eyes. He was shameless and he would have been an assassin but I still could sense him, and I could feel his goeíç on my neck and right shoulder.

"Like a bee to yellow petals, he came into our trap ... seeking the yellow nectar," Tamayo said, " ... the only one that can cure the malady in their hearts."

I saw Cao smile now behind him. Old Tamayo leaned forward, looking at me directly. "You saw everything before its time, Guaikán Columbus," he said. "I must grant you that. But you are not worth a crap as a behike man. You hurried my ceremony, put it through before its time, and my mind is very confused. Why did you open my heart only to set me up to kill?"

I could only look away. I knew, of course, he was right. I should have waited and seen the sequence better. In the midst of my peacemaking, I doubted not my own revenge.

Tamayo continued. "I am not angry with you," he said. "I found my own way to make peace. I thought to myself: Tamayo, this Castilla might be the last one you get to kill. I wondered: What should I give a dying Castilla, that he can take with him? And I had an idea. So we made a hot fire, found a large sun-caved stone and heated it red. And there I melted the gold bar. I melted it and melted it.

"Then, it was morning. Once more, Valenzuela cried for water. I opened his mouth and gave him the molten gold."

He saw me grimace and glared hard at me. He was right. I had no call to grimace, since he had done my bidding.

"And how did he like the golden water?" I asked, acknowledging his right to exalt in the cruelty.

"You know," Tamayo relished the moment, "he didn't like it much."

The warriors both laughed, and I joined them. I wasn't reluctant anymore, but laughed sincerely at the perfect irony of Tamayo's torture. It is true: I am no peacemaker, not now, not anymore.

The two men told me the rest, too, how they disposed of the bodies and how they swore their whole group to secrecy, all the captains and Cao. I recognized their valor. "You have saved your cacique," I told them.

"In the next few days, we are to go prepare for the peace parley by the lake," Tamayo told me, more directly, obviously feeling better for having reported the deed. "I think it may have been our last ambush."

As they walked away, I felt sad in my knowledge—about them and about me. I am not sorry about any of it, but I am glad its over.

Two hundred eleven. *My paper runs short.*

This is the last of my paper now. Tomorrow, we travel back together, Catalina and I. We have camped by ourselves for two weeks on the outskirts of the action, gathering word. We kept to our own when Mencía's camp moved without us. It was late July. Barrionuevo's ship was spotted and signals of smoke went up. A launch landed days later and guaxeri were soon available, cutting wood within earshot of Barrionuevo's soldiers, who then "captured" our woodsmen. From that point, everything functioned as planned. Two captains in canoes came up to the lake. Julia was sent out and contact was made. Enriquillo prepared his delegation of captains with more than half of their seasoned men, some seventy warriors, all ready for battle. Barrionuevo, I was told, came in with some fifteen men and few weapons.

It hurt me to have to hear of the parley second-hand. Silverio went back and forth for five days while Barrionuevo and Enriquillo made their peace. Silverio is a good boy, but not the best relayer of words. I knew from his reports that the parley was going well, but his lack of detail was frustrating. Tamayo himself came to see me. He had been sent by Enriquillo to tell me that pardons were granted all-round, that six of his captains would be deputized, and that a tract of land big enough for a town with good fields would be allotted. "The Castilla captain gives his word for the Queen. All Indians who are not slaves can live in our new lands."

Two hundred twelve. *Staying away from the peacemaking.*

Staying away as the peace between Enriquillo and Barrionuevo was made, for once I was satisfied not to be in the center of things. It is enough to know I have a place.

I know that Enriquillo's decision to press for a territory of refuge for all Indians appears in the treaty, which will establish such a community. Barrionuevo is as generous as he was encouraged to be back in Santo Domingo.

Of course, there are not so many Indians left now, and more and more Africans. It is not so difficult to give up the Indian labor. Anyway, I see that Enriquillo gains more concessions without me who has chastized Las Casas for the same opinion. Oh, and that poor friar, whom I have sent on a devious and misguided trail, God keep him, please. Truly my heart pays the price for my involvement in these affairs.

Two hundred thirteen. *Feeling the good friar.*

Silverio, Catalina and Enriquillo's captain Romero joined us. We have started on our ride back to Yakimo. We will take a barge out of Yakimo and sail to Santo Domingo.

Today, I could feel the good friar. I walked down an open path for a distance, behind Romero and before Catalina and it was the friar's legs and step that I could feel in my limbs, the length of his legs and of his neck, the way his neck stretches as he walks. I could feel his goeíç in the swing of my arms and my own step and I was very nervous. He must be angry with me.

Two hundred fourteen. *Last of the paper on the ship.*

This is the last of my paper, this half a sheet. Catalina tells me of an areito Mencía sang for her, the one with the story of how the men fought with each other in the old days, became mean and lost the women, and how Deminán and his three brothers lulled the female again into humanity. She said this is everyone's topic in the camps. In that areito, there are many instructions of how men are to care for women. The men talk about what Enriquillo has said, about settling down, farming peacefully, finding wives. There are messages from many, many Indians, all over the island, who want to settle with Enriquillo.

Two hundred fifteen. *Indians as dignitaries.*

We leave our horses now with Silverio. Catalina and I go by barge to Santo Domingo and Captain Romero accompanies us. The citizens at Yakimo came out to see him and even clap for him as for a dignitary. There is genuine happiness for a peace that every day seems more and more possible. We are well fed by the main citizens of Yakimo.

Two hundred sixteen. *All that I can fit.*

I can squeeze but a few more lines into this sheet. The barge leaves today. The baby boy is safe. Our Taíno-ni-taíno survives one more generation, and a place is marked, reserved for the future! And there are other worthy recognitions. I want to write but there is no more space for my mark. Xán, Xán Katú. This is all that I can fit. Grateful am I for the gift given and for the friendship of the courageous priest to whom I now return. Tau-ti-carayá.

Folio VII

Last testaments

In the convent, news of Las Casas ... In my room, a letter from the good friar ... A year's wait ... Preparing for marriage ... I hear of Enriquillo ... Journey to the new community ... I see Enriquillo again, on his deathbed ... At last in our bohío ... Final testament, 1539 ... A letter from Las Casas, the New Laws ... A note for Las Casas ... They will remember, my young generations ...

Two hundred seventeen. *In the convent, news of Las Casas.*

I write at the convent, on these few sheets I put away here. Thus, I will write some pages more, although everything is doubly painful in this Castilla place and in this Castilla mind.

Catalina and I are separated once more. We have no place to be together, and even our marriage is yet to be properly announced. Among our people it is so easy to just be, but here we must watch every move.

I long for Catalina immensely. I dread where I am and want to go.

For one thing, Abbot Mendoza is rude in his disappointment at my wanting to take a wife. "You were close to vows with our order," he said. "You have learned from us the Holy Sacraments.

Consider the seriousness of your decision."

Like everyone else, of course, he knows about my problem with Father Las Casas. He mentions it not, but he watches me differently, all the monks do. Only Father Remigio is warm to me as usual.

Two hundred eighteen. *In my room, a letter from the good friar.*

In my room, on top of my papers, I found his letter. But the good friar is gone, refusing to even countenance me.

June 10, 1533

To a Dieguillo who is a *diablillo*:

I have read all your papers. Thus I know of your deceit doubly, once on the trail, walking for nothing, and now again, from your own words that tell so many lies. I know I can find deceit in these papers on your desk, as I leaf through them again, what I read before and the much I had not seen. So I see your calumnies against Cúneo, who was a gentle soul, and I know could not have treated your cousin so badly. I must laugh at your assertions of heathen curses destroying the mind of the Admiral; then, to read of your inebriations with the cohoba vapors and of your infernal nightmares in the nether regions, oh, wonder that you are still the recalcitrant heathen; I lament the wastefulness of all your years of Catechism, all that patient instruction, first from the great Admiral himself, and then myself and so many others, all of us thinking you might take your vows someday, only to read right here in your room that you are a fornicator of old women (and in the past few weeks!), a frequenter of Barcelona girl whores, you who have walked through all that is holy of our sacraments, you who have taken the blood and corpus of our Christ and have assisted in all of our sacred rituals ... how could you deceive me this way? How, how, how could you betray me in such a manner, Dieguillo? You are a true devil,chameleon, changing your colors with the shades around you. Was it vanity, lizard, fear that I might take your glory that made you betray my cause of unity with your people?

I credit you for this only: I know now with certainty the little trust of your pages. I see with ease how wrong you are about so many things. Is it perhaps your luciferous cohoba— is that what burns your head clean of sincere thought? Why, for instance, do you pick on Pané, that simple good friar who recorded so many things about your people? And why do you vilify Velázquez, claiming that he killed his wife, when he was one of the truly refined people to come to the islands? Of course, he was a conquistador—but his own wife? No, Diego ... But you know what a great fibber you are.

I thought to destroy these pages, but I will leave them that you may read and re-read your own profanities. I know not all your shenanigans, but you are securely beyond redemption, and I would venture even less to consider what penance you might make for your brutish and odious twists of mind.

Consider, of course, that we are no longer friends. When you return, I shall be moved to another residence. I desire not to see you again. As for our shared ideas on Enriquillo's defense, feel released completely from any and all obligations. I certainly do. In fact, I shall visit the camps soon, Bringing the sacraments and planning for their new settlement. In the event of our coincidental meeting, do not bother to recognize me. Consider our years of convent life sufficient and ponder the fate of our apparent friendship, a fetid swamp now where once ran a transparent stream.

Las Casas.

Looking at my papers, which are out of order still on my table, I can tell by the round ink stains where he sprinkled holy water on the them. He opened my cohoba bundle, too, which I left behind and he broke in half four green parrot feathers given to me by Baiguanex.

Two hundred nineteen. *A year's wait.*

Catalina and I are made to wait one year. Abbot Mendoza has agreed to seek her free woman status, but we are instructed to prepare for one year, save our pesos and then set up our home. "If you are to be married, then let your Christian home be an example to your new generation," said the Abbot.

I see Catalina in the market on Wednesdays and Saturdays and at Mass on Sundays. We sit together and chat and we lock our ankles together under the benches.

Two hundred twenty. *Preparing for marriage*

I stay to myself thankfully, while in the convent. I go nowhere most days, but dedicate my hours to latching together square pig-traps, which Catalina sells for me at four pesos a cage. I make three or four pig traps a week and they all sell. Pigs are everywhere in the woods, and they produce great damage against all tuber crops.

With forty pesos we put away per month, in a year we will have what we need. I want to put up a good bohío and get a few cows for beef steers and raise young horses. I will plant my yuca already this year, for the crop will take a full turn of the seasons and will be ready when we are. I can always keep making pig-traps and Catalina makes a fine hammock. We will live thus.

I look not for Enriquillo, nor for the camp at Boyá. Even that urge has left me, and I am motionless in their relation. I ponder his words at our final meeting, and I hesitate not in seeing the meaning he dictated in my strategic actions. I know he is right. Once again I realize how the covered man continues to suck at my Taíno marrow.

I cannot write much more. I feel my urge in this activity leaving me, too. This play of words I have been at most of my life, as interpreter and now in this writing, tires me. I am robbed of enough memories by this Castilla activity, images in words spilled to the page so that my inside mind can no longer see them.

Two hundred twenty one. *I hear of Enriquillo.*

Ten months it is today since our return from the Bahuruku, ten new moons. I saw Silverio today, my young helper. He has married and has his own bohío at Boyá. He looks quite firm and robust. I asked about Enriquillo.

"He is frail, cannot sleep and is often irascible."

"Is he ill?"

"His lungs hurt him and he doesn't sleep."

I asked about the behike, Baiguanex.

"He never came in, we have not seen him anymore," he said.

Two hundred twenty two. *Journey to the new community.*

I have decided to visit Enriquillo at Boyá. It is a bit of a journey from Santo Domingo, and I traveled with Silverio for nearly a month. This is truly the last that I will write.

Leaving Azua and entering the cacique's community, we ran into a party of horse riders, six men in long capes and sabers. They stopped to greet us, and a voice I don't forget said out loud, "The clever Dieguillo, I believe, what convenience."

It was Oviedo, the gold-counting historian. He went on addressing a companion.

"My Duke," he said. "This Indian right here will resolve our question."

"Dieguillo," he said, turning to me "the Duke wonders how the Indians of the first years saw us. Did you think we were human beings or angels?"

"I said many times you were angels, in those first days," I responded, to avoid conflict. "And many of my people believed me. I believed it myself for a while."

Oviedo laughed. Silverio was impatient but quick to realize they had us surrounded, out-armed and out manned.

"And when did you start realizing that we were humans," asked the Duke. I saw my opening and responded.

"I once thought you might be angels, but, if the gentlemen will forgive an Indian's honest opinion, I never have thought you human at all."

Oviedo might have been angered, but he was too jovial that day. "Our cacique has quite the stamp," he said. "He likes his cups, too, Duke. You ought to see him."

"Only with the Castillian wine," I replied. "My own mabí root-beer I can drink and drink. It never gives me a headache."

"Saliva beer," Oviedo said, pulling on his horse and laughing loudly. "It's a wonder the Indians don't drink piss."

The Castilla group following Oviedo reined their mounts away from us without another word, cantering away, the shod hooves of their powerful horses throwing clods of mud.

August 24, 1535

Two hundred twenty three. *I see Enriquillo again, in his deathbed.*

Doña Mencía is the same, perhaps a little heavier. Her hair is turned quickly gray.

She took me and sat me by Enriquillo's hammock. He looked very old, thin and coughing in great fits. But he greeted me warmly.

"Look how you find me," he said. "Uncle, I knew I would not last long."

"You are bound to get well," I said. "You were always strong."

"Its all spent, my wax."

"Rest and gain strength, you magnificent cacique," I said to my Enriquillo boy. "You have a long life ahead."

I felt foolish for not coming earlier, as he wanted to speak with me. But his comments were all about problems of the community. For one thing, the Castilla had promised twenty cattle and had delivered only six. Then, his deputized men, including Tamayo, helped track and recapture two escaped Africans. Many Indians in the community disliked Tamayo tracking runaways for the Castilla. "Its a big problem for everybody," Enriquillo said. "Even here, they come talk to me about it. But I no longer see the workings of things. I only know that without our warrior discipline, everyone goes this way and that. On the other side, I know Tamayo's angers and they continue to grow. Tamayo is angry all the time. He doesn't think through his decisions."

Enriquillo coughed for a long stretch. A cloth he held was stained red. I felt so badly for him and for Doña Mencía but such matters as the Castilla not keeping their promises to us or of Tamayo participating in the tracking and hunting of cimarrons, I cannot contain.

"I liked the Bahuruku, our mountain trails," the cacique said. "The behike was right to stay away."

I wondered about Baiguanex, but said nothing.

"I only hope he doesn't die alone," Enriquillo said, looking at doña Mencía standing nearby. "At least I know I won't die alone. She will sing me to the spirit world."

"Come back," Doña Mencía said, as we parted. "Tell us more of your stories."

I promised I would, though truly, I lack the strength myself for such a trek again.

Two hundred twenty four. *At last in our bohío.*

I have left the convent with Catalina, not toward the mountains but to the edge of the sea on the savannah, to an area apart, what Castilla now call "vacant lands." We picked a place by a good stream, by a ridge she knows well, a place of fertile earth on her old people's lands.

Building our bohío, which we do alone, a rider came to see us, sent by Silverio. The young cacique died on September 27, nearly a week ago. Last night, when I complained to the fates about the young cacique, wracked with problems and now coughed to death, this after so many years of hard work for his people, Catalina shook her head at me. "My young husband," she said, "remember our old saying, 'No good deed goes unpunished.'"

May 5, 1539

Two hundred twenty five. *Final testament, 1539.*

Fearing that I may pass on without assigning these matters, I am resolved here to put down a dispensation of my worldly goods.

I own:

—a bohío that I share with my wife, Doña Catalina Díaz de Colón and this bohío, of course, belongs to her person even more than mine as the four directions of our bohíos always belonged to the female.

—a herd of ten horses, including five mares, two colts, two geldings and one stallion. This herd belongs to Doña Catalina.

—a herd of six beef cattle. This herd also belongs to Doña Catalina.

Of these two herds, I want Doña Mencía's people, on her behalf, to pick two mares and two cows, for their community.

—Several pigs, all of whom will remain to doña Catalina.

—All my cunukus, in preparation or planted, belong to Doña Catalina.

—My personal belongings of correspondence tools, personal tools and clothing, one machete, three good lariats, two saddles and bridles, all of that I leave with Doña Catalina.

—Finally, these pages which I have kept all these years, the early ones and the later ones, these items I leave to Father Remigio of the Convent of Dominicans, in the town of Santo Domingo. May he keep them for what they are, the incomplete record of my people's affairs in the years since the coming of the Castilla to these islands of my heart. Maybe they will last, maybe they will burn. I only know his: From the sky of our beautiful seas, the stars they will not cause to fall.

Signed,
Guaikán (Diego Colón)

Two hundred twenty six. *A letter from Las Casas, the New Laws.*

(Editor's note: Lastly, Diego Colón's papers included the following letter to Diego by Father Las Casas, Some four years after his last testament. A partial reply was written by Diego on the back side of the same letter. Apparently it was never sent.)

Text of Las Casas letter of May 20, 1543:

Dieguillo, old friend,

Last night I faced the evening breeze here on the coast of Barcelona. The coast and its smells reminded me of you, and I realized I have forgiven your actions toward me on the closing days of the Enriquillo war.

Furthermore, I want to apologize to you for my harsh words so many years ago. I have crossed the ocean time and again since then and, as they say, "much water has passed." I remember those first days, too, when you were the first Indian I ever saw, there at Seville, you and your parrots. And that was more than fifty years ago! Certainly, I hope you still have your health and that your marriage to Doña Catalina Díaz has gone well.

Facing the ocean here in Barcelona, I realize also that I miss our conversations about the early days and about the Indian causes. It was precisely that breeze from the ocean, the one you always said "spoke" to you, that seemed to carry the memory of your face and words to me. I realize, too, how much your smile back then as a boy has stayed with me. In some hidden way I believe the hand of God guided my eyes to that smile, which to this day represents the Taíno smile, the Taíno character to me. It was that quality in your island people that always tugged at me, eliciting finally from my heart a pledge to assist your race. This I have continued to do, since I have seen you last, and the urge is upon me to inform you about it. Again, I see the Lord's mysterious mind at work in my actions.

Since last I saw you, I have traveled once to Panamá and to Nicaragua, where I have seen the most dismal conditions endured by your mainland relatives. Thus, the work on the mainland in behalf of the Indian communities is quite dramatic. I was engaged in attempting to curtail the wars of conquest of the tribes. There, I did travel among the Maya Caxiqueles and Kekchies, and developed a way of singing to them in order to obtain a peace without horror, without war. This went well for a time, until certain conquistadors argued that it was not proper, as their rights of tribute and slavery they can obtain only through a war of conquest. Thus peaceful conquest they considered high treason.

(The law they don't respect in its spirit but will twist at will, if allowed by its language and interpretation. But then, you always told me that!)

I was run out of Nicaragua and, in Guatemala, Pedro de

Alvarado conspired to have me assassinated. The wheel repeats itself, dear Diego, and the abuses and cruelties suffered by your people in the islands are continuing here. I abhor it all, my Dieguillo, as I have seen again the new slave markets of Panamá and Nicaragua, where your copper people are herded by the hundreds, nay, by the thousands, branded, distributed and sold, mother torn from infant, husband from wife. Pity the mainland Indians, Dieguillo, the conquest continues.

To Perú I tried to sail, but the winds would not carry me, though I certainly have all the needed testimony to condemn Pizarro and all his henchmen, how they have tortured and quartered those innocent towns of the mountains. To be sure, the methods of conquest used on the islands they have refined on the mainland, where everything is bigger and more abundant.

The War of Enriquillo, dear Diego, was one great mark. I see now how it set a standard for caution, for the option other than war. Men like Fuenleal (remember him?) have continued their masteries in México, Yucatán and Guatemala—men who knew the suffering of the island Taíno—and who could see that a second generation could still rebel and dangerously assail the Spanish cause. This is of some help now, as I campaign here at the Court, petitioning the sovereigns and the Holy Pontiff himself, Pope Paul III, on behalf of the Indies.

Allow me to outline some recent changes that have me highly enthusiastic for a new chapter and many new verses with which to curtail abuses and protect the Indian.

In 1537, after much lobbying, the Pope issued his *Bulla Sublimis Deus,* a bull upholding the rationality of Indians. It rebukes those who argue that the Indians are "beasts of burden that talk," by proclaiming, as we have so many times, "all the peoples of the world are men." It was this bull that allowed us to contain Pedro de Alvarado in Guatemala, finally. Alvarado, who was branding and selling Indians in a wide open slave trade, was opposed by Bishop Francisco Marroquín, also a Protector of the Indians. We petitioned also and the oidores agreed to let me attempt a peaceful conversion for five years.

Thus it happened, Diego, you should have been there to see it. We wrote songs of peace in the Indian languages and our merchant friends, Indian, mestizo and white, sang to the tribes along the rivers, telling of the One True Lord and his Gift of Redemption. Cacique after cacique came into the fold, Dieguillo, all happy to be baptized. Juan of Atitlán was first in July, 1537, but by January, 1538, most of the Kekchi caciquedoms were with us, what we named the *Verapaces*, the True Peaces.

This is where everything went bad and the encomenderos began attacking me in earnest. This is where they declared it their "right" to make war on the Indians, even if the innocents had come to offer peaceful tribute! But these new conquistadors are evil men, Dieguillo, raping and killing at will and they must be stopped before the whole continent is consumed, as were the islands, before a whole race of people is exterminated.

Thus, now I can write that we have the New Laws, which were passed by the Court in 1542. The New Laws completely prohibit Indian slavery and even disallow the encomienda. This is the victory we have sought from the Crown, a sword with which to apply the final remedy, a remedy that should not drag on forever but must be followed up with vigor and be decisive!

Thus, Dieguillo, you can see that we are finally gaining the proper resources for our campaign. It pays to persist in one's commitments, for the justice of our One True Lord turns slowly, but it turns.

You will hear a great deal about these New Laws in years to come. They go on and on and will protect every facet of Indian existence and will be the backbone of our decisive campaign.

I hope this letter finds you well and you will consider the importance of the work of redemption for our human condition.

Your friend in Christ,
Bartolomé de las Casas

(A response from Diego is found on the back of the three pages of Father Las Casas' letter. Dated in 1546 and titled, "A note for las Casas," it is indecipherable in parts.)

Two hundred twenty seven. *A note for Las Casas.*

Once again, I reread the good friar's letter, now three years in my possession. I wish I could speak to him. I had the opportunity two years ago, when he came through, but I did not seek it. I had not the heart nor the time for a meeting. Catalina was dying then and I had not the inclination to shift my attention from her.

... [illegible] ... , they were pelting him with stones, hating him as never before. His monks, those that did not desert him right away, could find no food in town and were jeered whenever they appeared on the streets ... [illegible] ... then, last year, his flounted New Laws, were revoked. In Mexico and Peru, the colonists rebelled against the Crown of Spain. "Don't take away our Indians," was one of their banners. The other one was "Without Indians to work, the conquest means nothing."

Oahh, guatiao Las Casas, everything you do is good and yet does nothing! So how am I to respond?

I have no health, I would say. Catalina is buried, I would say. Like the final grains of the hourglass, my remaining suns are counted. Our world as we knew it is destroyed, our people are one in one hundred of what they once were. Such is what I would say.

Of our Indian boys and girls, some farm the land, others have gone back to the bush. Catalina took in three young guaxeri. I have taught them what I know of the tracking cure, and they trail the spirit like Taínos ... I am proud of those boys ... [illegible] ... "Each of you teach three more," I told them.

Two hundred twenty eight. *They will remember, my young generations.*

Fray Remigio is here. He brings me plantain, rice and beans, and I have my yuca patch. Now I give the friar everything, all the pages to put away. It is time he took them. Now I draw this sketch, what my father taught me, the real message of our people. Someday they will remember it, my young generations, someday in dreams its meaning will return to them ... [illegible] ... that way, because in the black of our eyes we were good ... it does not die ...

Postscript

The treaty with Enriquillo resulted in the settlement of the Indian community at Boyá, in south central Hispaniola. About four thousand Indian people settled in the free Indian community, where Enriquillo officiated until his death a year later. The Boyá community persisted and, although intermarriage and migration eroded the Indian jurisdiction, Indian ancestry persists in the families of the region today. Around the time of the settlement with Enriquillo, other Taíno groups, in Cuba, Santo Domingo and Puerto Rico, sought refuge in the mountains of their respective islands, and thus small enclaves of Taíno ancestors survived, some into the Twentieth Century. Of course, the Taíno people, in intermarriage with Iberians and Africans, are a major genetic root of the contemporary Greater Antillean population. The Greater Caribbean islands were under Spanish domination until the end of the nineteenth century. About Diego Colón, the Lucayo, nothing more is known.

Glossary

Adelantado. Spanish military title of Forward Commander.

Alguacil. Marshall or policeman.

Ampolleta. Hourglass filled with sand that was turned over every half hour to keep time on long voyages.

Anacaona, Taíno cacica of the Xaraguá region, sister of Bohekio and wife of Caonabó.

Areito. Taíno word describing traditional dances and recitations among the Taíno caciques and behikes.

Axí(es). Taíno word for pepper (Capsicum Spp.)

Axiaco. Taíno-derived word, still in use, to describe a Caribbean corn-based stew (*axiaco* that is mixed in with some of the islands' root crops.

Asturias. Region of Spain.

Bahuruku. Mountain range in the southwest peninsula of Española, 150 kilometers of coast and 100 kilometers into land. According to Las Casas, it contained a mountain made of salt. It also contains present-day Lake Enriquillo.

Baibrama. Taíno ceremonial cemí and spiritual entity associated with fertility of crops, particularly manioc. *Baigua.* Taíno word describing a plant used by fishermen to drug fish in the water.

Baiguanex. Medicine man of Enriquillo.

Baracoa. Taíno word meaning, "existence by the sea," describes a town in the northeast coast of Cuba.

Barbacoa (Barbecue). Taíno word describing method of cooking and drying foods by stacking the raw foods in grates, adding tomato, peppers and other condiments.

Batey. Taíno word describing a plaza or ceremonial field where areitos and ball games were celebrated.

Bayamanacoel. Taíno ancestral character who assisted in the creation of the islands by spitting a guanguayo on Deminán.

Bayamo. A large town in eastern Cuba today, still named for its old cacique's name.

Behike. Taíno term for medicine man or healer.

Bejuco. Taíno word still used to describe various types of vines, used as medicinal purgatives and as cord rope for tying and construction.

Bohekio. Cacique of the Xaraguá region of Española.

Bohío. Taíno word for home or house, it also described the island of Española.

Boricua. Person or object of Puerto Rican origin.

Borikén. Taíno word to describe Puerto Rico, means "land of the valiant cacique."

Brío. Castillian word describing high energy or spirit.

Brujo. Castillian word for male witch.

Cacicazgo. Hispanicized Taíno word describing the territory of a cacique.

Cacique. Taíno word describing a regional chief.

Caguayo (a). Taíno word, still in use in Cuba and Puerto Rico, describing a longish tree reptile.

Caximba. Taíno word for tobacco pipe.

Caymán. Taíno word describing Cuban swamp alligator. The word has been used poetically to describe the island of Cuba.

Cajaya. Taíno word describing shark.

Caiciju. Taino grandfather of Guarionex, noted for his prophecy of the coming of the Spanish.

Camagüey. Taíno word for a region and a city in central/eastern Cuba.

Caona Taíno word describing gold.

Caonabó Taíno or Ciguayo chief of the region of Maguana, in Española.

Caracol. Taíno word for spiraled sea shell.

Carib. Caribbean Indian people from the Lesser Antilles, a term chosen by the Spanish for people allegedly cannibalistic.

Carey. Taíno word describing the large sea turtle (Chelonia imbricata), used here as a personal name.

Casabe. Taíno word, still in use, to describe tort made from yuca or manioc root.

Castillian. A subject or the language of Castille, a Kingdom, now region, of Spain.

Ceiba. Taíno word for silk cottonwood, a sacred tree;name of Diego's first wife.

Cemí. Taíno word describing wooden and stone statuettes representing various spiritual entities.

Çibanakán. Taíno word describing a place of many stones.

Çiboney. Indo-Antillian word describing a people in central and western Cuba and in the southern Cuban keys.

Çibukán. Taíno word describing net sack used to squeeze juice from the scraped yuca.

Ciguayo. A tribe of Indians from north and eastern Española; a captain under Enriquillo.

Cimarrón. Escaped African slaves who joined the Taíno mountain camps, or "palenques."

Coaybay. Taíno place of the dead.

Comarca. Spanish word designating a territory or "commons" of land for a village or a community.

Coatriskie. Taíno word describing female spiritual leader of rainy winds at sea.

Cocuyo. Taíno word describing the Antillean firefly. Oviedo notes the cocuyo was used for night time travel. A hunter of mosquitoes, the cocuyo was also introduced under netting and in bohíos at night as a form of pest control. The practice of lighting the night trail with a bottle full of cocuyos is still current in eastern Cuba.

Cohiba. Taíno word for tobacco plant.

Cohoba (Piptademia peregrina). Ground up dust, or snuff, used by the cacique, behike and ni-Taíno to enhance their visions and to communicate with the ancestors and other spirits. It also describes the ceremony of cohoba.

Cohobanax. Fictional name encompassing the word, cohoba, as root, with "nax" added to describe an elder in that ceremony.

Converso. Castillian word for converted Jew.

Copei (copai). A tree on whose broad leaves a message could be written.

Cubanakán. Taíno word describing "center of the island" of Cuba.

Cunuku. Taíno word describing a planted field of yuca and other crops; an Indian homestead.

Deminán. Taíno ancestral character, one of the four directions and four winds, an adventuresome creator of much of the Taíno cosmological world.

Digo. Taíno word describing a plant whose root and leaf produces a cleansing lather used by the Taíno to bathe.

Dragas. Word used to describe "little people" by Iberian (Gallego) peasantry.

Duho. Taíno word describing ceremonial seat or stool low to the ground and fashioned from wood or stone.

Encierro. The gathering of the bulls prior to a bull run.

Encomienda. Spanish system of giving Indian villages to specific conquistadors, to whom they were entrusted to be Christianized in return for free labor.

Enriquillo. Taíno cacique (d. 1535), whose thirteen-year-war Diego describes in the present journal.

Escarmiento. Spanish word for a serious warning.

Española. Present day Haiti/Santo Domingo, variously known as Bohío and Quisqueya, and renamed Isla Española by Columbus. The word is also anglicized to Hispaniola.

Fascineroso. Spanish word describing a torrid or agitated person.

Fernandina. Christopher Columbus's first name for Cuba.

Ganadero. Castillian word for cattleman.

Goeiç (a). Taíno word for "spirit of (in) a living person."

Gonzalo. A captain under Enriquillo.

Guaikán. Taíno word describing remora, pilot or suckerfish, Diego Colón's Indian name.

Guamax. Taíno cacique of the Baracoa area of eastern Cuba.

Guamikina. Taíno word describing a "chief or head man," the name given to Columbus by his early hosts.

Guamo. Taíno word, as with caracol, describing a conch.

Guanguayo. Taíno word describing spittle of mixed cohoba and tobacco juice, spat on Deminán's back by Bayamonacoel.

Guanahabax. Name combining Guanahani, the island and bax, for principal man.

Guanahani. Indian name for the Bahamian island first sighted by Columbus.

Guanahanikán. Name combining Guanahani, the name of the island, with "kan," Taíno for center, as in Cubanakán, an Indian region in central Cuba.

Guanin. Taíno word describing a shiny metal or copper.

Guarikén. A Taíno expression, registered by Las Casas, meaning "Come, look and see."

Guarionex. Taíno cacique of the region of Magua, in Española.

Guarocuya. Taíno name of Enriquillo.

Guásima. Cuban "Tree of Life," sacred to the Taíno and their Guajiro descendants.

Guatiao. Taíno term for friend, particularly one with whom a name has been exchanged.

Guaxeri (later Guajiro). Taíno word meaning "one of us," or "countryman."

Guayaba (Psidium guajaba). Taíno word describing a sweet fruit with high ceremonial importance.

Güira. Taíno word for gourd (Crescentia cujete).

Hacendado. The owner of an hacienda, or large ranch or farm.

Hamaca. Taíno word for hammock, the hanging net bed of the Taíno.

Hatuey. Taíno cacique from Española who retreated to Cuba during the conquest.

Heniken. Taíno word describing a vine that was made into rope.

Hicara. Taíno word for receptacle made out of a gourd.

Hicotea. Taíno word describing fresh-water turtles.

Higüe. Taíno word describing "little people," who normally live around a stream or spring.

Himagua. Taíno word for twin.

Hutía (Soledonon paradoxus). Rodent of the West Indies, eaten by early Taíno and present-day guajiro.

Hyen. Taíno word describing the poisonous juice of the yuca after squeezed from the scraped pulp.

Iguana. Taíno word describing large, edible lizard (I. tuberculata).

Inriri. Taíno name for woodpecker (Melanerpesportoricensis).

Itiba Cohahubana (also Atabey). Taíno female deity, mother of the Supreme Being.

Jaba. Taíno word for sack or carrying bag.

Katsi. Taíno word for moon.

Kwaib. Term used by contemporary Carib chiefs of the territory in Salybia, Dominica, to describe their people.

Lucayos. Taíno-derived word describing the Taíno inhabiting the small Bahamian islands.

Macana. The war club made of the palm tree used by the warriors.

Macanear. To hit, verb in common usage in West Indies. From the Taíno word for war club or coral ax, macana.

Macorixe. A little-documented Caribbean indigenous people identified at various times in Española, Jamaica and Cuba, noted for their archery.

Macoutí. Taíno word, meaning back sack.

Maguacokío. Taíno word meaning, "covered men with swords that can cut a man in half with one strike."

Mahá. Taíno word, describing the largest snake in the Greater Antilles, non-poisonous.

Maguana, a Taíno cacicazgo in south central Española, led by cacique Caonabó at contact.

Maize. Taíno-derived word for corn; Maisi Point, eastern most point in Cuba.

Mamey. Taíno name for a tropical fruit.

Manaya. Taíno word meaning stone hatchet.

Manso. Castillian word for tame. A manso was an Indian living in the Spanish hold.

Manatí. Antillian sea cow.

Manigua. Taíno word for high grass country, also wild country.

Maraca. Taíno word describing rattle made from a gourd.

Marién. A chiefdom and territory of Española.

Maravedí. Spanish copper coin with limited purchasing power.

Matinino. Caribbean island(s) reputedly inhabited by Amazonian women.

Mencía. Wife of cacique Enriquillo, a leader of noble Taíno lineage.

Naboria. Taíno word describing a class of workers, not clearly slaves, that served Taíno society in domestic and field work, likely from earlier migrant groups to the islands.

Nanixi. Caribbean Indian word for "my heart, my love."

Ni-taíno. Caribbean Indian word commonly used to describe the rank of principal people, council of elders, just under the cacique families.

Ñame. Likely Taíno word for edible sweet tuber, or sweet potato. There is dispute as to the Amerindian or African origins of this word.

Oidor. Castillian word for a type of judge or "Hearer" in the colonial Spanish legal system.

Opia. Taíno word describing the spirit of humans and animals after death.

Opiyelguobirán. Taíno cemi and guardian spirit of the Spirit World.

Palenque. Mountain hideaway or guerrilla camps of Taíno later joined by escaped African slaves; the palenque forms the basis of Caribbean mestizaje.

Repartimientos. The act of "giving out" or "splitting" of lands with Indians attached to form encomiendas.

Romero. A captain under Enriquillo.

Sinrazón. Castillian word or concept, meaning action, usually brusque, "without reason."

Taíno. Caribbean Indian word commonly used to describe the aboriginal inhabitants of Cuba, Hispaniola, Puerto Rico, Jamaica and other lesser islands.

Tamayo. Enriquillo's principal captain.

Turey. Taíno word describing the sky and a type of medallion worn by chiefs.

Urayoán. Boricua (Puerto Rican) cacique, sometimes written as Broyoan.

Vara. Spanish measurement, approximately 0.84 m.

Xaguahiguatú. Taíno word used by Diego to describe a fertility ceremony. It translates as "fire in the loins."

Xaiba. Taíno word describing Antillian fresh water crab (Callinectes diacanthus).

Xamayca. Taíno word for present-day Jamaica.

Xaraguá. Territory of cacique Bohekio, in southwestern Española.

Xiba. Taíno word describing stone and woody mountain.

Xíbaro. The Puerto Rican native peasant, "man of the rocky and wooded mountain."

Xikí. Taíno word for a tree that has a very hardwood.

Ya. Taíno expression connoting a strong or vital spirit.

Yaguasa. Taíno word describing indigenous Cuban duck.

Yakimo. Port town in southern Española.

Yara. Place near Cuban city of Bayamo, where Hatuey was immolated.

Yoruba. Tribal people from Western Africa, many of whom were brought to the Caribbean as slaves.

Yuán. A reconstructed Taíno word for penis, from iu(yuca), the form of the tuber, and ia or an, vital force.

Yuca. Taíno word for manioc, a primary tropical root crop.

Yúcahuguama Bagua Maórocoti. Supreme Being in the Taíno cosmology. A triple name meaning "one who brings the yuca," "rules the sea" and "is without ancestral grandfathers," born of woman only.

Yukaieke. Taíno word describing village or settlement.

Yunque. A promontory form found near the ocean, in Cuba and in Borikén, flat plateau cutting off the top.